BESS

A Novel by
Georgina Lee

Grosvenor House
Publishing Limited

All rights reserved
Copyright © Georgina Lee, 2014

The right of Georgina Lee to be identified as the author of this
work has been asserted by her in accordance with Section 78
of the Copyright, Designs and Patents Act 1988

The book cover picture is copyright to National Trust Images

This book is published by
Grosvenor House Publishing Ltd
28-30 High Street, Guildford, Surrey, GU1 3EL.
www.grosvenorhousepublishing.co.uk

This book is sold subject to the conditions that it shall not, by way of
trade or otherwise, be lent, resold, hired out or otherwise circulated
without the author's or publisher's prior consent in any form of binding or
cover other than that in which it is published and
without a similar condition including this condition being imposed
on the subsequent purchaser.

A CIP record for this book
is available from the British Library

ISBN 978-1-78148-882-9

"I assure you, there is no other Lady in this land that I better love and like."
                                        Queen Elizabeth I.

Dedication

For my husband and daughters, with love

Acknowledgements

I am very lucky to have my husband Bob, who has always encouraged me to fulfil my dreams. My daughter Lauren, and my friend Tessa, spent many hours proofreading and giving me valuable feedback, for which I'm very grateful – many thanks to all of you.

Image 94085 – Elizabeth Hardwick, Countess of Shrewsbury (Bess of Hardwick) 1590, attr. to Rowland Lockey, Hardwick Hall, Copyright National Trust Images/John Bethell.

Image 184795 – Copyright National Trust Images/ Robert Morris.

List of Main Characters

Elizabeth Talbot (Bess) – **Countess of Shrewsbury**, previously Lady Elizabeth St Loe, Lady Elizabeth Cavendish, Elizabeth Barlow, nee Elizabeth Hardwick.

George Talbot – 6th Earl of Shrewsbury, fourth husband of Bess, Knight of the Garter, Member of the Privy Council, Lord Lieutenant of Yorkshire, Derbyshire and Nottinghamshire, jailor to Mary Queen of Scots.

Lady Frances Pierrepoint nee Cavendish – eldest daughter of Bess and Sir William Cavendish.

Sir Henry Pierrepoint – married to Frances, son-in-law of Bess.

Henry Cavendish – eldest son of Bess and Sir William Cavendish, stepson and son-in-law of George Talbot.

Grace Cavendish nee Talbot – daughter of George Talbot, stepdaughter and daughter-in-law of Bess, married to Henry Cavendish.

Sir William Cavendish – son of Bess and Sir William Cavendish, married first to **Anne Keightly** then **Elizabeth Wortley**.

Sir Charles Cavendish – youngest son of Bess and Sir William Cavendish, married **Margaret Kitson** then **Catherine Ogle**.

Elizabeth Stuart – nee Cavendish, daughter of Bess and Sir William Cavendish, married **Charles Stuart,** 5th Earl of Lennox.

Mary Talbot nee Cavendish – daughter of Bess and Sir William Cavendish, stepdaughter and daughter-in-law of George Talbot, wife of Gilbert Talbot, became Countess of Shrewsbury on the death of her father-in-law in 1590.

Gilbert Talbot – son of George Talbot, stepson and son-in-law of Bess, husband of Mary Cavendish, became 7th Earl of Shrewsbury on the death of his father in 1590.

Lady Arbella Stuart – only daughter of Elizabeth and Charles Stuart, Bess' granddaughter, had a claim to the English throne.

Agnes – personal maid to Bess.

Joseph – secretary to Bess.

Edward St Loe – brother of Sir William St Loe, (from Bess' third marriage) and enemy of Bess.

Queen Elizabeth – Queen of England from 1558 – 1603.

Frances Cobham – lady in waiting to Queen Elizabeth and friend of Bess.

Lady Dorothy Stafford – lady in waiting to Queen Elizabeth and friend of Bess.

Mary Stuart – deposed **Queen of Scotland.**

The Earl of Huntingdon – commanded to guard Queen Mary.

Lord Burghley – previously Sir William Cecil, Lord Treasurer, loyal advisor to Queen Elizabeth for most of her reign.

Sir Francis Walsingham – Principal Secretary and spymaster to Queen Elizabeth.

Duke of Norfolk – high ranking Catholic aristocrat.

Robert Cecil – son of William Cecil, (Lord Burghley) 1st Lord Salisbury, Secretary of State to Queen Elizabeth and then James I.

Hersey Lassells – young man in Shrewsbury household where Queen Mary is imprisoned.

Sir Ralph Sadler – commanded to guard Queen Mary.

Robert Dudley, Earl of Leicester – Queen Elizabeth's favourite, Knight of the Garter, Master of the Horse, Privy Councillor.

Margaret Stuart, Countess of Lennox – friend of Bess, mother of Charles Stuart, grandmother to Arbella Stuart.

Charles Stuart – son of Margaret Stuart, husband of Elizabeth Cavendish, father of Arbella Stuart.

Sir Amias Paulet – Queen Mary's jailor after George Talbot has been relieved of the post.

Mr James Starkey – Arbella's tutor and chaplain for Bess.

Master Dodderidge – elderly servant of Bess.

Sir Henry Brounker – sent by Queen Elizabeth to question Arbella.

Robert Deveraux, Earl of Essex – stepson of Robert Dudley (Earl of Leicester), Master of the Horse, Member of the Privy Council, Lord Lieutenant of Ireland, favourite of Queen Elizabeth.

Timothy Pusey – loyal steward to Bess.

Edward Seymour – grandson of Lady Katherine Grey and Lord Hertford, Arbella proposed marriage to him.

John Stapleton – Catholic friend of Henry Cavendish.

Henry Grey, Earl of Kent – distantly related to Arbella Stuart.

Eleanor Britten – housekeeper and mistress of George Talbot.

Master McLean – lawyer.

James Stuart – King James VI of Scotland (1556 – 1625) & I of England (1603 – 1625) son of Queen Mary of Scotland and Henry Stuart, Lord Darnley.

John Stanhope – one time friend of Gilbert Talbot, later his enemy.

Mistress Digby – gentlewoman and neighbour of Bess, attended her on her deathbed.

Dr. Hunton – attended Bess on her deathbed.

Prologue
London – February 1565

Freezing and bitter blasts of air blow down on the mourners standing beside the open grave in the churchyard of Great St. Helen's in Bishopsgate. The grey sky holds a threat of snow and a few tiny flakes high enough to hit the bare branches of the trees. The church bell ceases it's clanging; the priest pauses with a frown to wipe his reddened nose with a handkerchief. The people round the grave are finely dressed in expensive velvets and furs, their pendants and rings set with gold and precious stones. In vain the ladies fight to keep their hoods in place as the wind spins itself around them. They try to stifle the stench from the city, always a hazard on a windy day, with delicately woven silver pomanders, filled with aromatic spices. A group of soldiers in uniform stand solemn and dignified, oblivious to the weather, there to pay their respects to a well loved Captain of the Guard.

As the priest intones the words of burial, everyone glances surreptitiously at the widow dressed in deepest black, who stands stiffly apart from everyone, her eyes never leaving the face of her brother-in-law, Edward St Loe. Outside the graveyard, a small group of onlookers are braving the cold to gawp at the ceremony. Although not as good as a burning or an execution, it is entertainment, of a sort. They notice the expression on her face too, for it is impossible to ignore.

The look she gives him is of a piercing intensity. Had it been one of love, he would have been basking in its passion. But it is not of love, or any gentle emotion that would have given some warmth on that winters morning. It is an unblinking and unremitting stare, full of hatred, designed to bore into his very soul. But he is the only person there who appears not to notice. He too is staring, but at a fixed point in the distance as he shifts from one foot to another. Not once does he glance at his late brother's wife. It is as if she does not exist.

The coffin is lowered into the ground, and when the priest finally closes his prayer book there is an uneasy silence, broken only by the crows plaintively cawing as they circle overhead. With an effort, the woman shifts her gaze to the newly dug ground below, and gracefully bends down to pick up a handful of earth to throw over the coffin. The gravediggers move forward now, their spades at the ready, eager to get their job done and return to the warmth of their brazier.

People begin to turn away, they too are anxious to get indoors and out of the cold. If they wait a moment, they will see her blink away the tears she has tried so hard to hide from Edward. But he is already striding back towards his coach, his simpering wife in his wake. A handful of the mourners remain and they gather around the woman, whispering soothing platitudes. "I will see justice done. He will not get away with murder," she murmurs fiercely.

No one doubts it. She is known for her determination and strong will. They nod in agreement and lead her away from the grave towards the coaches waiting to take them to the sanctuary of the queen's palace, where wine and beer will flow freely for the remainder of the day at the drinking – the usual event that follows a funeral at Court.

Thus the Lady Elizabeth St Loe of Chatsworth in Derbyshire, better known as Bess, lays her third husband, William, to rest. But the worst of her personal battles has yet to be faced.

☙❧

April 1565 (two months later)

The two coaches are in convoy, as they make their way north along the muddy and rutted road. The long journey from Somerset to Derbyshire has not been aided by a catalogue of bad luck from the beginning. The weather has got warmer now that spring has arrived, but heavy rains have flooded the highways and lanes, causing delays along the route and the drivers refuse to travel until the weather improved. Within the first week, a horse becomes lame, one of the grooms hits his head on a low stable beam and a tooth-drawer has to be found for one of the servants who had a painful abscess. The more experienced travellers in the party know such setbacks are commonplace and that it is only a matter of time before there is another problem. It is therefore not a great surprise when suddenly there is a lurch to one side, and the sound of splintering wood as the front coach hits a large rut in the road. The driver curses, having been distracted for just a few moments, and pulls the four horses to a standstill. The servants in the second coach exchange a look of alarm, as they too have had to stop abruptly. They sit wedged together amongst chests of clothes, sheaves of documents, coins and valuables.

Bess' maid, Agnes, had fallen asleep and cries out to be so rudely woken up.

Both the drivers get down to examine the damage to the wheels and there is much muttering and shaking of heads. Inside the first coach, Bess and her fourteen-year-old son, William Cavendish, sit waiting. They are travel weary and both long to be in the comfort of their home, but they know that no amount of shouting orders will make a difference. Patience is needed when travelling.

"Is there any food left? We might as well eat while we are not moving. Shall I call a servant?"

William gets up to open the door.

"Leave them. Their work will start again soon enough."

Bess looks gloomily out of the window, resigned to yet another delay. He pulls the wicker hamper out from under the seat and opens the lid. Inside there are two capons, some salt fish, assorted cheeses, figs, almonds and a custard tart. He realises he is hungry, and has not eaten for several hours.

"Will you join me, lady mother?"

He begins to assemble a meal for himself on a silver plate. Bess shakes her head.

"I do not have much appetite. This dispute over your stepfather's will has upset me, especially so soon after his death."

"You did not seem upset in the Court of Probate."

"Just because I do not show emotion, it does not mean I am unmoved. I know Edward hates me, which I can bear, but I will not have William's last wishes overruled. I have been expecting trouble over the will. When a man who has children from a previous marriage leaves everything to his widow and her heirs forever, it is bound to cause problems. I never thought it would be his daughter Margaret who contested it though, Edward must be behind it."

William cuts himself a chunk of cheese and reflects for a moment.

"I think everyone was surprised that he left nothing to his two daughters."

Bess looks indignant and opens her mouth to reply, but he is quick to speak first.

"I know, they already had generous dowries."

"He was a generous man. His death was so sudden, I never had a chance to say goodbye."

He looks sympathetically at his mother.

"What will happen now?"

"I shall continue the legal fight over my husband's home of Sutton Court and try to prove that Edward murdered him with poison."

She sighs; her eyes filled with unshed tears. "I know it is almost impossible to prove. He may never be brought to justice."

"Well, you have done everything possible for the moment. We shall soon be home and other matters will occupy you."

The carriage door opens and the driver's face appears, looking grim.

"My lady, one of our wheels has cracked. Not badly, but if we continue carefully we will still reach Wirksworth by nightfall."

"My mother and I could move to one of the other carriages and go on ahead," William ventures.

The driver shakes his head. "I would not advise it, master William. To separate would be dangerous; there is always the risk of robbers. We should continue together without delay."

"Very well; let us get on."

Bess waves him away and puts a cushion behind her back.

"I am going to try and sleep for a while. I suggest you finish eating and do the same, William."

She closes her eyes and William studies his mother for a few moments as he chews on some almonds. He knows she is an extraordinary woman, quite unlike the mothers of his school friends, who had been shocked to discover that Lady St Loe deals directly with lawyers and bailiffs, with no male family member to speak on her behalf. He has never seen her at a loss for words or unsure of herself. Sir William Cavendish, his father and Bess' second husband, died when he was only six and he can barely remember him. Longing to be given some responsibility for the running of her business affairs, he knows that will have to wait a few more years. His mother has told him that his education is very important if he is to succeed in the world.

The coaches rumble on slowly through the Staffordshire countryside, which will soon give way to the open windswept moors of Derbyshire. William tries to rest, but cannot settle. He wanted to ride alongside the carriage, but Bess forbade it. For a while he contents himself by looking out of the window. There was hawthorn blossom in Somerset but, as they move further north, the signs of spring disappear and the temperature falls. He should have been studying at Eton with his elder brother Henry, but before he returns to his studies he is determined to make the most of his freedom.

It is several hours before they see the outskirts of Wirksworth where they are to spend the night and have the wheel changed. The landlord of the inn is slightly nonplussed to find such a distinguished guest on his doorstep unannounced, but he rallies quickly and is able to provide his best letting rooms for Bess, with hot water, fresh linen and a hearty meal. The driver is sent off in the gathering dusk to find another wheel while the servants chat to one another as they unload the valuables into Bess' chamber. By closing time the wheel has been replaced and everyone is in bed, for Bess has ordered an early start in the morning and, God willing, Chatsworth is now only a day's ride away.

After a breakfast of bread, butter and omelettes, washed down with ale, the party leaves at daybreak. A watery sun breaks through the clouds as they make their way onto the open road, and Bess throws coins out of the window for a handful of beggars. Then she settles back under several blankets and opens some letters to re-read. Already she is compiling a list of tasks to do when she arrives home. On his mother's suggestion, William reads Chaucer, which is one of his schoolbooks, and for the most part, the journey passes in companionable silence, only stopping briefly to water and feed the horses. By mid-afternoon they reach the edge of the Chatsworth Estate and the familiar blue of the Cavendish Livery is visible on the doors of the wayside dwellings in the hamlets. Tenants doff their caps and women curtsey along the way, curious to see their mistress again after her recent loss. Bess puts away her papers and watches the approach with a rising sense of anticipation. They pass large swathes of hilly, open moorland where her sheep step nimbly over narrow streams as they graze amongst yellow gorse bushes. The trees are not as tall here; the ever-present wind cuts them short like an invisible scythe as they grow up from the damp and stony ground.

She never fails to be in awe of the craggy cliffs and rocks that are the hallmark of her home county, so unlike anywhere else she has visited in England. Roads are little more than tracks that have been carved over many years by travellers passing through, for they do not often stay. Most visitors find the landscape dark and forbidding, with great rocks scattered down the hillside as if they were dice thrown haphazardly and left forever where they landed. Strangers in winter often find the county bleak and snowdrifts can be many feet high. Travellers have been known to disappear, their frozen bodies only found after the thaw. The summers are short and arrive suddenly, almost without warning, when the hillsides are covered with purple and pink heather which change colour as the sun passes overhead, casting long shadows on the grey rocks. To Bess growing up, it was all magical and majestic in turn, and she loves and respects its power and drama. At last the house itself appears in the distance, silhouetted against the sunset, the river sparkling beneath it.

William leans out of the window to get a better view. Even the horses sense they are almost at the end of their journey and quicken their pace. Bess and Sir William Cavendish bought it sixteen years previously when she had persuaded him to move from London during all the uncertainty of Queen Mary's reign. Bess began to build on to it a few years later and now there are four towers and a large quadrangle.

As the carriages draw to a halt, there are shouts of excitement and the large wooden door opens as the children run out to greet them, closely followed by their nursery maids and Joseph, the steward. Bess is first out of the coach and gathers the younger ones around her skirts, delighted to see them.

There is Mary, the youngest, and Elizabeth, aged nine and ten years respectively. Her eldest daughter, the dependable and matronly Frances, is next to reach her. Only seventeen, but already happily married to a wealthy neighbour Henry Pierrepoint, she has travelled from her home nearby to be with the rest of the family. Bess caresses her cheek, touched that she is there to welcome her home.

Henry, her eldest son and heir, stands and waits until his mother notices him, aware that, unlike William, he does not have permission to be home from Eton. Bess raises her eyebrows at him and he shrugs his shoulders in a gesture of defiance, although just fifteen, he looks older and worldly wise for his years.

Charles is the last to be greeted, two years younger than William, he gives her a shy hug and she ruffles his hair fondly, remembering that soon he too will be off to Eton with his brothers. Bess looks at Joseph, and notes with relief that he is smiling too. Hopefully that means nothing untoward has happened since he last wrote to her. After all the greetings are over, Bess takes charge.

"Now I am going to bathe and change my clothes and then we shall have our supper together."

"Are we really to eat with you, lady mother?" Mary looks suitably pleased.

"Yes, my love, you are. Then afterwards I want to see Henry in my study."

Henry smirks, completely unconcerned. Bess turns to the nursemaids.

"Have the children been good?"

"Most of the time m'lady," one of them is bold enough to reply.

"Then they shall be rewarded with presents tomorrow, when the unpacking has been done."

There are more squeals of delight as Bess disengages herself from them.

"Now, go indoors, I must speak to Joseph." They all surround William and disappear indoors.

She approaches him as he stands silently on the edge of the group. He is a short, thin man with rather a solemn expression and little sense of humour, but Bess knows she can trust him implicitly; she would not have left her domain to anyone else.

"Welcome home, your ladyship." He bows formally. "My condolences on the loss of Sir William. The manner of his death shocked us all."

"Yes, I find it hard to believe I shall not see him again. But I have employed spies who are trying to find some evidence against his brother. I know Sir William did not die of natural causes."

Joseph nods in sympathy.

"But it is good to be home, Joseph. I have been away too long. What news since your last letter?"

"The list of petitioners waiting to see you grows ever longer and the administration of all the estates needs your attention. But the rents are all paid up..."

"And my building work?"

"Progress has not been a fast as you would wish, but work is always slower in the winter."

"But some progress has been made since I left?"

"Yes, your ladyship."

"Good. I will go through everything with you tomorrow. Tonight I shall spend with my family.

Thank you Joseph, I do not know what I would do without you."

He bows again and turns towards his own quarters. Bess makes her way through the Great Hall, and gathers up her skirts as she climbs the stairs to her bedchamber. Always quietly efficient, Agnes has already laid out a clean gown on the oak carved four-poster bed, and is fussing over the temperature of the bath water that the servants have carried up from the kitchen. Bess rescued her one day as she was passing through the streets of Derby in her coach. Agnes' uncle, her only relative and a sadistic drunk, was beating her so hard that Bess feared he would kill her. When she ordered the coach to stop, and then challenged him, he expressed sneering surprise that a fine lady should show so much interest in her. With eyes as black as pitch and her limbs trembling uncontrollably, Agnes had stared in wide-eyed terror as Bess descended from the carriage and stood in front of her tormentor. She told him if he did not stop at once, she would summon the magistrate and he would find himself on a charge of attempted murder. By this time, a small crowd had gathered to witness the spectacle of Bess berating this well-known scoundrel, and knowing her reputation, they had no doubt who would come off the better.

Within seconds, he had disappeared down a dingy alleyway and the two women were speeding towards the safety of Chatsworth, where Agnes soon filled out with three good meals a day and a safe bed to sleep in at night. She quickly proved to be an invaluable aid to Bess, for she was willing, hard working, good with a needle and could dress her mistress' hair with dexterity and skill. Unsurprisingly, after such a rescue, she was devoted to Bess and would have died for her if the situation arose. It was Agnes who had given instructions before they left home so hastily for the preparation of Bess' homecoming. The floor is laid with fresh herb rushes, and a pretty bowl of dried lavender sits on the window seat, its delicate fragrance filling the air. Amongst other personal items on the bedside table, there is a likeness of Sir William St Loe, painted just after they were married. She regards it for a few moments with sad affection, for the few years they had together were very happy.

A log fire burns in the stone fireplace; it's warmth so welcoming after the long journey. Beautiful tapestries, embroidered by her own hand, hang on the walls and heavy Persian rugs are draped over two oak storage chests. The servants finish their work by sprinkling the surface of the water with dried rose petals before curtseying and closing the door. Bess undresses with Agnes' help, and sighs with pleasure as she lowers herself into the soothing water. Closing her eyes, she relaxes for the first time in weeks. Agnes bustles about warming her clothes in front of the fire, and pours her mistress a glass of wine.

"You must rest m'lady. These last few weeks have been a great trial."

"When have you ever known me to rest?" replies Bess wryly.

"Seven years of marriage, and now for the third time a widow – what bad luck! I wonder that you have found the strength to carry on. There are many women who would have been overcome by such grief."

Agnes starts to gently sponge her mistress' back. Bess sips her wine and allows Agnes to carry on talking, for there is something reassuring about her concern. And she is the only person that Bess would allow to talk to her in such a manner.

"The late master will be sorely missed for sure and the children losing a stepfather is hard for them. And all this nasty business with Edward St Leo as well, as if you have not got enough to cope with. With all the travelling to Somerset to the late master's home ..."

"Sutton Court," murmurs Bess, only half listening.

"Yes m'lady. And I suppose you will want to build more and more. To be sure, it all looks very fine when you have finished and the third floor you are adding to this grand house will no doubt be a picture. But while all the work is being done, there is so much noise and dust, banging of hammers and sawing wood. Those workmen will shout and whistle all day, every day."

"Then you will be pleased to hear I am thinking of extending and improving my childhood home of Hardwick Hall, far enough away from hammers and whistling workmen. One day I may even build a new house there."

"And what does your dear mother think of these plans?"

"I think it will please her, despite the inconvenience of the workmen. When my father was alive, it provided a good income from managing the land. I was just a babe in arms when he died, and my poor mother was left with a young family of seven children."

Agnes makes sympathetic noises as she helps Bess out of the bath and wraps a towel around her. "You have come a long way since those days, m'lady."

"And still further to go, with God's help."

Soon she is dressed, and sits while Agnes combs her long hair, which hangs in lustrous curls to her waist. Bess peers at herself in the looking glass. The tiredness and travel weary look have gone from her face, and she is now relaxed and at ease. Although not beautiful, her complexion and colouring are very attractive. The unusual combination of her reddish flaxen hair and sparkling mint green eyes, similar to the queen herself, prove an alluring magnet for men, and she is never short of admirers. She has a natural charm, but beneath it lies the strongest of characters. Agnes thinks to herself that it will surely not be long until her mistress remarries.

With one last look, Bess sweeps out of the room, leaving Agnes to start the unpacking from the chests that have been brought up. In the courtyard, the grooms carry lanterns as they attend to the horses and bed them down for the night. The kitchen is full of noise and steam as the preparation of the food is underway, delicious smells of roasting meat waft outside. Bess' three Irish wolfhounds languish in front of the stone-carved fireplace, her striking portrait on the wall looking down on them as servants bustle about their work.

The table in the Great Hall is set, pitchers filled with weak wine and ale, the children sit talking and arguing, their nursery maids nearby. Bess stands for a moment in the doorway and savours the scene. Her beloved children, for whom she has such high hopes, are growing up fast. Now that she is again a widow, she knows that this can only be achieved by careful planning on her part. Their future has always been a priority. There is much to think about and Bess realised long ago that the best person to rely on is herself. Her pragmatic nature tells her that she has to get on with her life for there is no one who will do if for her. Not for the first time, she is at a crossroads and the decisions she takes in the next year will be pivotal in realising her hopes and ambitions, not just for herself, but also for her children. But tonight, she is happy to be home and to put such thoughts aside. Her family is waiting and she hurries forward to join them.

ෂ෨

September 1567 (Two years later)

There is a great deal to keep Bess occupied as she mourns the loss of her third husband and the time passes quickly. From her previous marriages she has inherited land, property and mines, which she carefully manages, for she is an astute businesswoman and likes to be in control of her finances. She spends many hours each day closeted with Joseph in her study as they read and discuss contracts and building plans; she is always building and lending money. All her investments must be overseen to ensure their profitability. Farms managers and bailiffs report to her weekly, aware that she does not suffer fools gladly.

Bess runs Chatsworth House and its land as efficiently as if it was one of her many businesses and personally supervises much of the household management. A dairy provides butter, cream and cheese all year. There is a brewing house for ale and beer, together with a laundry, stables, coach house, fish farms and a dovecote. Bee hives supply honey and beeswax for furniture, the acres of gardens and the vegetable plot are tended by a team of gardeners. Different varieties of herbs grow in abundance and are used in cooking and around the house for moth proofing and sweetening linen. Wheat and barley grow in nearby fields. Fresh eggs are available daily from the poultry farm and there are deer, rabbit and wood pigeon in the park. Mutton, pork and beef are on the menu often, except of course for fish days, every Friday and during Lent. The huge kitchen is always busy and noisy, even when there are no visitors. It's vaulted ceilings rise high above the hearths, the brick ovens and roasting spits where servants work in the heat all day, carrying out orders from the old and irritable French cook who presides over everything with a fearsome reputation. He is not beyond slapping the more lazy boys round the head when they let the fire go out, or are slow to pluck a chicken. In the middle of it sits the huge oak table, above which hang a large variety of kitchen equipment such as pots, knives, frying pans, cleavers, axes, graters and chafing dishes.

With such a large household and family to manage as well, Bess has little free time to call her own. But it is outdoors where she loves to think and make decisions, walking at any time of year amongst the many symmetrically arranged flower beds, hedge walks and knot gardens that surround the house. Here she can sit and contemplate, as the trickle of water fountains and birdsong are the only sounds, and where sweet scented roses, gillyflowers, primroses and lavender are grown. It is one of her favourite pastimes to picnic with the children in the orchard. In a good year, there can be plenty of apples, cherries, pears and figs for them all to enjoy.

Today she is in the garden with Elizabeth and Mary. It is one of those late summer days when the sun is still warm, and ripening blackberries wait to be picked from the hedgerows. Rugs and cushions have been laid out under the shade of the trees and she watches her daughters play skittles, amidst much laughter and inevitably some arguments. The air is hot and humid, there is no cool breeze, so she fans herself and enjoys some candied apricots from a bowl nearby. A wasp lands on a fallen apple and she swats it away. Having been busy all day, she allows herself a rare hour of relaxation and lies back, her half-closed eyes focusing on a couple of butterflies as they dance overhead.

"Lady mother, you are not watching! You promised to keep score." Elizabeth's voice rings out across the grass and Bess sits up, shading her eyes against the setting sun.

"We do not need mother to keep score, I can do it perfectly well!" Mary is indignant and throws down the ball before flopping down beside her mother.

"It is too hot!" she complains.

"You are giving up because you were losing," Elizabeth says smugly as she joins them, sitting down neatly and hugging her knees. She starts to pick some daisies and make a chain.

"Tell us about father."

"Again?" Bess laughs and shakes her head.

It is information that they never seem tired of hearing and she obliges, a smile on her face as the memories surface.

"I married your dear father when I was only nineteen and he was forty. Because he had proved himself in the Court of King Henry, he was rewarded by a knighthood and made a member of the Privy Council."

"What did he do to earn such an honour?"

"He was an accountant, a very good one too. Your father was a clever man, and like me, not high born." Her voice becomes wistful.

"You could not wish to meet a kinder man, I saw him as not only my husband, but the father I never knew. Our age difference of nineteen years never bothered either of us. He taught me all I know about business and finances, I owe him much. We were always so busy during those years, having you children and giving splendid parties. We knew everyone of importance," she adds with pride.

"Tell us what you planned with him for the future." This time it is Mary who poses the question. She rolls over and looks at Bess earnestly.

"It was our ambition to create a dynasty."

"What is a dynasty?" Elizabeth looks up from her daisy chain.

"A family that rules by wealth and power. We only wanted the best for our children. You will all marry well; I shall make sure of it. The boys will have the best education that money can buy and there is no reason why you should not rise to the top of the tree. I have vowed to continue these plans without your father by my side."

Her two daughters look at her in wonder; it all seems too much to contemplate.

"Was he very different from your first husband?" asks Elizabeth

"Very much so. Arthur was the son of a neighbour; he was like my own family, not wealthy, but able to live in some comfort. We were both young and the marriage was arranged by his father; we did fall in love though, and I nursed him through his final illness. We were only wed for eighteen months."

"It must have been hard to have all your husbands dying."

"Mary! Do not be so tactless!" exclaims Elizabeth.

"It is all right, she means no harm," Bess reassures her. "It was hard, but it has made me a stronger person."

"And a richer one," Mary observes.

"Now you go too far, child!" Bess frowns at her precociousness.

"Well I for one, will miss our papa William," says Elizabeth. "He was not like a real soldier at all, more like a big brother." She has finished the daisy chain and leans forward to tie it round Bess' neck.

"When you are older, you will realise it is not always easy to have stepchildren, my own are grown up now and I rarely see them. But I could not have asked for a better stepfather for you all." She smiles. "Thank you for this, Elizabeth; it is very pretty."

Just then, their attention is caught as one of the youngest servants walks towards them and they watch him approaching. They have not heard a carriage approach and Bess is not expecting any more letters today. He bows and looks slightly flustered.

"Well, what is so important that you disturb me now?" she asks.

"Beg pardon your ladyship, there is someone to see you in the Great Hall. She will not give her name and says she knows Master Henry."

"What has that to do with me?"

He hesitates. "It might be best if you came at once, m'lady."

She gets up reluctantly and follows him inside. The servant waits by the entrance as Bess makes her way towards the figure sitting at one of the trestle tables. The person who has so unceremoniously arrived is a young girl. Bess estimates quickly that she is no more than fourteen. Dressed in clothes that have seen better days, her pretty face is hollow and tired. She stands up rather awkwardly and gives a brief curtsey. Now Bess sees that she is heavily with child.

"M'lady, thank you for seeing me."

Her voice is surprisingly strong, but she leans on the table for support as her hands shake.

"You had better tell me why you are here. I do not usually receive visitors unannounced."

"I think you should know ..." She swoons suddenly and falls forward in a faint, as the servant rushes forward to help Bess as they place her in a nearby chair.

"Go to the kitchens and get some ale," Bess orders.

She watches her recover as she thinks of what to do. It is obvious that she is going to claim that Henry is the father of her child and she has come here for some recompense. There have already been rumours about Henry's sexual exploits that have reached his mother's ears but she does not wish to believe them. She had hoped that the discipline of Eton would have curbed his behaviour, but the opposite seems to have happened. The servant returns with a pewter cup and places it on the table. The girl's expression is wary as Bess watches her drink.

"What is your name, child?"

"Charity Tanner," she mumbles in reply.

"How old are you and where are you from?"

"I am nearly eighteen, my home is near your son's school. My grandfather has an inn."

"You are not eighteen are you? Do not lie to me or it will be the worse for you."

Charity slams the cup on the table, the contents spilling out.

"I am not afraid of you just because you have a grand house and you are the lady of the manor. Henry used me and then left, that was not very gentlemanly of him was it?"

"Do not dare to address me in that fashion or I will have you thrown out! Anyone can see that you are not eighteen."

Neither speaks for a few moments, then Charity's voice is subdued.

"I did not know where else to go. My grandfather says he does not want me and a screaming brat in the house. Henry told me everything would be all right. It has taken me nearly a month to get here."

"You travelled from Windsor on your own?"

She nods and a tear rolls slowly down her cheek.

"How do I know you are telling the truth?"

"Write and ask your son. If he denies me he deserves to roast in hell."

Bess has heard enough and calls back the servant.

"John! Take Charity to the servants quarters, tell one of the women to help her wash and find some clean clothes, feed her and find somewhere for her to sleep."

"Yes, m'lady."

"I will write to my son and see if he will vouch for you. In the meantime you may stay here until I decide what is to become of you."

"Thank you, m'lady"

She watches as the servant helps Charity and they make their way to the kitchens. What a cruel irony that the girl is called Charity! It would be several days before Henry would be able to return her letter and she would not have put it past him to ignore it. She hurries back to her desk and picks up her quill to write to him. The letter is brief, and to the point, and will be taken to Eton at first light tomorrow. There is another matter to occupy her that afternoon. Although Bess is far removed from London, she is in constant correspondence with friends and important members of the Court. They are concerned to hear of her welfare and naturally tell her all the latest social gossip, of which there is always plenty. She likes to be kept up-to-date. Everything is of interest, Queen Elizabeth's latest remarks, political developments, unfolding scandals. She still has the network of spies set up during her second marriage to Sir William Cavendish and they are handsomely paid for their trouble. Consequently, a large numbers of personal and business letters arrive almost daily, carried by riders, from Court and her other properties and businesses in Derbyshire, London and Somerset. There are regular letters from her mother, sisters and half-sisters, as well as friends living locally. Her only brother, James, a year older, has always been a poor letter writer. But everyone has been scandalized by the rumour earlier in the year of the Scottish Queen Mary's possible involvement in the murder of her husband, Lord Darnley.

Recently she has received some unusual letters that are of a more personal nature. Turning the key, she opens a drawer and places two of them on her desk.

The first is from the brother-in-law of her friend, Frances, and the other from an old acquaintance. She reads:

Palace of Whitehall

London

My Lady St Loe,

It is too long since we have had the pleasure of your company at Court. Now that the period of mourning for your late husband is over, I hope you will consider me as much more than a friend, for my loving feelings for you cannot be repressed any longer. My sister—in—law, Frances, tells me that you are thinking of returning to Court and I would be overjoyed to see you again.

My fervent wish is that you will allow me to speak frankly to you about the future that I so long to share with you. I pray God send you good health and long life. Written this day xviii of August 1567. I remain your most devoted friend,

Henry Cobham.

Frances has been quietly arranging for Bess and Henry to be in each other's company as often as possible at Court. Bess likes him well enough, but he is a little too eager to please her, which she sometimes finds irksome. She turns her attention to the other letter, which is more direct and she cannot not help but smile when she reads it.

York House

London

Sweet Bess,

I hope you do not consider me too bold in addressing you thus, but I cannot help myself. I have long admired you for your beauty and charm. To watch you suffering alone the trials of widowhood yet again has been a torture for me as I have been unable to help you as I would have wished. Now I feel that our time together has come and, with your permission, I would like to give you the protection you deserve. I am well placed to do so and you may be assured of my devotion and love. I would also love your children as my own. It has not escaped my knowledge that others are vying for your hand, but I know you to be steady enough to choose wisely. I pray you to look kindly upon me and return to Court without delay, for you are much missed. My prayers and thoughts continue to be for you as I wait for your answer on this iv day of September 1567.

Written by the hand of him who would be yours,

John Thynne.

She lays the letters down and reflects for some minutes. The parchments have a smell of the London Court, indefinable and exciting. Always attractive to the ambitious, it is here that great matters of state are decided. A few aspiring men rise to high office, while others fail and are sent away to live the remainder of their days in obscurity. Others are found guilty of treason and pay the ultimate price. In contrast, there is lavish entertainment with banquets, plays, tournaments and music; life here is to be enjoyed wherever possible.

Foreign ambassadors and clergy clamour with everyone else of importance for the attention of the queen, who has now been on the throne for nine years and shows no signs of marrying. The extravagance here is beyond ordinary peoples' dreams and there is always a heady mix of seduction and intrigue. It is hard not to be impressed by it, not to want to be part of it. But it can be a claustrophobic, dangerous place and Bess has lived through years when it was safer to be a long way from Court. She knows she will have to make the journey down to London again and the time is fast approaching. Several weeks ago she received another letter from the queen who had hinted that Bess should feel ready to return, she would be most welcome. Not exactly a command, but close enough for her to feel it is time to start planning the journey. Bess decides to write to her mother and ask her to stay with Mary and Elizabeth whilst she is away, for she will be there for some months. In anticipation of the visit, she has already ordered new French gowns and some knitted silk stockings that ladies of quality are now wearing. Most importantly, she will take a present for the queen, an expensive silver cup that she has specially commissioned. Bess had once arrived without a gift, but the queen received her with such a coolness of manner that it was a mistake she will never make again.

She lifts her head to look out through the open window and thinks about returning to the garden again, but Elizabeth and Mary are nowhere to be seen, and she suspects they have probably gone to see the new pony that arrived yesterday. The servants are gathering up the rugs and cushions to bring them inside as the dogs sniff at the skittle balls before wandering away in search of some other scent. Dusk is beginning to fall and the shadows are lengthening. The thought of a family evening for once makes her a little restless.

There is one more letter in the drawer and she pulls it out as if it was fragile. Running her forefinger gently along the heavy seal, she is aware of its power and all it represents. The spidery writing therein reveals it is a love letter too, but more restrained and formal than the others. She has met the writer a number of times in London, for he is a Knight of the Garter and often at Court, as well as being Lord Lieutenant of Derbyshire, Yorkshire and Nottinghamshire. Of similar age to Bess and a widower, his wife died nine months previously. He is very wealthy and from one of the most distinguished and noble families in England. The letter says that he has been thinking about Bess a great deal, how highly the queen always speaks of her, and how he finds himself ever more impressed by these endorsements of her character and also wishes to see her soon. Bess stares out of the window, deep in thought.

She knows the financial worry that her mother, Elizabeth, endured when she was widowed.

After three years of struggling to run the family farm on her own, Bess' mother remarried a local man, Ralph Leche, whom Bess regarded as her father. But he eventually ended up in the debtors prison and once again, Elizabeth found herself having to beg relations for help. Bess is determined never to be in such a position herself. Replacing all the letters in the drawer, she turns the key with a satisfying click. She knows what has to be done now to ensure those cherished ambitions for herself and her children become a reality.

☙❦❧

Westminster Palace, London. December 1567 (3 months later)

One evening the queen stands in her bedchamber as her ladies-in-waiting help her to dress for the first of many Christmas feasts in the coming month. A handful of gowns lie discarded, her majesty having changed her mind several times about what to wear. Bess and her friend, Frances Cobham, are helping her into the detachable sleeves of a yellow silk gown, while Blanche Parry and Lady Dorothy Stafford, also friends of Bess, comb one of her red wigs ready to place over the royal head. The atmosphere is light-hearted as the queen is in a better mood, having finally agreed to the removal of a tooth two days before, which had been causing her a lot of pain. The ladies dart about attending to her, their gowns a rainbow of colours in the dark oak-panelled chamber. In less than an hour, *the toilette* will be complete, but first the queen decides to be a little mischievous. She teases Frances about her brother-in-law, Henry, who has made no secret that he hopes to marry soon.

"He does not discuss such matters with me, your majesty," Frances responds when the queen asks about his intentions.

"Then he should, for your opinion, as a woman, is worth ten times that of a man when it comes to love. Would you not agree, Bess?"

"I would, your majesty." Bess was seemingly engrossed in her task.

"But what of the rumours? For example, I have heard that Henry is making overtures to a certain widow and so far, she has not indicated her preference."

"We have not heard these rumours, your majesty."

Dorothy is quick to reply as she sees that Bess is uncomfortable with the conversation.

"Why yes, it is the talk of my Court. The lady concerned has several admirers. Sir John Thynne is one such man. They say he is going round like a lovesick calf."

She gives Bess a teasing look.

"At his age, your majesty?" Blanche murmurs.

"Love knows no age limits. We none of us know when or where Cupid's arrow will strike. I believe Lord Darcy is smitten with the lady too."

Bess bows her head and remains silent. She knows that this talk is not vindictive but she wishes the queen would change the subject. They all know that the 'lady' is Bess herself.

"And there is another mystery contender causing much speculation." Her eyes sparkle at the thought. "I shall say no more. Now make haste, I long to be dancing and I can hear the musicians getting ready."

Finally they leave the chamber, the queen a vision of embroidered extravagance, sparkling precious stones and exquisite lace ruff, her face painted alabaster white with lead powder, all the better to show off her red hair and green eyes. As she descends the stairs, a sweet cloud of rosewater surrounds her. The courtiers are silenced as they look up and bow low, for no one may outshine their queen.

The sight that greets her is one she loves to see. The Great Hall is decked out in bunches of red berried holly and trails of ivy. Snowy white cloths with swags of coloured ribbons decorate the long tables, and candles burn on the wall sconces alongside banners of the queen's coat of arms. The air is heavy with wood smoke from the huge log fire in the inglenook fireplace, and with the costly perfumed musk oil worn by the courtiers. They too are ostentatiously dressed in their finest clothes of silks, furs and velvets, as they look forward to the evening. Servants hurry in and out of the vast kitchen, their arms weighted down with seemingly endless silver platters containing a wide variety of meat and fish dishes, which they carefully place on the tables.

Afterwards the guests will partake of elaborate marzipan sweetmeats, gingerbread and figs, as they drain flagons of spiced wine and beer. The centrepiece of the confectionery is a large sugar paste replica of Whitehall Palace edged with gold leaf, a masterpiece, which the cook has taken many hours to prepare. The dancing will continue long into the night or whenever the queen retires, but she has been known to dance until dawn, much to the frustration of those who would rather be in their beds, either alone or with someone else. The musicians play in the gallery above, although the noise of everyone talking and laughing does much to drown their playing. Bess sits with the other ladies and listens to their chatter. She is in a particularly reflective mood. Having been here for several weeks now, it is not easy for her to enjoy some time to herself.

Her duties as lady-in-waiting involve being in attendance to the queen on a daily basis. There is always some task to do: assisting with the queen's toilette, attending to the royal wardrobe, sewing and mending, caring for her jewellery, taking dictation and writing letters, applying cosmetics to the queen's face, embroidery, reading aloud to her or playing chess and backgammon. At Court there is plenty of entertainment to amuse everyone. There are always musicians and dancers, plays to watch, masked balls, banquets and gambling. The queen also loves hunting and falconry whenever she can spare time from her state duties. As a high-ranking lady-in-waiting, Bess is privileged to have the ear of the queen in her private chambers, which is much sought after, hence everyone approaches her asking for favours or to intercede on their behalf. Some are not beyond offering bribes, but Bess takes her duties very seriously and conducts herself with dignity and poise, not becoming involved in the more giggly chatter of the younger ladies who are, in fact, slightly in awe of her. They look up now as she prepares to leave the table, wondering if all the rumours about her suitors are true. She whispers to Blanche that she will be back shortly.

"Bess, are you sure it is wise? No one may leave without the queen's permission. What if her majesty notices?"

They both look to where the queen is laughing with the Earl of Leicester, their faces close.

"I will explain and she will understand."

Blanche looks skeptical.

"I am not sure that she will."

Bess puts her hand on her friend's shoulder. "You worry too much."

She makes her way along the back of the hall to the stairs and hurries to her chamber. It is not so warm once out of the hall, and she pulls her mantle round her as she walks. Luckily the fire in her chamber still gives out some heat and she is glad of it. Only a matter of minutes after she sits at her desk to write, there is a knock on the door. She is startled; someone must have seen her leave. Has the queen sent someone to fetch her after all?

Covering the letters quickly, she bids them enter. To her surprise it is George Talbot, the Earl of Shrewsbury, the writer of the third letter. She immediately curtseys and he responds by bowing low and asks, a little cautiously, if he may speak to her. Bess hesitates, as the queen forbids male visitors to the apartments of her ladies-in-waiting, a fact that everyone knows.

"It is not allowed, your grace."

"What I have to say will only take a few moments, Lady St Loe."

"Very well."

As he passes her to stand by the window, she catches a hint of sandalwood in the air and becomes acutely aware of his masculine presence in the confined chamber. Bess pushes the door so that it is almost shut and waits, folding her hands demurely in front of her with her eyes downcast, as is proper. The earl is tall and slim, his cropped hair and long beard accentuate the serious expression in his dark eyes. His clothes are made from the finest red velvet and silk embroidery, trimmed with sable, a fur that must only be worn by peers of the realm. He clears his throat and speaks quickly in a hushed tone.

"I had hoped to spend some time alone with you since you have been at Court, but your duties have prevented me from having that pleasure. I realise of course that the queen's service must take priority, but for man such as myself, who is in love, it is a hard cross to bear."

Bess looks suitably embarrassed. She raises her head to meet his gaze but betrays no emotion.

"You cannot be unaware of my feelings for you. Your recent letter has given me hope that we have a future together," he says.

"Forgive me, your grace, but may I ask why have you chosen to honour me in this way?"

"Why should I not? You are one of the most sought after ladies of the Court. Your many virtues attract not only myself, but others. It seems you can have any husband you choose."

"On the contrary, for you are the one who may have the pick of the ladies at Court. You are the highest ranking aristocrat after his grace, the Duke of Norfolk. There are many who would desire to be your wife."

She looks at him seductively and murmurs modestly, "I would bring little to the marriage."

"I disagree. I believe a marriage between us could be mutually beneficial."

"In what way?"

"We cannot discuss this matter here. Are you able to meet me tomorrow morning after breakfast in the queen's privy garden?"

"Her majesty has a gown fitting, so I should be able to slip away unnoticed."

"Good. Until tomorrow, my lady." She stands aside for him to leave and stopping in front of her, they look into each other's eyes for a few seconds to exchange a look of understanding, before she closes the door behind him. Taking a deep breath, she goes over to the looking glass. Her face betrays nothing except her usual calm expression. Calling for Agnes, they begin the task of choosing what to wear for the meeting. Bess knows she cannot underestimate the importance of seeing him alone tomorrow morning. For the moment at least, the feast is forgotten.

☙❧

The following morning Bess dresses carefully to see the earl. She has decided on a pale lilac gown with a deep burgundy velvet cloak, together with her favourite headdress of cream pearls.

Agnes helps her with undisguised excitement, knowing her mistress has an assignation, but not with whom.

"Good luck, my lady," Agnes whispers as she leaves the chamber. She is rewarded with a brief smile from Bess, who will not admit to feeling slightly apprehensive.

The queen has woken with a headache and told the dressmaker to wait until she feels better. Blanche is her sole attendant and she will not allow anyone else to apply cold herbal compresses to her forehead, so the other ladies are at their leisure. A few have slipped away to quieter parts of the palace for secret trysts with their lovers, whilst others sit around in their bedchambers reading, playing cards or gossiping. Usually the Great Hall is filled with courtiers hoping to speak to the queen, but this morning it is deserted, save for a few servants sweeping the floor.

Bess walks purposefully through a side door and makes her way across the courtyard. The morning is damp, and she silently curses her soft leather shoes, which look pretty but do not keep her feet dry. Above her, a wisp of wood smoke from the many chimneys that burn within the palace drifts downwards, and she coughs as it catches in her throat. Two female servants carrying baskets of laundry look at her curiously as they pass. In a couple of minutes she arrives at the entrance to the gardens and pauses to compose herself, smoothing the folds of her gown and adjusting her headdress. She soon sees the earl, sitting on a bench, looking expectant. He jumps up when he sees her approaching, and she curtseys in response to his formal bow.

"I have laid a rug for your comfort this morning." Inclining her head at his thoughtfulness, she sits gracefully, arranging her skirt with care.

"You are very kind."

"I would not wish you to be cold on such a day." Remaining standing, he fiddles with his gold rings and she smiles to herself at his nervousness.

"I will come straight to the point, by your leave. Since my dear wife died earlier this year, I have been brought very low and I have come to realise that I miss the company and companionship of someone to share life's journey. I can think of no-one better than you."

"Your grace, I am honoured that you should think of me in this way. But I should remind you that I am not a slip of a girl to be dazzled by a title or wealth. I have buried three husbands and I have no desire for a fourth."

"Do you not have feelings for me, as I have for you?"

"I am very fond of you, but marriage ... I am not sure."

"But what can I do to help you decide in my favour? I would do anything, I mean what I say."

Bess savours those last five words before replying.

"You mentioned yesterday that a marriage between us could be mutually beneficial. I assume you are thinking of joining our two families together by the marriage of our children, are you not?"

"Yes!" he says quickly, and sits down beside her, his eagerness all too visible.

"You have no doubt heard that some years ago I arranged for my daughter, Catherine, to marry the Earl of Pembroke's son, Henry, and for my son and heir, Francis, to marry the earl's eldest daughter, Anne."

"I remember."

"So, your son Henry Cavendish would marry my daughter, Grace. One of your daughters would marry my son, Gilbert; thus uniting the Shrewsbury and Cavendish families."

"It should be my Mary. She is only twelve, so I would not consent to a full marriage until she was of age."

"Of course, my own Grace is but eight years old, and I would wish the same for her." He pauses before continuing, "but your son, Henry ... ?"

"You have heard tales of his behaviour."

"I confess that I have and it worries me."

"Let me reassure you. Henry is young and immature. With the right guidance, I am sure that he will settle down, and by the time Grace is of age, he will be ready for marriage and its responsibilities. I am afraid he has mixed with some bad influences at school."

"Just so, the young can be reckless." He is thoughtful for a few seconds. "But I am not averse to making my proposition as attractive as possible for you. You will not find me ungenerous. In short, I am willing to consider whatever conditions you propose."

Bess is silent as she gets up from the bench and begins to walk up and down the path. He watches anxiously.

"I must keep Chatsworth as my own," she says eventually.

"Yes, if that is your wish. I would have control of your Barlow, Cavendish and St Loe lands for my lifetime."

"Then they would revert back to me."

"Of course."

"I wish for these agreements to be drawn up legally, there must be a marriage jointure."

"Naturally. You may have your own lawyers draw up the documents. We can agree on the finer points later."

"No, I would prefer us to be clear at the outset, I do not wish any misunderstanding between us."

He looks mildly surprised but shrugs.

"What else do you desire?"

"I wish for the rents of several of your properties to be made over to me for my lifetime together with the manors of ... " she pretends to think about it. "... Handsworth, Over Ewedon and, shall we say Bolsterstone, given to me outright?"

"Yes, that would be acceptable to me. I do so dislike discussing these financial marital arrangements. I find it quite distasteful, but of course it must be done."

"I would also like us to buy Sutton Court, my late husand's home, from his daughter."

The earl makes a gesture of mock surrender. "Is that everything?"

Bess looks uncomfortable but she knows it must be said. "We have not discussed the marriage bed."

"We have not," he agrees. "Are you worried about it?"

"Not worried, but I am forty and past child bearing. I am not sure what we should expect from each other."

He takes her hand and gently guides her so that they sit together.

"My love, do not fret. Our past marriages have given us both sons and daughters enough. But I would hope we shall enjoy each other, not only in the bedchamber, but as companions through the rest of our lives."

"We are not young, I have some grey hairs," she says ruefully.

"As do I. Such matters are unimportant. Our two families will be joined together and we can grow old as we watch them thrive."

"You do not want a young wife to warm your bed?"

He chuckles and shakes his head as if the idea is amusing.

"You told me I could marry anyone I chose. It is you Bess, who lifts my heart. I do not want some empty headed young woman who is younger than my children."

Bess smiles at the idea, but he becomes serious.

"Do you want a marriage only of convenience?"

"Do you?"

"I confess I do not, for I find you the most beautiful and desirable of women."

He kisses her hand before adding shyly, "How do you find me? Am I agreeable to you?"

"Most certainly, I have found you more than agreeable for a long time."

"So if I consent to all your conditions, will you agree to marry me?"

She nods, unable to hide her delight. "Yes, I will marry you after our children's betrothal."

"Then I am the happiest man alive."

He puts his arm round her waist, not caring now if they are seen and Bess responds to his kisses. She is going to be Elizabeth Talbot, Countess of Shrewsbury. At that moment she has to stop herself from shouting it from the rooftops.

ርሄ୪ጋ

The Earl of Shrewsbury's London Residence. December 1568

It is evening and Bess waits for George to come home. He is late back from his audience with the queen, and should have returned over two hours ago. The servants have been instructed to have his supper ready within minutes of his arrival, and a boy is given the task of watching and waiting by the kitchen door. From here, there is a good view of the River Thames with it's numerous rowing boats, barges and wherrys that carry passengers and goods up and down stream, even at this late hour. They glide past the murky shadows of buildings and alleyways frequented by thieves and beggars, who loiter there each sunset. Voices carry to the far banks where swans huddle together as the gentle swish of the oars stroke the dark lapping water. The air grows colder as the night progresses, and a fog descends, swallowing the shapes and figures so that eventually it cloaks everyone and everything. But inside, Bess has both light and warmth. She peers at intervals through the windows, although she can see nothing.

In the ten months since Bess and George Talbot married, there has been a mixed response at Court to the news. The queen and Bess' friends all expressed their delight, but there were others who had not been so generous. There is still whispering in corners that Bess is a fortune hunter, a scheming, gold digger who would no doubt see this fourth husband into an early grave too. But other news has been occupying the gossips, which is far more interesting. The country was shocked in May at the news of the Scottish Queen Mary, whose nobles rebelled and forced her to abdicate in favour of her baby son, James. She fled Scotland and is now under guard in the north of England. Meanwhile, Bess has been busy in Derbyshire with her eldest daughter Frances, for the birth of her first grandchild, a daughter they named Elizabeth, who quickly becomes known as Bessie. As soon as she felt Frances and the baby were well enough, Bess travelled to London, anxious to be on hand for George if needed.

At last the lights of the Shrewsbury barge come into view and it moors up silently. The kitchen boy runs back inside to tell the cook, who begins to hastily put the finishing touches to the supper. A servant carries a lit torch as he escorts George to the house, followed by his secretary weighed down with books and documents. Bess hears him speak briefly, then the door opens and he comes towards her with outstretched arms. He looks tired, but smiles at her before they embrace without speaking while the servants are already laying food on the table.

"Come and stand by the fire, you look so cold," she urges him when he has washed his hands from the silver jug and bowl on the table.

"I would have been home sooner, but I kept being delayed by people stopping me to talk."

They wait as wine is poured and the servants leave, shutting the door behind them. She cannot contain her curiosity any longer.

"Well, husband, what news do you have?"

He takes a long swig of wine and helps himself to a dish of roasted venison and peacock in jelly. Bess toys with some pickled conger eel, but she cannot eat until she knows what has happened at Court today. George relishes her impatience and wipes his mouth on a napkin, his expression gives nothing away.

"George, please!" she pleads.

This time he looks smug and leans back in his chair.

"You may rest easy, Bess. I have been chosen by her majesty to guard the Scottish Queen Mary. She told me there was no one she could trust as much as me for the task. I am now a member of the Privy Council," he adds proudly.

"This is wonderful news!" Bess can barely contain her excitement.

"At present Mary is being held at Bolton Castle, as you know. She is shortly to be moved, but it has not been decided where she will go yet."

"To the Tower of London perhaps?"

"No, that is considered too close to the queen. Sir Francis Walsingham and Sir William Cecil want her to be kept in the country. Tutbury Castle in Staffordshire has been suggested; it was used as a hunting lodge by my family, but needs some work before we take up residence."

"We, why do you say "we" husband?"

George pours himself some more wine.

"Her majesty is keen for your involvement. We are both to watch Mary and report to Sir Francis Walsingham on what she says and does."

"Is she truly a threat to the throne?"

"It is believed so, certainly a focus for Catholic unrest. Remember how she called herself Queen of England after the death of her first husband, King Francis?"

"I see."

"You seem troubled?"

"Not at all, I am just thinking of how this will change our lives."

"It will not be for long, a year or two at the most."

"What will happen then?"

"The queen will decide her fate in due course. No doubt marriage to a foreign prince or she may take the veil …"

"That would hardly be appropriate!"

"No, perhaps not. Her alleged involvement with the murder of her second husband Lord Darnley would of course preclude it. That is not for us to worry about. Our task is to guard her well and keep her majesty and Sir Francis informed. It should not be too arduous. The queen will provide an allowance of course. We will have to journey to Tutbury shortly and make preparations. Her majesty has made it clear that Mary is to be accorded every comfort expected for a queen."

"I long to see her. They say she is very beautiful."

"Do they?" He says it a little too quickly.

"And very accomplished."

"You will see her soon enough and be able to judge for yourself. But do not fret my Bess, I only have eyes for you."

"I should hope so."

"That is another reason why the queen chose me. I am happily married and unlikely to fall in love with her."

"I would certainly not wish you to fall in love with anyone!"

George smiles at her indignation, then becomes serious.

"It is said that men are swayed by her beauty and cannot think properly. The queen needs her jailor to be immune to such behaviour. Also of course we are both of the new faith and loyal to the queen. This is a job not without danger, Bess. The Scots and English Catholics believe she is the rightful Queen of England and will stop at nothing to place Mary on the throne. You know already of the attempts on our own queen's life."

"But think of the prestige it will give us! We shall prove that we are up to the mark. We will rise in her majesty's estimation. Who knows what other honours she will bestow on you?"

Her eyes shine to think that George has been chosen for this important job, amongst all the others at Court.

"Steady Bess, let us take one step at a time. First we must prepare Tutbury to be fit for a queen. We shall travel there and assess what is needed, there is not much time."

Bess is already beginning to think of the necessary arrangements. This is an exciting end to their first year of marriage.

ଔଌ

Queen Mary stands in the middle of the chamber in Tutbury Castle where she is to be kept under guard and looks at everything with distaste.

"This is an outrage! Am I still to be locked up like a common criminal? It is shameful enough that I am bundled about like an unwanted parcel from place to place. But now you expect me to occupy apartments that are only fit for being pulled down. When am I to see your queen? Is she aware of these appalling conditions?"

George and Bess watch from the chamber door, having escorted her and her ladies from the main gate. Preparations have been hurriedly taking place for the last few weeks to make the castle ready, which is no easy task as it has been empty for years. The journey from Bolton Castle in midwinter has been especially tedious, and the travellers are cold, tired and dispirited. Coach after coach has just driven through the gates of Tutbury, and the courtyard is full of horses and various members of Mary's court as they disembark and look at the surroundings without enthusiasm. The Chief Guard tells George that Mary had been taken ill en route, and thus delayed their arrival. He adds that it had been very trying to travel under the conditions of security that he was obliged to use, and he is heartily pleased to find they had arrived without mishap. George nods grimly, anxious to move her to safety. After being formally welcomed by the Shrewsburys, she is ushered towards the tower where she is to be lodged. Inside, the fire does little to dispel the chilly temperature and despite her best efforts of bringing tapestries and furniture from Chatsworth, the accommodation is not what Bess would have wished. Studying her charge now, with fascination, she cannot help but think, so this is the queen who has scandalised the country. But Mary does not at this moment seem capable of such behaviour and she often touches the crucifix that hangs round her neck, as if to reassure herself of its presence.

At twenty-six, she has a statuesque figure and is as tall as George himself, with pretty, dark eyes and fair hair. Her legendary beauty has not been exaggerated, but closer inspection reveals her to be very pale and there is an air of fragile vulnerability about her. She speaks with a lilting Scottish accent although French is her first language, having been brought up since the age of six in the French Court. Everyone knows of her past history. It is a sorry tale of passion, recklessness and lust which has brought her here as a prisoner, a potentially dangerous adversary to the throne of England. The full story is even more shocking than first thought.

Two years previously, whilst Mary was heavily pregnant, she witnessed the fatal stabbing of her loyal secretary, Rizzio. Her courtiers were jealous of him and resented his alleged interference into their political affairs. Lord Darnley, her husband, was suspected of some involvement; his womanising and heavy drinking led Mary to think about divorcing him, but that would have made her heir, James, illegitimate. So when Lord Darnley was found dead in the garden after an explosion, it seemed a little too convenient. Mary had also fallen in love with James Hepburn, the Earl of Bothwell, a Scottish noble whom she had met in France. Controversy surrounded their marriage as it was alleged he abducted and raped her beforehand.

Rumours were rife that she had claimed she would follow him to the end of the world in her petticoat. Unsurprisingly, her Scottish barons, horrified by these events, forced her to abdicate and will keep her baby son James until he is old enough to rule. Despite raising an army, Mary had to admit defeat of her army at Langside; she then miscarried twins and never saw Bothwell again. Forced to seek sanctuary from her cousin, Queen Elizabeth in England, she now faces an uncertain future. These last three years of her life have been very eventful and she has shadows round her eyes to show for it. Her loyal ladies-in-waiting stand like sentinels in the corner. Mary insists that she is not parted from them. Their disapproval of the present proceedings is palpable as they stare in tight-lipped hostility at George and Bess. Mary goes to the window and her gaze lingers on the view of the surrounding countryside, which is pleasant enough, but isolated, with no sign of habitation for miles.

Her heart had sunk when she saw Tutbury as they approached it earlier. It is surrounded by a high wall with only one entrance and is not the most prepossessing of buildings. She and her ladies wrinkle their noses delicately at the dampness, which is evident as soon as they are inside. The plaster walls are cracked and the timber frames going rotten, for it is used rarely and has been neglected in recent years. Layers of dust, mouse droppings and cobwebs have been hastily swept away, fires lit under disused chimneys and windows cleaned, but nothing can disguise these unsavoury surroundings. Her voice quivering, she continues her complaints to George, who looks slightly awkward as he waits for a chance to reply.

"I came to Queen Elizabeth for sanctuary, as one cousin to another. If our situations were reversed, I would not have insulted her by providing such a place. It is hardly fitting for an anointed queen such as myself. I cannot stay here, I command that somewhere else is found for me."

"I am afraid that will not be possible, your majesty. My queen wishes you to remain at Tutbury and I can assure you that every effort will be made to make you comfortable," says George.

Mary's lip trembles and she sits down, her hand on her forehead. "Have you any idea how it feels to be treated in this way? My own barons have turned against me, I have lost everything. They took away my son, my dear James. I feel as if I have lost an arm without him." She begins to sob.

"Now I am alone in England and without friends. I hope I shall be allowed to hear Mass and worship, as I have done all my life; your queen will allow it will she not?"

Turning her eyes beseechingly on him, George hesitates, aware that Bess is watching closely.

"You must rest now, you are tired after the journey."

"I will have some refreshments sent up for you and more fuel for the fire, your majesty," Bess tells her. "You have your ladies here with you. I am sure we can think of ways to improve these conditions, can we not, husband?"

"Indeed, if at all possible," George replies stiffly.

He regards her in dismay as her sobbing continued unabated. Women crying always make him cringe with embarrassment. Her ladies glide forward to help her, speaking softly as they offer comfort.

Bess curtseys and George bows uncertainly before they leave. He turns the key and looks at Bess. Now that she is finally here, there seems an air of unreality about Mary's very existence here. To have the care of a Scottish Queen in England, where she is to be kept as a prisoner is an unprecedented event. Neither Bess nor George have any experience of being a jailor, let alone to a person of royal blood. They are just about old enough to remember the fate that the two Queens Anne Boleyn and Katherine Howard suffered when they were taken as prisoners to the Tower, and subsequently beheaded on the orders of their husband, Henry VIII.

George addresses two of the guards who are to be permanently stationed at the entrance to Mary's chamber.

"No-one is to enter or leave without permission from myself or the countess."

"Yes, your grace."

They stare ahead, aware of the seriousness of their orders. There will be no card playing or drinking on this watch. Bess suddenly becomes brisk.

"I will send up a tray of hot food at once. The room is not warm enough, it will have to be kept warmer otherwise she will die of cold. She will need extra bed covers and more candles."

"But that will mean more cost."

"We have no choice. She is a queen and must be treated as one. Those are our instructions."

"What about her entourage? There is over sixty of them, all standing about and waiting in the hall. What are we to do them? Why were we not told there would be so many?"

"We will ascertain who is the most senior, they can have chambers. The others will have to be content with whatever we can offer for the time being."

Bess turns towards the kitchens and hurries away. "Will you arrange for more wood to be sent up at once at once?" she barks over her shoulder to him before disappearing round a corner. George walks slowly back to his study. Queen Mary has only been here less than an hour and already he can feel a headache coming on.

०३৪०

Bess and George are not able to speak freely until later that evening when they go to bed. The headache has now become a vice like grip and he feels exhausted. Leaning back against the pillows, he watches as Bess climbs in beside him and she smiles encouragingly.

"I think once we have everything to our satisfaction, the Scottish Queen will soon settle in to her captivity. She must accept her situation, there is no choice."

"She was very emotional this afternoon," he replies.

"Would any woman not be emotional under these circumstances?"

"Do not expect me to sympathise with her, Bess. She has brought all this on herself."

"I know, but I cannot help feeling …"

"It is not our place to have feelings!"

His voice is harsh. "We have been given a task and we must carry it out. I hope you are not going to side with her because she is a woman!"

"Of course not. But a little compassion would not go amiss." Bess snuggles up beside him.

"We will do our duty as required."

"I am glad to hear it." George closes his eyes in an attempt to end the conversation, but Bess has other ideas.

"She is fifteen years younger than me. Would you call her beautiful?"

"Does it matter? I have no opinion on the matter, Bess."

"Nonsense! You must have an opinion."

"I have not given it any thought, there are other more important matters on my mind." He hopes she will leave the subject alone.

"Of course you have! I must be vigilant, I do not want you to become enamoured of her. I can see why she is believed to be beautiful, although I thought she would be somehow more ..."

She frowns, searching for the right word.

"... worldly, especially after all she has been through. Are you listening to me?"

"Yes." He kisses her forehead absent-mindedly. "Do not imagine I will fall under her spell. There is no chance of that happening when I have you as my wife. Now can we go to sleep?"

"Husband, we have the Queen of Scotland under our roof and in our care. I am far too excited about it to sleep. I will take some tapestries to her tomorrow and ask if she would like to work them with me."

"Does she really need all those attendants with her? Quite unnecessary in my view," he observes.

"It would appear to be the case, I did not think there would be so many. I am concerned that Tutbury will not be able to cope with such a number, it is not a large castle is it?"

"No, we have never had more than two score people staying at one time. With the servants and guards as well, we shall be a very large household to feed and shelter, more like four times that number. Then there are supplies to organise."

George opens his eyes now; his mind begins to race with the thought of everything that needs to be done.

"We will have go further afield if we cannot obtain enough locally." As always, Bess is ever practical.

"Hmmm. That will cost more."

"The queen must increase your allowance if needed."

They look at one another doubtfully. "I am sure she will do so. Then there are the arrangements for the privy. Tutbury has never had to cope with so many people before. I fear it will need sweetening sooner than we had previously planned."

"Then we shall have to move elsewhere whilst it is carried out."

"The thought of moving her makes me break out in a cold sweat."

"Hush! She has only just arrived; she will not need to move for a while yet. I will befriend her and try to gauge her thoughts and plans. You, of course, will do your duty as her jailor. Do not fret; we have good servants and guards around us. They are loyal and will help to carry out our queen's wishes."

She turns to blow out the candle beside the bed and the chamber is plunged into darkness.

"Bess, I am sometimes afraid that I am not up to this task."

"You must not think that – her majesty would not have commanded you to do it if she thought you were not the best person."

"I could not have refused." They both know this is true; to have done so would be unthinkable.

"How long do you think she will be kept as a prisoner?"

"Oh George, I really do not know, a year perhaps,"

"A year would not be so bad."

"One thing we must remember though," Bess whispers. "If, God forbid, anything should happen to our queen ..."

"Do not even think it!"

"... if anything should happen, then Mary would take the throne."

Neither speaks and he reaches for her hand, for such a thought is treasonous.

"We must take care not to alienate her," George says cautiously.

"I know."

"Then there is Sir Francis Walsingham, he has such a way with him that even someone innocent like myself feels guilty when he looks at me; and I have done nothing wrong to warrant his accusatory stare."

Bess gives a soft laugh. "Yes, I am not looking forward to reporting everything to him either. But we shall be together to help one another. And it will not be forever."

"True."

"Just think of how the queen will reward us. And of the prestige it gives us amongst the Court."

He does not reply and turns away. It is too late for such conversations and he longs for sleep.

She moves position too and settles down to sleep, trying to push the niggling misgivings about Mary's care to the back of her mind. All her friends have been very impressed with the news that the Shrewsburys are to act as Mary's jailors. It is a clear sign from Queen Elizabeth that they are trusted and loyal members of her court. Bess cannot help but feel some sympathy for Mary. She is obviously someone who allows her heart to rule her head, has made some catastrophic errors of judgement, and is therefore paying the price. The thought of ever being separated from her own children and kept as a prisoner in a foreign land fills Bess with horror. She resolves to show Mary some kindness, which, if matters did change in Mary's favour, would only be to Bess' advantage.

George is lying beside her in a stew of worry and anxiety. This task is going to be more of a challenge that he had first believed. There are so many aspects of her security and care to plan and carry out. Already he has spent a considerable sum of money and Queen Elizabeth has not paid him a farthing yet. He should have penned a letter to Sir Francis by now telling him of Mary's arrival, but he would have to do it in the morning. He tries to ignore the pounding of his heart and the pain from his gout, which has flared up again. Sighing heavily, he pulls the covers closer and resentfully notes that Bess is now snoring lightly.

On the other side of the castle, Mary is tossing and turning in her bed as she listens to the steady breathing of her sleeping ladies. She is very tired after the journey and the shock of seeing her accommodation, which was not at all what she had expected. She misses being outdoors and the freedom of riding or walking wherever she chooses. Most of all, her baby James is always on her mind and she worries whether he is being looked after lovingly, although she has been assured that he is being well cared for. When she had been told that the Earl of Shrewsbury and his wife were to be her jailors, she tried to find out as much as possible about them. She knows that the earl is rich and powerful, and that Bess has been married three times before. Naturally they are both of the new faith and enjoy Queen Elizabeth's favour. Her first impressions of them are that the earl is a fussy, nervous man, but his wife seems sympathetic and slightly in awe of her. Mary realises that somehow she must turn events to give her some advantage. She is still a queen after all and they are merely subjects. Throwing back the covers, she gets up and walks over to the window. The moon shines silently on the icy ground and all is still outside. Beneath her stands a lone guard, his breath visible in the cold air. She can just make out the figures of two more at the entrance gate. There are many more, some of whom have ridden with them from Bolton Castle. Escape is not going to be easy. She wonders again what her followers are planning, for she has every faith that God will come to her aid.

Shivering, she gets back into bed and tries to sleep, but it is just before dawn when she finally closes her eyes and her unhappiness is blotted out for a few precious hours.

ɷʚ

Bess is as good as her word and the next morning, after breakfast, appears at Mary's door with a servant carrying her needlework basket and some embroidery panels. She finds her charge and two of her ladies-in-waiting reading quietly in a circle round the fire. The ladies have been unpacking Mary's belongings for the chamber looks more comfortable with velvet cushions and heavy drapes at the windows to keep out the draughts. On a chest at the far end there is a large crucifix with two candles on either side, together with a Bible and rosary. Bess curtseys and waits as Mary closes her book.

"I see you have brought me something to pass the time, countess."

"I have, your majesty. I hear you are a skilled needlewoman. I too, love to sew. If it would please you, I thought we could sew together."

The servant lays the basket and tapestries on the table and leaves, eyeing Mary carefully as she does so.

"I have all the time now to devote myself to such an occupation. Pray be seated."

One of the ladies-in-waiting pulls up a chair for Bess and she sits down. To her surprise, she sees that a silk canopy has been erected since her last visit yesterday, which Mary goes to sit underneath. Intricately embroidered, are the words: *En ma fin est mon commencement.* She notices Bess looking at it.

"Do you speak the French language, countess?"

Bess flushes, she is sensitive about her lack of formal education.

"I do not, your majesty."

"It translates as 'in the end lies my beginning' – it is my cloth of state."

"It is very fine." She cannot help but feel at a disadvantage to this young and beautiful woman sitting in front of her. Mary seems to have recovered her composure from yesterday and, even in the captivity in which she finds herself, there is no doubt she has a regal bearing. Reaching into a coffer beside her, she brings out some examples of her own work, which feature Biblical and classical themes and places them in front of Bess.

"You are very accomplished, I have rarely seen work of such a high standard," Bess eventually observes grudgingly, as she studies them.

"Thank you. I have some pattern books too, we can use for inspiration."

They begin to thread needles and start to sew. The ladies-in-waiting, both called Mary, sit apart, also sewing. For a time the only sound is the crackle of the logs that burn in the grate.

"I hope the extra wood and bed covers are to your liking. And your chef prepared your meal this morning as you wish," says Bess, her head bent over her work.

"I have little appetite."

"Then we must find dishes to tempt you."

"With no access to the fresh air, I doubt I shall want to eat very much. I am used to being outdoors."

"I am sure exercise in the open air will be permitted."

"I should like that. I miss riding very much, I am accustomed to riding every day."

"It could soon be arranged, if that is your wish."

"I have only ten of my own horses here, I need more. Your queen, does she ride well?"

"She is an excellent horsewoman and hunts whenever her state duties allow."

Mary pauses to cut a thread. "I hope to meet her one day."

Bess remains silent as Mary warms to her theme.

"Yes, all our communication is through letters and representatives, which is not the same at all. If I could only speak to her face to face, I would be able to reassure her that I am no threat to her or her kingdom. Do you think it is likely we shall be able to meet soon?"

"I do not know – perhaps it will be possible."

"As woman to woman, queen to queen, we have much in common."

Bess cannot help but raise an eyebrow in disagreement. For how could Mary who had been thrice married, accused of murder and adultery, made to abdicate her throne, a strict Catholic and a mother of a child who had been placed in the care of others, have much in common with the Protestant Elizabeth who was by her own wish called 'The Virgin Queen'?

Mary laughs, clearly amused at her own joke. "Do not be alarmed, countess! I realise that my past is very different from your own queen in many ways. But she was kept in the Tower, as a prisoner by her sister Mary, was she not? That much at least, we have experienced together."

"Those times were very dangerous, we are all glad to have them behind us," replies Bess, and changes the subject quickly, holding up some embroidery threads.

"Look at these colours, so beautiful."

Mary makes a noise of agreement while studying her work.

"Come, countess, I am not stupid. I know why you are here with me." Her voice is silky and her eyes remain downcast on her lap as she works her needle.

"You wish to know my intentions, my plans, in fact everything about me so that you can report back to that spymaster Walsingham. Can you deny it?" Bess puts her needle down and looks at her steadily.

"I will not lie to you, your majesty. I have been asked to report about you, it is true. Would you be surprised if it were not the case?"

"Nothing about the court of your queen would surprise me."

Bess leans forward, her voice low although there is only the four of them in the chamber. "But I am not without sympathy for your present situation. Fate has brought us to this place at the same time. Neither of us really wants to be here. I myself would much rather be at home in Chatsworth, where I have every comfort, and I am close to my dear family. You of course, would rather be in Scotland as reigning queen over your people and with your baby son." At that, Mary's eyes began to fill with tears, and Bess puts her hand over hers in a gesture of comfort.

"We must make the best of it and trust in God to help us."

"I know, I know, but it is so hard. If only I knew how long I was to be kept as a prisoner. Am I really so much of a threat?"

"I fear so."

"I would do nothing to harm your queen, you must believe me. I have been most cruelly used. My only wish is to return home."

Mary drops her needlework and begins to sob uncontrollably. Her ladies begin to fuss over her and Bess stands up, realising that it was not a good idea to mention her son. The change of Mary's mood has been sudden and taken Bess by surprise.

"I will take my leave, your majesty. Hopefully when I return, you will be feeling better and we may resume our work." Disappointed, she leaves, but is determined to return as soon as possible. But as the weeks stretch into months, the two women eventually establish a routine that suits them both. They enjoy sewing, and find it is not unpleasant to sit beside the fire in the mornings and work whilst talking to one another. The hours pass peacefully enough, and when George looks in on them sometimes, he feels excluded from their air of feminine solidarity and awkwardly leaves them. Mary believes that Bess is sympathetic towards her plight and for her part; Bess basks in the role of exclusive companion to her. In the afternoons, Mary is permitted to walk in the grounds with her ladies while George watches anxiously from an upstairs window as the guards patrol nearby. Sometimes in the evening, Bess returns for a game of cards before supper. She finds Mary seems content to listen to Bess speak of her family and building plans. Mary in turn tells Bess of her childhood and her time in France as the wife of the

French king. They tactfully avoid any mention of Mary's more recent life, by unspoken agreement.

"What do you speak of?" George enquires as they eat supper one evening. Bess waits until the servants have closed the door.

"Nothing important, you may be sure. Inconsequential talk that a man would find very dull."

"But tell me anyway. I am curious."

"Very well. We speak of the weather, which is always a safe subject. She tells me of the Scottish highlands and I tell her of the Derbyshire moors. We discuss hairstyles in the English and continental courts, fashion, the best cures for some ailments. She tell me of her childhood and the women who influenced her, her mother, Mary of Guise, the French Queen Catherine de Medici, Diana de Poitiers …"

George holds up his hand, already bored. "Enough! I have no interest in such female chatter."

"Well, you did ask. I would have thought information from intercepting her letters was enough to keep you occupied."

"I was only wondering if she mentioned this idea of her marriage to the Duke of Norfolk? Several of her supporters have suggested it." He gives a snort of derision.

"She calls him 'My Norfolk'!"

"No, and I did not ask her about it. That would not be a subject she would discuss with me. In any case, she is still officially married to Bothwell."

"That could be easily annulled or she could divorce him, she has grounds enough."

"Where is Bothwell now?"

"Last I heard he was languishing in a Danish cell. I doubt he will ever be free again."

"Hmmm. She has not met the Duke of Norfolk has she?"

"No, why?"

"He might be Catholic like Mary but physically ..." she looks askance at him.

"Yes, he is not the most attractive of men, I agree. But she will be attracted to him as a prominent member of the English Court. He of course will want the power that marriage will give him as King of Scotland."

"Can you imagine him so triumphant over the Earl of Leicester and William Cecil if that was to happen? He dislikes them both so much."

"I would rather not. They are aware of the suggestion, but no action has been taken yet."

"Why not?"

She notices him struggling to place food on to his spoon, and sees that his hand is swollen, but knows he will not thank her if she offers to help. George suffers with arthritis and it has worsened lately.

"An Englishman would be preferable to a foreigner who might raise an army against us."

"But Norfolk could raise the Catholics in the north."

He does not reply and she frowns.

"Does the queen know?"

"No one has dared to tell her."

There is an uneasy silence. Bess helps herself to more meat but he has pushed his plate away.

"So, how do you find the Scottish Queen?" she asks conversationally.

He drains his goblet and pours himself more wine. "You have seen for yourself, she is highly strung, very emotional, I do not understand why she has these vomiting episodes so often. She complains all the time."

"About what does she complain?"

"Everything. The apartments are too small, too cold. The smell of the privies is overpowering when they are emptied each week. The wine is inferior; her horses are not being cared for as she would wish, her food lacks variety. I could go on. It is all very taxing."

"She is just not used to this way of life. You must try to understand."

"Understand!" George splutters. "I understand that she is costing me a small fortune in coal and wood for her fire and the fires of her attendants. That is before all the cost of extra food for everyone here."

"But you have your allowance."

"I have not seen any sign of it yet. So far, I have paid for everything from my own purse."

"Write again to the queen, she has probably forgotten."

They both realise that this is a false hope, as Elizabeth is known to be very careful with money. He stares miserably at Bess, and she tries to rally him.

"Write tomorrow and tell her majesty that you are out of pocket. I have some letters to go to Court myself. By the end of the week I warrant there will be a bag of coins for you."

"I hope you are right."

"But have you asked the queen if we could move Mary to Wingfield soon? You realise everyone is remarking on the smell from privies now!"

"Yes, yes. She has given her consent. You are to go ahead and prepare it."

"I shall travel tomorrow, we will all be much more comfortable there. Which part of the house is Mary to have?"

"The chambers that overlook the orchard. We shall be in the suite over the entrance porch so that we may see who comes and goes."

Bess looks pleased; she dislikes Tutbury as much as Mary does.

"Will she be allowed more freedom there?"

He grunts and pushes his chair back to stretch his legs.

"Up to a point. Why do you ask me?"

"I feel as much a prisoner as she does. We are tied here and cannot venture far."

"You are not so much a prisoner as I am. You will be able to travel tomorrow and have a rest from these onerous duties."

"Are they so very onerous, my dear?"

"Yes, I am afraid I find them to be so."

"After so short a time?"

George moves away from the table to stand by the fire, wincing in pain from his gout. "I can see how this is going to be already. Mary will be a constant thorn in my side, and I shall be out of pocket for my trouble."

"There is no reason to think that. These early days are troublesome, but Mary will settle down and realise that if she is co-operative and does not take part in any plans to take the throne or escape, she will be win our queen's favour."

"Bess!" He looks at her sternly.

"She has already proved herself capable of trying to escape from her Scottish captors. Letters are coming and going all the time between her and her supporters. You do not believe her to be capable of such honesty do you?"

"I wish to give her the benefit of the doubt. She seems so sincere when I talk to her and I cannot help but think she may be our queen one day."

"Will you stop thinking such a treasonable idea!"

"There is no-one to hear us speak of it. We do not know what will become of the Scottish Queen."

"We know that she is the centre of all Catholic hopes for the throne to replace our queen. Even as we speak, there are those who are plotting such an event with great fervour. That is why we must be on our guard at all times."

"Everything will be better when we are in Wingfield, you will see. The queen will send you some money, Mary will be happier with her apartments, the spring weather will be warmer so we will use less fuel, and I will send for the physician to attend you for your gout." She gets up and stands on tiptoe to kiss his cheek.

"There, now if you have finished your supper, shall we have a game of Primero?"

He nods reluctantly and Bess calls for a servant to clear away before setting out the cards.

It was to be the first of many evenings when George needed cajoling over Mary and his care of her.

○§○

Much to the relief of Bess and Mary, the whole household is moved to Wingfield Manor within a few days of this conversation. Despite George's security worries, the journey goes as planned, and as it is April, the gardens are full of blossom which adds to the sense of well being after the gloomy surroundings of Tutbury. Bess and George are so frequently in and out of Mary's chamber that George decides to be constantly unlocking the door to her chamber is cumbersome and inconvenient. As long as the outer doors are secure, he begins to allow Mary some freedom within the house. A Scottish visitor appears one afternoon and requests to see his queen. He has various gifts, which after looking at them, George can find no reason to keep from her. Mary is delighted to receive him, and Bess has refreshments sent up from the kitchen for them.

That night, Bess and George are sound asleep when there is a scratching at the door of their chamber and it is flung open to reveal Mary, in her nightshirt, carrying a lit candle.

"Countess, you must help me!" she cries and approaches the bed.

Bess sits up, befuddled, and peers into the darkness at her.

"How did you find your way here? Are you quite well?"

"No, I am not!" She begins to pace up and down in agitation. "My visitor today has brought me such bad news. I hardly know how to tell you."

"Is it your son, James?" asks Bess kindly.

"No, it is not my little boy." As she comes closer, they see that her face is red and swollen with crying. "My visitor today brought me such bad news. I ... I am at such a loss."

Bess gets up and manoeuvres Mary into a chair as George looks on in horror.

"Now you must tell us everything. What did your visitor tell you that was so terrible?"

"He told me that I am seen as an adulteress by my people, they do not understand ..." she wails, rocking backwards and forwards.

"They are not aware of my whole story. But there is worse, they are calling me a murderer! Their own queen! I dread to think what lies have been spread about me and I am not there to defend myself. It is too much to bear. I am at such a loss, what am I going to do?"

Bess looks at George who is becoming more furious by the second. Agnes appears, disturbed by the noise, but Bess waves her away and she retreats, her face a picture of alarm.

"Please your majesty, you must calm yourself. I am sure it is not as bad as you believe."

"Yes, it is. You do not understand. I have no friends; there are no plans to return me to Scotland where I belong to rule over my people, where I have been brought up since birth to govern. I am at the mercy of your queen who sees fit to keep me under guard day and night. What is to become of me?"

She starts to rub her blotchy, tear stained face nervously, as her eyes dart around the chamber.

"I will be a prisoner forever, always under guard. I shall never see my son again or hold him in my arms! What have I done to deserve such treatment?"

Further wails and sobs follow this exchange and Bess stands beside her helplessly. George beckons for her to come to him.

"How did she get past the guards? Get rid of her! Can we have no peace even in our own bedchamber?" he whispers, highly embarrassed to be seen *en deshabille* by the Scottish Queen.

"I am trying!" Bess retorts angrily. "If you think you can do any better, please do so."

They glare at each other and George pulls the covers up towards his chin. "Escort her back to her chambers at once, queen or no queen, I will not have this behaviour."

He reaches for the keys beside the bed and gives them to Bess.

"Take her back and lock the door this time."

"You are the one who unlocked it!"

"You made no objection at the time."

"I cannot just leave her in this condition."

"Her ladies can deal with her. It is not our responsibility to calm her when she is told what is merely the truth." Bess bites her lip, but helps Mary to her feet.

"Come, your majesty, you must go back to bed. I will take you, lean on my arm."

Mary allows herself to be taken back along the corridor, continually muttering to herself that she is a true Christian and why has God forsaken her? Her ladies are waiting anxiously in the doorway, unsure of what to do. Bess speaks to them quietly, but firmly.

"Your mistress needs a cold compress on her eyes. I have tried to calm her. The news from her visitor has troubled her greatly. How long as she been like this? She will wake the whole house." Mary's senior lady-in-waiting looks at Bess with concern.

"Since vespers. We could not stop her crying or going to your chamber."

"The earl has told me to lock the door again; he was not best pleased to have been disturbed in this manner. We will return in the morning, I bid you good night."

Bess shuts the door against further exchange and turns the key. The guard looks at her anxiously.

"I am sorry, your grace, I could not stop her. I did not feel I was at liberty to touch her, she is a royal person," he adds feebly.

"It must not happen again. The earl is furious and he will see you in the morning." She hurries back to the bedchamber where George is now glowering as he holds out his hand for the keys.

"Have you locked it as I said?"

"Yes, of course. Apparently she has been crying for hours."

She climbs back into bed, pumping up the pillows as she does so.

"What did she expect us to do about it?" he asks irritably.

"I have no idea."

"How did she get past the guards?"

Bess says nothing. It is not perhaps the right moment to tell George that the guard on duty tonight is a callow youth who had obviously been overwhelmed by Mary's status and hysteria. "This is a serious breach of security, we must take steps to make sure it never happens again."

"Yes, we will, husband. But no harm was done in the end and she is back under lock and key once more."

"Now I am wide awake. I doubt I will sleep again tonight," he says resentfully.

Bess lies down and closes her eyes. Mary's hysterical outbursts are becoming more and more frequent and there is no doubt it is tiring to witness. George seems particularly affected by it, and is unsettled after each episode. He is obliged to write every day to Walsingham and Cecil with news of Mary, as they need constant reassurance that all is well. The happier mood that had descended on arrival at Wingfield is quickly being eroded by Mary's behaviour, and he can see no way of improving matters.

౧୫౨

A few weeks after this nocturnal visit, Bess presents herself at Mary's door one morning with the usual intention of sewing with her. She is greeted by one of her ladies, looking very concerned.

"Our queen is ill, your grace; she has a fever and we cannot rouse her."

"Take me to her." Bess follows them to Mary's bedside and is shocked at her appearance. Lying inert on the bed, her breathing is shallow and drops of perspiration trickle down her flushed face.

"Are there signs of ... ?"

The lady-in-waiting is quick to reassure her.

"No, we do not think it is the plague, there is no rash or swelling."

Bess looks relieved as such an illness is always of great concern and usually fatal, also it would spread like wildfire amongst everyone.

"I will send for our physician."

"No, your grace, she would not wish to see your physician; her majesty has her own, here amongst her Court. He knows her well and she would want him to treat her."

"Very well. You may tell the guard to summon him at once."

Within minutes the physician appears, followed closely by George, who pulls Bess over to the corner.

"What is wrong with her?"

"She looks very ill, but there are no plague symptoms, praise be to God. Her physician will be here shortly. I suggest you wait outside, for the ladies do not approve of you being here."

He glances round the chamber and sure enough, Mary's ladies are eyeing him disapprovingly, so he leaves quickly. Bess and the physician emerge after an hour, the latter looking full of his own self-importance. He is a stocky little man with a habit of licking his lips before speaking in his broad Scottish accent.

"Well, what is your diagnosis?" George asks anxiously as he locks the door again.

"Can we talk privately?"

"Downstairs," replies George curtly and leads the way.

Once in the privacy of a chamber away from Mary's apartments, the physician turns to them gravely.

"My queen is seriously ill and I blame the conditions under which she is kept to be responsible. It is most disgraceful that she is locked up and denied freedom. The strain of such a life is affecting her majesty's health, which has never been robust. I have never seen her as bad as she is today …"

George holds up his hands impatiently, "… what is your diagnosis?"

"My diagnosis," he emphasises each syllable with a haughty stare at him, "is that Queen Mary is suffering from an imbalance of the humours, caused by her unsuitable and inappropriate captivity by yourselves. This has weakened her body and she has succumbed to the epidemic of influenza that has been claiming victims throughout the land for the last eighteen months. I have seen all the symptoms before. This is very alarming and you would do well to inform your queen at once."

"And your treatment?" Bess speaks before George, who looks too stunned to respond. The physician turns his gaze on Bess with reluctance.

"My treatment will consist of bleeding and purging. Her majesty will need a special diet that I myself will formulate. I will also consult the stars to ascertain the most propitious time to act. She will need constant attendance day and night."

"Will she survive?" George finds his voice at last, although it is little more than a whisper.

"If God is willing," he replies coldly.

"We shall do all to help in this matter," Bess tells him. "You must inform us how we may be of assistance for her majesty to recover. Her health is most precious to us."

He looks disbelievingly at Bess before bowing to them both.

"I must return to my patient. You will be told what is required shortly."

The physician leaves them and George sits down heavily in his chair.

"This is a calamity! You know this influenza epidemic has killed thousands of people. God's bones! What will they say in London? How has she caught it? No one else is ill."

"You must write to Sir Francis at once," she pauses, her face thoughtful. "She would be far more comfortable at Chatsworth."

"No, I am not moving her again." George shakes his head. "Every time I dread an ambush from her supporters."

"How will they possibly know? If we move her tomorrow it will be quite safe. It is only eight miles and the roads are good at the moment."

"I am very reluctant, Bess."

"Husband, she cannot be properly cared for here. The number of her household has doubled which has given us the same problem with the privies as we had at

Tutbury. It would only be for a week or so to give enough time for sweetening of the privies here, then she can return if she is well enough."

He still looks doubtful but she continues.

"Now that most of her Court are boarded out, they will not need to come here during the day so that will help the situation."

"I suppose what you say does make sense."

"I think it is for the best, I will make the arrangements and inform the Chief Guard. Will you tell her or shall I?"

"You can tell her."

He does not want to face the stern Scottish faces in Mary's bedchamber twice in one day and sits down at his desk.

"All will be well, George," she reassures him before leaving.

"You have more faith than I," he replies and picks up his quill to write again to Sir William Cecil. He is finding the care of Mary ever more troublesome.

○8∞

As soon as permission is granted, the whole household moves to Chatsworth where Mary slowly recovers from the influenza. Thankfully only a handful of the household succumb to it as well, much to the relief of everyone. Bess is able to enjoy some time at home, a rare luxury these days. The house is quiet, the children are all away. Henry is at Court, acting as a gentleman page for the Earl of Leicester, William is studying at Cambridge and Charles is still a pupil at Eton. Elizabeth and Mary are serving as gentlewomen in different noble households, as Bess did. They will learn the social skills required at

Court and make important friendships and contacts that will help them in later life. Frances and little Bessie, living nearby, visit whenever they can.

Bess has time again to devote herself to the administration of her lands and properties, spending hours once more with Joseph as they work to keep the books and accounts balanced. She misses the challenge and stimulation of the work, but George is not so happy. He considers the security at Chatsworth to be inferior, and is constantly checking on the guards and locks, scanning the road for signs of an approaching kidnap attempt and is generally on edge all the time. It is a relief for him when everyone is back at Wingfield again.

One afternoon, not long after their return, he is standing in the Hall talking to his manservant when there is the sound of fast approaching horse hooves through the open front door. The servant goes to look, as George waits, his face tense.

"It is the rider from the queen, your grace."

They watch as he dismounts, taking some letters from the leather pouch round his body. The rider has spared no horses to arrive at Wingfield in the shortest time. Dishevelled and dirty, he doffs his cap and hands the letters to George, who quickly opens the one bearing the Royal Seal. Starting to read it, he frowns. The rider clears his throat and George looks up in annoyance.

"You may go," he tells him sharply.

The servant indicates for the rider to follow him to the kitchen, where he will be given some refreshment after his long ride. The letter is brief, but to the point, and he swears under his breath.

"Bess! Bess? Where are you?" He begins to walk towards her study.

"She is outside, your grace," one of the servants replies, as she carries some linen upstairs.

He finds Bess in the rose garden, talking to the gardener.

"Read this!" he fumes and hands her the queen's letter. The gardener bows his head and tactfully disappears out of sight. Bess scans it quickly then looks at him angrily.

"So her majesty has finally discovered that the Duke of Norfolk and the Scottish Queen were planning to marry – and she blames you for not informing her."

"Why am I to take the blame? Cecil, Walsingham and Leicester all knew about it. Not one of them had the guts to tell her!"

"How did she find out?"

"I do not know; but it was bound to happen sooner or later."

"I can well imagine the queen's rage. Now she orders us to take Mary back to Tutbury."

"To punish her, I imagine. But look …" he jabs at the last sentence with his arthritic finger.

"Lord Huntingdon is to come and 'assist' me! What an insult!"

"Perhaps she thinks you are still recovering from your recent illness."

"Her majesty knows I am quite well now. I have written several times to reassure her. No, it is a deliberate undermining of my authority. This is the thanks I get!"

"It is an insult to both of us."

"How can the queen question my trust and loyalty?"

"I know, husband. It is very unfair," she replies and touches his shoulder.

They stand dejectedly for a few moments, with George barely able to contain his fury. "The implication is that I am not capable of this task."

"I am trying to remember the appearance of this Lord Huntingdon; do you know him?"

"We met briefly, a few years ago. He is a strutting peacock, he will relish this opportunity to show off his authority, damn him!"

"He will be here tomorrow, that does not give us long."

"Oh my Bess, what a task we have been given!"

She can think of nothing that will comfort him and suggest they go back inside. Bess had been due to sew with Mary that afternoon, but somehow she does not have the will for it now and shuts herself in her study with her paperwork and instructions that she is not to be disturbed. George wanders around the house and gardens, finding fault with anything and everyone wherever possible. From their upstairs window, Mary and her ladies watch and listen, but it doesn't take them long to find out what has made their jailors so annoyed. The household waits with a sense of dread for the arrival of the Earl of Huntingdon.

ଓଞ୍ଚ

By noon the following morning, their newly arrived guest and his pistol carrying men have made a thorough search of Mary's chamber. Drawers are pulled out and upturned, their contents thrown on the floor, rugs lifted, boxes and chests opened and examined, even the clothes of her ladies are rifled through, much to their chagrin. They have been given no explanation for the search, and after the respectful handling by the Shrewsburys; they are shocked at the violence of the actions. Mary herself stands apart from it all. After her initial surprise, she is now calm.

"What is it that you seek to find?" she asks. Bess and George wait in the doorway, both fuming in silence. The Earl of Huntingdon has not been swayed by Mary's looks, and is not intimidated by her royal status. He has been given his orders and will carry them out, to the letter. "Do you have something to hide?" he asks brusquely.

"I have nothing to hide," Mary responds quietly. "You may search all you wish, you will not find anything."

He grunts and after another ten minutes, has to admit defeat.

"Queen Elizabeth gave orders for your chambers to be thoroughly searched."

"For what reason?"

He gestures for the men to leave. Bess and George move out of the way, regarding them with annoyance.

"Do not pretend you do not know the reason, madam!"

There is a gasp from Bess to hear Mary addressed in this way and George can remain silent no longer.

"You forget yourself Huntingdon! You are addressing an anointed queen."

He ignores George and stands threateningly in front of Mary.

"The proposed marriage between yourself and the Duke of Norfolk has come to the attention of Queen Elizabeth who is extremely displeased. No one of royal blood may marry in England without the permission of our queen. Perhaps you had forgotten that you are now a prisoner on English soil?"

"I am hardly likely to do so am I?"

"The Earl of Shrewsbury tells me that your household numbers sixty or more attendants. That is far too great a number. You will have to reduce it to thirty by the end of the week." He walks toward the door. "Oh, and you are to return to Tutbury as soon as possible." At this, Mary's face looks crestfallen. He pauses in front of the Shrewsburys.

"I suspect some of your servants of being sympathetic to the Scottish Queen, they are to be dismissed at once."

George and Bess can only look at him in resentful mortification. He then turns on his heel and strides out of Mary's apartments, leaving everyone to come to terms with the imminent new regime.

꽃

There is worse to come though. The Earl of Huntingdon is waiting for them in the Hall. He accuses Bess of being too friendly with Mary, and that both of them treat her with too much affection.

"I have treated the Scottish Queen with respect, as is her due," Bess replies firmly.

"You spend every day in her presence. She has given you gifts," he says meaningfully.

"We sew together, that is all. She has to pass the time somehow. I have a few small trinkets from her, it is true."

"Can you deny that you enjoy her company?"

"Where are these questions leading? Is it a crime if I enjoy sewing with her?" Bess is becoming even angrier and suspects that the Earl of Huntingdon has taken too much on himself. George stands beside her, his face like thunder.

"Countess, you and your husband have incurred the queen's displeasure. This plan to marry the Duke of Norfolk can never come to anything. Did you encourage it?"

"Of course not!" George opens his mouth to speak but Bess holds up her hand to silence him.

"Our orders are to treat the Scots Queen with the respect and dignity her royal personage demands. At the same time, we are to watch her and report back on anything that could be regarded as dangerous. How are we supposed to do that if we do not spend time with her?"

"There has been far too much freedom allowed. Well, that is all going to change. We leave for Tutbury as soon as possible."

"It will take a few days to organise the move," Bess says defiantly. "We have carried out our duties to the best of our ability. Queen Elizabeth will not find anyone who is more loyal and trustworthy than my husband and I. You have performed your duties here with no finesse whatsoever. I will be going to London myself shortly and I shall speak to Sir William Cecil about your behaviour. I'll warrant he will not be pleased with you."

There is an awkward silence then Huntingdon gives a short laugh.

"Speak to whom you choose, countess. Like you, I am also just doing my duty. Make the arrangements to leave as soon as possible." Powerless to protest, they watch him leave and look at one another.

"I did not know you were planning to go to London." George sounds peeved.

"I was not, but I think it would be a good idea. We can put our case directly to the queen. We need to tell our side of the story."

"But you will help the move back to Tutbury first?"

"Of course, I would not leave you to do that on your own."

George looks at her gratefully. He leans on the stick he had started to use and pulls himself up with some effort.

"Is your gout troubling you again?"

"It never really leaves me. My arthritis has got worse these last few days too."

"Shall I recall the physician?"

"No, Bess, he can do nothing. I am getting old."

"Indeed you are not, we are of an age."

"Yes, but you are the picture of health, sweetheart."

It is true. Bess at forty-two looks years younger than her husband, who is only a year older. The contrast between them has begun to show only months after they had started to have the custody of Mary.

"I wish I could do more to help you, but I do have business interests that need my attention," she tells him.

"Yes, as do I." They begin to walk along the corridor. "But you must go to Court and see everyone. You must put our case most strongly. I only wish I could go with you, instead of which I have to suffer the company of Huntingdon. Think of me when you are enjoying the diversions of the Court." His voice has become full of self-pity and Bess has to stop herself from tutting at him. Instead, she promises him that she will, and hurries away to prepare for the journey.

൏ൢ

Bess has been glad of an excuse to travel to London after the months of being tied to supervising Mary. After the household has been moved back to Tutbury, she loses no time in making arrangements to leave. George is envious and keeps saying he wishes he could go with her. She promises to try and limit the damage done by the Duke of Norfolk's proposal and to write to him every day. He watches as she settles into the Shrewsbury coach with Agnes at her side, and the retinue makes its way along the narrow road until they are out of sight. He goes to his study and shuts the door, feeling very sorry for himself. Their journey proceeds with relative ease, and by the end of the week they are comfortably accommodated in private chambers close to the queen's apartments. Bess promised George that her visit would be as short as possible, so Agnes is sent out shopping on her behalf to the newly built Royal Exchange in Cornhill. Here she will buy from the many shops such as haberdashers, milliners and apothecaries. Bess loves to shop, but she will have to wait until her next visit to browse for herself. She has requested an audience with the queen, Sir William Cecil and Sir Francis Walsingham, which is scheduled for the following morning. The court is full of the news that Duke of Norfolk has been sent to the Tower in disgrace. But the gossips say the queen has calmed down by now, much to Bess' relief. As the queen's diary is very busy, she can only spare half an hour, so Bess knows she will not have long to put her case. After breakfast they assemble in the Privy Council chamber and once the usual pleasantries are over, Bess hastens to reassure them.

"The earl and I were as shocked as yourselves by the news that the Duke of Norfolk was hoping to marry the

Scots Queen. It would be unthinkable without the permission of your gracious majesty. I believe both of them are deluding themselves to imagine it could ever happen."

"Indeed." The queen looks tired today, which no amount of white complexion paste or lavish costume can disguise. "We have heard of it in good time. They both continue to be a thorn in our side. Norfolk is a constant nuisance. I know full well that he coverts my crown and that he considers a mere woman as myself quite incapable of ruling well," she says.

"But you constantly prove him wrong, your majesty." Sir William and Sir Francis nod in agreement, murmuring assent. Bess continues, warming to her theme with words she has been rehearsing on the journey.

"We would never allow such a union to happen whilst we were responsible for her safe-keeping. We would rather die than surrender the Scots Queen to anyone who would plot or harm your gracious majesty. All our household, the guards, the servants, from the highest to the lowest, are of one mind and that is to guard our charge with the utmost care and determination. All her letters and those of her ladies are intercepted and passed on to Sir Francis. Everything that comes into and out of her apartments is thoroughly searched, she is constantly watched whenever she goes outdoors to take the air and never left alone. I can assure you all in the strongest terms that my husband and I remain proud to be of service in this most important matter, and we will continue to be vigilant for as long as your majesty desires."

This speech, delivered so eloquently, seems to satisfy them all and the queen rewards her with a smile.

"I know it to be so, Bess; the news did not come as a complete shock. I have long suspected Norfolk of such deceit and arrogance. Obviously they can never been allowed to marry for I would not be able to sleep soundly in my bed." Then she turns to Sir William. "Do you have the Scots Queen's letter?" He produces a parchment from his sleeve and, with his eyes on Bess; he gazes at her with foreboding.

"I have received a letter from the Scottish Queen about you, countess," he says.

"Really? And what does this letter say?"

"It says that I am not to listen to your schemes and accusations about her."

Bess is genuinely surprised, which quickly gives way to incredulity.

"Why should I have any schemes or accusations about the Scottish Queen? It makes no sense to me!"

"It does not surprise me," Sir Francis says drily. "She is full of schemes and plots. And she is obviously worried about what you may say to us about her."

For once, Bess is at a loss for words and the queen sees her distress.

"We take no heed of the letter, do not be alarmed."

Her reassurance goes some way to calming Bess, who is struggling to stay in control of her emotions. "Tell us Bess, I have long wondered, what do you talk about?"

The queen echoes the thoughts that have been on everyone's' lips at Court. Bess thinks quickly. "We speak of very trivial matters. I would not presume to ask her any questions of a personal nature. Our time is spent sewing and working on our embroideries and tapestries."

"But you must speak of something!"

"So my husband tells me," Bess smiles.

"Nonetheless we should wish to know."

This time is an edge to the queen's remark.

"Naturally we discuss the colours of our threads and the designs we are going to use. We talk of nature, the weather and of fashion …"

"So you are two women together and you do not gossip!" Sir Francis is skeptical and the two men exchange a look of knowing disbelief.

"It is not beyond the realms of possibility. Do you gossip with her, Bess?" persists the queen.

"I am most careful in my speech to the Scottish Queen. I know that I must always be on my guard with her, as I am sure that she is likewise. If I am to spend time with her, as you so graciously commanded, then the hours cannot be spent in silence. There is our sewing as I have said, and we play cards. She also reads with her ladies and spends many hours on her knees in prayer. Under supervision, she is allowed some fresh air each day. She knows that I have the ear of my queen and that I report to you. I think that she does not trust me. After all, it is my word against hers is it not?"

"Of the two of you, Bess, I would believe your word against hers."

Bess is relieved, in that at least she is vindicated. Then the queen's voice becomes strident.

"But the security of the Scottish Queen still remains of the greatest importance. We have given Huntingdon absolute charge of her for the moment. I know this will be difficult for you and the earl, but we must consider what is the best course in this matter."

No one speaks for a few moments. Sir Francis has fixed his gaze on the wood pattern of the table in front of him. Sir William gives Bess a warning look as the queen stands up. The audience is over. They all rise then, and Bess curtseys while the men bow.

"Sir Francis, come, I have some questions for you." She sweeps out, her gown rustling and Bess is left alone with Sir William. He closes the door firmly. "Have you a few minutes, Bess?"

"Of course."

They sit down again and she waits for him to speak.

"You must let these matters run their course."

"My husband will be very upset. He does not deserve such treatment."

"Huntingdon will not stay long at Tutbury."

"How can you be so sure?"

"It is not his style. He likes to be seen as someone who gets results quickly. You will soon be left alone again to continue your duty. I should have thought your husband would welcome the chance to share the burden with someone else."

"On the contrary, he sees this interference as an insult to his loyalty and integrity. Huntingdon was rude and brash in his dealings with the Scottish Queen and spoke to her very disrespectfully."

"Have you grown to like her?"

"She can be very charming when she wishes. So far, I have found little to dislike about her. But after the letter she sent you, I can see I shall have to be more careful."

"And the earl, your husband? How is his relationship with her?"

"He finds her emotional and demanding. Her episodes of crying are certainly very exhausting, for all of us who have to deal with her."

"Yes, he writes of it often."

"But all this is known to you already, my friend. What do you really wish to find out?"

Sir William strokes his beard slowly. "It is vital that we have knowledge of Mary's intentions. We are keeping a close eye on certain northern lords who support the Duke of Norfolk, and are sympathetic to Mary's Catholic cause. Anything that might be relevant must be reported to us at once. You and the earl are our eyes and ears."

"We do our best, Sir William. It is not an easy task and to be frank, one that is costing a lot more than first thought."

"Ah yes, I wondered when you would mention the cost."

"It is a sore point with my husband. Would you please mention these costs to the queen for us? I am afraid his requests are ignored."

"Of course, but do not expect too much." He gathers his papers and staff before getting up.

"The queen knows that you both had nothing to do with the Duke of Norfolk's wish to marry Mary, but such incidents make us nervous. We have no doubt the duke will try again, we must be ready for him."

"When will her captivity end?"

"If you mean when will the queen decide what is to become of her cousin, I cannot tell you. Be patient, you will not have to wait much longer and Huntingdon will be gone."

She stands up too and they begin to walk into the corridor.

"Have a care when dealing with the Scottish Queen. I would advise you not to become too familiar."

"I think you are right, I see her in quite a different way now."

They part outside Sir William's study and Bess hurries back to her chamber to prepare for the journey back to Tutbury. She has yet to understand how she is going to distance herself from Mary while at the same time, try to find out her plans and schemes. The numerous invitations that Bess has received from friends at Court, who are keen to find out about Mary, will have to be declined for the time being.

༺༻

As 1569, the first year of Mary's imprisonment draws to a close, Bess and George have become resigned to the Earl of Huntingdon's presence and an uneasy truce descends on Tutbury. The building itself seems to cast a spell of doom over everyone with its dark, dingy corners and musty chambers that no amount of airing with roaring fires can remove. The servants hate it here too, and there is much grumbling in their quarters at the end of most days. Mary receives and sends letters almost daily, all of which have to be checked by George and the Earl of Huntingdon. She writes to friends in Scotland and France, as well as priests and foreign ambassadors, telling them she has been upset to hear that the Duke of Norfolk was sent to the Tower in October. But she denies knowledge of the attempt to free her in a rebellion called The Northern Uprising, one of many failed plots, and no evidence is found to implicate her.

Meanwhile Bess feels increasingly frustrated with their continued role as jailor. Her sewing times with the Scottish Queen continue, but there is a wariness now on both sides, which makes the atmosphere strained.

One afternoon, Bess asks to see Mary's latest work. This time Mary seems reluctant, but passes her the hanging, which consists of two branches of a tree, one with fruit and one without.

"This is very unusual, your majesty." Bess looks at it carefully.

"I may as well tell you, countess, it was intended as a gift for the Duke of Norfolk."

"Really? Could you explain the meaning to me, although I have a fair idea of its implication?"

"Oh, it has no real meaning. It is merely a pretty design."

"I think not. Look at the motto you have placed here." She points at the Latin wording, unable to trust herself to pronounce it: *Virescit Vulnere Virtus*. Mary pretends to peer at it.

"Oh that – I do not remember sewing it. I probably saw it in one of my books and copied it."

"Would you translate it for me, please?"

"*Virtue flourishes by wounding,* is the meaning," she replies after a pause.

Frowning, Bess picks it up and spends a few moments studying it intently.

"I see now what you have done here. The unfruitful branch represents our queen and the fruitful one predicts the result of the union between yourself and the Duke of Norfolk. What a pity that such exquisite work has such a dangerous message."

Bess puts the hanging down as if it is contaminated.

"Are you going to confiscate it from me?" asks Mary.

"Not at all. It is yours to do with as you will."

"I do not expect you to understand."

"It is not my place to understand."

"But you will report to your queen will you not?"

Bess does not reply. Mary sighs and starts to put away her needle and thread. "My sewing is a way for me to express myself, my feelings and hopes. You may make of it what you will. I suppose I shall be stopped now."

"I will not prevent you from sewing, your majesty, but I would advise you not to let my husband see this particular work, or any others of a similar nature."

"Your husband is more sympathetic than you think. We understand one another and have grown very close these last few months. When you are away, he seeks my company, it is only natural. Men have always been attracted to me, I cannot help it. Your husband is lonely without you, but we have a warm friendship that is based on mutual respect."

Bess does not rise to the bait and regards her impassively. Mary goes to sit under her canopy, where she always feels superior. "We pass the time amicably by playing chess or cards. Has he not mentioned it to you?" she asks innocently.

"He has not. Nor would I wish to hear it, if it were true, which I doubt."

"Oh, it is true you may be sure, countess."

"I do not believe you."

"Why do you not ask him?"

"I do not need to ask him. He is your jailor and I trust him implicitly."

"Can any man be trusted implicitly?"

"I speak of my husband, not yours."

Mary flinches at this barb and Bess walks to the door.

"To embroider such tapestries is at best provocative, at worse, treason. You would do well to keep it out of sight. I shall say nothing for the moment."

"Is that because you wish me to continue working on your own tapestries?"

"I am grateful for your help, but do not think to outwit me by filling my head with tales of my husband's lack of propriety. I know him better than you do."

At that moment, Mary's ladies come into the chamber and the conversation is brought to an abrupt end. As Bess makes her way back to her apartments, she hopes that she will not regret her actions. If Queen Elizabeth was to even hear of this work, she would be furious, and with good reason. On the other hand, if Mary was to ever become Queen of England, such thoughts are never far from Bess' mind. Later that evening, Bess and George are together in the dining room after supper. She sits at the table composing a letter to Charles at Eton; he seems homesick and she is thinking of how she can cheer him up. George is reading some letters. A knock on the door makes them both look up and the Earl of Huntingdon strides in, full of his own self-importance. "I have some news which may be of interest to you both."

George puts down his letters with a sense of dread. "Well?"

"I am to be relieved of my duties here."

"We have had no orders to that effect."

"You will be told soon enough."

George and Bess look at one another in disbelief. Huntingdon's stance is even more arrogant than usual.

"How has this come about?" Bess asks.

"I have requested it. My work here is finished, now the situation is under control. You may carry on what I have started."

George can barely contain his fury. "What you have started! You have done nothing that I could not have done myself."

"But you did not."

"It has been easy for you. You have come here for just a short while. You have not had to endure months of looking after the Scottish Queen as we have, or the expense of paying for her household."

"You were glad to be given the task were you not? I heard how you preened about the Court and basked in the decision to make you a member of the Privy Council. Not so pleased now are you? I am well rid of this Godforsaken place, cut off from everyone and dancing attendance on that Scottish adulteress and murderess. You are welcome to her care!" He turns to go but Bess stands up, and when she speaks, her voice is low as she glares at him angrily.

"My husband was entrusted with the care of the Scottish Queen because he is one of Queen Elizabeth's most loyal subjects. Your presence here has not been welcome and you might remember that one day, the Scottish adulteress and murderess of whom you speak, might be your sovereign queen."

For the first time, Huntingdon looks uncomfortable.

"I cannot think that will ever happen."

"It is a possibility. She will certainly not forget your treatment of her."

"I have only been carrying out the orders of our queen."

"With malicious pleasure, we are witness to that!" Bess snaps at him.

Huntingdon then approaches George and lowers his voice. "You would do well to keep that wife of yours under control. She will be the death of you."

George is taken aback. He is not accustomed to being spoken to in such a manner.

"Your words are very offensive. I think you had better leave at once."

"With pleasure."

He gives a mock bow before leaving. Bess can hardly contain her anger.

"Who does he think he is? Has he forgotten who you are?"

"Let him go, Bess. We are well rid of him."

"Are you going to let him get away with speaking to you like that?"

"You have already told him what we think."

"So you believe I was wrong to speak my mind?"

"I think it would have been wiser to leave it to me."

"But you said nothing."

"You did not give me a chance."

"It is all my fault is it? You have been far too easy with him from the beginning. If you had stamped your authority when he arrived, he would not have dared to be so rude."

George starts to read his letters again. "I am not discussing this any more, Bess. I am tired, and if what he says is true then we shall soon be back to normal."

She throws her quill down on the table.

"Normal? I have forgotten what 'normal' means. I am going to bed!"

He takes no notice and she gives a cry of frustration as she slams the heavy oak door shut before going upstairs, where not even Agnes' devoted care can improve her mood.

◦≽◦

A year later

The handsome young man is standing with apparent ease before Bess. A member of her household, his name is Hersey Lassells and his behaviour is causing concern because Mary has started to show him more attention than usual. He is tall with sparkling blue eyes and cuts a handsome figure in his breeches. Bess studies him closely for a few moments before she speaks.

"Master Lassells, this is the third time I have to question you about your relationship with the Scots Queen. You are still very friendly with her."

"I am just being polite, your grace."

"Your courtesy seems to extend beyond mere politeness. I have noticed that you try to see Queen Mary as often as you can. You frequently volunteer to carry out tasks and favours for her."

"She likes me and tells me I am handsome."

"Does she indeed?"

"I feel very sorry for her."

"Why?"

"She should not be kept locked up. She has done nothing wrong."

"Do any of the other servants feel the same as you? Do you talk to them about her?"

"No. They would not understand. I am closer to her than anyone else."

"Have you done anything to bring this closeness and favouritism about?"

"I am not sure of your meaning."

"It is a simple enough question. What have you done above and beyond the usual service for Queen Mary?"

He does not reply and Bess gives a sigh. "I advise you to tell me the truth. I will find out soon enough."

"She has sworn me to secrecy."

"Do you not realise that your friendship with Queen Mary could cost you your head! Is that what you want?"

"I am only trying to help. I see no harm in it."

But he shifts nervously and a look of alarm comes across his face. He cannot meet Bess' unrelenting glare and stares at the floor.

"Queen Mary has given me a gold ring," he mumbles.

"Why?"

"I am to give it to the Duke of Norfolk as a token."

"Go on."

"She said … she said if I helped her to escape, then she would make me a lord."

Bess raises an eyebrow.

"Then I would be of higher status than you."

"You think that is likely do you?"

"I do not see why not."

"Then you have made a grave mistake. You will never become a lord through the favour of a captive queen. I shall have to dismiss you."

"When Queen Mary escapes, as she soon will, then you will be proved wrong and I shall laugh in your face."

"You will do no such thing!"

Bess slams her hand on the desk and he jumps nervously.

"You are a conceited and brainless oaf who has been flattered by the attentions of the Scottish Queen! The game you play is a dangerous one."

A thin line of perspiration has broken out on Lassells' forehead and he begins to bluster.

"I ... I have the assurance of Queen Mary that she will protect me. She has promised me ..."

"Then you are a bigger fool than I thought. You have been duped and led astray by someone who has used their charm for their own ends. The Scottish Queen has no power to grant you anything."

"What will happen to me?"

"As I said, you are dismissed and you may think yourself lucky that I am not sending you to London for questioning by Sir Francis Walsingham."

"I beg your grace not to send me there. I have done nothing, I swear." He produces a gold signet ring and places it on the desk.

"Here, I still have the ring in my safekeeping. You take it and do as you will with it. I want no further dealings with the Scots Queen, as God is my witness. I realise now that I was wrong."

She sees that his hands are shaking.

"You have been lucky this time," she replies as she picks up the ring.

"If you wish to live long enough to see your children and grandchildren, you would do well to stay out of trouble from now on. Pack your bags and leave at once. Someone will escort you out of the grounds. Forget about the Scottish Queen. Get as far away as possible. Find a wife and live simply in the country."

He nods miserably.

"Yes, your grace. Thank you."

She instructs the guard outside the door and watches the two of them until they are out of sight before turning to see George approaching.

"Who was that?"

Bess explains briefly and he becomes anxious at once.

"You have dismissed him! How do you know he will not continue these plans? I should have been told about it."

"You may rest easy, George. He does not have the wits to be any threat. Mary will deny it all of course. As soon as I mentioned Sir Francis to him, he nearly fainted with fright."

"Where has he gone now?"

"I neither know nor care."

George sits down heavily and mops his brow. "Sometimes I feel that we spend our whole time waiting for something to happen. It is all very vexing."

"Yes, I do not think people realise it is a great strain for us."

"But more of a strain for the Scottish Queen. She does not look well since her freedom was curtailed even more. I hear the Pope has declared our queen a heretic," he says gloomily. "Thus making Mary a figurehead for Catholic rebellion."

Bess shakes her head. "There will be more trouble to come."

They look at one another in silent agreement. It is a depressing thought.

ଓଃଡ

1572

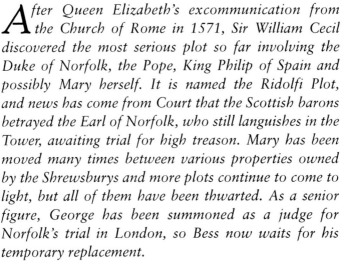

After Queen Elizabeth's excommunication from the Church of Rome in 1571, Sir William Cecil discovered the most serious plot so far involving the Duke of Norfolk, the Pope, King Philip of Spain and possibly Mary herself. It is named the Ridolfi Plot, and news has come from Court that the Scottish barons betrayed the Earl of Norfolk, who still languishes in the Tower, awaiting trial for high treason. Mary has been moved many times between various properties owned by the Shrewsburys and more plots continue to come to light, but all of them have been thwarted. As a senior figure, George has been summoned as a judge for Norfolk's trial in London, so Bess now waits for his temporary replacement.

The January morning is bright, but cold, as Bess stands to welcome her visitor riding towards the gates of Sheffield Castle. Her spirits are unusually low, having recently heard of the sudden death of her mother; although they did not see much of each other in recent years, Bess will miss her. She has just come from the Scots Queen's apartments where the mood is tense as Mary has been on her knees praying since dawn for the

Duke of Norfolk, as he faces trial. George left the previous day with a great deal of fuss and constant reminders to Bess about Mary's care. He had hoped to see the man sent to replace him, but time has run out and he could not delay any longer. Bess is pleased he is having a respite from his duty and although he grumbled as usual, he is secretly relieved.

Nearby on the banks of the Rivers Don and Sheaf, groups of people are buying and selling their wares at the daily market. Live chickens squawk in cages, bloodied cuts of meat hang from hooks; women with baskets of onions and fresh bread call out over the general melee. The stallholders are also shouting to attract the attention of passers-by, offering eggs, cheese and cooked pies. Small boats come and go, some carrying passengers, others with more commodities such as leather purses and tools. A handful of hungry beggars stand as close as they dare to the suckling pig that is being roasted on a spit over an open fire, while some ragged urchins crack an icy puddle with a stone. From her apartments, Mary cannot see any of this activity as her high windows face into the courtyard, but she can hear the voices and she longs to be in the fresh air with them. Through all this mayhem, her visitor steers his horse cautiously and looks about while the drawbridge is lowered for him. The guards salute, as they are expecting him, and he continues into the courtyard to find Bess outside the main door. She watches as he dismounts stiffly from his grey mare and stretches, before walking over to greet her with a formal bow, removing his hat with a practised flourish. He is a short, wiry man of advancing years, a diplomat, Member of Parliament and administrator. Having accepted this task with reluctance, he would far rather be at home in his manor house at Stanton, some thirty miles north of London; but Lord Burghley trusts him implicitly and the two of them have known each other well over many years. Although Bess has never met him until now, she has heard of his somewhat unusual marital arrangements and his distaste for life at Court. More importantly, he played a key role in meetings with the Scottish delegates over the future of the Scots Queen and has met her on several occasions.

"I assume I have the honour to address the Countess of Shrewsbury? I am Sir Ralph Sadler. Good day to you."

"Sir Ralph, you are very welcome. I'm afraid my husband has already left for London and you have missed him. I am to brief you on the security arrangements, but first, please come this way."

Bess leads him into the Hall and beckons for a servant to serve their guest a silver goblet of warm mead. He looks around at the surroundings with appreciation. "This is a most comfortable dwelling; quite unlike Tutbury I believe?"

"You have heard about it?"

"Oh yes, Huntingdon was damming in his description."

"I imagine he would find nothing of good to say about his stay with us."

"Believe me, I have spent much time in draughty Scottish castles. I doubt Tutbury would be any worse."

"Despite the respite it will give him from the care of his prisoner, my husband did not wish to take part in the trial. Up until this treason was discovered, he was a great admirer of the duke. But he knows his duty."

"Quite so," he drains his goblet and sets it down on the table." I would like to go to the Scottish Queen at once. Then I can see my quarters. My manservant will arrive shortly, he can sleep on a truckle bed if necessary."

"Of course. Please follow me, Sir Ralph."

Bess leads the way along stone flagged passages and up curving stairs, unlocking sturdy oak doors until they reach the entrance of Mary's chambers. The guards stand to attention and Bess unlocks the final door with the largest key that hangs from her waist. They find Mary still on her knees in front of a large crucifix, a rosary in her hands, with her ladies praying behind her. Bess and Sir Ralph pause and wait for Mary to finish. Then she makes the sign of the cross and her ladies help her to stand.

"Sir Ralph Sadler, your jailor in my husband's absence, your majesty," announces Bess.

Mary looks him coolly up and down before sitting on her chair beneath the canopy. Sir Ralph bows and she acknowledges it with a curt nod.

"We meet again under less happy circumstances, Sir Ralph. And what sort of jailor will you be, I wonder?"

"I shall be a fair one, I hope, your majesty."

"Given that my very captivity here is unjust, that is hard to believe. You must excuse my cynicism. I have suffered at the hands of some of my jailors since I fled my native Scotland. Look well upon my face, does it not already show the signs of old age? So would anyone who was kept under guard day and night. I was once considered a beauty …" her voice trails off and she looks at Sir Ralph under her lashes.

"Sir Ralph is here as your jailor, not to comment on such trivial matters," Bess tuts in disapproval.

"My queen has asked me to send you her best wishes and thanks you for the gift you sent her," he says.

"I am pleased that she liked it. I would have preferred to give it to her myself, but my requests are always refused. Am I such a danger to the crown that my cousin will not be in the same chamber as me?"

"I cannot answer that question. But you must realise with plots to kidnap you coming to our ears all the time, my queen is very reluctant to give you much freedom."

Mary gives a light laugh.

"I do not think that is the whole reason. I think your queen is jealous of me, of my many accomplishments and my beauty, which is universally acknowledged."

"I can assure you that is not the case," Bess interrupts.

"No indeed," Sir Ralph agrees quickly. "Our queen has no woman to equal her."

"Ah! Loyal subjects I see. Of course it is not only your queen who keeps me here. Her spymaster Walsingham and her other lap dog, Cecil, oh, I beg your pardon, Lord Burghley, as we must now call him, are also to blame. It is amazing what people will do to advance themselves," Mary replies waspishly.

"Rather like Hersey Lassells," Bess reminds her.

"I do not know this man. Is he a member of your household?" Mary's voice is all innocence.

"Not any more. I have dismissed him. I would be obliged if you would refrain from trying to involve my servants in your escape plans."

"Me? Nothing could be further from my mind."

"Please, ladies, there is no need for discord." Sir Ralph places himself between them.

"You may wish to know that I shall not be requiring any food on certain days of the week as I intend to fast and pray for the Duke of Norfolk," announces Mary.

Sir Ralph looks perturbed at this announcement but Bess is matter-of-fact. She is determined that Mary's histrionics shall not be allowed to have centre stage.

"Sir Ralph, I suggest we leave the prisoner for now and return in the morning, when she is in a more co-operative frame of mind."

Mary looks at them sharply. She has never been called *the prisoner* before now. Bess feels she has the upper hand and jangles her keys for good effect. Sir Ralph realises he is fighting a lost cause between the two women and after bowing again, makes a hasty retreat from the chamber. Bess gives Mary one final withering look before following him, locking the door behind them. Sir Ralph stops in the corridor.

"I must ask you for the keys now, countess."

"Of course, they are all here, the outer doors as well as this one."

He examines them carefully before peering through a nearby window.

"My primary aim is to keep her safe from any more attempts to release her. Can we talk somewhere more private?"

"This way, Sir Ralph"

As soon as Bess has shut the door to the chamber, he wastes no time in telling her his news.

"The latest escape plot has come to light. It seems it was hatched by two local squires, Francis and George Rolleston …"

Bess interrupts him impatiently. "It was I who first heard of this plan." He looks surprised.

"Oh, then you will know that Mary's major-domo, Beaton, was also involved."

"He met the two brothers one early morning on the moors; they were seen by the guards. The plan was for Mary to escape down a rope, and hence to the Isle of Man. This is old news, Sir Ralph."

Bess cannot not help but feel a little smug. "Evidently," he replies shortly. "Beaton – has he been questioned?"

"He is too ill I am afraid; I do not think he will live much longer."

"Why was I not told more of this plan before I left London?"

"I can only think letters have gone astray. Events can happen very quickly here."

He produces a document and places in on Bess' desk.

"Are you aware that two of your servants are implicated?"

"Surely not!"

"John Hall and Hersey Lassells were definitely part of it. Did you have any prior knowledge of their intentions?"

"No, I had no idea that they were part of a serious plot; I am shocked to hear it. Lassells was a dim-witted, arrogant young man and I questioned him over a period of time. I did not think he was any threat."

With a pounding heart, she picks up the parchment and reads it quickly while he waits.

"And John Hall?" he asks when she has finished, her expression anxious.

She tries to keep her voice steady.

"I believe he was in the service of my husband for a number of years. He was a troublemaker and voiced his disapproval when the earl and I were married. He was dismissed, as was Lassells."

"Well, there are those who suspect you of conspiring with the Scottish Queen."

"Then they are wrong!" she retorts angrily. "I would never side with her against our own queen. I am a loyal and faithful subject. Lassells was duped by Mary. It is one thing to talk about an escape, but quite another to carry it out. It seems I gave him the benefit of the doubt when I should not have done so." She frowns, embarrassed by her misjudgement of the situation.

Sir Ralph picks up the letter and regards her with sympathy. "Then you would do well to write to London and explain yourself."

"I will do so at once." Bess pulls parchment, quill and ink out of a drawer and begins feverishly to compose her defence. Sir Ralph watches in silence, his face thoughtful.

☙❧

1574

The weeks and months pass into years. Bess and George realise that they are playing a waiting game and the wait so far has been five years. Mary and her entourage have to be moved to different locations time and time again, if not for sweetening of the privies, then because there is a greater risk of an escape attempt. When this happens, the seaports are told to be on high alert, and there is increased tension where she is residing at the time. The guards, usually bored with their routine, become nervous and edgy, sometimes fights break out and George has to restore order quickly.

Mary's health is unpredictable. Sometimes she cannot leave her bed because she complains of severe headaches, stomach pains and vomiting, then she recovers quickly, and is granted permission to ride or take the waters at Buxton. It is now two years ago that the Duke of Norfolk was found guilty of High Treason and sent to the block, which was more cause for Mary to lament and bemoan her situation. But George has recently heard a rumour that she will soon be returned to Scotland, an idea that he clings to as he goes about his duties each day.

Sir Francis believes that Mary is constantly plotting to kill the queen and seize the throne of England for herself. He monitors her correspondence with ruthless efficiency, but as yet can find no evidence against her. He paces back and forward impatiently, as the bespectacled code breaker works for hours deciphering the many letters that pass through Mary's hands. Sir Francis knows Elizabeth will not act precipitously in this matter, but he believes there will be no rest until Mary is dead. So the waiting and watching continues.

Bess begins to spend more time away from this task. She misses her home and family, together with her businesses. People stopped envying them long ago, and now there is an element of pity that the duty has continued for so long. George catches sight of himself in the looking glass and does not like what he sees, for the last few years have prematurely aged him. The pain from his arthritis and gout has etched itself as deep, downward lines around his mouth. He sleeps badly, worrying about money and Mary escaping. Unable to walk far without leaning heavily on a stick, he is torn between doing his duty and accepting that he is not well enough. He is not pleased to discover that Bess has invited her friend Margaret, Countess of Lennox and her son, Charles Stuart, to visit Bess at Rufford Abbey, Nottinghamshire, in the spring. He reminds her that the countess is the mother of the murdered Lord Darnley, Queen Mary's husband, as well as the granddaughter of Henry VII. But this invitation will not be well received at Court for the queen dislikes Margaret and is suspicious of her loyalty. Once Bess has made up her mind to do something though, she will not be stopped, and after some heated discussions with him, she takes her unmarried daughter Elizabeth, to Rufford with her.

The two countesses are walking in the gardens the day after their arrival. It is a fine April morning and a freshening breeze stirs the branches of the lilac trees that are about to blossom. A gardener has started a bonfire and the earthy, acrid smell blows over them briefly as they make their way past herb beds of aromatic rosemary and thyme. He removes his hat and bows as they pass, and Bess acknowledges him with a nod. Margaret is a lively companion and they enjoy one another's company. Since her arrival though, she has been uncharacteristically quiet. Bess suspects there is something on her mind and waits for it to surface in their conversation.

"When did you last see the Scottish Queen? I can hardly bring myself to speak her name, such is my hatred for her." Margaret's voice is brittle as she asks about her daughter-in-law.

"I know, I would feel the same given your circumstances," Bess replies, knowing that Margaret suspects Mary of involvement in her son Henry's death. "She leads us all a merry dance with her demands and conspiracies. I am glad to be out of it whenever I am able, for it wears me down."

"And your husband? Has he fallen in love with her yet?"

"Do not jest, Margaret! The subject causes me much concern."

"I do not mean to upset you Bess, forgive me, but surely he is not so weak as to be taken in by her superficial charms?"

Bess cannot bring herself to tell her friend that is exactly what has happened, in her view. "No, of course not."

"He is caught in the middle of you both. An unenviable position for anyone. He has a weighty task on his hands, but I should imagine you are a great help to him."

"Not as much as I should be," Bess says regretfully. "I hate to be there, locked up like a prisoner myself with no-one allowed to visit. It is a wretched existence, miserable and lonely."

"I am sorry to hear it. Is there no sign that her captivity will end?"

"I wish I could say there was, but no, it has been five long years now."

"At least you can have a respite from it."

"For that I am grateful. If not, I fear I would go mad."

"You are too strong for that to happen, Bess. You are the last person I can think of who would succumb to such a malady."

They look at one another and smile. For a minute they walk in silence, under the pergola where an old vine flourishes each summer, then between a shady avenue of tall lime trees leading towards a fine expanse of lawn at the back of the Abbey. Here they see Charles and Elizabeth practising archery, amidst much laughter. Margaret and Bess pause to look at the two of them together. Bess breaks the silence.

"They make a handsome couple, do they not?"

"They do indeed. Elizabeth is not yet married, is she, Bess?" Margaret is well aware of the answer to this question and regards her friend with an air of conspiracy.

"Alas, no. She is my only daughter still unwed. I have not found anyone of sufficient status for her."

"How old is she now?"

"Nineteen at her last birthday, of similar age to your Charles. Do you have any plans for him?"

"Not as yet." Margaret stops and turns to face Bess. "We are old friends, Bess. May I speak frankly?"

"Of course."

"I find myself in financial difficulty, it pains me to speak of it, but I must. You know that we do not receive any income from the Lennox estates, and that the Lennox lands now belong to my grandson, the boy King James, Queen Mary's son. If only I could resolve the future of my son Charles and my financial crisis at the same time."

"I may be able to suggest a solution that would please both of us," Bess says softly.

Margaret looks shocked. "I hope you are not thinking that Charles and Elizabeth could be married. We would need permission from Queen Elizabeth for such an event and I doubt she would grant it."

"Come Margaret, do not pretend you have not thought of it yourself and it is the reason you are here with me!"

"I could say the same to you, Bess. The idea had occurred to you months ago when we met, can you deny it?"

"We understand each other perfectly. Elizabeth has a dowry of four thousand pounds."

"And Charles has sufficient status, I think you will agree."

"What a splendid couple they make!"

Once again, they look over to the pair, who are running hand in hand towards the trees. He is blond haired and slim, whilst she has her father's quiet manner and dark eyes.

"They do seem very happy in each others company," Margaret muses. "Elizabeth has always been a sweet girl."

"We need to be sure they spend time together over the coming week. It might be helpful if you took to your bed for a few days, Margaret. Then I could nurse you back to health, and the two love birds will have a chance to be alone and get to know one another."

"Why must I take to my bed? Why not you?"

"Because everyone knows I am never ill!"

Margaret laughs. "All right, it will be me." She suddenly looks troubled. "But I am worried about the queen …"

"We shall present her with a *fait accompli*."

"She will not like it."

"She will have to accept it."

"I think it is worth the risk," Bess tells her. "The queen shows no sign of marrying and will soon be past child bearing. Think of any child that Charles and Elizabeth produce, it would be a Stuart, a potential heir to the throne of England and Scotland after the boy King James." Bess' eyes sparkle and Margaret grips her hand in excitement. "Can it really happen?"

"We can make it happen."

They link arms and start to walk back inside, keen to put their plan into action as soon as possible.

◊

Within a week, Bess returns to Sheffield Castle to face George with the news.

"Married already!" he gasps.

"You should be pleased, it is a good match."

"Have you lost your senses, Bess? I cannot believe you could be so reckless!"

"Well your attempts at finding a husband for Elizabeth all came to nothing, I had to do something."

"You have done something all right, this is a calamity for us. The queen will be absolutely furious. She would never have given her permission for such a match."

Bess arrived back just before dark without Elizabeth, who is with her new husband and mother-in-law on their way to Settrington in Yorkshire. Trying to find the right moment to tell him that Elizabeth and Charles Stuart were now husband and wife was tricky, but she decides to come out with it as they get into bed that night.

"It is true she will be none too pleased, at first, but I think she will come round, eventually."

George looks as if his eyes are going to pop out of his head, and can only stare at her in horror.

"All will be well, husband, you will see. They fell in love, who are we to place obstacles in the path of true love?"

"What fanciful nonsense!"

"Wait until you see how they look at one another. He is besotted with her and she with him. I am sure it will not be long until I have another grandchild, and a very special one."

"The queen will annul the marriage and declare any child illegitimate. Your grand plans will come to nothing."

"There is no reason for an annulment, everything was done properly. We made sure of it."

"I wager you did! How long has this little scheme been in the planning? All the time you have been neglecting your duties here with me and I thought you were busy with household and business matters. As usual, you have deceived me, and now it will look as if I were a part of it."

"No-one will think any such thing, you exaggerate, George. And I do not deceive you, when have I ever done so?"

He scowls at her in frustrated anger. "You cannot help yourself, it is part of your character to claw your way up to wherever or whoever it is that you have set your sights upon. Have you any idea what the consequences will be for all of us?"

Bess takes some rose salve and rubs it in her hands. "I am ready for it. Sometimes risks have to be taken."

"You might be ready, but what about the rest of us? You and your infernal ambitions!"

"My ambitions have done nothing but good for my family. I only want the best for them; is that such a crime?"

He shakes his head in despair.

"I shall have to convince them that I knew nothing about it. Gods blood, your Elizabeth is now Mary's sister-in-law and aunt to the boy king."

"Yes," replies Bess calmly, settling down in the bed and getting comfortable.

"You have thought all this through very carefully, have you not?"

"Of course. You do not think I would entertain such an arrangement lightly, do you?"

"It is all too late now. I must try and explain it to Lord Burghley. I can see you going to the tower for this. I shall say I knew nothing of it."

"Then you will be lying, for I mentioned it some months ago."

"Did you? My memory is not what it was; anyway I shall deny everything."

"If I am sent to the Tower, then so be it. A short visit will be worth it."

"How can you speak of it in that way?"

"I am thinking of the future, the long term future. Where are your ambitions, George?"

"Having been born into one of the finest families in England, I have had no need of such schemes," he replies with a sneer.

"How fortunate for you, some of us have had to work hard for position and wealth."

"Do you think I have not had to work for royal favour? All those years commanding armies when I spent years away from my first wife, Gertrude, when I was Lord Lieutenant in those northern counties, and my duties as Chief Justice …"

"I am not saying you did not work hard."

"Well, what are you saying?"

"I mean that what you take for granted because you have had since birth, some people have to obtain through their own endeavours."

"Yes, and this is the result, a hole in the corner marriage without royal permission. Did Margaret Lennox forget she has already been sent to the Tower twice?"

"If Margaret Lennox has to return there, she will be familiar with the surroundings."

"That is a heartless comment and not worthy of you."

"Margaret knew the risks just as I did. She obviously felt it was worth it, the means justified the end."

"Does your daughter realise the seriousness of it? The queen could punish her too."

"I doubt it. Margaret and I will be seen as the instigators of this marriage."

"I do not know how you can discuss it so calmly."

"It makes a change from discussions about Queen Mary, of whom I have become heartily sick in recent months."

"As if I have not got enough to cope with! You have added to my burden when it is your wifely duty to support and obey me. You must never put us in this position again."

"I shall do whatever is necessary to secure the future of my family."

"Are you listening to me, or am I talking to the wall?"

Bess closes her eyes and does not reply. George gives an exasperated sigh and gets up. "I repeat I do not want you to do anything of this nature again. You have gone too far Bess, and your disgrace is mine."

He paces backwards and forwards awkwardly, his face mottled with anger.

"I mean what I say! As my wife it is your duty to obey me in all things. I will not have you putting my name in jeopardy for the sake of your detestable ambition."

He stands over her and she can feel his breath on her cheek. She opens her eyes and sees he is close to losing his temper.

"I am sorry, husband," she eventually responds meekly. "You are right of course. I shall consult with you before matchmaking again."

Looking down at her upturned face and beguiling eyes, he thinks she is not sincere, but what's done is done. She reaches for his hand.

"Did I tell you that Mary and Gilbert are coming for the Christmas festivities? They will stay until Easter, so she will be here with me for her lying in."

"When is my first grandchild due?" His gruffness cannot disguise the pride in his voice.

"They think in the middle of February. We have permission for them to stay; only the midwife may attend her. I only wish we could have all the family, I miss them so."

"I know you do."

He pulls his hand away, still furious.

"I must take some more opium, my pain is bad tonight."

"Can I help?"

"No, I can manage," he mumbles as he leaves the room, limping from his gout.

She watches as he struggles to turn the door handle. The physicians do not seem able to help his arthritis, and now his hands are becoming quite deformed. She silently thanks God that her own health is good. By the time George returns, she is sound asleep and he blows out the candle, hoping for an undisturbed night. The repercussions of Elizabeth Cavendish's marriage to Charles Stuart, so skilfully engineered by Bess and Margaret, have yet to be felt, and George is all too aware of its potential to cause damage to himself and his family.

C3&O

The earl's prediction that the queen would be furious came true. Within a week, letters were arriving at

Sheffield Castle from Bess' son Charles and George's son, Gilbert, who at twenty-one years of age respectively, were now at Court. They wrote of the gossip and speculation that the marriage has produced, to say nothing of the queen's rage. Sir William Cecil, now Lord Burghley, wrote to George and warned him that the consequences could be serious. Margaret, Charles and Elizabeth were all commanded to appear before Queen Elizabeth, who promptly sent Margaret to the Tower. The two newlyweds were told to remain at their house in Hackney until the official enquiry was complete. Bess was luckier and was able to use the excuse of attending the birth of her grandchild, born to Mary and Gilbert the following February 1575, which she begged the queen to allow. It was a boy they called George and is the first male child to one of George's sons.

Margaret was eventually released from the Tower, and in time, the queen forgave Bess. In November 1575, a year after the wedding, Elizabeth gave birth to a daughter, Arbella. Sadly Charles Stuart died of consumption only six months later, which helped to ease Queen Elizabeth's anger. But there are now serious problems surfacing within Bess' marriage that threatens to destroy it.

03&0

1577

A group of young courtiers stand idly in an antechamber at Greenwich Palace watching Bess with some speculation, taking wagers as to what will happen when she comes before the queen. Some think she will be publicly humiliated and sent back to Derbyshire in disgrace, while others are convinced that a stay in the Tower will be her next resting place. It is the first time some of the newer members at Court have seen the Countess of Shrewsbury and they eye her curiously, for her reputation as a woman of substance is well reported. Today she is dressed in a new amber coloured gown with heavy brocade panels, her hair elegantly dressed by Agnes in the French style and she wears a large gold and ruby necklace with matching earrings.

Having arrived a week ago, she was told the queen has been ill and unable to receive her until now. Keeping her eyes on the floor, she breathes deeply and hopes the wait will not be too long. She has not seen the queen since the marriage of Elizabeth to Charles Stuart. Blanche told her that she has been forgiven, but nonetheless she is naturally apprehensive and has thought very carefully what she will say.

At last the door is opened and a page beckons for her to enter. Bess makes her way towards the queen, who is seated on her ornate, gold leafed throne. She wears a magnificent purple gown of the finest silk, with intricate silver embroidery that glimmers in the shafts of sunlight falling through the window. A multitude of sparkling emeralds and cream pearls adorn her head, some entwined around her red wig. On her neck rests the most exquisite, heavily starched, white lace ruff, the biggest that Bess has ever seen. In contrast, Lord Burghley stands beside her as usual, sombrely dressed in black, holding his staff, and with his face giving nothing away.

Bess curtseys deeply and dares to raise her head, but the queen regards her with a sisterly affection and extends her ringed hand, which she kisses optimistically.

"Bess, we are pleased to see you at Court. Come closer, let me see you"

"Your majesty, I trust you are quite recovered?"

"Quite recovered, yes, it was a trifle really, but my physicians are cautious."

"Your health and well being is our greatest concern."

"That is reassuring, I am surrounded by well-wishers. You must sit, Bess."

They smile at one another and Bess sits on the step at her feet, an honour only granted to a favoured few.

"Your gifts were very welcome, I always know that you will find something to please me that bit more."

"I am glad you are happy with them. I thought the jade silk gown particularly fine and perfect for your majesty's fine colouring."

"I shall wear it tonight and you shall tell me if it is perfect or not."

"I must hear your news for you can make me forget all my cares of state. How I miss you at Court! You do not come often enough. How is the earl?"

"My dear husband is well and sends you his best wishes for your continued health and happiness."

"And the Scots Queen, how does she fare?"

"She can do no wrong in my husband's eyes."

"Is that so? You are not jealous of them are you?"

Bess pauses, torn between her pride and an honest answer.

"I find it hard to see them together. You will think me foolish."

"Not at all. We all know the Scots Queen's character and her capabilities."

"He spends a great deal of time with her. I do not know what they find to discuss."

"How do you know this? I hear you are with them but seldom."

"I am told by my servants, who are very loyal to me. When I do go there, I feel an outsider, as if I am an intruder. Our days of sewing together are long gone."

"Perhaps that is just as well. I would not wish you to become too friendly with her."

"There is no danger of that your majesty, for I find I have a strong dislike for her."

"There is much to dislike. But perhaps you should spend more time at Sheffield or wherever she is being held, then you would see for yourself and take steps to distance them from one another."

"I have spent much time in the past and neglected my other duties and businesses, which I have been content to do, as it was by your gracious command …"

"But now …?"

"I wish to be at home, with my family at Chatsworth. I serve no purpose now as a jailor to the Scots Queen, she tells me nothing when I do see her, and our relationship is very strained."

"I see."

"It dates back to when she wrote to you, my lord, and accused me of scheming and telling lies. I truly believe she wishes to cause conflict between my husband and myself."

"This is the sort of situation that I was hoping to avoid." The queen frowns and looks at Lord Burghley for affirmation.

"It must be hard for you, countess," he says. "But to reassure you, we do not take her words seriously, you need not be concerned."

She looks doubtful. "There is nothing I can do to stop the Scots Queen, but I do try to be a good wife, if only my husband would allow me to live again with him."

The queen takes her hand and her voice is kind.

"You have carried out your duty and have done it well. The Scots Queen remains a threat to my throne, but I know the earl will continue his vigilance. I have been reflecting on your daughter Elizabeth, I was angry with the marriage at first, it should not have taken place without my permission …"

Bess lowers her eyes and prepares for her wrath.

"… but time moves on. How is she coping with widowhood?"

"Elizabeth is a worry to me. Since the death of her husband she has hardly eaten or slept, but stares all day through the window at the river and trees. She hardly acknowledges Arbella, and leaves her care to myself or the nurse."

"What does your physician say?"

"He has not been able to help. He says she has a form of madness brought on by the shock of Charles' death. He says women are sometimes afflicted after the birth of a child."

"And his treatment?"

"He recommends shaving her head and bleeding."

The queen instinctively touches her red wig. "Oh! I hope that has not been carried out!"

"No, I would not allow it. I believe in time, she will find her path in life once more; she has lost her way, that is all. We will look after her and make sure she is cared for, with plenty of rest and good food, but it breaks my heart to see her thus."

Tears begin to swell in her eyes and the queen leans forward to put her arm around her friend.

"Do not distress yourself, Bess. I am sure that all will be well in the end."

They are silent for a moment as Bess struggles to regain her composure. "Forgive me, your majesty."

"Not at all. It must be a great trial for you. You have not told me of Lady Arbella, how old is the child now?"

"She is but two years of age and the bonniest little soul you can imagine!" At the mention of her granddaughter, Bess' eyes light up, her tears momentarily forgotten. "She is a source of such joy to me, and I see her every day. I have just had a portrait of her commissioned and it hangs at Chatsworth. I am every day hopeful that your majesty will visit us soon. Derbyshire is not so far, and I have some splendid building work to show you."

"I should like to visit your beloved Chatsworth, Bess, I feel I am missing something very special. It is finding the time to come that is difficult. But I shall try at the end of our summer progress. It is not so far from Buxton, I believe?"

"A days ride in the summer, with good weather, your majesty. And we are honoured that the Earl of Leicester is to take the waters at Buxton and stay with us."

"I shall think on it and speak to Lord Burghley."

He smiles at her encouragingly and Bess decides to press on with other important issues.

"May I be so bold as to ask you of another matter? The Scottish government is refusing to acknowledge Arbella's claim to the Lennox title …"

"Yes, I believe that is the case."

"I would be most grateful for your majesty's help in this matter. I have written several times and pleaded on her behalf, but I know that your intervention would carry so much more weight. She is the legal heir, daughter of Charles Stuart, she should have what is rightfully hers without question."

"Of course. I will do what I can Bess, but you know I have no jurisdiction over the Scots. I can only appeal to their better nature. But we shall invite Lady Arbella to Court when she is older."

"Thank you, your majesty. I shall pray for a satisfactory outcome."

"We shall speak again. You will dine with me tonight."

They both get up and Bess curtseys once more.

"I am your devoted servant, as always."

The ladies-in-waiting, who have been watching from the corner, immediately stand and follow her through the door. Bess breathes a sigh of relief that the meeting has gone well and accompanies Lord Burghley out of the chamber. They pass through the throng of courtiers who are still standing idly and gossiping. Having noted Bess' relaxed demeanour, it is concluded that the queen has been lenient towards the Countess of Shrewsbury, and that she is still welcome at Court. Some smile as she passes by, and she thinks how fickle they are, one minute condemning her, the next fawning over her.

"Are you in good health, my lord?" She notices that he leans more heavily on his staff than previously.

"I have been better, countess. My duties continue to occupy me by day and night."

"Her majesty relies on you, I know you work harder than ever."

He gives her one of his rare smiles. "I think there are few people who would be allowed to enjoy the favour of the queen after such an event as your daughter's wedding. You were wise to stay away until the dust had settled."

"I am favoured indeed, I never forget it."

"Her majesty admires your determination. You have a strength of character unusual to most of your sex. That you have been chosen as a wife by two of her majesty's most loyal subjects, speaks louder than any words of praise."

"You are very kind, my lord"

They have reached the door of his study and he holds the door open for her. "But your husband writes to me about you almost daily. I would speak with you now, please come in. Some wine, countess?" he indicates to the servant, who pours two goblets and leaves them alone. They sit and Bess waits for him to speak first.

"It is not a task I relish, that of intermediary between a married couple, but I hope as a long standing friend of you both, you will allow me to speak freely."

She nods, and he takes a deep breath, clearly embarrassed.

"The earl tells me that you are extravagant, always wanting more money for your family and building work. He says that you have deliberately gone against his wishes several times, and complains that that you are coming between him and his son, Gilbert."

She is mortified; it is unbelievable to her that George has been writing about their marriage to a third party. But when she answers, her voice is strong and gives no hint of her inner turmoil. "My husband was upset about Elizabeth's marriage at the time and chastised me for my part in bringing it about. I have promised him that I will not do such a thing again without his approval and I have kept my word. I am entitled under our Marriage Settlement to payments from him, and there are amounts outstanding. He says he does not have it to give, which I find unlikely. As for Gilbert, it is true that on occasions he takes my side instead of his father's, which does brings difficulties, but I cannot help it if he feels more empathy with me than his father. These are domestic matters common to all families, I cannot think why he is taking up your valuable time with it."

Lord Burghley is not comfortable about mentioning this matter to Bess, but he has agreed to speak to her in order to pacify George. He shifts in his seat before continuing. "He seems to think you are the cause of all his problems."

"How can I be? I am not responsible for everything."

"I agree, but he has somehow got it into his head that you are. He also blames your son Charles, for coming between Gilbert and himself. I hear they are still close since they were educated together."

"He has bothered you with this pettiness? I am sure you do not wish to be burdened with our problems. You have great matters of state that are far more important."

"He also writes to her majesty and the Earl of Leicester about your troubles."

Bess is now incredulous and beginning to become angry with George. Lord Burghley wishes he had never started this embarrassing interview. He spreads his hands in a gesture of finality.

"I think enough has been said. I would not presume to offer advice to either of you. You are now aware of your husband's views, I cannot do more."

"May I ask how often my husband writes to you?"

"Almost daily. His letters have increased in number and complaint since last year when his daughter Catherine died," he hesitates, unsure if he should continue.

"What is it my lord?"

"Have you noticed any change in his behaviour lately?"

"I am not sure of your meaning."

"There is something about what he writes that is … not right."

"He has been very tired of late." Bess tries to think. "He still frets over the cost of the Scots Queen to his purse and his gout and arthritis still give him much pain."

"This is different. I have noticed an irritability in his letters, a lack of patience, an irrational thread that runs through all his correspondence."

"He is irritable yes, but who would not be with such ailments?"

"You are probably right, I am imagining it. Forgive me Bess; I wanted to mention it to you whilst you are here at Court. I fear I may have made matters worse."

"No, you have not. I appreciate your frankness and I am glad you have spoken to me about it. I will try to find out what is troubling him. I am sorry that you have been bothered, I had no idea that he was writing to you."

"I hope you will not allow my words to affect our friendship."

"Of course not," she murmurs. "Thank you, my lord. I realise it has not been easy for you to discuss this matter with me." They both stand and he responds to her curtsey with a formal bow. In the corridor outside she tries to calm her thoughts then looks down in puzzlement at her hand, which feels wet. She has been clenching her fist so tightly that she has drawn blood.

༄

1577

The talk with Lord Burghley has disturbed Bess more than she cares to admit. She longs to speak to George about it, but that conversation will have to wait until she sees him. In the meantime, she stays at Court for a few more weeks, enjoying the atmosphere and spending time with her old friends such as Dorothy and Blanche. There are the usual banquets and masked balls to entertain visiting dignitaries, the opportunity to buy and show off the latest fashions, and to see others and be seen. As always, gossip and intrigue is rife and, despite her promise, it is a chance for Bess to indulge in some speculative matchmaking, a subject still close to her heart. But at the end of the visit, she is ready to return to Derbyshire and entertain the Earl of Leicester, who is to take the waters at Buxton. His health has been poor lately and the queen has given instructions to George for his diet. He is to stay at Chatsworth on his way back to London and his presence will be a great coup for the Shrewsburys, with the surrounding Derbyshire nobility anxious to be included on their guest list. On the morning of his expected arrival, the house is in a flurry of activity.

"Hurry, his grace will be here soon," Bess orders her servants as they put the finishing touches to the bedchamber prepared for him.

"Is everything ready?" George comes in from outside, having scanned the park for signs of their guest's entourage.

"I think so."

She looks around and gives a nod of satisfaction, dismissing the servants. The earl is to be given the best accommodation that Chatsworth has to offer, and Bess hopes the queen will stay in it one day. There is an elaborately carved oak bed, which dominates the chamber, lavishly hung with thick scarlet damask curtains. Soft featherbed mattresses are covered with sweetly scented linen sheets, embroidered with the Shrewsbury Coat of Arms. Brightly coloured tapestries of biblical scenes have been hung around the walls and new woven rush matting placed underfoot. Bowls of dried lavender sit on the windowsill and vases of delicate pink roses fill the air with their lingering scent. A silver edged looking glass hangs on the wall opposite a large oil painting of the queen, beneath which is a table bearing a silver ewer, basin and comb, together with several linen towels. A large chest has been covered with Bess' favourite Turkish carpet, taken from her own chamber and a close stool in the corner completes the accommodation. A door to a small chamber leads to where his servant will sleep. Less ornate bedchambers have been prepared for the other gentlemen in the party.

"I hope all goes well," George fingers the curtains nervously.

"It will," Bess responds confidently. "It must. I have long waited for such a visit. The Earl of Leicester is the nearest we have to a king, and we will be one step nearer to the queen herself coming here. She was very positive when I spoke to her about it."

"You are aware that he has permission to meet the Scottish Queen."

"That will be an interesting encounter."

"In what way?"

"Well, to see how he responds to her charms, of course. Most men seem to be smitten, even yourself."

"What do you mean?" he replies angrily, reddening.

Bess walks over to join him at the window and avoids his gaze. "You spend a great deal of time with her. I have seen how you fawn over her, yes, your majesty and no, your majesty. It makes me sick to my stomach."

"I do no such thing! I have to watch her; you know that is my task! I most certainly do not fawn over her as you say. Your imagination is overactive. I care nothing for her other than she is my prisoner."

Bess turns to face him and her voice was icy. "You can deny it all you choose, I know what I see with my own eyes."

"Nonsense!"

"I still cannot forgive you for writing about our troubles as you did. It is so disloyal to discuss our private lives with others."

"Oh do not start about this again! You have made your feelings very clear since you arrived back from Court.

"Why should I not? I was so angry, have you stopped writing and complaining about me and Charles?"

"I shall stop when you cease your endless demands for money, and you behave like a wife should do to her husband."

"I cannot do more! What is it you expect of me? To agree with your every thought? To have no mind of my own?"

"Now you are being foolish."

"When was the last time I asked you for money? I wager it is so long ago that you cannot even remember."

He gives a grunt of displeasure and sits on the bed.

"Do not sit there!" she shouts. "You will crease it before he arrives!"

Scowling, he gets to his feet and listens impatiently as Bess continues, her strident voice carrying through the open window.

"You do not pay me what I am due, you have broken your word to me and I have no redress. All you do is complain about me to everyone, it is so humiliating! No doubt you discuss me with the Scots Queen as well …"

"I do no such thing!"

"Of course you do – I can imagine the two of you, all cosy in her chamber while I am at Chatsworth. What do you tell her about us?"

George does not get a chance to reply as a servant comes running in, slightly breathless.

"Your graces, the Earl of Leicester approaches."

"Tell the other servants to take their places," Bess orders. "Come husband, let us do all well for this important guest. Nothing must mar this visit."

George looks at her in bewilderment. He cannot cope with sudden changes in mood. Without replying, he brushes past her, his fingers gripping his stick awkwardly and they hurry downstairs to the courtyard.

A group of six gentlemen are dismounting from their horses, as Bess and George appear to welcome them. The Earl of Leicester is not mounted, but sits on a litter;

the bandage on his leg hides a painful boil. Servants rush forward to help him and Bess curtseys deeply, her face a wreath of smiles.

"Your grace, we are deeply honoured by your visit to our humble home. You and your friends are most welcome."

"Bess, you are kindness itself." He steadies himself and reaches for her hand, kissing it gallantly.

"And your husband, good day to you."

He gives a courtly bow towards George who bows in return.

"You know my brother of course, and may I present my fellow travellers, all fit and well after taking the Buxton waters and enjoying a very strict diet." His eyes are twinkling in amusement. There is general laughter at this comment, which Bess understands to mean the opposite. George regards them stony-faced as he bows again, missing the joke.

"I trust the Chatsworth food was to your liking?" Bess teases, referring to the daily feasts she sent over to Buxton during their stay.

"More than ample Bess, but you know we eat only a modest amount and drink very little."

There is more ribald laughter from the men, and Bess shakes her head in mock disapproval.

"Then I shall have to give any surplus to the poor for I have ordered a sumptuous table to be prepared for you tonight."

"Lead me to it, lady, for I will do my best for you." He takes Bess by the arm and they walk inside, leaving George to follow after the others on his own. The next week is spent entertaining the earl as lavishly as possible. Despite the pain in his leg, he insists on hunting every day, presenting a logistical problem for the servants, who have to carry him everywhere. There is plenty of prey to be found with deer and game birds in the park, the fish ponds have had extra stock added and there is always hawking as a change. Every meal consists of a wide choice of meats and fish, pasties, bread, salad herbs and sweetmeats, washed down with plentiful amounts of ale and the best claret.

In the evening, there is entertainment in abundance with music, dancing, plays, card games and gambling. Bess has hired extra musicians as well as dancers and actors from Derby to perform each night. Her family joins the guests: daughters Frances and Mary with their respective husbands, as well as her sons Henry, William and Charles. Arbella's mother, Elizabeth, makes a desolate appearance, her widow's black gown doing nothing for her pale and grief stricken features. Bess excuses her after the first two days and tactfully the earl does not remark on her absence.

Naturally the earl is keen to meet the Scottish Queen and George escorts him to her quarters the following day with much deference. Bess follows, not wishing to miss out on the encounter. Mary has been expecting him, although she feigns surprise when he appears at her door.

"May I present His Grace, the Earl of Leicester," George announces.

Mary gives him a smile before extending her hand. The earl bows low and kisses her ring briefly.

"We are pleased to meet you at last, much has been said about you, my lord."

"Then we have something in common already, your majesty." Mary laughs and her shoulders relax.

"Please sit and talk to me, I have few visitors." She looks at George and Bess. "Still here? Do you not trust his grace?"

"On the contrary, but we must remain in the room." George sits himself down and looks out of the window. Bess arranges herself beside him, making sure she has a good view of the two of them.

"I hear you have been taking the waters at Buxton." Mary looks at his leg. "Has it helped your health?"

"Alas no, my leg will take longer to heal but I have enjoyed my visit to Derbyshire. It is a beautiful, if sometimes bleak county."

"I would not know, I see little of it."

There is awkward silence then Mary asks sharply "How does my cousin, your queen?"

"My beloved queen is well and send you her good wishes."

Mary gets up abruptly, obliging everyone else to stand. She goes to the door and tries the handle.

"You see how it is, I am trapped like a caged animal. The good wishes of your queen mean nothing. Perhaps you would ask her how long she intends to keep me here? Or her lackey Walsingham? He seems to know everything!"

The earl frowns. "I know nothing of your captivity or date of release. I do know that several attempts have been made to release you for dark intent against the throne of England."

"Lies! All lies! I have no knowledge of such attempts."

He exchanges a glance with the Shrewsburys and his manner softens.

"Please your majesty, let us sit down again and talk calmly of other matters. I have not come here to cause you further misery."

Mary hesitates but returns to her seat. Her ladies sitting at the other end of the chamber have looked up in alarm, but reassured by his words, resume their sewing. Everyone sits once more.

"Why have you come here then, my lord? Is it out of sheer curiosity? Or have you run out of entertainment and thought it would be fun to see a captive queen?"

"Certainly not. My reasons for requesting to see you are so that I may reassure my queen of your well being, and convey any request you may have. Also because yes, I am curious to meet you. Who would not be?"

She laughs softly at his reply.

"I have been equally curious to meet the man who has had so many honours bestowed on him by his queen. Your talents must be numerous, my lord."

"I strive to serve my queen to the best of my ability."

"Then she is lucky to have you. I wish I could have been better served."

"It would have been my honour to serve you, had life been different for us," he says. Mary responds with a coquettish look, which is not lost on Bess, who cannot help but glower from her seat.

"Perhaps I can tempt you to a game of chess? My ladies grow tired of playing me all the time."

"I would be delighted, your majesty, but I must warn you I play well."

"As do I."

They move to the table where the chess pieces are set up and begin to play. Mary is all smiles and charm, having lowered her voice so that the earl has to lean towards her.

"This game could carry on for hours," George whispers to Bess after a few minutes.

"I know. Can we not stop it?"

"I think not. We have no reason and the earl is clearly enjoying himself."

"This is typical of her, she is as cunning as a fox," she hisses back at him, her eyes glaring at them.

"Hardly Bess! It is but a game of chess."

"Can you not see what she is doing?"

"No, but I can see you wish to tell me."

"Flirting with him, of course! Can you imagine the anger of our queen if she could see them both now? Look, she is touching his hand as she moves a piece."

"Hush! They will hear you."

"I do not care!"

"Be silent! There is nothing we can do. Leave now and I will stay with them."

"But …"

"For once in your life do as I say, Bess." His stern expression is enough to convince her that it isn't worth an argument, especially with Mary and the earl only a few feet away. She stands up reluctantly, curtseys, and with a final disapproving look at George, she leaves the chamber. Mary and the Earl of Leicester do not even notice she has gone.

സ്ഥ

After the earl and his party leave, Bess begins making preparations to return Mary and her court to Sheffield Castle. Each time she is moved, which is frequently, it involves a great deal of packing and unpacking, loading and unloading of carts and logistical planning. George hates moving her anywhere because of the ever-present threat of kidnap. Bess always hates to leave Chatsworth, but she has commissioned some building work at

Sheffield Manor Lodge, within the grounds of Sheffield Castle, and wants to see for herself how it is progressing. It is decided that Arbella will remain at Chatsworth with her mother Elizabeth, but that Bess will return there as soon as possible. Arbella has come to bid farewell to her godmother on the morning of the journey.

"I hope we shall meet again soon, little one," says Mary as she crouches down to stroke her cheek. Arbella gives a curtsey as she has been taught, before leaving with her nurse. But Bess lingers after the nurse has carried Arbella away.

"Was there something else, countess?" Mary asks.

"Only that I wonder if your majesty has considered that my granddaughter, the Lady Arbella, has a stronger claim to the throne than your own son, James?"

Mary narrows her eyes and looks at Bess with pure hatred.

"Is there no end to your ambition? Of course my son has the greater claim. It will not be your family that will provide future kings and queens, but my own Stuart blood. You are very impertinent to even think that there could be any other outcome." She gives an ironic laugh. "Your husband agrees with me. I pity that poor little girl with you with you as a grandmother. Arbella is an innocent, but you will ruin her life with your schemes and your plans."

"You should know, having ruined your own life, the truth can be painful, can it not?"

"You would not know the truth if it stared you in the face! Your husband has said as much to me on many occasions."

Mary moves away to sit under her canopy and watch Bess' reaction.

"I think your majesty is mistaken. My husband would never discuss our private affairs with you."

"Are you quite sure? How well do you know your husband? What do you imagine we talk about on those long days and nights when you are at Chatsworth, with your own little court? We are very cosy here in my prison and sit together in front of the fire. Yes, we are very content in each other's company."

"I know what you are doing, I know that you wish to cause strife between the earl and myself. Do not imagine that he is your friend; he is your jailor and his first duty is to our beloved Queen Elizabeth, who, unlike you, is worthy of the crown that has been placed upon her head."

"After what you have told me of her reputation, I do not believe she is worthy at all. Why, it is common knowledge that the Earl of Leicester shares her bed, amongst many others," she adds.

"I have told you nothing!" Bess replies defensively. "If you wish to believe Court gossip, that is your choice. I give no credence to such scandalous lies."

"Who will believe you have told me nothing? We have spent many hours together. People will assume we have talked about everything and anything, including your queen."

"How dare you suggest that I have been disloyal!"

"I dare because I am a queen myself. It is not for you to speak to me of what I may or may not say."

"No, it is not." Bess' eyes glitter dangerously. "But you gave up your rights when you behaved so badly and shocked the world. You did not act as a queen did you? You behaved as a common harlot! There! I have said it and you may make of it what you will."

"What do I find here?" George's voice rings out across the chamber and they both swing round to see him standing in the doorway, like a teacher who has found two fighting pupils. Neither woman responds. Bess has not taken her eyes off Mary who sits apparently at ease, looking guileless. Tight-lipped, he bows towards her.

"It is time for you to leave. The guards will escort you to the Hall, where I shall join you shortly. Your ladies are waiting for you."

Mary gets up and smiles sweetly at George before leaving. No sooner has she left than George shuts the door behind her.

"Do you realise everyone could hear you?"

"That woman is evil. Do you know what she said …?"

He holds up his hands impatiently.

"We do not have time for this now; the coaches are ready and we must make haste."

"You will not believe what she has been saying about you."

"About me?"

"Yes, husband, about you. But as you say, we do not have time." She makes to leave, but he puts his crooked hand on her arm.

"Tell me."

"Tonight, I will tell you tonight."

George nods reluctantly and releases her. They do not speak again for many hours.

෪෨

One month later

The surrounding fields of Sheffield Manor Lodge shimmer in the July heat and everyone complains of the high temperature. Mud on the roads is dry and cracked, giving travellers an uncomfortable ride as they hope for a breeze to cool the stifling air in their coaches. Wheat and barley crops are already golden, but only half the size they should be, due to lack of rain. The grass has withered to a brown stubble, which crackles underfoot and the ripening wild blackberries are as small as currants, showing no promise of a healthy crop. Cattle stand motionless under the shade of trees, and the farmers look hopefully at the cloudless, azure blue sky each morning. At night, the suffocating air hangs as heavy as a blanket around restless bodies that toss and turn with heavy sighs in their beds, unable to sleep. Lying awake in the darkness of their chambers, they wait for sunrise on another unbearably hot day.

Servants are slower in their work and the cook grumbles that the food is going off much more quickly than usual. The workmen that Bess has commissioned to hang new tapestries and upholster furniture in the Hall are working hard, although their fingers are made clumsy in the heat. Every so often they call out to one of the passing serving girls for a drink to quench their thirst, despite being admonished by their foreman. But their biggest worry is leaving sweat stains on the fabrics; the foreman has worked for Bess in the past and knows she will not pay if the work is not to her satisfaction.

Mary, enclosed with her ladies and her court in the Turret House nearby, spends much of each day lying on her bed with a herbal compress pressed to her forehead. She finds the heat very oppressive and complains bitterly about everything to her ladies-in-waiting, who are kept busy swatting the flies that manage to gain entry through the narrow windows. Her gentlemen courtiers venture outside to sit in whatever shade they can find, whilst the ladies constantly fan themselves, their close fitting costumes chaffing their skin. They long to dangle their feet in the cool water of the river as a peasant would without qualm, but it is not ladylike, so they just become more irritable and lethargic. The panting dogs lie listless in the shade, and only when it is cooler in the evenings do they show any sign of activity.

Bess sits in her study, hard at work with Joseph and William, who by now is proving a great asset to his mother. They mostly work in silence, only broken by the scratching of quills. Through the open windows, the sound of birdsong and the bleating of sheep floats in, occasionally interposed with snatches of conversation between servants going about their tasks in the courtyard and outside the kitchen.

Suddenly the door is flung open and George is before them, his expression twisted and angry. The grip on his stick is such that his knuckles are white and shaking. The three of them look up expectantly, but before anyone can speak, he addresses himself curtly to William and Joseph.

"Leave us!"

William glances at his mother who gives an imperceptible nod and they hastily put down their quills and hurry out, closing the door quietly. Bess raises her eyebrows, but her manner is mild when she speaks.

"George, whatever do you mean by bursting into my study in this manner?"

"Have you told the workmen they may spend their nights here until the work is finished?"

"Yes, I see no harm in it."

"Do you not realise that the Scots Queen is only yards away in the Turret House?"

"Of course, but there is no danger, she …"

"Why do you always go against me?" he shouts.

"I never go against you, husband. You have the only keys to her apartments, the workmen do not pose a threat."

George's face is damp with perspiration as he thrusts it over the desk between them. In his temper, he can hardly enunciate his words, and spittle has gathered in the corners of his mouth.

"I am in charge here, not you! If I say the workmen cannot stay overnight then that is how it shall be. Who are you to countermand my authority?"

"Do not raise your voice to me in that manner!"

"I shall raise my voice to anyone I choose."

Bess stands up and looks him square in the face.

"You may be in charge of the security of the Scots Queen, but I am in control of the household and it is just as well that I am, for otherwise it would all fall about our ears. If the workmen stay here, it will mean less time will be spend travelling for them, thus meaning the work will be completed more speedily and cost us less."

"I have already spoken to John Dickenson about this matter and it has been decided."

"You did this without consulting me!"

"You did not see fit to consult me, but took it upon yourself to give orders."

"Why should I not? Am I not mistress here?"

"You may be mistress, but it is my money that pays for all your work."

"Do not start to complain about the cost of everything again. Your wealth can easily afford to pay for it. I have never known anyone so obsessed with money."

"Is that so? You display a fine show yourself of wanting more and more money to fill your coffers. What do you know of my wealth? What do you know of except your own ruthless character? I have never known a woman to be so greedy and ambitious."

She is stunned by his depth of feeling and her eyes widen in surprise. "It pains me to hear you say such cruel words to me. Why are you acting in this way?"

"Because I am tired of all your interfering and constant demands for money. If it isn't more building, it is more furniture or gowns or some luxury for Arbella. That child is thoroughly spoilt. Mark my words, she will bring nothing but trouble in the future."

"Do not bring my Arbella into this argument!"

"Are you ever to stop giving me orders? It is not your place to do so. The security of the Scots Queen must come first in all matters. I would have thought you of all people would have appreciated it. But you are so wrapped up in all your business dealings …" he throws some of the desk papers in the air, "… that you forget

I am your lord and master. It is I who have elevated you to the status of countess and this is the gratitude you show me. It is an outrage that I am so belittled by you. There can only be one head of the household and that is I. You would do well to remember it. I wonder that your other husbands were so badly abused by you. Perhaps it sent them to early graves, all of them."

Bess visibly pales at these words and when she replies her voice trembles with emotion.

"I never forget that you are my lord and master. I have always held you in the highest esteem, but you have no right to speak of what passed between my husbands and myself. Since all of them have left me proof of their love and devotion by their bequests after death, it is clear that they at least, considered me to be a honourable wife. Your words have hurt me deeply."

His eyes flicker and he taps his stick a few times on the floor, realising that he has gone too far.

"Yes, well, perhaps I spoke hastily about your husbands. I regret those words to you."

She cannot trust herself to respond and gazes unseeing at all her papers, which are now in disarray.

"I have told the workmen they may not stay and that is an end to it," he says dismissively.

"So you have countermanded my instructions?"

"I have, madam."

"You had no right to do so! You have made me look foolish in front of everyone!"

"I think you can manage that without any help from me." He turns to go and looks over his shoulder at her. "Do not interfere again or I shall have to take the appropriate action. I shall use all my powers and the law against you. It is time you realised I shall not stand for your wickedness. I rue the day we got married, for you have brought me nothing but misery and debt!"

Bess stares after him as he goes through the door. No one has ever spoken like that to her before.

※

After this argument, Bess cannot concentrate on her work and after finding Joseph and William sitting on a bench outside, she tells them she is going for a long walk. They watch as she strides out towards the river path within the Shrewsbury land, her head down, clearly deep in thought. After the initial shock of George's outburst, she begins to think through what has caused him to be so critical of her. There is no doubt that his behaviour has changed over recent months. Usually he would have left such matters for her to deal with as she saw fit, but it seems that his complaints about her have been festering in his mind for a long time. Gilbert remarked to her recently that he thought his father's behaviour was irrational at times, and that he was becoming very irritable. Lord Burghley had said much the same. It was true that he found looking after the Scots Queen very costly, and there was the constant worry of her escape, which if it ever happened, would inevitably mean his downfall with Queen Elizabeth; he would be stripped of his positions and banished from court, possibly forever.

Bess knows he would move heaven and earth to prevent this from happening. But he has other problems that contribute to his mood. He has been asked by the Privy Council to intervene in a quarrel between two local landowners, and it seems to be a never-ending feud. Then there is his physical health; this is harder for Bess to understand, as she has never had a day's illness in her life. Eventually she is ready to return to the house and find George to reconcile, for she loathes being on bad terms with him. Making her way past the stables, she notices that his horse is missing.

"Where is his grace's horse?" she asks the groom.

He doffs his cap. "The earl left an hour since."

"Did he say where he was going?"

"He mentioned Bolsover, your grace."

Bess nods, and hides her surprise. So George has left in high dudgeon, without saying goodbye, something that has not happened before. She continues inside and finds a letter on the hall table with Lord Burghley's seal, which she quickly opens and takes to her study to read in private.

Palace of Whitehall

London

Countess,

I write to inform you and your husband of the Scots Queen's latest methods of communicating with her supporters. Your own discovery of writing on bolts of cloth and inside the heels of shoes worn by her ladies—in—waiting, has been very useful. We have also found invisible writing in between the lines of books sent to her. Our agents have intercepted these books, copied the contents, and replaced them, so that the Scots Queen is none the wiser. Although the writing is in code, our agents are able to decipher their meaning with accuracy over a period of time.

The recent report of the theft of the Scots Queens' jewels has caused us a great deal of concern, and her majesty is most displeased to hear of it. Although likely that the Scots Queen herself has sold them to fund another escape attempt, the fact remains that somehow they are no longer in her possession. Her majesty has commanded me to emphasis to both of you again, the vital importance of vigilance and through searching of items arriving and leaving the apartments where the Scots Queen resides.

Please thank your husband, the Earl of Shrewsbury, for his kind invitation to stay with you when I come to Buxton next week. I had hoped to see the Scots Queen on this visit, but Her Gracious Majesty Queen Elizabeth has not granted permission for this meeting to take place.

I trust this letter finds you in good health.

Written this day 28 July 1577,

William Cecil, Lord Burghley.

Bess now wishes that George had not left so abruptly. Apart from what the servants might think of his departure immediately after their argument, she needs to make him aware of the contents of Lord Burghley's letter. Despondently, she puts it away and prepares to spend the hot and humid evening alone.

○❦○

August 1577

Early preparations for Lord Burghley's visit are just as intense as they had been for the Earl of Leicester. Extra supplies of food and drink are brought in by waggons to be unloaded by burly men, puffing and panting with the exertion as they make their way to the Chatsworth kitchen. Bess has hired help from nearby villages and ordered cleaning of the house from top to bottom. New tapestries for the remaining bare walls arrive and are hastily put into place. Wood and silver are polished until they gleam and the larder is full of joints of beef, mutton and pork. Servants spend hours plucking chickens, turkeys, geese and pigeons. Freshly killed haunches of venison add to the list of meat waiting to be prepared. The Chatsworth fishponds yield a good supply of carp, pike, sturgeon and tench with oysters and anchovies arriving in barrels from the coast.

A team of laundry maids work all day and into the night, washing linen and ruffs, while carpets and rugs are taken outside and well beaten for dust. The dairymaids are kept busy making extra butter and cheese, and the brewery dispatches kegs of ale to sit in a cool corner of the basement. Some early apples are picked from the orchard and made into pies, sitting alongside elaborate sweetmeats and marchpane. Joseph hurries from one room to another, supervising and giving orders.

After a heavy thunderstorm, the summer weather is cooler and by the time Lord Burghley has been to Buxton with George, the temperature is more comfortable for everyone. On the morning of his expected arrival, Bess orders fresh flowers to be cut from the gardens and brought into the house. There are bunches of fragrant roses, lilies and wild flowers from the hedgerow, providing the finishing touches to the chambers. Bess is satisfied as she surveys the work before hurrying upstairs to change. She is slightly apprehensive about seeing George for the first time since their latest row, but in front of Lord Burghley, he is all smiles for such an honoured guest.

Everything does not go according to plan however, when a letter arrives later that afternoon with news of another escape attempt by Mary. George has to rush back to Sheffield, leaving Bess and the family to entertain Lord Burghley. Unlike the Earl of Leicester, he does not wish to hunt or fish, so Bess has to find other, more sedate amusements for him. They spend some of the two days by walking gently around the gardens or watching the others playing bowls. Bess also shows him her latest building work and some horses she has recently acquired. But work follows him wherever he goes, so a certain amount of time is spent answering correspondence from the queen and the Court. There have also been brief visits from neighbours, the Manners family from nearby Haddon Hall, and Sir John Zouche and his family from Wingfield. Lord Burghley leaves feeling well fed and rested, with promises to Bess that he will do all to encourage the queen to visit as soon as possible. With much bowing, curtseying and waving, everyone watches him depart with his small retinue, and the family make their way to the Hall with Bess to relax and reflect on the event. There is a general feeling of relief that their important guest has gone on his way after a successful visit, for such visitors from London are rare.

It is not often now that the family are all gathered with her and she has enjoyed these last few days with them. Her gaze scans their faces, one by one. There is Henry, now twenty-seven, his hair already receding and his face showing signs of burning the candle at both ends. Frances and Mary are talking animatedly together, as sisters do. William, Charles and Gilbert are standing at the window, laughing over some joke with Frances' husband. Elizabeth, who by now seems a little better, has managed to join them for short periods over the last week, although she is still quiet and withdrawn. Grace, Henry's wife, sits apart, her thin lips pinched in a line; she finds the Cavendish family *en masse* noisy and overwhelming. She has always been in absolute awe of her mother-in-law, only responding meekly when Bess speaks directly to her. At times like this, she is acutely aware that she has not produced any heirs from the marriage, and she looks wistfully at the five grandchildren as they are taken back to the nursery. There is Bessie, Robert and Grace (children of Frances and Henry), little George (son of Mary and Gilbert) and Arbella, all having being presented to his lordship with great pride by Bess.

Mary is the daughter who is most like her mother, strong willed and outspoken, although she does not have Bess' striking hair colour, or her business acumen. She turns away from Frances now and they both smile.

"Are you pleased with the visit, lady mother?" asks Mary after a few moments, knowing by the look on her mother's face, that she is delighted.

"Very much so, Chatsworth is looking at its best, and Lord Burghley will return to London and tell the queen what a wonderful time he spent with us. It should tempt her to visit; that is my dearest wish. Yes, I am very pleased; it could not have gone better. You all played your part, as I would have expected. Apart from Henry of course, who could not help but drink too much of my good wine." She regards him without pleasure.

"Come, lady mother, I am here am I not? I could have been listening to musicians or looking at my horses, which I would have much preferred, but I chose to be a dutiful son and spend two boring days fawning over Lord Burghley."

"It was the least you could have done! Why can you not be more like your brothers? Why must you always be a disappointment to me?"

"Not always, lady mother, remember he did become MP for Derbyshire five years ago," Frances reminds her.

"How long did that last?" she replies bitterly. "He never sticks at anything, no ambition, no thought for me or his family." The company exchange resigned looks, once Bess starts to complain about Henry, it usually ends badly. "To think that Chatsworth is entailed to you and there is nothing I can do about it. And you always take my husband's side against me; do not think I am unaware of it. Such disloyalty is despicable. Perhaps you forget that it is I who pays your debts, not him."

"Your husband, the earl, at least has a better opinion of me." Henry drains his glass of wine and sets it down on the table before getting to his feet. "You expect too much, you always have. I am only flesh and blood. The truth is that I will never be good enough for you, so I have given up trying."

Charles and William both speak at once.

"Henry..."

"You never even started to try!"

Bess sounds resigned when she speaks to him again. "I have given you many chances, but you have thrown them back in my face. You are the talk of the county, an embarrassment to us all. I am ashamed of you. I am only glad your poor father is not here to witness it. And still you have no legitimate heir, although plenty of bastards around the county and beyond!"

There is an uncomfortable silence and Grace blushes with shame.

"Come wife, we shall leave this merry gathering and return to the comfort of our own home." He holds out his hand and she duly stands up, unable to look at anyone. Bess gets up and walks over to her.

"Grace, I am sorry for my harsh words, I sometimes speak when I should remain silent. I know you are a good wife to him, you deserve better."

They embrace and Bess kisses her softly on the cheek.

"Write to me," she whispers. Grace nods and sketches a curtsey to the family. Henry is impatient to go now; this was only what he expected. With no further exchange, they both leave and Bess returns to her seat, shaking her head.

"What a shame father could not join us," says Gilbert, trying to defuse the situation.

"Yes, he felt guilty enough at having a few days at Buxton, then having to hurry back to his charge. A rest from his duties would have done him some good," Bess replies.

There is a brief silence, then Frances stands up. "Who will join me for a game of cards?"

Everyone goes to the table except Bess and Gilbert. A servant refills their glasses and Bess indicates for Gilbert to move his chair nearer to her, as the cards are dealt amidst some noisy repartee between the siblings. "Has your father spoken any further to you about our argument the other day?"

"He has been much troubled about it."

Bess regards Gilbert as a friend, and they are quite close. In appearance, he is like a younger version of his father, with a long face and deep set, inquisitive eyes, which look back at Bess with disarming honesty.

"As I have myself," she replies.

"I told him of your offer to dismiss the groom he so disapproved of the other week."

"And what was his reply?"

"He said that he doubted you would agree to a man of his choosing."

"I would try – I still think he is happier when he is not with me."

"No, that is not true."

"I am sure that he prefers the Scots Queen's company to my own."

"What makes you think it?"

"He feels sorry for her. They have grown close over these years of captivity and she is an attractive woman who knows how to appeal to a man."

"Do you not think her attractiveness has waned in recent years? Her health is not good and I hear she wears a wig."

She gives the semblance of a smile. "That just makes her more vulnerable to your father. I have thought about it a lot, Gilbert. The Scots Queen has no power over anyone anymore, yet she is an anointed queen, an unusual combination. She is still entitled to our respect and to be treated with dignity. The relationship between them is more complicated than you might think."

"I do not see how, she is a prisoner and he is her jailor. That seems simple enough to me."

"That is because you do not know her determination to escape and be crowned Queen of England. Your father's constant denial of any impropriety between them, smacks to me of a guilty conscience."

Gilbert looks shocked. "Are you serious? Do you really think he has fallen in love with her?"

"I believe he has formed an attachment to her, which goes beyond what their relationship should be. I have my spies wherever she is being held. They report to me of lengthy talks late at night, of laughing together, of his laxness in her captivity and his pleasure in her company."

"Can you not spend more time with him?"

"He does not wish it, Gilbert. We seem to argue all the time now and I have much work to keep me here, which I cannot neglect.

"Is that all?"

She hesitates and reaches for her glass to give herself time to reply.

"Truth be told, I prefer to be here at Chatsworth, it is my home and more comfortable in every respect. When I am staying wherever Mary is being kept, whether it be

Sheffield or anywhere she is housed, I am restricted so much. I am not allowed any visitors to cheer me, so I cannot see you all. I am constantly having to attend to the Scots Queen, for she is always complaining of some trifle …"

"… but it is the same for my father."

"Yes, I know, but he does not seem to miss home and family so much. He could ask to be relieved of this task, which I know it is having a bad effect on his health and his purse, but he does not ask the queen because his pride will not allow him." On the other side of the Hall comes the sound of laughter from the card players. Bess lowers her voice. "But I have heard rumours of a very serious nature against your father."

"Do you mean the child he is supposed to have fathered by her?"

"You know about it?"

"There have been rumours at Court to that effect for some while. I am sure there is no truth in them."

"How can you be so sure?"

"You yourself have told me that her ladies never leave her side. My father may be many things, but I do not believe he would take advantage of her in that manner."

"Is there much gossip at Court about it?"

"A little, I think there is bound to be."

Bess is suddenly weary of the discussion.

"Let us join the others, I am feeling lucky tonight."

They walk over to the card players and are soon enjoying the game, the conversation forgotten. It is to be the last time they are all happy for a while.

೦ಶ೭೦

3 Days later (10 August 1577)

As the time approaches midnight, the house is quiet and everyone has retired to bed. The servants, scattered around the house and stables, fall asleep quickly, exhausted by their labours from the day. Moonlight casts its shadows over the wooden floors and the house creaks as it too settles for the night. In her comfortable bedchamber, Bess sits as Agnes attends to her *toilette;* it has been another long day of spending time with the family, and they are both tired. Finally, Agnes helps her mistress into bed and curtseys, leaving Bess alone. Tomorrow everyone will be leaving, except William, Elizabeth and Arbella; the house will quieten down as houses always do, after visitors. Yawning, she blows out the candle before listening to the familiar sounds of her home through the open window. The soft gurgle of running water from the river nearby, a dog's isolated bark, a couple of owls hooting – content and relaxed on the deep feather mattress, she eventually falls asleep.

She is woken about two hours later by some raised voices through the wall, which she recognises as Mary's and Gilbert's. Something is wrong. They sound distraught and she lights a candle before getting up and hurrying to their bedchamber. Without pausing to knock, she opens the door and freezes. The sight that greets her is one of anguish and pain. Mary is standing beside George's cot, a candle in her hand. Tears are streaming down her face, for she is experiencing every parent's worse nightmare. His little body, that only a few hours ago had been running around with boundless energy, is limp and lifeless. Gilbert sits immobile nearby, staring at his son in disbelief.

By this time, family and servants appear and watch in horror as she moves forward to look closer, with a terrible sense of foreboding, for she knows what she will find. Bess stifles a cry as Mary falls into her arms, and the room is racked with their sobs. Charles finds a servant and tells him to ride to the physician without delay. He goes over to Gilbert and puts his arm on his stepbrother's shoulder.

"My dear friend, I am so sorry, so very sorry."

"Too late, it is too late," groans Gilbert, burying his face in his hands.

"But he was well! So full of life yesterday ..." Mary cries.

Bess is speechless with shock as she clings to her daughter and wonders how she will have the strength to tell her husband, for he dotes on his grandson as much as anyone else. No one sleeps for the remainder of that night, and it is not until the first rays of the sun appear as a red streak in the early morning sky, that they return sadly to their beds.

The night has brought back painful memories for Bess herself, as she lost two of her own babies,

Temperance and Lucres, some years ago. With a heavy heart, she sits down at her desk to write to family and friends, but first she must compose George's letter. Picking up the quill, she cannot stop her tears spilling onto the parchment. For a long while afterwards, she is inconsolable.

☙❧

1578 – Westminster Abbey

Seven months later Bess finds herself at another funeral, but this time, it is someone of her own age being buried, and not a child. From the grand edifice of Westminster Abbey, muffled bells are ringing in the early morning sunshine, the sound echoing across the Thames with haunting regularity. Bess watches with the other mourners as they wait for the coffin of Margaret, the Countess of Lennox, to be lowered in the Chapel of Henry VII, her final resting place.

She has not seen Margaret since they plotted the marriage of their children three years previously, although they had corresponded regularly. Her death has been very sudden and taken everyone by surprise. The whole court is in attendance, including the queen herself, sitting in great state apart from the congregation, and looking especially regal with her jewels sitting heavy around her neck and head. There is some whispering as to the cost of such a spectacle as no expense seems to have been spared by the queen for her royal cousin, despite their stormy relationship over the years.

"Well Bess, this was a shock. They say she dropped down dead," Blanche Parry murmurs as they begin to file out behind the queen.

"At least it was quick," responds Bess. "Better than a slow agonising end."

Blanch nods in agreement. "How will this affect little Arbella?"

"The Scottish Regent does not accept Elizabeth as her guardian, which has caused her much anguish, as she fears Arbella will be taken away from her."

"I am sure the queen will intervene and make Arbella her ward."

"I hope so. Arbella should inherit the Lennox English estates at least. I am not so sure about the Scottish, we may have a fight on our hands about them, as well as the Lennox title."

"Poor wee mite. Is Elizabeth any better?"

"She seems to have accepted her fate, but I don't think she will ever be quite the same. But at least she plays with Arbella now and seems to dote on her."

Blanche smiles. "As do you."

"It is true, she is the sweetest child," Bess says proudly. "I have had her horoscope charted which shows that she will hold the highest rank in the country."

"Have a care, Bess. This is dangerous talk and the queen is but a few yards away."

They glance towards the back of Elizabeth who has stopped to speak to someone. "Do not fret, Blanche, I know what I am doing in this matter."

"Does your husband know of your ambitions for Arbella?"

"He knows of some of it. I do not tell him all, for he worries so, and chastises me for my dreams."

"Well he might. Can you not lower your sights for her?"

"Certainly not! She has royal blood. I want this to be recognised and for her to have what she is entitled to. You know I recently commissioned a portrait of her."

"But she is not yet two years of age!"

Bess pretends not to hear. "It is in in full Court dress and the Lennox motto will be inscribed – 'I endure in order to succeed.' I shall hang it at Chatsworth in a prominent position where everyone can see and marvel at it."

"Very commendable."

Blanche knows better than to challenge Bess, especially as this is neither the time nor the place. They wait as the Earl of Leicester escorts the queen to her coach. A crowd has gathered to watch the spectacle, all in sombre mood to match the Court. There are a few cries of "God save the queen" – but for the most part they are silent. The bell continues its relentless tolling. Blanche shivers and pulls her cloak tighter, looking for her own coach in the queue.

"Are you going to the drinking, Bess?"

"I hope to slip away early. There is much to do and I have little time for such events. The queen has granted me a formal audience tomorrow, and I must have all clear in my mind."

"Then will you join us afterwards? Come for supper, it is just the family."

"I would like to very much."

They kiss briefly on each cheek and go their separate ways, Bess to her waiting coach and Blanche to her own. On the short journey back to Whitehall, Bess is deep in thought and takes little notice of the crowds of beggars that shout as the coach passes along the crowded streets. Her dear friend, Frances Cobham, was not at the funeral. She had decided to leave Court three years previously, when her name was mentioned by one of the Shrewsbury servants during interrogation by Walsingham as being too friendly with the Scots Queen. Bess is wary of communicating with her now, although she is sure there is no truth in it. Margaret had been a life long friend too, and the marriage of their children had brought them even closer. But Margaret would be missed, not least because she was very active in looking after Arbella's interests while she was at Court. Now that she is dead, it will be left to Bess alone to fight for her granddaughter's rights. George has made no secret of his relief that Margaret was no longer alive.

"She cannot get you into any more trouble now," he tells her. "That woman has been a bane to everyone she came into contact with!"

"That simply is not true," replies Bess. "She did not get me into trouble, as you say. I am not so easily swayed."

"No, for you are as stubborn as an ox."

"That is unkind. Some would call it a strength, not a weakness."

"I am not one of them." He suddenly becomes angry. "If only you were like my first wife. She knew how to behave. She always supported me and never went against me. It is a pity you do not have such virtues."

"I suppose you mean she always did as you bid her, something I have never been guilty of."

"No indeed, let me assure you madam, you fall very short of an ideal wife!"

At this, George had stormed out of the chamber and left Bess puzzled and hurt by his accusations. Sitting alone in her coach, she mulls over again what he had said. Such outbursts are becoming more commonplace, and sometimes he seems determined to pick a fight with her over trivial matters. She knows his failing health contributes to his mood, and also that her own robust constitution is a constant source of annoyance to him. There is nothing she can do about either of these matters, and the queen shows no sign of releasing him from his task as jailor to the Scots Queen. But now Bess has more pressing matters to occupy her, and Arbella's security and future needs her full attention. George will have to take second place for the time being.

ಚಿರಿ

1578

In the autumn, Bess has to make another interminable journey to see the queen, who has moved to Richmond in an attempt to avoid the plague. George sent her again to petition regarding his expenses for the Scottish Queen. Not only does he want an increase of the allowance but also payment of the backlog of monies owed, neither of which the queen has so far shown any sign of handing over. Bess has also been trying all year to secure an increase of the pensions awarded to Elizabeth and Arbella. Margaret Lennox left Arbella all her jewels, to be given to her on her fourteenth birthday, but the Scottish executor claims they have been stolen and Arbella has yet to receive them. Another disappointment for Bess was that Queen Elizabeth has confiscated Margaret's English properties and land that should now belong to Arbella.

"Somehow we must pay for Margaret's funeral and her debts," the queen tells Bess, who has to bite her lip from a confrontation with her. She dreads telling George that her trip has not been successful. He is waiting for her as the coach pulls into the courtyard of Sheffield Castle; his cloak wrapped tightly against the bitter north wind. Hardly has Bess stepped down from her seat, than he is questioning her.

"Here you are at last! I have been standing for hours in the cold. Well, what news do you have for me?"

Bess brushes herself down and stretches, chilled and stiff with travelling. "We were delayed by one of the horses shedding a shoe."

She makes a gesture to greet him with an embrace, but he pulls back and she hides her embarrassment in front of the servants, who are unloading trunks and attending to the horses.

"Are you well, my dear?" she asks as they go inside to the warmth of the fire in the Hall.

"I am never well, you know that. I am ever anxious to hear of the queen's response to my request."

"If I may just catch my breath ..." Bess takes a cup of warm mead offered to her and stands in front of the fire warming herself. "Has all been well in my absence?"

"Of course, I am quite capable of running everything without you."

"How is my little Arbella?"

"The Scots Queen has been playing with her all morning. The little madam has just left with her nurse to buy a toy from the market, I expect them to return shortly."

"With the guards?"

"Naturally."

"And Elizabeth? Is she still well?"

"I believe so. I have seen little of her. Everyone is in the best of health, except me," he adds.

"I am sorry to hear it, husband."

George sits himself down by the fire and looks morosely at the flames.

"The family will join us tomorrow and stay a few days."

She smiles. "How I miss them all! Now I must wash and change."

"Not before you have told me your news."

"Can it not wait? I have much to do now I am here."

"No! It cannot wait, such matters may not be important to you but I am worried sick about the cost of keeping Mary. It is going to bankrupt me!"

Bess tries to keep her exasperation to herself. Tired though she is, she knows George will have to find out sooner or later.

"I am afraid I do not have any good news for you from her majesty. There is to be no increase, and she did not assure me that the backlog would be paid any time in the near future."

"Did you make a point of asking?"

"Of course."

"Then you clearly did not put my case as well as you should have done! I suppose it was not a priority and that your pleas for Arbella were more important. That is typical of you, all you think about is your own ambitions. It is always the same."

"I promise you that I tried very hard to persuade the queen. I explained that the cost of food and fuel for Mary and her Court was much higher than the allowance. I said that you were still carrying out your duties with the highest sense of responsibility and vigilance. I begged her majesty to ease the burden of your debt, believe me. You can ask Lord Burghley or Sir Francis or the Earl of Leicester, who will all vouch for my efforts on your behalf. They told me that there is no money to pay you."

"I would not demean myself by asking them! It is you who is to blame here!"

"No, George, I am not to blame for the queen's refusal! It is most unfair to accuse me when all I have done is carry out your wishes. I have travelled all the way to London and back, in this bitterly cold weather for you …"

"It was not for me! You went for yourself, for your own agenda and your spoilt granddaughter. I know you too well! Others may think you are charming and without guile. The Earl of Leicester has already written to me praising your conduct on this visit, but you are nothing better than the women who stand at the quayside selling fish!"

"George! The servants …" She knew he would be angry, but had not thought his reaction would be so violent. He stands up and shakes his stick in her face.

"I care nothing for the servants! They know what you are like; they have seen it for themselves. You have a wicked tongue in your head, I see evidence of it every day."

Bess loses her temper with him now. She is cold, tired and fed up with his constant criticisms. To fight back is contrary to the behaviour of a good wife, but she cannot help herself.

"I have done my best for you with the queen! No one could have tried harder than myself. If you are so short of money why have you commissioned a new house in Worksop with Robert Smythson as your designer? Hardly the actions of a man on the brink of bankruptcy!"

"That is no business of yours. You have commissioned enough work on your beloved Chatsworth, which by the way will be quite outshone by my own building."

"So we are in competition with one another are we? I had not realised. It hardly seems necessary for you to undertake this project, as we both know you have more houses than you have fingers on your hands."

"How I spend my money is my own affair."

"It does not stop you complaining to Lord Burghley and Sir Francis though does it? They must be heartily fed up with your constant stream of letters. Every day so I hear; there must be quite a collection by now."

"How easy it for you to sit in judgement! Last year I spent over £1,000 on fuel and wine that was not provided for in the allowance. Mary and her Court are wilfully wasteful with my money; there was another £1,000 for pewter and plate. I am allowed sixpence a day for guards but I only receive payment for twenty-four, when there are twice that number. The bill for paying my servants last year rose by £400, as I must pay extra to secure their loyalty. But you are not interested in all this, are you?"

"Why should I be? These are matters that I cannot control. Your wealth should be more than enough to pay for all of this, if managed correctly," she adds under her breath.

"What is that supposed to mean?"

"Some people are better at keeping their money than others."

"When do I have time or opportunity to oversee my finances? I am forced to leave it in the hands of others. I do not have the luxury of giving it my full attention, my role as jailor is all consuming. If you were here to help me more often then perhaps I would not be in this muddle."

"Yes, of course! Blame your wife! Everything is all my fault, how convenient for you. It is nothing to do with you at all. Why do you not ask the queen to release you from this task? Let someone else struggle with it? No, you would rather complain and be a martyr, it suits you so much better."

"I will carry out her majesty's commands to the best of my ability. She continues to tell me that I am the best person for this job. It would be an admission of defeat for me to relinquish this position."

"Let us not pretend your pride is at stake here – you want to continue to be close to the Scottish Queen. I am not a fool, I know …"

"Lady grandmother!"

There is a little voice from the doorway and Arbella stands with her nurse staring at the two of them with dismay.

"My darling jewel, come here my love."

Bess immediately changes her mood and crouches down with open arms and a beaming smile to receive her granddaughter, who runs towards her with unsteady steps. George grunts in frustration and annoyance before taking himself off, his stick making a clacking sound on the flag stone floor. The nurse keeps her eyes downcast and pretends not to notice, for such arguments between the master and mistress are now commonplace.

಍಄

1582 – 1584

❖

More sorrow for Bess and the family, when her daughter Elizabeth dies, leaving Arbella an orphan at the age of seven. Her daughter-in-law Margaret, who was married to her youngest son Charles, also dies in the summer after giving birth to a baby boy, who tragically never survives. George has his share of grief too, when his son and heir, Francis, dies of the plague; this means that Gilbert becomes his heir. The rumour that George has fathered a child by Queen Mary will not go away, and he becomes convinced that Bess is responsible.

There are more disagreements over money, and by 1583, George is refusing to see his wife, despite receiving conciliatory letters from her. But in 1584 matters between George and Bess reach a crisis point, and he effectively declares war on her.

Annie Carter, long time tenant on the Chatsworth Estate, places her baby granddaughter in the wooden crib, and pulls the blankets gently around her swaddled body. Having spent the last two hours trying to placate her, Annie wearily returns to her bed. She is looking after her son's child while his wife is ill. Her son is one of the house carpenters and unable to care for the child himself. It is a task that she is glad to do, but hopes it is not for too long, as she is not as young as she was, and coping with little sleep does not come as easily as it used to. Her husband, the head gamekeeper, snores gently as she snuggles down beside him and soon she is fast asleep too. Their cottage stands on its own, a rare statement of his status, at the end of the small hamlet and near the Norman church.

In the moonlight, all is quiet and peaceful, but just as the clock on the church tower shows two o'clock; there is the sound of horses hooves clattering on the paving stones nearby. Annie wakes with a start, thinking it is the baby, but she has not stirred. Then there is the sound of raised voices, so loud, that Annie thinks they are just below the window. She creeps out of bed to look and stifles a gasp. For down below at the entrance to the churchyard, a group of armed men are chasing a rider as he runs towards the church entrance. He has evidently dismounted, for his horse is being rounded up by one of the men. She does not hesitate, but goes round to the other side of the bed to wake her husband.

"What is it?" he groans sleepily.

"Come to the window, someone is being attacked," she whispers urgently.

Her husband is a large framed man with fingers like sausages, who never shies away from trouble. For someone so big he is out of bed in a trice and peers towards the church, where the lone figure is seen opening the door and disappearing inside, his would be assailants not far behind. They increase their shouts and wave their weapons, frustrated that they are unable to follow. Some disappear round the side of the church to see if there is another entrance, but they return after a minute and look upwards towards the clock tower.

"What shall we do?" asks Annie.

"Nothing," her husband replies. "Come back to bed, we have seen nothing."

She is puzzled but joins him, waiting until they are under the covers before she asks him the reason. "Did you not see whose livery the men were wearing?" he mumbles, his eyes already closed.

"No, did you?"

"They are the Earl of Shrewsbury's men. I wager they are chasing one of the Cavendish sons on his orders."

"How can you be sure?"

"I could see their coats with the Shrewsbury arms on the back."

"Was the earl himself there?"

"I doubt it. He would be no use on such a raid and only get in the way."

"But which of the three sons could it be?"

Her husband thinks about it.

"It would not be Henry, he is liked by his stepfather. It could be William, although I did not think he could run so fast."

"Maybe the threat of all those men spurred him on"

"No, my money would be on the youngest, Charles."

"But why?"

"He must have done something to upset the earl."

"Something quite bad," she says. "Whoever it was, he must have been frightened."

Her husband turns over, wishing to get back to sleep again.

"There is nothing you and I can do. He is safe in the tower if he has locked all the doors properly. We shall seek him out in the morning."

Annie wants to talk about it some more, but within a minute he is asleep. She lies listening to the men disperse, and then the only sound she can hear is her husband snoring and the steady quick breathing of her granddaughter, oblivious to it all.

At the entrance to the church, Charles just manages to shut and secure the heavy door before the men reach him. Completely terrified, he pauses for a moment to catch his breath before sprinting towards the staircase that leads to the tower. There are two more doors that he locks, his hands shaking as his feet stumble on the stairs, clambering ever upward before stopping at the top of the tower to peer through the narrow aperture. Panting with the exertion, he can see the men looking up at him, shaking their fists and circling about. A few have gone round to the back of the church to see if there is another entrance, but Charles knows there is only one door. At that moment, the full moon comes out from behind a cloud and he also sees that the men are all wearing the Shrewsbury Coat of Arms on their backs. In a few minutes they disperse, and all is silent again.

After one final look to satisfy himself that the men have gone, he slumps to the floor in frightened relief; sweat pouring down his face, horrified to be the object of their attempted violence. At a loss to understand the reason for the ambush, his feelings give way to anger that he is now forced to remain here until daylight, some five hours away. Having been dining with friends nearby, he left quite late, but had been hoping his journey would only take an hour and he curses again, for he could have been in his warm bed now instead of sitting on a stone floor. Then a thought occurs to him. How did the earl's men know he would be there at that time on that particular road to Chatsworth? Were they just lucky or had they been tipped off by someone? Either way, it is not much use to him now. He knows his mother will be furious and she will want to confront George at the earliest opportunity.

A chilly wind is blowing through the openings of the cramped space and he pulls his coat more tightly round himself in an attempt to keep warm. He hears scrabbling and sees a mouse running along a beam. A stale, rotten smell makes him swallow the reflex to retch and he curses again to himself in the darkness.

Charles spends the remainder of the night huddled in a corner. He cannot sleep and strains his ears constantly for any more sounds that the men have returned. It gives him plenty of time to think. He is mystified by his stepfather's behaviour. Up until recently, George has been pleasant enough towards him and at one time encouraged his friendship with his own son Gilbert. But now, it is clear that any goodwill between them no longer exists. He can hardly wait to tell Bess about this frightening incident. Charles is no coward, he got into scrapes as much as any other pupil at Eton, but tonight he knew he was completely outnumbered and had no chance of reasoning with a mob of weapon wielding men, even if they were wearing the earl's livery. When dawn arrives, and a grey light begins to filter through the darkness, he gets up and stretches his chilled, stiff limbs. Carefully retracing his steps out of the church, he takes some deep breaths, as the air is fresh and pure after the confines of the tower. Tenants from some of the dwellings are already stirring and trails of smoke rise up from chimneys. He stops in front of a man chopping firewood.

"Do you know if any of the earl's men are still in the area?"

The man, recognising Charles, stops chopping to tug his forelock and nods slowly.

"I have not seen sight nor sound of them, sir. Last night were a bad business. Never seen the like before."

"I have been forced to spend a cold, uncomfortable night in the church."

The tenant's wife appears, her face full of curiosity and concern.

"Can we offer you some ale, sir?"

"Thank you mistress, I will go on now, if I can find my horse."

"Is it a chestnut mare? Over there, behind the oak tree."

Charles thanks them again before going over to his horse. His expensive saddle has not been stolen, so he concludes that robbery was not the motive for this attack. He mounts, nervously looking about, and half expects the mob to reappear, but he completes the last mile in safety. When he finally arrives at Chatsworth, the grooms are already up and working in the stables. He hands his horse over to their care and makes his way inside through the large kitchen, where the servants look at him in surprise and curtsey. On his way, he picks up a couple of freshly baked rolls that are cooling on the table and eats them hungrily as he goes to his bedchamber. His manservant appears, full of apologies, and disappears to bring hot water and clean towels for him to wash.

"Her grace, your lady mother is downstairs in the Hall, sir," he tells him as he helps him to change.

"Is she indeed?" replies Charles in surprise.

Bess is an early riser, but this is too early, even for her. He hurries down to find her standing by the door with one of the estate bailiffs, John Smyth, and they both look concerned.

"Charles – I have been worried about you. Where were you last night?" she kisses him and he explains what happened to delay his return. When he has finished, his mother is predictably angry.

"This is unbelievable!! You could have been badly hurt, how dare he do such a thing!"

"I am afraid it could get worse, your grace."

John is a mild mannered man who has worked for the Cavendish family since he was a boy. His brow is creased in concern and he looks between Bess and Charles anxiously.

"We have heard of another plan, worse than the two events that occurred last night."

"There were two ambushes?" Charles asks.

"As I was telling her grace, some of the tenants in Rowsley were woken in the middle of last night by the earl's men breaking down the doors to their homes, smashing window panes and furniture. They had fierce dogs and terrified the people out of their wits. Old widow Peters collapsed with the shock of it."

"What do you mean when you say it could get worse?" says Bess.

"I have heard of a rumour that the earl is planning to storm Chatsworth and remove items that he believes belong to him." John looks apologetic and shuffles his hat from hand to hand. "Nicholas Booth was there too," he adds.

Charles looks quizzically at him.

"Your stepfathers land agent, sir. A tough man, and one I always try to avoid. He told the tenants they must pay their rents to the earl and not you, your grace. I am sorry to be the one to tell you." He tries to hide his dismay, but it is all too obvious in his voice. "This is something I never thought to see. I advise you to leave Chatsworth immediately and take any valuable items with you. I think he will most likely do it under cover of night."

"Yes, that is his style," remarks Charles bitterly. "Ashamed of his actions, he knows they are wrong so he uses the darkness to hide."

"How have you discovered his plans, John?" Bess asks him.

He gives a shy grin. "My daughter-in-law is a friend of one of the wives of his men. She walked the seven miles yesterday to tell me, and I rode here at first light."

"I am grateful to you both," she responds. "Now this is what I want you to do. Return here tonight before dark with some of your strongest men, and we will at least have some manpower. I will barricade myself in my chamber ..."

"No!" exclaims Charles and John simultaneously. She looks at them sternly.

"You question my orders?"

"Lady mother, you must leave here tonight with Arbella. It will not be safe for you remain in your chamber."

"But I cannot just leave ..."

"Yes, you must. What would happen if the men were to break down the door?"

Bess throws up her hands in a reluctant gesture of defeat.

"Very well, I shall take Arbella with me to Hardwick Hall until it is safe to return. But I resent having to leave my own home in this way."

John leaves with the assurance that he will return tonight with his most trusted men. Bess looks at Charles with concern.

"My poor boy, you must have been so afraid."

"I was afraid, I am not ashamed to admit it."

Servants have begun to lay the table for breakfast and the house is beginning to wake up; they move into the Hall beside the warmth of the fire.

"I wonder will the earl be leading the men when they come here?" Charles asks, rubbing his hands in front of the flames.

She stares at the hearth, her expression thoughtful.

"We shall have to wait and see. I am more concerned as to the reason this has come about. Why does he continue to resent me so much?"

"Perhaps because he is jealous that you purchased Hardwick Hall from your brother last year with cash, which he does not seem to have?"

"Possibly, I know he was furious at the time, but I was pleased to have it at last. I shall build a magnificent new house that will stand for centuries to come."

"But all this trouble with your husband has been brewing for a long time."

"I just wish he would not write to the queen, Lord Burghley and the Earl of Leicester about our troubles, but he continues more than ever. To write to the Earl of

Leicester in this manner, when he was broken hearted after the death of his baby son, was unforgivable."

"And also a blow to you, as Arbella was just betrothed to the little one, was she not?"

"My dreams came to nothing that time, it was very sad, as it always is to lose a child."

"Why did the two of you arrange that marriage?"

"We hoped that the queen would declare Arbella her heir, and Leicester believed his family would be one step nearer to the throne. The Scots Queen was against it of course; she always thinks I am aiming too high for her niece. But I care not for her opinion any more. Her days are numbered."

Charles is intrigued. "What do you know about her future?"

"Sooner or later the Scots Queen will make a mistake and incriminate herself. We both know what the end result will be. My husband is not within his rights to expect to take the money from my Chatsworth rents, but he has been doing it all the same."

"He must know he is in the wrong."

"But he will still try to frighten everyone into doing what he wants."

"Does he not care for his good name any more? No-one will look kindly on these attacks and he will be thought a bully to wage a war on his wife and her family."

"I know. He is desperate. You have not seen him as I have, these last years, worrying and fretting over the cost of all his expenses as if the whole world was his responsibility." They stop talking as a servant enters with a tray of food and places it on the table.

"We have woken Joseph and he is on his way to see your grace," she says, having found out already, in the way that servants do, that something is seriously amiss. Why else would John Smyth appear at dawn and Sir Charles be out all night unexpectedly? She curtseys and leaves, eyeing Charles under her lashes, for he is a handsome and charming young man. The cook has prepared fresh omelettes and there is also warm bread glistening with butter and golden honey beside pints of beer and wine to wash it down. They sit down and Charles attacks the food with relish, all the excitement has made him hungry.

"Did any of the tenants come to your aid?" Bess asks as she picks up her spoon and starts to eat.

"I should think they were all too frightened to come outside. They must have heard shouting and the barking dogs, I do not blame them. I saw a couple looking through the upper window; I think it was the gamekeeper's house.

"He may be needed as a witness."

"But to resort to this violence … has he ever struck you?" Charles has to ask although he suspects that Bess would never tolerate such behaviour.

"No, my dearest boy, he has not, so you need have no fear. He has become angry on occasions and waved his stick at me, but nothing more."

"Not yet at any rate," he observes.

She appreciates his thoughtfulness, grateful that he should ask such a sensitive question. Of her three sons, she feels Charles has always been the most vulnerable. Since losing his wife two years ago after only twelve months of marriage, and then his baby son William, he has struggled to overcome his grief and she hopes he will remarry and find happiness again before too long. "I will send someone to fetch William; I want you to stay here with him for a while until we know what the earl is planning. You will both lead our Chatsworth men against him and his men. I know it will not be a pleasant task, but we must pray for God's help. Once it is clear that there is nothing of value here any more, they will go away. I do not want you going about the country until this has all settled down, you must promise me." He knows she is right to be cautious and nods in agreement.

"I have this day now to make preparations," she continues. "I shall arrange for my valuables to be packed and moved with me to Hardwick. The carpenters and locksmiths can get to work making the entrance doors and windows more secure."

Charles looks worried and Bess squeezes his hand. "If he thinks to get the better of us, we shall prove him wrong. My family can rise to any challenge and he will regret starting all this trouble."

Then Joseph descends the stairs quickly and they are pleased to see him.

"Ah, Joseph," responds Bess. "You find us eating to keep our strength up. There is much to do today."

༃༄

As darkness descents, the preparations at Chatsworth are almost complete. All day the servants have neglected their usual tasks and have been busy wrapping Bess' most treasured and valuable possessions into straw lined crates; after which they are loaded onto waiting waggons outside for hasty transportation to Hardwick Hall, about eight miles away. Two carpenters have installed a substantial oak beam across the main doors to reinforce it. The downstairs windows have been boarded up, an unsightly result, but William believes it to be necessary. Across the narrow bridge that spans the river, bales of hay are being assembled to delay the earl's men after Bess makes her escape. She looks around her home and is almost brought to tears to see it so stripped of her belongings. Her beautiful tapestries, valuable silver plates and goblets, carved oak chairs, oil paintings are all gone, leaving empty gaps and spaces on the walls and floors. Agnes waits by the door, having supervised the loading of Bess' extensive jewellery collection and chests of coins.

"Come, your grace, Lady Arbella is already in the coach, we must leave now."

"Have you my pearls? I should so hate to lose them."

"Of course. I have everything, but we must make haste; they could be here at any minute"

Joseph looks worried, it would be very unfortunate if Bess were to meet the men on the road. William and Charles are examining the pistol that is usually kept under lock and key; they are disagreeing over who should have it.

"Stop arguing at once!" Bess tells them. "I hope you will not need to use it. Charles, you must find another weapon, but this is not the place for your sword."

"Lady mother ... please leave. We shall do our best, try not to worry."

William's calm voice belies his fear. The earl's men also attacked some of Charles' tenants last night at his manor house in Stoke; but when William told his brother earlier, they agreed not to tell their mother for the moment. A servant helps her to put on her cloak, and she looks at her sons with pride.

"I wish your dear father could see you." They smile briefly before ushering her and Agnes through the door.

"You must not return until you hear from us that it is safe to do so," William tells her as she kisses them both goodbye, before mounting the steps to her coach.

"Send word as soon as you are able. I shall pray for you this night," she replies.

As the driver sets off at a brisk pace, William and Charles watch it leave and turn to look at one another.

"Are you ready for this?" Charles asks him.

"As ready as I will ever be," he replies with more confidence than he feels, and they hasten inside to order the securing of the doors. Now all they have to do is wait.

☙❧

The atmosphere in the house has become even more tense. John and the men he has brought, sit around talking in low voices. Four men have been posted as lookouts on each of the towers, and even some of the women servants have decided to help by keeping watch. In the kitchen, the cook is enthusiastically kneading bread to take his mind off everything, while the kitchen maids are torn between being excited and terrified. The evening drags on and nothing happens. Joseph has forbidden the men to play cards and the only alcohol they are allowed is the weak small beer. He wants them to be alert and ready for whatever happens. The female servants sit about, too nervous to go to bed, but some of them fall asleep on their chairs or on the steps of the stairs. The bolder ones flirt with the men as they take the refreshments round, ignoring Joseph's disapproving look. William and Charles wait by the main door, pacing up and down restlessly. They have discussed their plan of defence, such as it is.

"I will reason with them first of all," William tells him. "Then if it does not work, we shall try to hold the door for as long as possible."

Charles does not look optimistic. He saw for himself last night how threatening the mob were, and he does not rate their chances very highly. They do not say much to each other now, the tension is too great, and in any case, everyone is listening for any noise, which might herald the arrival of the earl's men.

"Our lady mother should have arrived by now," Charles says.

"I pray God she is safe," William replies.

Just then they hear a shout from the lookout in the west tower, who has run into the hall.

"They are coming, Sir William, I can see many torches!"

"How far away?"

"I cannot say for sure, I think by the bend in the river."

"That will only give us a few minutes," Charles estimates. William checks his pistol again and the men stand to attention.

"Resist as best you can, men. Have courage!"

The next few minutes seem like hours and the noise of the men's boots gradually becomes louder as they approach the house. Another man comes down from one of the other towers and tells William he thinks there are about forty men.

"Four times the number that tried to attack me," murmurs Charles.

Then there is the most tremendous hammering on the door, resonating round the whole house, the like of which it has never heard before. The women have been told by William to go upstairs, and they watch the proceedings with terrified faces from the relative safety of the gallery.

Suddenly it all goes quiet and they hear a lone voice shouting. William pulls back the small grill on the door to look through, and sees his stepfather standing in front of a mob of his men. By the light of their torches, he can see that they are holding makeshift clubs.

"They are well armed," he tells the others.

"Open up at once! " George commands.

"Who is there and what do you mean by disturbing us at this hour?"

"Is that you, William? It is your stepfather, the Earl of Shrewsbury. Where is my wife? I demand lodging for the night."

The two brothers look at one another in dismay. "This is madness, he has lost his wits," whispers Charles.

"The countess, my lady mother is not at home, your grace. Please take your men and go away. There is nothing here for you," William reasons unhopefully.

"Do not think to deceive me as your wicked mother has done! I will claim what is mine by law; it is my right as your mother's husband. I will give you one last chance to open the door or we shall break it down!"

"I repeat, please take your men and go."

He closes the grill and there is silence for a few moments.

"Maybe he will go away," William says to Charles who says nothing.

They hear the earl's voice again, muffled this time through the door, and there is some scuffling before the sound of footsteps retreating and a pause. Then, with a tremendous thud, the door is battered with massive force, causing the horizontal beam to quiver and shake. At the same time, the boards over the windows are hammered, shattering the glass to hundreds of shards. The women scream in terror and cling to one another. Some of them are on their knees in prayer. William orders the men to hold the door against the force and they are pushed back time and again by the battering, but they do not give up. Then the wood on the horizontal beam starts to splinter with a loud crack.

"It is giving way, sir!" one of men shouts above all the noise.

Within only half a minute it is clear the door is not going to hold.

"Stand back everyone!" commands William.

They take up safer positions further away and watch in dreaded anticipation as the mighty oak double door groans before their eyes. Splinters of wood fly out in all directions and the metal locks, so carefully put in place, crack into pieces onto the stone floor. Then the middle of the door gives way, a whole plank shearing off like a knife through butter. The faces of the earl's men are now visible, mean and determined, red faced and puffing from their exertions. With one last thrust of their ram, the door gives way entirely and they scramble through, breaking more wood carelessly as they do so. They stand slightly dazzled by the many candles from the wall sconces; their weapons raised, and look menacingly at the Chatsworth men. No one speaks as the earl is helped to climb over the pieces of broken wood. William and Charles regard him stony-faced. They think he looks unwell as he stands leaning on his stick in the middle of the Hall. He brushes himself down as if he has all the time in the world. William fires his pistol into the air.

"You have no right to be here! How dare you break into this house?"

"Take their weapons!" George commands." I thought to find you both here. No doubt on your mother's orders. I have a surprise for you."

He turns to look outside and a figure steps forward from the darkness.

"Henry!" Charles exclaims in disgust.

William moves towards his brother, but one of the earl's men blocks his path.

Henry appears slightly discomforted and not his usual carefree self. William and Charles look at him with contempt.

"You should have opened up," says Henry. "Now you are going to have to pay for a new door."

"Is that all you can say?" William is shocked to find his own brother on the side of the earl. "Do you realise the stress all this has put our lady mother through? And what about all the innocent tenants?"

"This can be done the easy way or the hard way. Our men outnumber yours and we have more weapons. Be sensible, brother, and let the earl take what he wants. Although I expect our lady mother has already creamed off the best of it. She is never one to miss a trick."

"Take that back, you scoundrel, or I will …"

"You will what?" interrupts Henry.

Four men are now restraining both William and Charles on either side, but they long to silence Henry with a few well-aimed punches.

George looks triumphant as he barks his orders. "Take whatever you can out to the carts! If anyone tries to stop you, use whatever force is necessary!"

Some of his men start to move the broken wood to make a clear walkway while others, carrying empty crates, go to search around the house. The servants eye them nervously as they stand with their backs to the walls. Joseph has kept silent until now, but he steps forward hesitantly.

"Your grace, is this really necessary? You are causing much distress by these actions."

"Ah yes, Joseph, the faithful servant! You have been very quiet in the corner there have you not? I wondered when you would give us your opinion. Do you think I wanted to do this? Do you think it gives me pleasure? No, it most certainly does not. Your mistress has forced this upon me, I had no choice."

"But to gain entry by force like this ..."

George shakes his stick in annoyance.

"You would do well to remain silent, as you were before. You are only a servant. If I had my way you would be out on the street."

Joseph bows his head and steps back into the shadows; he knows when he is beaten. The Chatsworth men have been rounded up into a corner and are surrounded, they do not want to risk fatal injury. William watches the theft of his mother's belongings with seething rage.

"For shame sir! This is my mother's house, left to her by my own father, who was twice the man you are. These are not the actions of a gentleman."

"You are in breech of contract by this dishonourable behaviour!" shouts Charles.

"You Cavendish men and your wicked mother have brought this on yourselves by your malicious gossiping," George replies.

"What are you talking about?" Bewildered, they both speak at once

George moves closer to them and lowers his voice.

"The outrageous rumour concerning myself and the Scots Queen is all your doing. Do not attempt to deny it! You think to discredit me in society but I shall make you pay for your actions. I am more powerful and my friends more influential than yours. I shall make you appear before the Queen's Council to answer for yourselves, yes, even your lying mother will be shown for what she is."

"You bastard! My mother is a good and loyal wife to you. She would never make any slanderous comment or repeat such gossip, and neither would my brothers or myself. I thank God she is not here to see this spectacle."

George loses patience. "Hold your tongue boy! How dare you use such language to me?"

He addresses two of his men standing nearby. "Take them both to the kitchens and tie them up. I do not have to listen to this nonsense!"

Struggling and kicking, William and Charles are led away, their arms behind their backs. They have failed to stop him and feel very frustrated. The kitchen is empty, the cook having hurried away to hide. William and Charles are handled roughly and bound with rope by their hands and feet to kitchen chairs. Linen gags are placed over their mouths as a final insult, and with much laughing from the mob, they are left alone.

Meanwhile upstairs, George goes from chamber to chamber muttering to himself and cursing under his breath. He sees the blank walls and dressers where the silver should be and the empty floor space in Bess' bedchamber where her money and jewellery is kept. He peers into a coffer being carried out by one of the men, and lifts out a worthless pewter jug in disgust.

"She has taken anything of value, damn her. Damn her to hell!"

In his rage he throws it across the chamber and it lands in the corner with a clatter. Descending the stairs in slow movements, he vows to have revenge on Bess if it is the last thing he does.

"We have taken everything we can find here, your grace," Nicholas Booth tells him.

"It has been a waste of time! All the valuables have gone. Where are those two Cavendish boys? I want a few words with them before we go." The two of them make their way to the kitchens, where William and Charles are trying to wriggle out of their restraints. "You have not heard the last of this! Tell your mother I will have my revenge, and this is just a taste of what is to come if she does not give me back what is rightfully mine."

William looks at him, wide eyed and tries to speak, but can only grunt in frustration. Charles regards him with hostility, as every fibre of his body yearns to throw his stepfather outside, and all his henchmen with him.

"Your mother uses you, just as she uses everyone else for her own ends, and one day you will realise I am right. I curse the lot of you!"

William shakes his head and the earl suddenly seems to crumble. He realises he is exhausted and leans on the kitchen table for a moment. His face is ashen.

"Help me out of here," he mutters.

Nicholas Booth offers his arm, and William and Charles watch their retreating backs with relief as eventually all goes quiet in the house, and they wait for someone to untie them.

○○○

At first light a rider is dispatched to Hardwick with a letter for Bess, detailing the events of the night, including the damage to Chatsworth. As William writes to his mother, he spares her none of the details. Several of their men have suffered bruises, cuts and black eyes in the scuffles and one has a broken nose, but it could have been much worse. The front doors are in a sorry state and will need completely replacing, as will the glass and frames in the downstairs windows. William and Charles survey the scene after George and his mob have left, and are filled with a sense of failure.

"We gave in too easily," says Charles. "We should have held out for longer."

"It would not have made any difference," William replies as they watch the servants sweeping up the broken glass and wood from the floor. "I was not prepared to lose any lives over it. How could Henry take his side?"

Charles shakes his head. "I know, it beggars belief. Have you been hurt?"

"No, only my pride."

"We will have a few bruises tomorrow."

"Where do you think he took it all?"

"Sheffield Castle I imagine."

"Now that he has what he wanted, his men will be sent back to their homes."

The two brothers look at one another.

"Are you thinking what I am thinking?" Charles' eyes light up at the idea.

"That we take it all back?" replies William slowly.

"Yes. Ride to Sheffield within the week, they won't be expecting us and we shall have surprise on our side. The earl will be busy with his duties as jailor. We could send word to our men to meet us outside the city with their carts, if we come from different directions, it will not attract attention. Then under cover of darkness, we can gain entry and bring it all here, where it belongs."

"You make it sound very simple."

"It is. I warrant the earl has put it all in a large chamber somewhere, until he can find time to allocate the different items to wherever he thinks to place them. Will it not be a jape for him to find the chamber empty when he goes to look?"

They both laugh. "Our men will be keen for revenge. They will need no persuading for this job."

"What will our lady mother think about it?"

"We shall not tell her until the deed is done."

"Then we need to start thinking about it at once."

William nods and in a quiet corner they begin planning their own offensive.

✿

Over the next few days the house is repaired; the front doors are replaced with finest oak from the estate, and the windows are made as good as new. True to their word, William and Charles organise a counter raid to return the stolen items, which is surprisingly easy and they meet no resistance. But Bess is still too afraid to return home and decides to remain at Hardwick with

Arbella for the time being. She has gathered all the Chatsworth men involved and personally thanked them, ordering John to hand out some coins to each one in recognition of their loyalty. They were not expecting any money and are pleasantly surprised.

Not to be cowed, Bess celebrates her fifty-seventh birthday in style and invites all her family to a lavish party, where they are joined by friends and neighbours nearby. There is the usual entertainment of dancing, music and a play, together with a particularly fine supper. Henry is conspicuously absent, and Bess is still so enraged with him, that to simply mention his name in her presence is enough to suffer a frightening glare from her.

The day after the party, she is sitting at her desk when a letter from Lord Burghley arrives. He writes that George has accused William of being insolent to him when he stormed Chatsworth. William has been arrested and is now in prison; also that George tried unsuccessfully to block a knighthood for Charles. Bess is furious and picks up her quill at once, dashing off a reply in which she says she will leave for London at first light tomorrow to come to her son's aid. She is hurrying along the passage to give the letter to a servant, when she almost collides with Arbella, now nine, who immediately curtseys, and gives her grandmother a broad smile.

"Arbella my love, should you not be at your lessons? You know how important they are."

"My tutor has the toothache and has gone to see the surgeon in Derby."

"So what are you doing with yourself?"

"I am reading in the garden and learning my Spanish verbs."

"Good. You may need to speak Spanish if you marry a Spanish Prince. And your music, have you been practising each day?"

"Yes, I set aside time for the lute and the virginals, as you ordered. My tutor is pleased with me."

Bess smiles down at her, but Arbella frowns and she is immediately concerned.

"What is it? Does something trouble you?"

"I thought you had ordered all the servants to call me highness."

"Yes, I have, in keeping with your royal status."

"Some of them forget."

"Who are they? Give me their names."

"I only know their faces," she replies. "One of them was making my bed yesterday."

"I will find out who is responsible and punish them. My orders are clear enough and everyone knows how to address you at all times. I will not have you spoken to without deference and your correct title."

"But lady grandmother, I am not really a princess am I?"

Bess bends down so that she is level with her.

"My sweet jewel, you may not be a princess in name, but your connections are as royal as any prince. Our queen, God bless her, will eventually look to you as her heir. You are destined for greatness, Arbella. According to the stars, your horoscope predicts that you will achieve all my hopes and dreams for you."

The child looks uncertain and Bess chuckles. "But it is not for you to fret about such matters now. I am making sure that your education is as good as that of the queen herself. You will be able to hold your own in the highest company and be very accomplished by the time you eventually go to Court. Apart from the her majesty, of course, you will easily outshine all the other ladies."

At this, Arbella jumps up and down in delight.

"When may I go to Court? I want to go to Court now."

"All in good time. We must wait for an invitation from the queen; and you are not ready just yet. But you will be soon, and we shall journey there together."

She pats her head affectionately.

"Now run along back to your books like a good girl."

Arbella curtseys again, and with her head held high, makes her way along the corridor, very pleased with herself.

CR&O

1584 – Buxton, Derbyshire

Queen Mary is sitting with George in one of his houses as they wait for the coaches to take them back to Sheffield Castle. She insists on bringing her little dog, which has been her constant companion for the last few years. George looks at it now with annoyance as it sleeps in front of the fire. For some reason, the dog has taken a strong dislike to him and growls in his presence. More than once George has had his ankles nipped, but Mary carries him everywhere and the two are devoted to each other, so he feels he cannot separate them.

Having had to request for permission from the queen for this visit, they have both enjoyed the change of scenery and relative freedom it has brought. With all his recent troubles, George was in need of a holiday, although he is never really able to relax as Mary's jailor. It is not their first time to Buxton and as it was used by the Romans, George feels this is reason enough to seek its benefits. The naturally warm spring water is said to have healing properties, and they have spent a week availing themselves of it; but now it is time for them to reluctantly leave.

"This visit to Buxton has done me so much good – I feel quite refreshed!" she says.

"I wish I could say the same. My gout is still just as troublesome," he replies miserably.

"But has it helped your arthritis?"

"Not at all."

"I am sorry for it."

Mary looks concerned and then her gaze wanders around the chamber. They are quite alone and she decides to take the opportunity to speak to George in confidence.

"I would like to discuss a very private matter with you."

"I hope your majesty feels that we may discuss anything of concern to you."

He gets up to check that the guards outside cannot hear their conversation and resumes his seat.

"Pray continue."

"I have been very hurt by the rumours that we ..." she hesitates and lowers her eyes in embarrassment, "... are lovers and that you have fathered my child."

George becomes very flustered and clears his throat several times. "I too have been deeply affected by this scandalous lie. It is an insult to us both."

"I understand such scandalous gossip is common at Court, but as you are a married man, and with myself as a queen, it is especially upsetting."

"I hesitate to tell you what I know, for fear of causing you more grief."

"You must tell me," she says.

"There is an innkeeper in London who has been telling everyone that he knows where the child is buried."

Mary looks horrified and her eyes immediately start to swell with tears.

"Please do not distress yourself, your majesty. I have instructed my sons to make enquiries on my behalf in London and find out as much as possible about it."

"And what have they discovered?"

"It seems this vile rumour was first heard over ten years ago."

"Have you found out the person responsible for starting it?"

"I have not; but I have my suspicions."

"As do I."

Neither speaks for a few moments. Then George moves his chair nearer to her. Mary lowers her chin and looks at him through her lashes.

"I am afraid I believe it was your wife, the countess."

"Then we are in agreement for I truly think that she did instigate the rumour, together with her sons, William and Charles. I have thought it for some time, but I did not want to believe that my wife would stoop so low."

"It is a wicked course of action for anyone to take."

"What really pains me is that everyone thinks she is so wonderful! I write to the queen herself, to Lord Burghley and Sir Francis Walsingham and they all take her side. No one will listen to me. I know they just humour me all the time. She manages to fool them all …"

"She is very clever, despite her lack of education."

"And her ambition knows no end! You have heard about her plans to marry Arbella to your son or to the Earl of Leicester's baby son before he died. She dreams of the child being Queen of England one day. It is all ridiculous, but she will not be swayed."

"Yes, I know all about it. She begged me to agree for Arbella to be married to James. I believe she will stop at nothing to obtain her goals. I had thought we were friends at one time and I used to enjoy her company, but after time, I discovered her true character."

"I have been sorely deceived by her ever since we married." She nods sympathetically and says, "The question is, what can we do about it?"

"We must take some action; she must be made to realise that she will not get away with such slander."

"I am going to formally complain to my cousin, your queen. She will have to take notice."

"We could both write to the Privy Council and demand that she and her sons must be questioned at length."

"They will not dare to ignore my requests over such a serious matter. I am deeply offended that our integrity is being questioned in this way. I know you to be a man of honour, my lord, and I have every faith in your judgement. You have been badly treated by your wife, who does not deserve you."

"I thank God that at last I have found someone who understands what I suffer."

"I understand much more than you think." She reaches for his hand, a gesture she has never made before, and his heart skips a beat.

"My captivity has been made less arduous by your kindness towards me. The last fifteen years have been the worst of my life, but I thank God that you have been there for me, otherwise I might have been under the care of a harsh man who showed me no respect. Whatever my future holds, I hope that we shall always remain friends."

He looks down at her hand over his own. It feels cool to the touch; her fingers are long and slender, he thinks they are a fitting place for her beautiful rings.

"As far as it is possible between jailor and prisoner, your majesty, it would also be my wish. I would have preferred to spend time with you under better circumstances but ..."

She withdraws her hand.

"Yes, history will not judge your queen kindly for my long imprisonment, but you are not to blame for it. We have got to know one another well, have we not? It is almost like a marriage, the two of us together all those years in such unusual circumstances."

Before he can reply there is the sound of a key rattling in the lock.

George whispers, "I shall write as soon as we return."

"I shall do likewise," murmurs Mary and bends down to pick up the dog, which has woken up and is now sniffing round her skirts. Within minutes they are on their way. At last George feels he has someone who appreciates what he is going through.

ଔଃ

As George and Mary begin to make their way back to Sheffield Castle, a distance of about twenty miles, Bess is in London at the Palace of Whitehall with Lord Burghley. He has requested a meeting with her and once she has ensured that William is to be released from prison, she readily agrees. They face each other now across his desk, and she thinks he looks even more tired than usual.

"There are two important matters I wish to speak to you about, Bess," he says. "Firstly, her majesty and the

Privy Council have decided to relieve the earl of his duties as jailor to the Scottish Queen."

Bess raises her eyebrows in surprise. "I see, may I ask the reason for this change of heart?"

"Your husband has recently allowed a fanatical Catholic, the Earl of Rutland, to visit Mary, against all the security guidelines we have laid down."

"I suppose that because Rutland is his first wife's brother, he thought the visit would be all right."

"Yes, it is possible that he was misguided enough to believe it, but we have never questioned his loyalty. His judgement has not always been sound lately."

He frowns and shuffles some papers on his desk, avoiding her eye. Bess thinks he is about to say more about it, but she is mistaken.

"Sir Amias Paulet will replace him, but in the meantime Sir Ralph Sadler leaves for Sheffield shortly."

"How will my husband be told?"

"Her majesty has written to summon him to London, and the letter will be waiting when he returns from Buxton; she wishes to tell him to his face."

Bess thinks of the relief it will bring to George; this has been his dearest wish for such a long time. "He will be pleased at the news," she says.

Lord Burghley nods gravely, before pausing to bend down and unlock a drawer in his desk. He pulls out a letter which she notices bears Queen Mary's seal; she has a sense of dread at its possible contents, which she thinks can only be bad.

"I have here a letter from Queen Mary that is written to our own sovereign Queen Elizabeth. I am afraid it contains some very damming personal accusations about you."

There is total silence in the room as Bess regards him steadily, her green eyes unblinking. She has been afraid of something like this happening. Now that it has, she is almost glad. It is not in her nature to be fearful, and she would rather face her problems, than imagine what they might be in the future. He lays the letter down on the desk.

"I think it would be best if you read it for yourself."

She reaches out for it and opens the thick parchment. She recognises Mary's handwriting at once, for it is very distinctive. The letter is long, and consists of a series of remarks, which Bess is supposed to have made to the Scots Queen over the past years that Mary has been a prisoner. She reads it with an ever-growing sense of horror, and feels her face blushing under his scrutiny. At the end of the letter, she looks up. "This is all lies, my lord."

"Of course, I give it no credence."

"Look at some of these wild stories – that I spent many hours gossiping with her, and promised I would help her escape! That our queen has Sir Christopher Hatton, the Earls of Oxford and Leicester as lovers. I have said she is vain, treats her ladies cruelly, we all laugh at her behind her back and ..." Her voice is barely a whisper.

"I can hardly bring myself to say it, that her womanly parts are deformed! Sweet Jesu, can you see me ever uttering such appalling and treasonous lies? I, who have always had the utmost respect and love for our great queen?" The words on the page have started to swim before her eyes and she puts her hand to her head to steady herself. Allowing her a few moments respite, he gets up and pretends to look out of the window.

"I see that she demands my appearance before the Council to answer for the accusation that I started the rumour of her pregnancy, and that my husband is responsible."

"It is within her rights, and the earl is also demanding it; their letters arrived at the same time," he replies. "I am so sorry, Bess. The queen has instructed me to set a date for the Council to meet. William, Charles and yourself will be required to answer their questions about this matter."

"And if we refuse?"

"I would not advise it."

"Does ... does her majesty know of this letter?"

"The queen only knows that they have requested a hearing. Sir Francis intercepted this particular letter before it reached her."

At this Bess allows herself to breath more slowly again. She knows that if the queen were ever to read this letter, the consequences could be very damaging to her and her plans for the family.

"It is so insulting, so cruel to accuse me in this way. Questioning the queen's virginity of all things! Why has she done it? What can she hope to gain by such slander?" She throws it down on the desk and struggles to remain calm.

"Perhaps by discrediting you, her own status will be enhanced." He gives her one of his rare smiles. "Do not be afraid, Bess, I shall keep this letter in my safe-keeping. Apart from us, only Sir Francis has seen it and his discretion is guaranteed, you may be sure. I do not know why she wrote it, but we think it shows that she is a desperate woman now, who will say anything to shift blame on to others. I think you are an easy target for her." He returns to his desk and sits down. "I will let you know when a date has been arranged, it will be soon."

"I treated her with kindness in those early years, she became like a younger sister to me. I never thought for one moment she was capable of such vindictiveness; and my husband continues to hound me. I cannot think what I have done to incur his displeasure to this degree. Once again my lord, I am in your debt."

He gathers up the letter and replaces it carefully in the drawer, turning the key and waving aside her thanks. "Believe me, the sooner we are rid of the Scots Queen, the better it will be for all of us."

The interview has only lasted minutes, but it seems like hours. Feeling hot, she wants to be out of this chamber, away from his gaze, and as far as possible from that poisonous letter that is surely burning a hole his desk with its malicious gossip. The phrases that Mary used are going round and round in her head. She begins to feel faint and quickly excuses herself. He barely notices as he is already concentrating on his work. In the passage, she stumbles towards the door that leads to the gardens, and the cold air hits her, making her gasp. Bent over double, she has a wave of nausea and blind panic as she leans against the wall for support.

"Are you quite well, countess?" She turns to see one of the younger ladies-in-waiting staring at her with concern.

"Very well thank you, I just felt a little hot." She pulls herself straight and smiles at the girl, who continues on her way.

Bess must not be seen like this, it is a sign of weakness, which the Court will seize upon, and the gossips will be busy again. Adjusting her headdress, she takes some deep breaths and prepares to walk back through the Hall, and past the ever-curious courtiers to the privacy of her chamber. She needs to be alone and gather her thoughts. How she wishes she were at home now! The noise of the courtiers talking in the Hall reaches her ears as she turns the corner. News that Prince William of Orange has been assassinated in the Netherlands is the main topic of conversation; it will mean that Spanish victory in the Netherlands now looks very likely. No doubt its possible consequences for England will be discussed late into the night. Bess has no interest in politics, but at least such news will keep people speculating and discussing the outcome; so attention will be diverted away from any gossip at Court, for the time being at least.

When she reaches the sanctuary of her chamber, she closes the door with relief, and leans against it for a few moments, her heart pounding. Agnes is on an errand for her and will be out for a couple of hours, giving Bess some time to herself. If Agnes could see her like this, she would be questioning her, and Bess does not want a fuss. She slips off her shoes and lies on the bed. The accusations in the letter have not shocked her quite as much as she led Lord Burghley to believe. Like everyone at Court, Bess is aware of such gossip against the queen, whispered in dark corners or on pillows between lovers. Such outrageous tales never see daylight, but they surface from time to time, furtively and secretly, like a forbidden game. But for Bess to be accused of telling Mary these lies about the queen, that in itself is a shock, and Bess is very shaken by it. This is the worst action that Mary could have chosen to discredit her. She wonders why the letter has been written now, when she has not spent time alone with Mary for many years. Being a victim does not sit easily with Bess; she has always been a fighter; for her rights, for her family and for justice. Now she finds she is without recourse, and must depend on the discretion of Lord Burghley and Sir Francis Walsingham to save her from exposure and disgrace. What if the queen was to read it and believed its contents? She goes cold at the thought. Getting up from the bed, she paces up and down, unable to keep still. There is no one she can turn to, because no one must know, not even her family. The less people who know, the better.

Eventually she begins to feel calmer; Lord Burghley and Sir Francis have given their word to keep the letter a secret, she must trust them. In the scheme of everything concerned with Mary, this is after all, a minor event; the spiteful ramblings of a deposed Queen of Scotland and the increasingly nasty behaviour of a husband who is fast losing credibility. With these thoughts she feels ready to face the world again, and when Agnes returns, she finds her mistress quite composed and looking forward to the evening's entertainment.

C380

Winter 1584 – 1585 London

In the time it takes Lord Burghley to arrange for the Queen's Council to convene, Bess is busy preparing her defence. Returning home is not an option until this matter is settled. She makes several journeys in her coach to the village of Holborn and consults her lawyer in Gray's Inn, who is one of the top members of his profession in the country. Her spies are ordered to urgently report to her for further instructions, and they set about their work without delay to discover anything that will help her case.

The hearing has been set for next week, and she summons William and Charles to her chamber at Court for the first of several meetings. It is early morning, and the two sons are slightly bleary eyed. William, his face set in a frown, clasps his mother's hand in a gesture of reassurance. Charles smiles at her encouragingly with confidence he does not feel. She greets them with a kiss, and tells them to eat the simple breakfast of buttered bread and honey that Agnes procured at such an early hour from the kitchen. Bess was unable to sleep with her mind so troubled and has been up since dawn.

"It is not just me who has been been accused of spreading malicious gossip and lies about my husband and the Scots Queen; it is you two as well. This is an insult to the Cavendish family, and we shall fight it every inch of the way."

"The earl has some powerful allies on the Council," says William. "He is not the only one with powerful friends," Bess replies with determination. "I have powerful friends too, but he will still have to prove that we began this rumour and produce evidence to that effect. Like us, he will have his spies around the Court and will send his friends to try and obtain information against us."

"Gilbert says his father's personality is not was it was. Apparently he is irritable much of the time and very impatient over small matters. The other day he went into a rage over a small piece of meat that was thrown away. The cook was reduced to tears and she said she would leave if he continued to complain," says Charles.

"All these disagreements must take a lot of his time and energy. He did not look at all well when we saw him at Chatsworth on the night he stormed the house," William observes.

"We must be completely prepared for this hearing. I want us to make a list of the sort of questions we shall be asked and have our answers ready. It is important that we present a united front and our stories coincide with one another."

"Will the earl be present?" Charles hopes he has other business to keep him from it.

"I would imagine he would want to be there to witness our discomfort."

"It will be the first time you have seen him for months, lady mother."

"Yes; your stepfather wants to be rid of me."

William and Charles exchange a look and begin to protest.

"It is all right, you need not leap to my defence. I know how he feels about me and I know there is nothing I can do now to save my marriage. It saddens me very much that I have failed, and it is made worse, because I do not think I have done anything that warrants his extreme reaction."

"It is almost as if he has become another person," muses William. "I was talking to an old friend last week who said that his wife's father had become very forgetful and aggressive in his dotage. Quite out of character for the old man and he now manages to upset all his family."

"Do you think it a form of madness?" asks Charles.

Bess and William look uncertain, but it is William who finally answers. "I think there is definitely an element of madness in the earl's behaviour. Unfortunately, because he is such a powerful figure, he can do much damage, unlike an ordinary man in his own home."

They reflect on this thought for a few moments before Bess returns to the matter in hand.

"Charles, I want you to use all your contacts at Court to find out what my husband is doing to obtain evidence against us. Speak to servants; it is surprising what they know. William, I want you to come with me to meetings with my legal advisors and help to devise a strategy. When we appear before the Council, it is important that we remain calm and do not lose our tempers. Do not allow yourselves to be over-awed by the proceedings.

Answer the questions truthfully and with sincerity. Just tell the truth and, God willing, we shall win the day."

"I am not looking forward to it," confesses Charles and he bites his fingernail anxiously.

"Neither am I," William agrees. "But there is time to prepare and we shall make good use of this week ahead."

She smiles, willing them to be strong. It will not be easy; the whole Court is aware of the hearing and will be watching closely. "Go now, Charles, I want you to report back to me every day. William, we need to start writing a draft statement for the Council this morning, we must get to work."

He kisses his mother's hand and leaves, aware that Bess is depending on him. William has already found quill and parchment. The breakfast sits untouched.

সঙ্গ

When George leaves Mary in the care of Sir Ralph Sadler once more, he believes he will return to his duties in a few weeks. Before his audience with the queen, he spends a few days entertaining friends at his grand house in Thames Street near London Bridge. They are a captive audience for his grumblings and grievances; forced to listen over many varied dishes of food and copious amounts of best claret. He tells them that Bess is a shrew, a liar and has a wicked tongue; they nod in agreement. They tell him that it does not matter if they are born high or low, some wives are like that, and it is the cross that men have to bear. After finally being granted an audience with the queen, he is disappointed to find that she is not particularly sympathetic towards his side of the story with Bess. She listens to his complaints but he notices she and Lord Burghley take care to be non-committal. When the queen tells him he is to be relieved of his duties, he finds himself with a strange mixture of feelings. Relief of course, for now he will no longer have to dip into his purse and worry every day and night about her security. Someone else will have that task. But a part of him will miss it too, the prestige and authority it brought, together with the company of Mary herself. There is no doubt in his mind that she is a captivating and fascinating woman that men find very attractive. Now he will not see her again; he will miss her.

Afterwards, he makes his way back to the house feeling tired and dispirited; the dusk has brought a swirling damp fog, which does nothing for his arthritis and he longs for the warmth of the fire and a hot meal. Once inside, he looks in briefly at his study where his desk is littered with half forgotten requests, bills and petitions. He has tried to sort it, but he cannot seem to summon the energy. Two months ago he dismissed his faithful secretary because he did not trust him anymore and thought he was plotting against him. Without his help, everything takes much longer. He shuts the door and goes to the dining room where the long oak table has been polished and gleams in the candlelight. It has been laid for one, with silver ware and fresh flowers.

"Good evening, your grace, are you ready to eat now?"

His eyes follow the sound of the voice in the corner of the room and he sees a young, attractive woman waiting for him. She steps forward from the shadows and curtseys; he is surprised for he does not recognise her.

"And the name is …?"

"My name is Eleanor Britton, your grace. I have taken over as housekeeper since Mrs Black had to return to Kent."

"Yes, of course."

He sits down, slightly discomforted, as she is very comely. Tendrils of dark hair have escaped from her cap and as she leans forward to pour his wine, he cannot help but notice her ample cleavage.

"Britton, I know that name."

"My nephew is the odd job man, John." She ladles out steaming soup and places the bowl in front of him with some warm bread.

"I will wait for your grace to ring when you are ready for the next course."

George grunts and picks up the spoon, he does not wish for her to see him eat, as his hands often let him down, riddled as they are with arthritis. She leaves silently, her movements deft and purposeful. The room is very quiet, so quiet he thinks he can hear his own heartbeat. He looks at the chair where Bess would sit when they dined together in the early days of their marriage. How could he have been so blind not to have seen her for what she really is? Why does everyone take her side?

Even the queen does not say anything against her. Knowing that the hearing is the right course to take does not make it any less stressful for him. The rumour has upset him to the core, making him angry all the time. He could not believe it when the Chatsworth items were brazenly taken back only days after he claimed them, but all his time has been taken up lately with the hearing. If only he did not feel so tired and could have some relief from the pain in his joints. There are times when he thinks the whole world is against him. He pushes his dish away and rings the little bell. Eleanor appears almost at once, bearing a tray of several hot dishes. He watches as she silently lays them before him, her eyes downcast.

"You live locally with your husband?" he asks conversationally as he begins to pick at the mutton pie.

"I am a widow, your grace. My late husband was of advanced years and died last Christmas."

"You have children of your own?"

"No, there is just me and John." She busies herself placing the dishes within his reach, and then goes over to put more coal on the fire. Through the cheap calico material that clings to her body, he can see her slim waist and the curve of her hips. She sees him looking at her and he hastily averts his gaze. There is a clatter as he drops the spoon and immediately she rushes to pick it up.

"My fingers ..." he mumbles, embarrassed, but she merely smiles kindly and hands it back to him.

"My grandmother also suffered with arthritis. It was very hard for her."

George swallows and for some reason finds he is close to tears. Staring at his hand holding the spoon, he cannot bring himself to use it. Seconds pass before he looks up and finds she is gazing steadily at him in a way no woman has done for many years. She gently takes the spoon from him.

"Will your grace allow me to help you?"

Mesmerised, he waits patiently as she scoops a morsel of pie and begins to feed him. Her body is now so close that he can see the threads of material in her smock. He wants to touch her very much.

"If your grace wishes, I can help you like this every day."

He opens his mouth obediently like a child and does not reply, but his eyes do not leave her face.

"I can do anything you desire; you only have to ask."

With a mischievous giggle, she takes his hand and gently places it on her left breast

George thinks he has died and gone to heaven. Mealtimes will never be the same again.

౸౹౺

November 1584 – London

The hearing has been set for ten o'clock the following Wednesday morning, and Bess sits waiting as William is huddled over some papers, doing some last minute writing. Charles paces up and down the chamber, his leather boots squeaking on the oak floor. They are staying at the Earl of Leicester's London house; a fact that has not escaped George's attention and predictably annoyed him. In the days leading up to the hearing, all three have been busy preparing their defence. It has not taken them long to discover that George is in the process of suing the writer of the book claiming the story is true. But the origin of the rumour is going to be hard to prove, although they are not sure what evidence, if any, George will bring to the hearing.

"Charles, you must eat," she urges him.

"I cannot swallow a morsel. I feel sick. I think I have eaten something that disagrees with me."

"You must overcome it; I need you to be strong. I do not know how long the hearing will last; it could continue for hours."

"Or days," William says.

"Oh no, I hope it will not be days." There is a hint of despair in Charles' voice; Bess gives an exasperated sigh. "For pity's sake Charles, sit down. You are making me nervous."

He returns to his chair and half-heartedly attempts to eat some breakfast. The time passes interminably; no one speaks. Finally Bess decides it is time to make their way to the Palace of Whitehall, where they are to appear before the Queen's Council. She has taken extra care with her appearance this morning, dressing in a sombre grey gown with a charcoal velvet cloak, trimmed with sable. A portrait of George looks down on them as they past through the hall, his face reproachful and aloof.

"Why are you doing this to us, George?" she asks it and shakes her head.

"He is jealous of the family," suggests William.

"I think he has lost his mind," says Charles and sometimes Bess is inclined to agree with him.

The whole Court has been talking of nothing else since George first made the accusation, and she knows that the outcome today will be closely followed. She is neither optimistic nor pessimistic, but determined to present her case calmly, which she believes will stand in her favour. Her greatest fear is that William or Charles will lose their temper, which could prejudice the case. All the members of the Council are known to George of course, and he has undoubtedly spoken to them already, to influence their decision. She knows they do not have a high opinion of a woman like herself, who is strong-minded when she should be compliant, and independent when she should be obedient to her husband. They climb into the coach and travel slowly through the busy

London streets, the wheels splashing through puddles in the damp and misty air. William and Charles have had their instructions from Bess. They are not to speak unless directly asked a question. They are not to look shifty or guilty, but they must look the members of the Council in the eye, and hold their heads up. William shuffles his papers again and again.

"We have done nothing wrong," Bess reminds them. "You bear the Cavendish name; you are your father's sons."

The journey is short and within ten minutes the carriage swings into a side courtyard and draws to a halt. They descend quickly, and climb the steps leading to the chamber where the hearing is to take place. To their dismay, there is a crowd of courtiers lining the route, who fall silent as they approach. One or two murmur "good luck," but for the most part they just stare curiously. William and Charles quicken their pace as they walk, nodding to a few familiar faces. Bess keeps her face neutral, whatever the verdict, she wants to remain dignified. She sees her lawyer waiting for them and he bows formally as they approach.

"Good morning, your grace. I am afraid I have bad news …"

"Already?" William says.

"I am not to be allowed to accompany you into the chamber."

"Why not?" asks Bess.

"Their lordships will not allow it. I must wait outside."

William and Charles look at Bess, but she is not flustered. "Very well. So be it."

"Are you not going to protest?" asks Charles.

"There is no point. I do not want to antagonise them before we have even started the hearing."

Before he can reply, the clerk of the court appears and tells them that the Council is ready to receive them.

"Thank you," she responds with a smile. They follow the clerk through the heavy door into a large panelled chamber, where three middle-aged men are sitting behind a long table. Bess recognises all of them as members of the Privy Council, and with a stab of disappointment, notices they are also all friends of George. The clerk of the Court sits down to the side and picks up his quill, evidently to record the proceedings. Then she looks to her right and sees that George himself is seated close to the table, a scowl on his face and his hand resting on his stick.

"Good morning, my lords." She curtseys and William and Charles bow. Bess turns to face George and her voice is light.

"Good morning, husband. I trust you are well?" He stares through her and does not respond. But she can see he looks haggard, his lips downturned and tight; she turns back, waiting for the chairman of the Council to speak.

"Good morning to you and your sons, countess. We all know the reason you are here before the Council, and I would like to proceed without delay."

William sees that no chairs have been provided for them and it seems they are expected to stand. He asks if they could sit down.

"You may not," the chairman replies abruptly.

"Quite right," they hear George mutter. Despite the occasion, Bess cannot help but suppress a smile. The chairman starts to read from a leathered covered book.

"Elizabeth Talbot, Countess of Shrewsbury, Sir William Cavendish, Sir Charles Cavendish, you have been summoned to appear before her majesty's Privy Council in order to be examined as to the source of a most damaging and scandalous rumour concerning Queen Mary of Scotland and George Talbot, the Earl of Shrewsbury. The nature of this rumour is that the said earl has fathered a child borne to Queen Mary of Scotland since she has been in captivity here in England. This rumour has caused much distress to both parties and they strenuously deny any such involvement has ever taken place. They accuse you of not only being the source of the rumour, but of repeating it to several persons over many years, thus enabling it to thrive."

He pauses for breath and looks at Bess.

"What have you to say on the matter?"

"Anyone who knows me will maintain I am not capable of these falsehoods, especially one that is in such poor taste. We absolutely deny these accusations, and we will vigorously fight any attempts to lay the blame upon us."

"But you do not deny that you and your husband, the Earl of Shrewsbury, are estranged from one another and are not living as man and wife?"

"It is true that we are estranged, much to my great disappointment, but I have no wish to damage the reputation of my husband or the Scottish Queen."

"But you do have a motive, being a spurned wife."

"I am not the only wife to live apart from her husband. On that basis every estranged wife has a motive to damage the reputation of her husband, whether he be titled or not."

"We have read your joint statement, and note that you suggest the pregnancy rumour could have been started because of a general dislike by the English of the Scots Queen. Explain yourself to us."

"My understanding is that this rumour began about ten years ago, possibly in a city tavern. The captivity of the Scots Queen has always been a subject of speculation and gossip. People will talk, especially after too much wine. I wonder that my husband has taken so long to feel aggrieved enough to demand action over it now. Our queen knows that the Scots Queen tried to cause problems between myself and my husband. I should not be surprised to learn that she has been instrumental in persuading my husband in this matter."

"Do not speak of Queen Mary in that insolent manner!" George shouts.

"I speak as I find," Bess replies, glancing at him with defiance.

"My lord, I must remind you that you are here as a bystander and have no right of speech. I must insist that you remain silent," the chairman tells him.

George bangs his stick impatiently. Then Bess delivers her *piece de resistance* and waits for their reaction.

"We will meet anyone face to face who claims that we are involved in any way with this rumour, and prove that they are lying."

Their lordships confer, looking more and more uneasy.

"May I speak my lord?" William finds it hard to remain silent, and Bess gives him a forbidding look.

"You may speak when it is your turn, Sir William. Countess, is it not true that you are on friendly terms with many individuals at Court and it would be quite easy for you to circulate such a rumour?"

"I did not realise that having friends at Court was an indication that I was a gossip."

George makes a snorting noise, and the chairman frowns at him.

"Do you have any evidence against us, my lord?" Bess asks, becoming bolder now that she gathers from the line of questioning that it is beginning to look unlikely. He sighs and pushes the book away from himself.

"Well, Sir William, what is it you wish to say?"

"Only this, her grace, the countess, would not demean herself by such behaviour and neither would I, or my brother. It is outrageous that we have been brought here today. The earl and his men attacked Chatsworth, causing my lady mother to flee in terror. He broke into the house by force with a mob of armed men and stole possessions that did not belong to him. My brother and I were gagged and tied up …"

"Silence!" The chairman holds up his hand but William is not deterred, "… but no action is taken against him!"

"William!" Bess says sternly, but he can only glare at George, who scowls back in equal measure. It is the first time they have come face to face since the night that Chatsworth was attacked.

"Instead I am sent to prison, for what is termed my 'insolence' in trying to defend myself and my family."

"These matters are irrelevant to the proceedings."

"These proceedings are a farce, my lord, and have been brought against us by the Scottish Queen and the Earl of Shrewsbury to publicly humiliate and discredit us."

George gets to his feet, unable to remain silent for any longer.

"Are you going to allow them to continually interrupt these proceedings or do I have to come round and take control myself?"

The chairman looks at George sternly.

"You are the person disrupting these proceedings! I must ask you again to remain silent or I shall have you removed from this chamber."

"He should not be here in any case," Charles says boldly.

"I will have silence!"

George sits down in frustration. The chairman confers again with the other two lords for a minute, then he looks up, but before he can speak, Bess walks forward to stand directly in front of them. "My lords, I repeat my question; am I right in saying that you have no real evidence against us?"

The chairman shifts uncomfortably, looking at George out of the corner of his eye. "The earl has not produced any evidence that we can realistically accept."

"You have before you my own evidence that certain prominent members of the Court deny any wrong doing on our part," she tells him.

He looks again at the names that Bess has called upon to take her side.

"Yes, it is an impressive list."

"What is happening?" says George, very disgruntled. "This is highly irregular."

"We may be able to close this matter to the satisfaction of both parties if you would swear on your knees in front of us," the chairman whispers to her.

Bess thinks for a moment. "If we do, have I your word that we shall be completely exonerated and the matter is closed?"

"You do, countess."

"Let me speak to my sons."

She steps back to William and Charles, who have not heard all that has just been said. When she tells them, they are furious.

"No! I will not kneel before them. How dare they suggest it!" William says.

"Nor will I!" agrees Charles.

"We have no choice," Bess tells them in a whisper. "Their lordships must be seen to take some action to satisfy the earl, or he will continue with his fight. If we do this, it will end it once and for all. It must be done; I am willing, you must follow my example."

In the meantime, George has approached the lords himself and is rapidly losing his temper.

"That will not be sufficient to exonerate them! They will swear anything. They are guilty I tell you. Look at them, laughing at me and plotting schemes to injure me!"

"We see nothing to suggest what you say. I must insist that you to return to your seat," the chairman tells him. "You have not produced any real evidence against your wife and her sons. There is no more that we can do."

George reluctantly sits down again, swearing under his breath as he does so. Bess gathers her skirts and gracefully kneels, her back as straight as a ramrod. Her face betrays no emotion; she will not give George the pleasure. But William and Charles cannot hide their anger and kneel beside her slowly, with many furious looks at their stepfather, whose expression by now has changed to superior satisfaction. The clerk of the court produces a Bible, which he gives to Bess. The chairman indicates for her to begin, and in a clear, loud voice she does so, her eyes staring straight ahead.

"I swear before Almighty God that I was not the author, inventor or reporter of the rumour that my husband, the Earl of Shrewsbury, had fathered a child by Queen Mary of Scotland. I also swear that whilst in the custody of the Earl of Shrewsbury, Queen Mary has always behaved with chastity and honour, as expected of a princess."

She hands the Bible in turn to William and Charles, who repeat the oath; their voices low pitched and resentful. The chairman nods and they all rise, as the clerk comes forward to take the Bible.

"Very well, countess. We shall report that we found no evidence against you and your sons. You are completely exonerated and free to leave."

"This is a travesty of justice! Can you not see her for what she really is?"

George is beside himself with frustration and rage. Their lordships get up quickly, gather their papers and with a nod to Bess, they exit through a side door, avoiding any further discussion with him. Bess turns to her sons and hugs them, the relief is overwhelming and they cannot quite believe it.

"We have done it!" she says. "We must go and celebrate!"

Grinning with delight, William and Charles slap each other on the back and follow their mother to the door. George is waiting for them and reaches out to grab Bess by the arm.

"You may have escaped this time, madam, but I have not finished with you yet!"

"Unhand my lady mother!" Charles is nearest and pulls his arm away.

"Do not presume to touch your betters! I will have satisfaction; you may have won this battle, but do not think you have won the war!"

He pushes roughly past them and walks towards his legal advisors waiting outside the door.

Bess looks at him with resignation before going past the courtiers. It is not hard for them to see who has come off the better this morning.

ଔଚ

Tutbury – December 1585

Mary is moved back to Tutbury, still considered the safest place for her. Her new jailor, Sir Amias Paulet, is quite a different character from George. In the damp and miserable surroundings, she becomes depressed and ill; maybe her days with the Shrewsburys were not so bad after all.

Mary is in her bed, where she has lain for the last few weeks. She is weak and dispirited, and complains of constant aches and pains. Her hysterical outbursts are more frequent, and after having George as her jailor for so long, she is finding it hard to adapt to someone else. Her once beautiful face is ravaged by her confinement, and the stress of her situation has aged her. It is now fifteen years since she was first brought here, and the plots to release her have all come to nothing. Over the years the conspirators have been tortured and executed, but Queen Elizabeth is very reluctant to pass the death sentence on Mary herself, without irrefutable evidence to condemn her. It sits heavy on Queen Elizabeth's conscience that Mary is an anointed queen, like herself.

Sir Amias visits her once a day and this morning he is in a particularly severe mood. She hears the rattle of the keys in the door and turns away to face the wall; she does not wish to see him. He comes into the chamber and regards her motionless body with sour distaste. Even if he were not her jailor, Mary would have a dislike for him, as she considers him to be an ugly, fat man without any charm or redeemable qualities.

"Your majesty," he says, managing to inject a contemptuous sneer into the words. "How are you this morning?"

His lips barely cover his yellow teeth and there is a greasy sheen to his face. There is no reply and one of her ladies appears from the other chamber.

"Her majesty is much the same as yesterday, Sir Amias." She places herself between him and the bed in a defensive position, which he neatly sidesteps to approach the bed.

"I must see for myself," he replies, as he peers closer.

Mary stiffens and shuts her eyes. She cannot bear to see him; his presence makes her skin crawl. None of the ladies like him with his condescending manners and judgemental remarks. They have come to realise now that life under the earl's care was infinitely better than his, and wish every day that he was back in his post, but they know he will never return.

"If her majesty could have some fresh air …" the lady-in-waiting ventures.

"Then open the windows!"

"It would be better if her majesty could be allowed to walk outside when she is feeling stronger."

"I cannot allow that to happen. My orders are quite clear and I am following them strictly. No one will be able to accuse me of being lax in my duties as jailor."

"Could the food be improved? We asked about it last week, but it remains quite inedible."

"The food is more than adequate. I myself eat the same as you all. To over indulge and crave pleasure from eating, is gluttonous and a deadly sin."

The lady-in-waiting sighs and tries another approach. "Sir Amias, can you not feel how cold it is? We have barely enough wood to heat one chamber. I am sure that if your queen knew she would be horrified at these conditions."

"Do not presume to know the feelings of our queen! It is not for you for make such requests. I am simply following my orders and you must realise that I have no real power here. I am merely an instrument in this unsavoury business."

At this, Mary turns over and opens her eyes. When she speaks her voice is raspy and interrupted by coughing, but her eyes blaze in her pale face. "You call the captivity of an anointed queen an unsavoury business! Yes, you are right, where else in the world would this be allowed to happen? Since you have taken over the post as jailor, my life has become unbearable; for you are a nasty, unpleasant creature with no Christian virtues to your name, despite your outward show of piety. You are unkind and harsh, and God will punish you, as he will punish all of you that have used me so ill." She has another fit of coughing and her lady-in-waiting holds a handkerchief to her mouth.

Sir Amias looks unmoved. "If you mean I have not indulged you as the Earl of Shrewsbury did, then I am content, for it shows that I have done my duty, and I will continue to do so to the best of my ability." He turns to go, but Mary cries for him to wait.

"What is going to happen to me? Does your queen hate me so much that I am forgotten and left to rot in this hell hole?"

"I can assure you that you have not been forgotten."

"You must know what plans there are for me? Will I be left to die here?"

"Why do you ask me such questions? I am merely your jailor and hold no such power over you."

"But you made me remove my dais and cloth of state did you not? Such action was nothing less than vindictiveness." She tries to sit up, her hands trembling as she clutches the sheets.

"I must know what is to become of me. I cannot bear it any more. Your queen has pushed me to the depths of despair; I cannot continue like this."

Sir Amias does not reply, but stares at her with his beady eyes. Mary dissolves into sobs and he makes a tutting noise. "Come, these outbursts are wasted on me and the sooner you realise it the better. Life has been far too easy for you here. This is not meant to be a holiday! You are kept here because you are a threat to the throne of England. My queen is generous in her treatment of you, considering your scandalous past …" He shakes his head disapprovingly and gives another bow. "I shall take my leave."

Once he is gone, Mary recovers and reaches under her pillow for the letter that has been smuggled into her apartments. She gestures for her lady-in-waiting to read it again to her and her face registers a glimmer of hope as she listens. She closes her eyes and tries to sleep, her mind repeating a name over and over; Antony Babington, Antony Babington. Could his name hold the key to her freedom at last?

ଔଃ

Chatsworth – February 1587

"So William, what news do you have to tell me?" Bess asks.

She has already received word from her contacts, not only from Court, but from Fotheringhay Castle, where Mary was taken after her arrest. William has just arrived from London and sits with his mother as she watches him eat a beef stew. He is dusty and tired, but all this is forgotten as he tells Bess what the whole country is talking about: the charge of High Treason against Mary, her subsequent trial, swiftly followed by her execution only a few days ago. Sir Francis Walsingham, after years of patient waiting, watching and gathering information, finally obtained some hard evidence with which to convict her.

"Where shall I start?"

"At the beginning, in case I have missed something."

"You remember Anthony Babington?"

"Yes, of course, he was a boy page for me and used to visit Mary when she stayed. He must have fallen under her spell at that time. I never thought anything of it, she always liked to spend time with children."

"And Thomas Morgan, the earl's secretary at Sheffield?"

"The man who spoke with a slight stutter?"

"Yes, after he left the earl's service he went to France as Mary's agent, but Sir Francis had him constantly followed. After a while, Babington also went to France and made contact with him before returning to England, where he became involved with a group of Jesuit priests as they travelled round the country in secret. Letters from Mary to her supporters were hidden in beer barrels and copied, after being deciphered. The letters were read by Lord Burghley, Sir Francis and Sir Amias Paulet, so they were all aware of her intentions. They had the help of a turncoat priest called Robert Gifford, who told them of a plot to kill Queen Elizabeth and rescue Mary. The Pope was to send his troops with the Spanish, and invade England with the help of English Catholics. Mary would be made our queen and Queen Elizabeth …" He makes a cutting gesture across his own throat and Bess stares in horror. "Sweet Jesu!" she exclaims. "My blood runs cold at the thought of it."

"Babington was arrested when this letter was discovered and together with his co-conspirators, they were sent to the Tower." His face becomes dark. "They were horribly tortured, lady mother."

She nods, knowing that it was inevitable. "And their trial?"

"A foregone conclusion of course, they were all found guilty and sentenced to death by hanging, drawing and quartering – whilst they still lived."

At this, Bess goes pale. "Surely not? That is so cruel."

"It is the truth. Some are saying it was the queen's command, whilst others say it was Lord Burghley's.

The men were dragged through the streets to Holborn, where a huge scaffold had been erected so that as many of the people as possible could witness it."

He takes a large swig of wine and wipes his mouth.

"Babington was forced to watch the first one before his own death and he cried out, 'Spare me, Lord Jesus!' towards the end. At first the crowds were shouting for their deaths, but when they saw the butchery, they expressed disgust for the manner of their deaths and shouted 'for shame' and 'have pity' as they watched and groaned with the violence of it."

"May God have mercy on their souls."

There is silence in the chamber for a minute as the two bow their heads before he continues.

"On the following day, the remaining conspirators were dead before the disembowelling and quartering was carried out."

"So the people made their feelings known and it was swiftly acted upon, by orders of the queen," Bess replies.

"I have never seen a hanging crowd so moved."

"But they still came to watch."

He shrugs, "such events have always held a fascination for the people."

"Was Babington allowed to speak?"

"No, he was not. Truth be told, he was in no fit state for speech."

Bess sighs, the story is one of horror, but she is forcing herself to know the details of Mary's death. She feels in a strange way that it is important before she can finally place her in the past.

"After Mary's trial, your husband was given the task of informing her that she was to die on the morrow."

"How do they say she took the news?"

"Apparently quite calmly, I think she wished to be seen as a martyr. Everyone knew the verdict would be guilty, although Lord Zouche, rather bravely I thought, said he did not agree and wanted more evidence. Her priest asked for more time, but there could be no delay once Queen Elizabeth had signed the death warrant with the royal seal. Lord Burghley was not going to take any chances."

"And the execution of Mary herself? I heard it took several blows of the axe to sever the head from her body."

He gets up to stretch his limbs after hours of travelling, and his voice hesitates as he retells the moment of her death. "There were gasps from the crowd, for it was badly done, one of her ladies swooned in anguish. After the executioner held up her head so that all could see, the red wig she wore in those last years was parted from her scalp to reveal her own thinning grey hair. There was a terrible moment when after the beheading, Mary's skirts moved, but it was just her little dog whimpering and cowering underneath."

Bess tries to imagine the scene, glad that she was not there in person.

"How many people attended?"

"The Great Hall at Fotheringhay was packed; Lord Burghley, Sir Francis Walsingham, Sir Christopher Hatton and Sir James Croft amongst others. She faced all of them bravely. The trial lasted two days, and she kept asking Sir Amias Paulet to identify the faces of men she only knew by name."

"It is hard to believe she is gone. The consequences will be severe."

"They say the queen is beside herself with rage and regret. She says that she gave no permission for the execution, and that the Council acted too quickly without her consent, despite the signed warrant in her own hand. Lord Burghley has been banished, Sir Francis Walsingham is at home because he says he is too ill to leave. Even the Earl of Leicester has been sent from Court."

"But politically, this could be a disaster for England could it not?"

"Spain will retaliate for her death, that much is certain. The belief is that they will launch an invasion attempt. We shall be at war."

He pushes his plate away and pours some more wine for them both. "But there is nothing we can do about it. These matters are out of our hands and we must trust her majesty and her advisors."

"As we always do," Bess agrees.

"But the earl rather gave himself away at the end," says William cautiously.

"What do you mean?"

"First, he had to tell the executioner to proceed, which they say he seemed to find very difficult. Then he cried like a baby when the axe fell for the last time, and everyone stared at him, can you believe it?"

"I can imagine," Bess is moved to reply.

"It poses the question why would he cry over the death of a traitor, and in public view?"

She has no answer to this question, but for her part, it is a relief that Mary is dead and can cause no further trouble between her husband and herself. But now, of course, it is too late to save their marriage.

CB&O

Wingfield Manor – June 1588 (3 years later)

The years pass and life for Bess continues with George still refusing to live as man and wife with her, despite her best efforts. The queen intervenes on more than one occasion to try and reconcile the pair of them, but to no avail. He is still withholding money he owes to Bess and has started to include Bess' daughter, Mary, in his outward display of dislike. But Bess has other matters to occupy her; the building projects at Hardwick and the future of Arbella, who is thirteen years old. The Scottish Queen Mary's son James, is now first in line to inherit the throne of England, followed by Arbella. However there are urgent matters of national importance to occupy the queen and her Privy Council – by June, England is on full alert for an imminent invasion by Spain. These are worrying times for everyone, nonetheless the queen invites Bess and Arbella to Court, and Bess does not need to be asked twice.

Once the invitation from her majesty has been received and read, preparations begin for the visit. Arbella is to have new gowns, and she will learn about the most important people at Court in preparation for when she meets them. Bess writes to her friends telling them of her imminent arrival so that arrangements and invitations can be issued for social gatherings. She leaves more instructions for the on-going building at Hardwick, declaring that she will be inspecting the work on her return. A trip to London is going to be a welcome diversion, and she is keen to remind the queen and everyone at Court that she has a fine granddaughter. Travelling in convoy, three coaches are loaded with boxes of clothes and hampers of food, together with gifts for the queen. Agnes travels in one coach with two male servants, whilst Bess and Arbella sit in the best coach, two chests of coins at their feet. Four, armed mounted outriders escort each coach. Arbella is on the edge of her seat in the coach for most of the time; keen to see everything they pass on the road. Small hamlets, villages and towns all merit her attention, each one individual and different. She watches the people stop and stare as the coach trundles along its way, some men tugging their forelocks as they recognise the Shrewsbury Coat of Arms on the side of the door. The women struggle to curtsey as they carry baskets or go about their daily chores, craning their necks to see the occupants and the sumptuous interior of the coach. Arbella sees that the people are dressed simply in drab coloured smocks and some have wooden clogs on their feet; children run along beside the coach, their high spirits soon dampened by the drivers, who fiercely tell them to go away.

From time to time, Bess throws money through the window for the beggars, a gesture she always makes when travelling, and one that George found infuriating. Arbella's eyes are wide as she stares incredulously at the fighting that ensues as they scrabble in the filth and mud of the road for the coins.

When they stop for the night at one of the inns en route, Arbella is aware that a great deference is shown to her grandmother, and nothing seems to be too much trouble. But everything is strange; there are new accents to hear, different food to taste, and as they travel south, more of the houses are made from timber, unlike the limestone or sandstone buildings of the north. Approaching London, the coaches slow to a gentler pace, as there are many carts and crowds of people, as well as livestock being taken to or from market. Bess has warned her about the place called Tyburn, where crowds gather to watch the hanging of thieves; their bodies left to rot for days as a reminder to others. Arbella looks at it in morbid fascination as the coach turns towards the queen's private hunting ground, Hyde Park. From there, they go on to Charing Cross where the River Thames stretches into the distance, with the royal palaces of Whitehall and Westminster on the right hand bank. Today, the quaysides are especially busy, with larger boats loading and unloading goods, the cranes moving backwards and forwards like a synchronised dance.

They are waved through by the heavily armed guards at the entrance to the palace. Once inside, the gates are shut behind them, and the drivers steer their horses through several courtyards where the busy throng of the streets can only be heard faintly. They see a tiltyard used for jousting and the royal tennis court, before passing under a gatehouse leading to the queen's privy gardens. When Bess sees it she cannot help but think back to that morning when George proposed to her there. It seems a long time ago now. Their journey finally ends in front of an imposing set of doors, and they are greeted by the queen's housekeeper who shows them to their apartments.

Bess and Arbella are to share a bedchamber, which Arbella does not like very much as she prefers to be alone. Then she can easily slip out of bed to gaze at the moon and listen for noises she has not heard before, breathing in the atmosphere and allowing herself to become almost intoxicated with it. With Bess sleeping only a few feet away, this is impossible. Already Arbella is looking forward to the day when she can be her own person, independent and free. It will not be long to wait she is sure. Bess herself has told her that she was married at an early age and Arbella is already thirteen. It is her dearest wish to have a handsome husband and children one day; she has every faith that her grandmother will enable her marriage to the most suitable man who presents himself. She also is impatient to be a part of the Court, to be admired for her clever mind as well as her beauty, for Bess has told her she has both these qualities in abundance.

She looks at her grandmother now, and although she loves Bess as a granddaughter should, she is also slightly afraid of her.

"Is this to be our bedchamber? Oh it is so very fine! And look, lady grandmother, the view from my window is vastly different from home. There are so many buildings, all the chimneys, all the people. I am so excited!"

Arbella is in high spirits and runs around their guest apartments at the Palace of Whitehall as Bess watches indulgently.

"To be sure, it is just right for you, my sweet. We shall have a happy time at Court, I am delighted to be here with you."

"Shall we see the earl, your husband?" she asks hesitantly.

"If he is at Court, he will be civil to me so there is no need for you to worry."

"He does not like me."

"I am sure that is not true," she goes over to her and lifts her chin up gently. "What is there to dislike about such a fine young lady as yourself?"

Arbella does not reply, but she has seen the way George looks at her and heard some of the many arguments between Bess and George over the years. Bess takes her hand and pulls her to sit on the bed.

"I must talk to you about this visit. I know you came here last year with your Uncle Gilbert and Aunt Mary …"

"It was so wonderful!" Arbella exclaims. "I sat at dinner with Sir Walter Raleigh, and Uncle Charles escorted me as if I was quite grown up. Lord Burghley was very impressed with all my accomplishments, but there was someone special who made a particular fuss of me."

"Oh, and who was that?" Bess asks, looking at her indulgently.

"Robert Deveraux, the Earl of Essex," she says dreamily. "I think he has marked me out very favourably as I noticed he hardly spoke to the other ladies at all. Is he much older than me?"

Bess' expression changes in an instant.

"No, Arbella!" she tells her sharply. "You must not encourage him. Be polite of course, but that is all. He is only a twenty-three-year-old soldier, but already a favourite with the queen. Last year she made him her Master of the Horse and no doubt there will be more honours in the future. If the queen sees you both together, she will be very displeased. Stay away from him."

Arbella scowls. "What did you want to talk about, lady grandmother?"

"You must make the best possible impression each time you come to Court. Everyone will be watching you and there are those who wish you to fail. You are young and you have a lot to learn, but you must stay close to me. Do not put yourself forward with the queen; wait for her to notice you, and speak only when she speaks to you. There are many names and faces to remember and I will ensure everyone of importance is introduced to you. Conduct yourself with dignity and grace at all times. You may not leave the confines of the Palace without permission of the queen. And do not wander round the palace as it is easy to get lost." Bess pauses. "Do you have any questions?"

Arbella looks annoyed at this list of rules and shakes her head stubbornly.

"Good. Now we must wash and change for dinner."

Bess disappears to the adjoining chamber to find Agnes, whilst Arbella falls back on the damask coverlet that lies on the four-poster bed. She gazes at the folds of the blue silk lining overhead and imagines Robert Deveraux looking at her adoringly, and asking her to dance above all the other ladies. It is a very pleasant daydream and is only interrupted by the servant bringing in a bowl and jug of hot water for her to wash. Arbella gets up and performs her ablutions, trying to ignore the stares of the young girl who has been sent to attend her.

"Why do you stare at me?"

"I beg pardon m'lady. I did not mean to stare."

"It is very rude to stare at your betters. Has no-one ever told you?"

"I am sorry." The girl blushes and twists her fingers nervously.

"You do realise I should be called 'highness', I am called it at home in Derbyshire, by order of my grandmother."

"Yes, m'lady"

"What is your name?"

"Patience, but my family called me Patti."

"And are you?"

"Am I what, m'lady?"

"Patient of course!" Arbella laughs, drying her hands on the linen towel. "This is my second visit to Court. I came here once before with my aunt and two uncles, but now I am with my grandmother."

"Yes m'lady, I know. She is the Countess of Shrewsbury."

"What is your age, Patti?"

"I am not yet ten and six."

"So you are only two years older than me. Come here." She guides her over to the looking glass and stands them side by side. Arbella looks closely at the reflections, whilst Patti squirms in embarrassment. "Keep still!" commands Arbella. "How tall are you?"

"I do not know, m'lady."

"I am slightly taller, see?"

Arbella stares at their reflections. She sees two girls of similar age, both fair haired and blue eyed. But that is where the similarity ends, for Arbella is dressed in the finest cream silk gown with heavily embroidered sleeves;

her earrings are costly teardrop pearls, held on with delicate gold clasps, her hands are lily white showing her to be a lady of quality. She is wearing silk stockings and soft velvet slippers, which Patti cannot help but envy. Patti does not wish to stand in her rough linen smock, trying to hide her chapped red hands beside this vision of pampered wealth.

"May I go now please, m'lady?" she asks, edging towards the door.

"Before you leave, are there many other ladies of our age at Court?"

Patti thinks for a moment. "No, I believe you are the only one m'lady."

"Go then," she replies offhandedly.

Patti curtseys and sidles out with the jug and bowl. Arbella has a pang of disappointment; once more she is to be in the company of adults. But her mood is not downhearted for long; a visit to Court is an event to be lived to the full. There are no lessons here, although she did have to promise her tutor, Mr. Starkey, that she would continue her reading of the classics when she had time; she knows she will be asked about it. With a sigh she sits on the window seat and waits impatiently for Bess to appear, already she feels delightfully overwhelmed with London and its attractions.

❧

The following morning, Bess and Arbella walk towards chapel with other ladies and gentlemen of the Court. The sun is shining and despite the imminent threat of invasion, everyone seems surprisingly blithe, as if nothing could possibly disturb the routine of the Court and its members. Arbella walks behind her grandmother, who is talking to her friend Blanche, but Bess is distracted by another friend who stops her, and the three ladies begin an animated conversation. After a couple of minutes, Arbella becomes bored with standing around, and decides to go into chapel alone. She pushes past other ladies who are at the entrance, and is surprised to find the Master of Ceremonies lowers his staff to block her way.

"What are you doing?" she demands haughtily. "Let me pass into the chapel."

"I must ask you to stand back and let other ladies precede you, Lady Arbella," is his reply, and he looks down on her with undisguised contempt for this slip of a girl, who has given herself airs and graces.

"I think not, sir! Do you know who I am? This is the very lowest position I could be given. Let me pass at once!"

By now everyone has stopped and turned to stare, including Bess, who is completely aghast at her granddaughter's behaviour. Arbella's eyes flash around the crowds of people watching her; everyone is waiting to see what she is going to do. She blushes, but holds her head high and tries for the third time.

"I say again, you must allow me entry before anyone else. I demand it! How dare you disobey me?"

Then from the back of the crowd, a male voice is heard, and it is like sweet music to Arbella's ears. " If the lady will allow me, I shall be honoured to escort her into chapel."

All heads turn to see the Earl of Essex, his tall, elegant figure swaggering through the crowd. His mouth is twitching, for he sees the situation as one of humour, rather than a breech of etiquette. He is looking particularly attractive this morning, and the ladies follow him hungrily with their eyes, admiring his shapely legs in breeches that are slightly too tight, and the muscular shape of his body beneath his doublet, left open a little too carelessly. Arbella's mood changes at once and she rewards him with a warm, adoring smile.

"Thank you, your grace," she says, her voice little more than a whisper. He looks down at her, his eyes caressing her face, and bends forward to whisper something in her ear; she giggles and places her small hand on his arm. The Master of Ceremonies reluctantly steps back to allow them to proceed. Once they are in the chapel, all eyes turn to Bess, whose face is one of absolute fury; then the gasps and whisperings begin, people shake their heads in disbelief, some smirk in satisfaction. Bess has never felt so publicly ashamed.

Within the day, Bess and Arbella are packed off back to Derbyshire. As soon as they are in the coach, Arbella tries to apologise again, but her grandmother is in no mood for reconciliation.

"You have disgraced me more than you can imagine, Arbella! Did you not listen to what I told you? I cannot believe you could be so stupid. Whatever were you thinking of?"

"I thought I was doing only what I am entitled to do."

"You are a slip of a girl, you know nothing of these matters. I told you not to put yourself forward, and within days of our arrival, that is exactly what you have done."

"I was tired of waiting for you."

"Then you are an impatient baggage who needs to learn her manners quickly. I thought you would be ready for a visit to Court, but I was obviously wrong. You are not ready, you have brought shame on both of us; the queen is furious, and now we are being sent home in disgrace."

"I have said I am sorry, lady grandmother."

"So you should be. It may be a long time before you are summoned to Court again. I cannot bear to even look at you at the moment."

A scarlet-faced Arbella shrinks back into her seat as Bess turns her head to look out of the window. She does not want to tell her that there may be other reasons for their dismissal by the queen. There is a real danger that should the Spanish invasion be a success, then Arbella could be used as a hostage and would be safer in Derbyshire. Also the queen is irritated by the kindness that the Earl of Essex has shown her. Everyone knows that she will not tolerate any rivals for the attention of her favourites. Bess is disappointed as well as furious, such visits are costly and this one has all been a waste of money, as well as humiliating; George will be delighted when he hears of it. She would have liked to stay longer, if only to see the Earl of Leicester, who by all accounts is unwell, although he is loyally preparing for the war with Spain. But it is at least a week before Bess is able to regard Arbella once more with her usual fondness.

ങ്ക

The Spanish Armada is defeated in 1588 and the whole country celebrates the victory. Mingled with this great achievement, is a sadness for Queen Elizabeth, as the Earl of Leicester, her beloved Robbie, dies soon afterwards. She had advised him to take the waters at Buxton again, but he never reached the town; she is grief stricken and for days will see no one. Bess is also saddened to hear the news, as he has been a good friend to her, particularly during all her marital troubles with George. Bess continues with the building work at Hardwick, although she lives with Arbella at Wingfield. She sees her husband rarely, but she knows he has spies reporting to him on her movements.

Shrewsbury House, Chelsea – 1590

"Sign here, your grace"

George adds his shaky and almost illegible signature to the papers that his lawyer has set before him. At a high price he can little afford, he has bought the Barlow lands that were left to Bess by her first husband.

"I should have done this years ago," George tells him. "I have had to watch my wicked wife profiting from all the sources of income that were left to her by her previous husbands – only one of whom could be called a gentleman, in my opinion. This will go some way to redress the balance."

The lawyer nods diplomatically and adds his signature as witness. He finds the household of the earl and his mistress to be slightly comical, what other way is there to describe an attractive, young woman doting on a sick old man? He would not trust Mistress Britton as far as the door, and as for the earl himself, his mind has definitely deteriorated. On several occasions the lawyer has had to remind his client of the purpose of their meeting, or answer his repeated questions on the same subject. Once he even forgot his own name, but

Mistress Britton is always at his side, ready to answer for him. "She does everything for me," he once confided to him.

The lawyer watches in embarrassment as George fumbles his hands over her buttocks. She pushes them away and tells him, "Not now George, we have company."

There is an awkward silence and the lawyer collects the documents before bowing and hastily leaving the chamber, breathing a sigh of relief that the business is done. Eleanor sits on the desk in front of him and he regards her with affection. For some years now she has been there for him and he is grateful. He knows she does not love him and covets his wealth, but these are small issues compared to being in her company. Just to feast his eyes on her is a treat and he lives in dread that she will leave him. Let people think what they will, he is past caring.

She thinks he looks every bit as old as his sixty-two years; his hair is sparse and grey, his eyes rheumy with heavy bags sagging down deeply lined cheeks. No longer able to stand upright because of his arthritis and rheumatism, his body is bent forward like a windswept tree. It is his mind that she is more interested in, because he is so forgetful it is easy for her to take an item, and tell him he said she could have it. She knows everything about his finances and reads every letter that comes to the house and every letter he sends. He has given her a free rein with the running of the household, and as long as he is kept well fed, warm and comforted, he does not ask questions.

When he complains about his children, she suggests he refuses to see them any more. When Sir Francis

Walsingham dies, she advises he writes more frequently to Lord Burghley instead. He revels in being petted and fussed over by her as no one has ever done so before, at least, not that he can remember.

"I have not long for this world my Ellie, you are my only comfort now," he croons at her as they lie in bed together. He likes to hold her as they fall asleep and while doing so, his thoughts invariably turn lately to his life achievements and death. After all these years, the insinuation that Bess made to him is still raw in his mind. She said he never had to work for what he achieved, and he cannot forget her words. With the great wealth and status of the Shrewsbury name, he has always enjoyed riches and privilege; it was taken for granted and never thought about from one day to the next. He cannot help but wonder if he had not been so highly born, he could have managed to climb the ladder of success as Bess' second husband, Sir William Cavendish, had done so brilliantly. But such men increasingly outshine those such as himself; he can think of several who have risen by their wits in the Tudor Court of Queen Elizabeth and her father. He secretly regards them with contempt. But he plans to out do them, even in death. He has been composing an inscription for his tomb, which has kept him busy, and provided some relief from the more mundane administrative work which constantly threatens to overwhelm him. Determined the inscription will not contain any reference to Bess, he ignored the surprised look on the face of the Latin translator when he told him. His marble sarcophagus will show him as a young man in plate armour and he likes the idea of having a hunting dog at its feet. Coincidentally the obvious choice is a Talbot, his father's favourite hunting breed. All his family would have to do after his death would be to add the date.

Eleanor is almost asleep. Each day she wonders how much longer she has to bear his touch or pander to his every whim, for the sight and smell of him revolts her. She hates his bony, deformed hands and the way his adoring eyes follow her about the room, as if he was a puppy waiting for attention. Sometimes she finds the key to the chest of money kept in his bedchamber and opens it, running her fingers through the coins and thinking of everything that she could buy. As she polishes the silver plate each week, she decides which of the booty she will keep and where she will place it in her new home. There are his oil paintings she likes too, as well as a striking clock, gold basins and some valuable jewellery that belonged to his first wife, some of which he has already given to her. But she wants the best pieces too and feels resentful that they are not already in her possession.

When George goes out, which is not often lately, Eleanor sits in the warm kitchen with her nephew John, and they plan how to spend his money. John is a lumbering giant, a sixteen-year-old spotty faced youth, with a thick neck and a mop of curly hair. He wishes to take it all now, but Eleanor tells him they must be patient. He is not very good at being patient, but childlike, he trusts her to do the thinking for both of them.

As autumn days turn to winter and the last of the leaves have fallen, George takes to his bed. He is ailing with gout and in constant pain. An old retainer visits him and George becomes very agitated, telling him in a tremulous voice that Arbella will cause a lot of trouble for Bess. After that he gradually becomes more and more confused, calling Eleanor by the name of his first wife, Gertrude, and crying that he sees Catholics at the foot of his bed and they should be killed before they do any more harm.

At one point he thinks the Scottish Queen is beside him, and he attempts to get up, but his strength is gone. Eleanor sits with him and makes him comfortable, trying not to show her impatience. One evening John stands at the door of his bedchamber and beckons to her.

"The old fool is taking an age to die. Can we not hurry his death a little?" he whispers. "I could do it now, it would take but a minute."

"Do not call him that, John!" she snaps. "Whatever else he is, I will not have him called a fool." She looks back at him as he lays defenceless in the bed, his eyes closed. "What are you suggesting?"

"A pillow over his face would be the quickest. He would never know, he is half gone already."

She frowns and thinks about it, murder is not to be taken lightly.

"I will give him one more night."

John nods, pleased that she has agreed, and goes back to the kitchen. He has already started packing and longs to be far from this place. Their plan is not needed in the end as George obliges them by taking his last breath on the morning of 18th November, and the two of them waste no time in the first hour after his death. Eleanor begins to ransack the house at once, and with John's help they load everything of value onto a waiting cart. By the time they have finished, the house looks empty, for she has stolen furniture and bedding too. "We must get away." John is sitting on the cart with his hands on the reins.

"Wait!" she says and hurries back inside to the earl's desk. She rummages in one of the drawers and finds a few property leases, which she quickly stuffs into her bag. Stopping by the open door to his chamber, she hesitates and goes over to him one last time. His face looks serene, all the troubles and pain have left his body.

"You were good to me, old man," she whispers softly. "I am sorry." She finds to her surprise that a single tear rolls down her cheek and she hastily brushes it away before John should see it. With a final look around the house, she runs outside to join him and they make their escape before anyone can stop them, the loaded cart causing much comment from bystanders until they reach the open road.

George's cold body lies alone in his bed, for the moment forgotten, estranged from his wife and family. His home looks bare and unkempt, the latch of an open window bangs in the wind and the remnants of a meal sit on the kitchen table. His desk is in its usual disarray, with some of the papers scattered on the floor. The fires have all gone out, and a chilly air blows through each chamber. It has taken only a few hours for an unlived-in atmosphere to pervade the walls. Torn between anger and grief, this is how Gilbert finds everything later that day. It seems all the neighbours have their own version of the events and are keen to regale him with stories of Eleanor and her nephew. Tight lipped, he listens wearily to them all, but makes no comment. He is now the seventh Earl of Shrewsbury, his wife Mary is the new countess, and Bess is widowed for the fourth time; but George will still manage to cause them trouble, even from the grave.

⁂

Wingfield Manor, Derbyshire

As soon as she hears of George's death, Bess sends for his lawyer to confirm the contents of his will. She cannot feel much sorrow at his passing after all that has happened between them, but she has no regrets. Her everyday life will not change very much; there will be more administration work from her Shrewsbury inheritance, but nothing that cannot be handled. Gilbert has written to tell her of the circumstances of his father's last days and that he must see her urgently. When he arrives, she is taken aback by his dishevelled appearance and wild manner. "Bess! Thank the Lord you are here." He gives her a fleeting kiss after bowing absent-mindedly and begins to pace the floor in nervous agitation. Such behaviour reminds her briefly of George, a thought she quickly dismisses.

"Did you know how badly the Shrewsbury estates have been managed over recent years?"

He does not wait for a reply and Bess sits watching him. She has already guessed which way the wind is to blow, and has prepared herself for when the moment comes that she is to tell him.

"I had expected my debts to be paid off when I succeeded to the title, but what do I find? There is little enough money to even pay the expenses of the lawyers. That scheming bitch Britton has taken everything she could carry away! All the Shrewsbury jewellery that should by rights be passed to Mary now, gold chains, silver plate, bedding – she has even taken cattle, can you believe it? My father spent a fortune on this new house at Worksop, and another in London; of course paying for the Scots Queen proved to be the biggest drain of all."

He sits down beside her and hangs his head in dejected misery.

"My creditors are closing in on me, they do not believe I have inherited next to nothing."

"Gilbert, you must calm yourself. Have some wine, it cannot be as bad as you say."

"I do not think you quite realise the seriousness of my situation – or maybe Mary has already told you. I know you women gossip amongst yourselves."

"Mary has mentioned it, only because she is worried. I can recommend someone to advise you if you wish."

"They will be no help," he replies and drains his goblet before sitting down opposite her. "I shall have to raid her house and take it all back."

"If she can prove it was all given to her, then it will not be so easy."

"She will not be able to prove anything! I cannot let her get away with it, Bess. This is such a mess! My two brothers have been named as executors, not me, his heir. I am hardly mentioned in the will," he adds in despair.

"When was this will written? Is is actually legal?"

"Oh yes, it is legal, signed and witnessed correctly. He made it six months ago, when he was well under Britton's control."

"Will your brothers agree to be the executors?"

"I think not, in which case I shall take over the duties myself, as is right and proper."

"But you will still have the entailed properties."

"What good are they without cash? I know my father kept about £10,000 as gold coins in one of the chests, of course it has disappeared and I doubt we shall see it again."

"You have a battle ahead of you Gilbert. If I can be of any help with the administration ..."

"As a matter of fact, you can help me."

He looks at her eagerly and leans forward, his eyes shining with hope.

"You will inherit a tidy sum from my father. More than you need. You could easily give up your widow's rights."

Bess gets up to stand facing the fire and does not reply for a few moments; he holds his breath as he waits, but feels confident about the outcome. But when she speaks at last, her voice is unequivocal.

"I am not prepared to do that, Gilbert. I am sorry you are in this position, but I cannot help you."

"It would be little enough to you, but everything to me. Look around Bess; you are a wealthy woman without your widow's portion. You would hardly miss it."

She turns to face him, her expression resolute. Gilbert stands up too; his fists clenched and he looks at her uncomprehendingly.

"You have helped Henry often enough! I have been more of a son to you than he ever has."

"Have you forgotten that I have loaned you money too, which you still owe me? Both of you need to control your finances better. When the dust has settled, you will be able to assess the situation and work to salvage what you can from it. I will help with ..."

"If you refuse to help me with the money, I do not want your help at all."

"Very well. You must take responsibility for yourself, Gilbert. You are now the head of the Shrewsbury family and you must behave as such."

"So at last you show your true colours!" He takes a few steps towards her then hesitates.

"Gilbert ..." she puts her hand out to touch his shoulder, but he jerks back roughly. His eyes are burning with indignation.

"I always defended you against all the gossips and people who speak ill of you, and there are many, believe me! But I can see now that they were right and I was wrong. You are greedy and ruthless, you only think selfishly of yourself. No one would listen to my poor father when he told us your true nature; we all thought he was exaggerating. But it seems he knew better than anyone. Well, do not trouble yourself, madam. Take your widow's portion and all the rest of it that you have stolen from your dead husbands, and when I am sent to jail for my debts, you may say to yourself, yes, it is I who helped put my stepson there! And tell your grandchildren the same! I hope you will be proud of yourself."

"Why should I agree to your demands?" she shouts passionately. "Why should I forgo what is rightfully mine? I have endured over twenty years of being married to your father, who has treated me with vengeance and hatred. He accused me of being the worst of wives and sullied the memory of my other husbands with his cruel comments. I have had the allowances owed to me withheld by him for years. He stormed my beloved Chatsworth and kept me from living there peacefully. He frightened my sons and tenants with his violent ways. Do you know how humiliating it has been for me to have his mistress flaunted around the city? All my attempts to reconcile with him and live as man and wife have been rejected. Do you really think I am going to walk away with nothing from this marriage after all that?"

Gilbert can only look at her with narrowed eyes; he knows what she says is the truth.

"No, I am not going to, even for you Gilbert," she tells him, her voice much calmer. "I love you as my own son, but I will have what is mine. You must find another way to solve your money problems."

"Is that your final word?"

"It is."

"Then there is no more to be said."

Bess holds his gaze steadily and watches as he storms out of the chamber. She hears him shouting to the servant for his horse and within minutes he is gone; the house resumes its silence again and it was as if he had never been. She stands still for a while; the chamber has become gloomy in the gathering dusk, a floorboard creaks and a blackbird swoops across the grass, it's song piercing the icy air. It has been a long time since she has had to speak out and defend herself. His words echo in her head – greedy, ruthless, selfish. She cannot allow herself to entertain even a shadow of doubt that she is doing what is right for herself. Gilbert asks too much of her. Maybe it had been optimistic to think she would not have to stand up for herself again. Her head has started to ache and wave of tiredness washes over her. She climbs the stairs to find Agnes, who will massage her neck and shoulders with scented oils to try and soothe away the cares of the day. Soon she will have to see Mary, who will not be at all surprised by her mother's decision.

ଔଓ

Within the week the lawyer waits in the Hall at Wingfield for Bess to receive him. He carries a bag with documents, which are so heavy; they have made his shoulder ache. Standing in front of the roaring fire, he rearranges his cloak and sees he has mud splattered on his boots, but it is too late to clean them now. Already he is impressed with the air of efficiency that the house seems to have. There is a quiet and purposeful atmosphere, the servants are all neat and tidy, bustling about their work unobtrusively; everywhere is clean and the rays of sunlight falling through the windows show no trace of dust. This is obviously a well run household and quite different from the late earl's love nest. He smiles to himself at the memory of it, but quickly composes his face when the servant beckons for him to enter Bess' chamber. He is intensely curious to meet the woman about whom his client has spoken with such rancour and hatred.

He walks before her desk and bows, looking up to see a woman in her early sixties, her shrewd eyes gazing at him with authority. She is dressed in black and exudes a confidence he has not seen before on any woman. Her faded red hair is kept neatly under a black velvet headdress, dotted with silver pearls of the finest quality. Her hands rest lightly on the desk, the fingers wearing several rings of gold and he can see ruby stones, some as big as cats' eyes. All around her there are stacks of papers and ledgers in neat piles, wall maps positioned around the room. On her desk he notices what he assumes, are likenesses of her family, but not one of her late husband. There is a steeliness in her manner; he can see it before she even speaks.

"Good day to you, Master McLean. This is my son, Sir William Cavendish and my steward, Timothy Pusey." She gestures to her right where William and Timothy are working at their desks and they nod their heads in acknowledgement, barely pausing.

"Please be seated."

He is grateful for the few moments it takes him to extract the papers from his bag while she watches him. All fingers and thumbs, he drops a few of them and hurriedly picks them up before apologising. Bess gives the barest of smiles.

"Thank you for coming to see me so promptly. I realise that it is a little unusual to see me as you are the earl's lawyer, but as I wrote to you, I am anxious to hear the contents of my late husband's will. Of course you are aware that we have been estranged over recent years, and I believe he has changed his wishes. I would obviously like to know if this is the case."

"Yes, your grace, your pre-marriage agreement is unaffected and still stands, of course. But I have to tell you, not is all as it should be with the late earl's estate."

"Yes, so I understand."

"The new earl has already met with me. My initial enquiries have found the Shrewsbury Estates to have been poorly managed over a number of years. This has lead to a considerable fall in revenue resulting in the late earl's estate now being much lower than expected. The late earl embarked on costly building works, as you know and made some unprofitable investments. There are also some missing items taken by …" He looks at the floor, too embarrassed to meet her eye.

"… his mistress, Eleanor Britton. My stepson has told me about it."

"I have advised him to try and re-claim these articles from Mistress Britton, but she is now countersuing and claiming the property was given to her by the late earl. At present we have no evidence that this was the case."

Bess raises one eyebrow and glances at William, who pauses mid-air in his writing, his face a picture of disgust. Master Maclean's voice becomes more positive.

"However your own financial position is much healthier, your grace. The land and income from your previous husbands' estates now revert back to you, and as the late earl's widow, you are entitled to a third of his estate."

"That is correct," she says with a nod.

"Indeed, Bolsover Castle, this present property Wingfield Manor, Shrewsbury House in Chelsea, the extensive properties in Derbyshire and Yorkshire as well as the lucrative coal and lead mines, the glass works and forges are all yours. The new earl owes you a substantial sum in loans, lead and cattle as you are aware."

"I have always enjoyed a good relationship with my son-in-law, but his attitude towards me has changed since the death of his father."

"May I ask the reason?"

"He thinks I should help him at considerable cost to myself. The large debts he has incurred over the years were offset by his expectations, which have come to little. When I made it plain to him I was not going to forgo my widow's rights, he will no longer speak to me."

"Well, it is not as if you need the Shrewsbury funds."

As soon as he says it, Master Maclean realises it is a mistake. Had Gilbert not already moaned about this matter to him? Had he not said that his stepmother is unyielding and stubborn? Bess looks at him coldly and for a few moments there is silence. When she speaks, he hears the hint of a Derbyshire accent in her voice, which comes to the surface when she is angry.

"You forget yourself Master Maclean! It is not for you to tell me what I need and do not need! My need is immaterial, it is what I am entitled to receive as the earl's widow that matters."

"I meant no disrespect, your grace. I apologise if I have caused offence," he says quickly. "It is highly unusual to find myself dealing directly with a woman in such legal matters. It is a pity the late earl did not have your flair for business."

"If you mean I am quick to see where some profit is to be made through loans or the purchase of property, then yes, I am not ashamed of it. I am a woman of business through necessity, and the future of my family depends on it. I will not allow anyone or anything to stand in my way."

"Such sentiments have brought you to this position today, your grace. As Dowager Countess of Shrewsbury, it seems you are now the wealthiest woman in England, after the queen herself."

"You would do well to remember it. If I am so wealthy, then I am also powerful."

"Indeed. I am honoured to have such a worthy adversary, your grace. No doubt we shall meet again before the judges in due course. But I warn you, the new earl is in no mood for compromise."

"I had wished to settle these differences out of court, but if my stepson thinks otherwise, then so be it."

Master Maclean stands up; keen to get back to his office.

"If that is all, your grace, I will take my leave. Good day to you." He bows and Bess merely nods curtly. As soon as he has gone, William puts his quill down and stretches his arms above his head.

"What did you make of him, lady mother?"

"Like all lawyers, he will doubtless charge too much, but that is Gilbert's problem. It is good to know my finances are in such a healthy state."

"Thanks to your management," he replies.

"But you and Timothy must take some credit too," she says and smiles as Timothy gets up to replace a book on the shelf. "We are a team are we not? What do you say, Timothy?"

He turns round; the book still in his ink splattered hand and regards her with familiar cheerfulness.

"Modesty forbids me to answer that question, your grace"

"I thought you would say so. But I value your work and the contribution you make."

"Thank you," he responds simply and she can tell that he is pleased.

"Why not take a walk to the laundry, where I believe your latest sweetheart is pining for you?"

William gives a chuckle and takes the book from him.

"I will finish this," he tells him.

Timothy pretends to be reluctant and starts to bluster with excuses, but Bess and William shoo him out and he disappears. Since the death of Joseph a few years previously, Timothy has proved himself to be a worthy replacement. Although very different in character from his predecessor, he has the same dedication and loyalty; these are qualities which Bess rewards generously as she knows the importance of reliable servants. Somehow he has reached the age of thirty-five and avoided marriage, but William believes time is running out and teases him that the laundry maid could be the one to snare him. As he is boyishly handsome with curly fair hair and a warm grin, there is no shortage of female admirers.

"I think a special drink is called for," Bess tells William and she goes over to a cupboard and produces two silver goblets and a flagon.

"I have been saving this finest claret for a special occasion." She pours them both a generous portion and they toast to the future.

"Hmmm, that is excellent" he savours the taste appreciatively. "How clever of you to have these agreements with the earl before you married."

"Was I clever? Or just practical?"

"You are both, lady mother, and much more besides."

"Stop this flattery, William! I just do my best."

"If father could see you now, he would be very proud."

"But we still have a long way to go."

"Do you mean with Arbella?" He frowns. "How old is she now?"

"Fifteen, nearly of marriageable age."

"I wonder the queen does not send for her. She is more than old enough."

"Her majesty will, in due course."

"It is very dull for her living here, she would much rather be at Court."

"I expect she would; no doubt she complains to everyone about it. I can do nothing except wait for the summons."

"She seems to think you could hurry matters if you wanted to."

"That is nonsense, of course I cannot influence the queen! Arbella will have to be patient, I keep telling her. The letter will arrive one of these days and we shall be ready for it."

William lowers his voice. "That tantrum she had the other evening …"

"Yes, it was the worse one yet. Such behaviour will not be tolerated at Court. I do wish she would try and control her emotions; it is most unseemly for someone of her status to shout and cry. She did not inherit that from your sister Elizabeth."

"It must be a Stuart trait."

"The Scots Queen used to be dramatic on occasions too. Crying and wailing to get her own way."

She shakes her head as if trying to erase the memory. "Now who is waiting to see me?" He picks up a list from his desk and reads from it.

"Three bailiffs to discuss the cattle figures and next month's sheep sales, a foreign sailor wanting to raise capital for some private ships and two local landowners hoping for loans."

"You can deal with the bailiffs, take them into the other chamber; show me the conclusions when you have finished. I will see the foreign sailor myself, then I want to go through the latest building costs with you and Timothy"

She straightens her headdress; it is time to get back to work.

☙❧

1590 – 1591

Nearly two months later, George is given a funeral that is fitting for his status, and Gilbert spares no expense, despite his lack of funds. He tells friends he wants it to be remembered for many years to come. Thousands of onlookers brave the chilly January morning and although Bess is not involved with the arrangements, both she and Arbella are seated in prominent positions inside the church. Gilbert's relationship with not only Bess, but also his brothers and some of his friends, deteriorates over the next year, as there are disagreements over legal matters arising from the will. Bess attempts an out-of-court settlement with Gilbert, but he does not uphold it. Mary now has little contact with Bess, preferring to maintain a relationship with Arbella instead. Bess continues to increase her property portfolio, acquiring land at Edensor and Little Longstone, from owners who have defaulted on loans she had made to them. Building is well under way of a grand new house at Hardwick, adjacent to the old one, from plans drawn by Robert Smythson, the architect. But at last, the queen sends for Arbella on her birthday, and it looks as if her life is about to change for the better.

ଓଞ୍ଜ

November 1591

Preparations for this visit are the most lavish and costly yet. Twelve wagons are needed to transport the family, together with furniture, bedding, linen and plate, as well as Bess' important business documents to London. A large flock of sheep and some oxen have already been sent ahead of the party to provide food in the coming weeks. The servants at the house in Chelsea have been told to prepare for an extended visit by the family, so chambers must be cleaned and aired, as well as extra food and fuel ordered. Bess brings her own cooks, butlers and kitchen servants to provide the standard of entertaining that is required. Forty servants are chosen to accompany the family, some ride on horseback, whilst other more senior ladies are in horse drawn litters. At Wingfield, all the family chambers will be closed up and remaining furniture covered with sheets, leaving Timothy in overall charge.

Weather permitting; he will be in daily contact with Bess through letters, so that she will not be out of touch with her many business interests. She rides in her cumbersome coach, with Arbella of course, chests of coins under their seats and with armed guards riding alongside. William and Charles with their respective wives and families have their own coaches, so the complete convoy is an impressive sight as they ride south, with Bess giving money to the poor in every town. She makes sure people know she is coming, by sending ahead a servant lad dressed in the blue Cavendish livery to warn the bell ringer.

For the visit, they are all to reside at Shrewsbury House, in the cleaner countryside air of Chelsea. Bess has extended it to provide extra accommodation and it provides easy access to Court, via the river. But before Bess can start to see, and be seen with the cream of Tudor society, she must have new garments made for herself and Arbella, as well as the important gift for the queen, which this year is to be an exclusively designed, heavily embroidered and beaded coat. Tailors work round the clock with Bess' own seamstresses to produce these clothes as quickly as possible. In the meantime, Arbella, now aged seventeen, poses impatiently for her latest portrait, which will show her standing and finely dressed in a cream gown with black detail, her hair flowing loosely down her back. After some arguments, she agrees to borrow a pearl necklace from Bess, but insists most of it is tucked inside her gown, as a gesture of defiance. Bess has bought her some new jewels because she still has not received the Lennox jewels from Scotland, left to her by her other grandmother. The artist suggests including some books in the portrait, as a reference to her education and intelligence, an idea to which Bess readily agrees. At one of the masque balls at Court one evening, they eventually see the queen, who seems to have forgotten Arbella's *faux pas* a few years earlier. She smiles as they both curtsey.

"We are growing old together, Bess," she tells her and searches her face keenly, for the two women are only a handful of years apart in age.

Of the pair of them, it is Bess who looks healthier, thanks in part to her strong constitution and common sense approach to life.

"It is I who am growing old, your majesty. You have not changed at all, and will never do so."

This is blatantly untrue and they both know it. Bess is secretly appalled to see the deterioration in her appearance, but her outward show of admiration never falters. The queen has lost more teeth, causing her cheeks to collapse. Those teeth that remain are blackened and unsightly. Her skin is heavily pitted from smallpox and damaged by the powered arsenic that she has painted onto it every day, when she appears in public. Sometimes she reveals her decollete with it's very wrinkled skin on her neck and breasts, much to the embarrassment of others. The usual array of fine jewels, sparkling stones and lavish costumes cannot disguise her aging body. But she carries on as she always has done, and everyone still treats her with the adoration and deference she demands and expects.

"So Lady Arbella, you have grown since you were last here." The queen looks her up and down, not unkindly, and seems pleased. "We are glad of your company now and there are some other young people at Court for you."

"I am fortunate, your majesty, and honoured to be here."

"We have not forgotten to find you a husband, the negotiations are continuing."

Arbella is all smiles as Bess watches approvingly. Then the queen moves on to someone else; Lord

Burghley, his hair and beard now snowy white, follows slowly behind, nodding at Bess as they pass.

"I thought the queen would speak longer with us," Arbella observes.

"Her majesty is very busy, we shall have more opportunities in the coming weeks. I shall request a private audience."

"I do hope I shall not have to wait much longer for a husband to be found for me."

Bess can only agree with this wish, it has been her fervent desire since the hour of Arbella's birth. Also, in truth, at sixty years old, she is finding the constant supervision of a young woman, especially one who is very different in temperament from her mother, to be a strain.

"I have promised to dance, I beg you would excuse me, lady grandmother."

Arbella hurries through the crowd, leaving Bess to find a place to sit. She reflects that her daughter Elizabeth would never have flirted with Sir Walter Raleigh as Arbella is so boldly doing now. Looking at the two of them as they dance, Bess strokes the lengthy five-string rope of pearls she wears round her neck for these occasions. She has commissioned a portrait of herself wearing them, for they are quite spectacular in quality, size and quantity. These beautiful pearls attract the attention, admiration and envy of almost everyone, which is the reaction she is hoping to achieve. The queen herself has some similar pearls, which Bess was so taken with, she bought her own. As they are so heavy, she is only able to wear them in all their glory for short periods. Above them she wears a large, delicately made white lace ruff, which together with the pearls, provides a contrast from the severe black gowns she now wears all the time. On her head she has a small gold edged black cap that drapes behind her neck, hiding her hair.

"Your grace, may I join you?"

She looks up to see Lord Burghley's son, Robert Cecil, standing in that awkward way of his beside her.

"Of course."

He half stumbles into the chair and they wait while a servant silently refills their glasses. Robert is physically stunted with a curved back that often gives him pain, although he would never admit to it. His rise in Queen Elizabeth's Court, under the expert guidance of his father, Lord Burghley, has been nothing short of meteoric, having taken over the duties of Sir Francis Walsingham, after his death last year. At almost thirty years of age, it is widely acknowledged (with bitterness by some) that he has a glittering career at Court ahead of him.

"Is your father not attending the festivities tonight, Master Cecil?"

"Alas no, the queen has excused him. He is not in the best of health and retires early each night. I am afraid the times when he works into the early hours of the morning are long gone."

He reaches into his silk waistcoat.

"He asked me to show you this miniature of the Lady Arbella, it is a copy of the one sent to Spain."

Bess takes the small gold edged portrait and studies it with interest. "For her proposed marriage to son of the Duke of Palma? It is a fair likeness. I myself commissioned another portrait of her recently, it hangs in my house at Chelsea."

"I was sorry to have missed your banquet last week. I hear it was very lavish with no expense spared."

She hands back the miniature and smiles at him. "I have been entertaining and seeing my old friends. Now that my finances are in order, I am able to spend as I wish."

"And lend money as you wish too."

"I help my friends, and am glad to do so."

"But you also lend to courtiers so that they may build grand houses for the queen to visit."

"You seem to be accusing me of doing something wrong!" She laughs lightly. "Do you not approve?"

"It is not for me to approve or disapprove, your grace. But you must admit it is very unusual for a woman to have such …" he searches for the word.

"… wealth? Power? Business acumen?" They both smile and Robert is quick to respond. "My father always said you have a manly understanding of money and business. There are many men who would dearly love to have your grasp of these matters." He looks around the Hall. "I can name at least half a dozen of such men within a few yards of us."

"I shall take that as a compliment," she says and gazes at him over the rim of her glass. At that moment, he sees a fleeting glimpse of a younger Bess, the one that captured the hearts of her four husbands. But the image fades as quickly as a petal falling from a rose.

"How long shall we have the pleasure of your company at Court this time?"

"Long enough to see a decision about my Arbella's future."

He grimaces, and sips his wine.

"On that subject her majesty will not be drawn. She enjoys the negotiations as you know, not for herself any more, but for others."

"As older ladies, you must allow us some diversions."

"I would not wish to curtail such activities for you." His voice is teasing but she realises the light-hearted banter disguises the seriousness of the subject. There are no two ways about it; Arbella is a problem for the queen, who is now well past child bearing, and made it very clear years ago that she will not marry. Many doubt that these negotiations with Spain for the marriage of Arbella will be a success, as it would be unthinkable to allow a foreign power to have control over someone so close to the throne.

Bess and Robert watch the others for a few minutes in silence. It is the usual scene of expensively clad courtiers, some watching and gossiping, whilst others are dancing energetically, their faces flushed in pleasure. The silver and gold platters of food are being cleared away and taken back to the kitchens by the numerous servants who deftly avoid the Court jester performing some acrobatics. The queen giggles like an empty headed milkmaid with the Earl of Essex and shows no sign of retiring to her bed, although it is nearly midnight. Robert turns back to Bess, his teasing manner gone. "You have been in London for some time now. Are you not curious to see how your building work is progressing in your absence?"

"By the time I return to Hardwick, the New Hall will be well under construction and the alterations to the Old Hall are nearly complete now. Everything is going well, but I always enjoy my time at Court. I believe I must be one of her majesty's longest serving ladies-in-waiting."

"Certainly, you are of a similar age."

"And seen many changes, yes."

"Did you hear about the play to be performed tomorrow here at Court?"

"Written by the playwright Will Shakespeare? About Henry VI is it not?"

"Yes, you may wish to see it as one of your late husband's ancestors has a prominent role."

Bess is intrigued. "In that case, I should certainly watch it, although I am not a great admirer of the theatre, unlike my sons, especially William."

Arbella flounces over to them, her face a picture of abject misery.

"Whatever is the matter, child?" asks Bess.

"Sir Walter has gone to dance with Bess Throckmorton again! I was hoping he would dance the Volta with me."

"How do you know the steps of that dance? It is not suitable for you."

Robert tactfully looks the other way and Arbella gives him a stony glare before sitting down heavily with a loud sigh.

"Some say those two have been doing a lot more than dancing," he whispers to Bess.

"So I hear. There is always some scandal to keep the tongues wagging. I have seen it all before, I am glad to be out of it, but there is some pleasure to watch it from afar."

He nods gravely and stands up, bowing with as much grace as can muster. "I beg you would excuse me, countess. Lady Arbella."

Arbella ignores him and Bess waits until he is out of earshot.

"You were very rude just now, Arbella! Robert Cecil cannot help his deformity; you are very un-Christian to treat him so cruelly. It is not the way to behave at all; you must show kindness and be thoughtful to others. Remember everyone is watching you, I cannot emphasise how important it is that you make the best of impressions whilst you are here."

She pouts and does not reply, but studies a loose thread on her gown. Exasperated, Bess taps her knuckles sharply with a spoon and Arbella looks up, her eyes brimming with unshed tears.

"Do try to look happier! How are we ever going to find you a husband if you are never smiling?"

It is a question that seems unanswerable at the moment.

꿍꿍

Shrewsbury House, Chelsea – April 1592

*B*ess and the family have been enjoying themselves in London for the last five months. The proposed marriage with Arbella and the Duke of Palma is no further forward and Bess is becoming increasingly frustrated at the lack of progress. Despite her grandmother's earlier warning, Arbella is still pining over Robert Devereux, Earl of Essex, although he is now married.

One spring afternoon Arbella finds herself on her own, Bess having gone shopping with friends; other family members are either out or occupied elsewhere in the house. She is restless, getting up and sitting down again several times an hour as she attempts to read or embroider. The view from the window does not please her, there is little traffic passing through this part of Chelsea. There are few ladies at Court that Bess will allow her to fraternise with, as they are not considered suitable for one reason or another. She has her own ladies-in-waiting, but they are older and always seem to be disapproving of her, no matter what she does. Tired of their veiled looks, she has dismissed them for the rest of the day.

She idly starts to scratch her initials with her ring on the stone window sill and has got as far as completing the letter $\mathcal{A}$ when she hears the clatter of horses hooves and a rider stops outside the house to dismount. To her horror and delight, she sees it is the Earl of Essex, and pulls back quickly from the window. There is a knock at the front door and after a moment, the butler comes into the chamber, his face showing disapproval.

"His Grace, the Earl of Essex is here, highness."

"To see me?"

"Yes, highness. I have informed him that her grace is not at home, but he wishes to stay nonetheless. Do you wish me to show him in?"

"Certainly, and bring us some refreshment."

Arbella rushes over to the looking glass to check her appearance. She wishes now that she had worn a different gown; he has surely seen this one before. When the butler announces him, Arbella literally goes weak at the knees, and has to hold on to a chair for support. He grins at her as if such a reaction is quite what he expected.

"Lady Arbella." Giving a sweeping bow he removes his hat, and she responds with a curtsey before gesturing for him to sit down opposite her.

"No, I shall sit next to you, all the better to admire your beauty."

She flushes and fingers her necklace.

"This is an unexpected surprise, your grace."

"Will you not call me Robert?"

"Very well, you may call me Arbella. My lady grandmother is out, I do not know when she will return."

"I have not come to see your grandmother."

He lights the tobacco in his pipe that most men seem to smoke nowadays, and inhales deeply before placing his arm along the back of the chair.

"My lady grandmother does not like the smoke from pipes." Arbella looks worried. "I fear you will have to put it out."

"Just one smoke will not hurt," is his reply and gives her his most inviting look. "Is the countess out spending her vast wealth again? They say she must have spent over £5,000 so far during this visit. How vulgar!"

She looks shocked to hear him speak so freely and he laughs. "Why do you not accompany her? I have yet to meet a woman who does not like to shop and spend money."

"I spend more than enough time in her company, I do not seek it out."

"No, I do not suppose you do," he replies thoughtfully. "It must be hard for you, especially as you are so young and alive."

A servant appears with a tray of sweetmeats and wine, she places it in front of them and curtseys before closing the door quietly behind herself. They pick up their glasses and Arbella begins to nibble on some marchpane.

"It is to be regretted that despite our noble births, we are at the mercy of others all the time," he says.

"Yes, I long to be able to choose my own destiny."

"You should be able to do so, and to marry where you choose, whether it be prince or pauper."

She wrinkles her nose. "I shall not marry a pauper."

"If you loved him, surely that would be enough. Love would overcome all difficulties."

"That is easy to say. Anyway, I never meet any men I would wish to fall in love with."

"You have met me," he teases. "Am I not your idea of the perfect man?"

To emphasise his point, he places the pipe on the table and in a swift movement he is kneeling on the floor in front of her.

"I hardly know …"

Embarrassed, she looks down, and he puts his hand under her chin to tilt it up again.

"I am sorry Arbella, I must not tease you, it is unfair. You and I are alone here, we could do anything we chose to do."

Their eyes lock and his gaze is hypnotic; she cannot break away from it.

"Anything at all," he repeats and gently strokes her cheek.

Arbella is feeling faint with desire for him and as his face looms closer, she feels his other hand sliding up the inside of her gown with practised ease.

"But Robert, your wife …" Her voice of protest is nothing but a whisper.

"Shhhh …" Their lips are now almost touching and she cannot stop herself from kissing him, something she has wanted to do since that shameful day he escorted her into chapel. She has never been kissed by a man before and she experiences a tantalizing glimpse of what she is missing.

Suddenly the mood is shattered as the door is flung open and Bess stands on the threshold, her face a mixture of surprise and anger. The pair look dumbstruck and quickly separate, Robert springing to his feet, and Arbella blushing deeply.

"Arbella, go to your room!" she barks, standing aside for her to pass. Arbella runs out without a glance at either of them. Bess takes her time and shuts the door before looking at him with contempt.

"So my Earl of Essex! Is this how you behave when I am not here?"

"You misunderstand, countess, I meant no harm, truly." He picks up his hat, which has fallen to the floor.

"You have acted without any respect for my granddaughter, who is still of tender years and …"

"… hardly tender, she is seventeen, old enough to be a woman and one with passions and desires."

"Which you have tried to take advantage of!"

"She seemed very willing to me," he replies lazily.

"How dare you suggest that Lady Arbella has encouraged you! I have a good mind to tell the queen of this attempted seduction. I do not think you would be so much in the royal favour then!"

"You must do as you please, but I doubt the queen would take any action against me. In case you did not know, I can do no wrong in her eyes." Placing his hat on his head at a jaunty angle, he checks it in the looking glass and she watches with narrowed eyes.

"People like you at Court will soon be dead," he tells her. "Your time is nearly over and a new order is coming. Arbella and I will be at the centre of it all. Your days are numbered, countess."

"On the contrary, it is your days that are numbered. You are a man with little judgement, and much arrogance. Your famous good looks, charm and birthright have brought you thus far, but I do not see a future for you."

"What would you know? An old lady in her dotage!"

"I have seen decades of life at court and I know who is going to win, and who will lose. You are a loser, and your ambition will be the undoing of you."

"So you can foretell the future! Your ambition does not seem to have done you any harm."

"My ambition did not pose a threat to the throne of England."

"Really? By marrying your daughter to Charles Stuart?"

"There is a big difference between you and me. I am loyal to the queen and you only have loyalty to yourself."

"Come, let us not part on bad terms. We could be useful to one another. If I promise not to seduce your little one, can we be friends?"

He has moved closer and she detects the smell of leather and musk.

"I do not wish to be your enemy," replies Bess carefully.

"Good, we are in agreement. I bid you good day, countess."

He bows before leaving, nonchalant and supremely self-confident, she is not at all surprised that her granddaughter is smitten with him. Going to the bottom of the stairs and looking up, she sees Arbella crouched at the top, evidently trying to listen to every word that has been exchanged.

"Come downstairs, child."

Arbella uncurls herself and descends slowly, apparently deep in thought.

"Are you all right?" Bess asks and beckons for her to come closer.

"I am, thank you, lady grandmother." She does not go to Bess but stands a few feet away, her arms stiffly by her side.

"Did anything happen between the two of you?"

"No."

"How long had the earl been here?"

"Not long."
"You did not invite him did you?"
"No."

Bess sighs that she is not more forthright. "You must not be alone with the earl again. I have already told you that you are not to become close to him and you know the reason. If I had not disturbed you, I shudder to think what would have happened."

Arbella is staring at the floor, then she looks at Bess who is shocked by the fierce passion in her eyes. "I could have married him! Why was he not put forward as a suitor for me?"

"No child, you could not have married him. That would not have been possible."

"Why not?"

"The queen would not have given permission," replies Bess wearily, tired of always being asked the same question and having to give the same unsatisfactory answer.

"You did not get permission for my parents."

"That was different."

"Neither of you want me to be happy!" she shouts. "I like Robert, he makes me feel good and he understands me as no one else does. You are jealous, both of you! I am young, pretty and clever! You are two ugly, old women who take pleasure in spoiling my life!"

There is a resounding slap as Bess' right hand finds sharp contact with Arbella's left cheek. In the few seconds of stunned silence that follows, Arbella's eyes start to fill with tears before she runs upstairs, her sobs reaching hysterical wails by the time she is out of sight.

Bess is shaking with emotion. She has never raised her hand to her own daughters and certainly not to her grandchildren until now. Going to her chamber and shutting the door firmly, she sits at her desk, alone and pensive, drumming her fingers on the wood. She feels no pride in what she has done, but Arbella was rude and what she said was very unpleasant. If anyone was to hear her speak of the queen with such hatred, the consequences do not bear thinking about. With a terrible sense of guilt, Bess realises that because she has spoilt and indulged her so much, this behaviour cannot all be blamed on Arbella alone. She hopes it is not too late to put it right.

ଔଃ

The return journey back to Derbyshire is leisurely, as Bess has acknowledged to herself that this will be her last visit to Court and she makes the most of it. She parts from the main convoy and stays with Sir Christopher Hatton's heir, Sir William, overnight. Then she is welcomed at the home of her daughter, Frances and son-in-law Henry, who are planning the imminent wedding of their daughter, Grace. Bess provides the dowry of £700, together with money for the two newlyweds to set up home. Her last visit is to another old friend, Sir Francis Willoughby, who has recently completed elaborate alterations to his house, which Bess wishes to see, as she is looking for decorating ideas for the New Hall, not yet complete. By the time her coach arrives at Hardwick, she is eager to put her plans into action.

ଔଃ

Hardwick Hall – August 1592

"Welcome home, your grace." The greeting that Timothy gives Bess as she makes her way through the front door makes Bess feel good to be back at last.

"I trust your visits were enjoyable?" A servant helps Bess off with her cloak and disappears to tell the kitchen that the mistress has arrived.

"Most enjoyable, thank you Timothy."

"There is a long list of matters needing a decision from you, but you already know about the most urgent."

"Yes, we shall sit down together with Sir William at first light tomorrow and make a start on the work. I would like to review the materials used for the building and the costs of wages for the last three months. Please have the figures ready for me in the morning."

"The books are already on the desk for you."

Bess smiles at him. "That is why I rely on you so much, Timothy."

He gives a brief bow and goes back to work.

Bess looks up to see William's wife, Anne, descending the stairs with care, as she is expecting their third child next year.

"Lady mother, you have made good time. We were not expecting you until this afternoon."

"Travel is always quicker in the summer." They kiss cheeks and Bess looks at her appraisingly. "Are you still feeling sick in the mornings?"

"Yes, it was especially tiresome yesterday. I do not want to eat breakfast for fear of making it worse."

"I was lucky, it was something I never suffered from with my own pregnancies, but you should try and eat to keep your strength up. The children are well since I left you last week?"

"Wylkyn has been fretting over a toy we left in London and little Gilbert has settled here again after the journey."

"I shall go up to the nursery later and see my little jewels."

They are interrupted by William who has appeared at the door of his study.

"You are back lady mother, how were all your visits? Any gossip?" He comes and kisses her hand as she laughs fondly at him.

"You know I do not indulge in idle gossip."

"Well, any news then?"

"I will tell you later, nothing of great importance. Where is Arbella?"

"She was here a minute ago, she must have gone upstairs."

"You have been escorting her when she goes in the grounds have you not?"

"Of course, we have been following your instructions and not leaving her alone outside."

"Is the building work progressing as it should?"

"Oh, very much so! You will be pleased when you see what they have achieved in your absence."

"I shall see the supervisor after I have washed and change, is Agnes upstairs?"

Anne and William exchange a look. "Agnes has not been well these last few days. I think the London visit has tired her out," Anne says.

Bess sent Agnes ahead with the others and is concerned to hear about her ill heath.

"I shall see her at once." Bess starts to climb the stairs. "Anne, will you tell the servants to serve some light food in an hour?"

"Of course"

The brief period that Anne has had in charge is now over, and she follows William back to his study before closing the door.

"How much longer will we be living with your mother, William?"

He has sat down and is already looking through papers. Outside there is the noise of hammering where the workmen are building and she pulls the window latch to try and deaden the sound.

"I do not know, why?" he replies, only half listening.

"This house is not big enough for us all. And your mother is ..." she hesitates, aware that his mother can do no wrong in his eyes.

"Is what ...?"

"You know what I am trying to say. She is a very strong character; it is never easy with two women in one house. Sometimes I feel she takes over our whole lives."

There is a catch in her throat as she says it, and William immediately looks up at her in concern. "I know she is not the easiest person to live with, but I would have thought in your condition, you would welcome having someone to run the house and servants. This is her home after all," he adds gently.

"I know, it is just that, she is such a presence everywhere. I feel nothing is my own."

"You must not think that!" He gets up and puts his arms round her. "As soon as the New Hall is finished, she will move in with Arbella."

"But where will we live? I do not want to be here, so close to the New Hall."

"Neither do I, my love. A new house will be built for us within a reasonable distance. Not too close, but not too far away; you need have no fear. The Old Hall will just be used for guests."

"What a pity we cannot have Chatsworth, I would so love to call it my home. Henry does not deserve it; and anyway he cannot afford to live there."

"He may not always have Chatsworth, Anne."

"What do you mean? It is entailed on him."

"He may want to sell it one day."

"Could we buy it?" she asks, excited at the idea.

"We shall wait and see. Now why not go and rest before we eat?"

He turns back to his papers and she realises he is not interested in further discussion. The banging and hammering seems to be getting worse, and she silently curses it under her breath as she goes to the kitchens to give Bess' instructions. The house feels very different now she is back.

Upstairs, Bess finds Agnes lying on her bed, clutching her stomach.

"What is it, my dear?" she crouches beside her and reaches for her hand.

Agnes can only look at her with wide eyes that are full of pain.

"Is it very bad?"

"I fear I cannot serve you ever again."

The effort of speaking causes her face to distort, and Bess is horrified at the rapid change since she saw her only a week ago.

"This is my fault, you were not well enough to visit London. I should never have let you come. You should have stayed here and rested."

Agnes shakes her head. "Ruby is not ready yet to take over from me."

"But she soon will be." A local girl, Ruby, has been with the household for the past year and has recently started to help Agnes with her duties.

"Do not worry about it. You must get into bed and rest. I shall send for Dr. Hunton right away, and he will give you something for the pain."

Agnes begins to cry, which Bess has never seen in all the time they have been together. She is full of concern for the woman who has been so loyal to her for more years than either of them care to remember.

"Come, I will help you to get into bed."

"No, you cannot, it would not be right, your grace"

"Nonsense! Of course I can help you."

Agnes does not have the energy to argue and allows Bess to undress her. The swelling of her stomach is all too obvious, and Bess sees it with a sinking heart. She pulls the covers up and tucks her in as if she was a small child.

"I will send to the kitchen for some broth, could you manage a little?"

Agnes nods, her eyes closed.

Bess draws the curtains with a final sad look before hurrying to give the orders for Agnes' comfort and dispatch a rider for the doctor. She decides to look at the building work now, and hoisting up her skirts, she makes her way upwards to what will be the Great High Chamber on the top floor. The overseer is checking the plans with one of the hundreds of workmen. They see her picking her way through the assortment of materials that are strewn across the floor; the noise of sawing, hammering and banging is deafening.

"On guard now, lad, here is the countess," mutters the overseer, and they stand up at once.

"Your grace," they say in unison and remove their caps, bowing deferentially.

"I have come to see the progress you have made in the eight months I have been away."

They begin to show her round the last part of the building work, pointing out areas of difficulty or particular importance. She spends several minutes intensely studying the plaster and stone work where intricate designs have been crafted to her own exact specifications. It shows the Cavendish and Hardwick heraldic devices over the fireplace, and as Bess still had not given up hope of the queen visiting, there are even royal devices entwined in her own. Stone for the walls has been brought from Bess' own local quarries, lead boarding for the roof from her mines and timber for the joists and beams from her forests; thus keeping costs to a minimum. The men wait with some trepidation, knowing her standards are very high.

"Have there been any more problems with supplies?" she asks, having in mind the problem they had with glass, which came from Gilbert's glazier.

"No, your grace, since you set up your own, they are able to keep up with demand. Would you like to see the most recent work of the carpenters and painters?"

"I would like to see it all," Bess replies firmly and waits for them to lead the way.

As they go round, she stops to talk to a few of the workmen, some of whom she knows by name, as they have worked for many years on her building projects. After nearly an hour, she is satisfied and finally goes back to the Old Hall to change. Ruby is waiting for her, her manner subdued.

"How is Agnes, your grace? She will not allow anyone to look after her."

"I am afraid she has not got long to live. I have seen such growths before and the result is always the same. I have sent for Dr. Hunton and he will be here very soon. Do not fret yourself about her, I shall make sure she is made as comfortable as possible for her last days on earth."

Ruby nods, fighting back tears. She washes Bess' face and hands with rosewater and helps her into a clean black gown and ruff. Bess becomes slightly impatient with her slowness, as Ruby fumbles to dress her.

"Leave my headdress for now, I am at home with the family," Bess tells her. "Unpack all my gowns, check them for any sewing needed before you send the soiled ones to the laundry, together with the ruffs. I remember there was a slight tear in the gown with the silver edging. Brush out the furs from the winter wardrobe and hang to air, clean all my jewellery and replace in caskets. I have my undergarments washed by Agnes, not the laundry, so you must do so too. My shoes will need to be cleaned and tell the boys who carry the water, I shall be bathing tonight. Do you have any questions?"

"No, your grace." Ruby hides her dismay at the thought of having to do these tasks without Agnes.

"I do not want Agnes disturbed and I wish to be told when Dr. Hunton has seen her."

Ruby curtseys and Bess returns downstairs again to join William and Anne who are waiting to eat.

"Arbella says she is not hungry," Anne tells Bess. "I have left her reading on the bed."

Bess does not reply, but it is clear she is unimpressed that her granddaughter has not appeared to welcome her, but her mood quickly changes when she looks at the food set out for them. Today there is boiled beef, cheese, manchet bread, venison pasties, roast chicken, a spiced custard pie, apple fritters and oranges. Several flagons of the best wine and ale complete the meal.

"I must go through the accounts with you and Timothy as soon as possible," she says as they sit down at the dining table and begin to help themselves to the dishes.

"Of course lady mother, it would not be the same without your signature on every page of the accounts book," William jokes and Bess shakes her finger at him in mock indignation.

"If I did not check every last entry, I would not be able to sleep at night."

Anne is not asked or encouraged to play any part in the running of Bess' many business ventures or even the household accounts, so she remains silent. Bess notices Anne looking left out of this banter and changes the subject.

"Have you told Anne about the land at Owlcotes?" she asks William.

"Not yet, I did not know if the purchase had gone through," he replies and Anne looks curiously at both of them as she tries to eat some cheese to stave off the nausea.

"I have bought some nearby manors so that I can build a house for you both at Owlcotes. The land is just right and I have found an ideal location to build."

"It sounds wonderful," responds Anne, hoping her voice sounds suitably grateful.

"Yes," echoes William. "It is very exciting. A brand new house, built to our own specifications."

"The manors were farmed by my father and grandfather before him, so they are special to me. I hope you will be pleased, the purchase was quite costly, but I believe it was worth it. Your happiness is very important to me."

She reaches across the table to touch Anne's hand.

"You are very generous, lady mother."

Bess smiles at them both, it always give her much pleasure to help her family; if only Arbella's future could be settled so well.

֍

Old Hardwick Hall – September 1592

Anne is asleep beside William, but in her dream the banging is getting worse. Louder and more insistent, it will not go away, as if there is a hammer inside her head. She hears it all day, and now at night, so it will surely drive her mad. But she knows it is night, so why are the workmen here?

With a start, she opens her eyes and realises it is not a dream; someone is hammering on the front door as if their life depends on it. Early morning light is edging in through the curtains and outside the birds are singing their hearts out. Is anyone going to open the door? It seems to have been going on for ages.

"William!" She nudges him. "The front door."

"Let the servants answer it," is his sleepy reply but she persists.

"They are not answering, you must go yourself."

Cursing under his breath, he lights a candle and stumbles out of bed, pulling his nightshirt down in an attempt to be decent. He gets half way down the stairs, when a young lad finally appears by the door and struggles to unlock the great oak door. A rider stands outside holding his horse's reins with one hand and a letter in the other. William strides forward to take it himself.

"Urgent letter from Lord Burghley, Sir William," announces the messenger breathlessly.

William bids the man to wait in the kitchen. He hurries back upstairs to his mother's bedchamber and knocks sharply.

"Come," Bess shouts. As he expects when he opens the door, she is already up and wide-awake, with several candles already burning.

"Is it one of the family?" she says, fear in her voice.

"No, from Lord Burghley." He hands the letter to her, his expression anxious.

Arbella, in her bed at the other end of the chamber, sits up in a daze, trying to focus and rubs her eyes. Sleepy servants emerge behind Anne as she waits by the open door, their candles flickering in the inky darkness. Letters that arrive at dawn are always important. They hear Wylkyn crying and his nurse trying to comfort him. Everyone waits as Bess holds the letter near the flames and reads it.

"He has discovered another plot to kidnap Arbella, convert her to Catholicism in Spain, where she will remain until the death of our queen, then return to claim the throne as rightful heir. There is a Jesuit priest involved who confessed under torture." She looks up, her face pale.

"God's bones! They are still trying to get her!" William says, clearly shocked.

Before anyone can blink, Arbella is swiftly out of bed and clinging onto Anne in desperation.

"Oh no, no! They will keep trying until they succeed! They know where I am, they will find me in my bed and kill you all!"

Then she swoons and collapses to the floor, almost pulling Anne down with her.

"There, there," William says soothingly, going over to help her. "You must not be afraid, you are quite safe here with us."

"I am never safe – I need a husband to protect me."

"We can protect you," Bess reassures her. "You must stay calm …"

"Calm!" shrieks Arbella. "You talk of calm, it is easy for you. It is not you they wish to kidnap! I must get away from here at once, far far away! I shall leave now."

She shrugs off William's help and gets to her feet, looking around in confusion. Anne puts out her hand to try and steady her, but Arbella pushes her away roughly.

"Careful, Anne is with child!" William says anxiously. "Go back to bed, my love, there is nothing you can do here," he tells his wife and she disappears gratefully, not wanting to have any more to do with this latest scene of Arbella's.

"Come here, child, and rest, you can share my bed tonight if you wish. Will that make you feel any better?"

Arbella looks at Bess as if she is insane and begins to laugh in a queer, high-pitched way.

"No, you old fool, that will not help me to feel better! I must think of what to do."

"Arbella!" William is horrified at her language, but Bess holds up a hand to silence him.

"Everyone return to your beds. I will deal with this."

"Are you sure lady mother? She is very unstable," William whispers as they watch Arbella darting backwards and forwards at the window, her hair dishevelled and wringing her hands repeatedly.

"Yes, an audience makes her worse."

He reluctantly leaves and closes the door on the inquisitive stares of the servants.

"You heard the countess, be about your work, the day is upon us."

Bess goes over to open one of her chests and begins to look at her gowns, apparently ignoring her granddaughter. After some minutes Arbella stops pacing and stares at the view, her fingers scratching the glass. Bess watches surreptitiously and carefully judges the right time to speak. Lord Burghley's letter has been hidden in one of the drawers, out of sight. Arbella begins to sigh and hold her head with two hands; Bess goes over to her quietly, she sees that her granddaughter's fingernails are so bitten down that there is hardly any nail remaining.

"Is your head giving you pain, child?"

"Yes," her reply is muffled.

"Then come and lie down, I will get you a warm posset to help you get back to sleep."

Bess guides her over to the bed, murmuring soft reassurances all the time and Arbella seems calmer, lying down quietly. Once her eyes are closed, Bess makes her way to the kitchen and waits while a lowly kitchen maid, already up and stoking the ovens, prepares a posset. But by the time Bess returns, the bed is empty and Arbella has gone.

"Arbella! Arbella! Where are you?" she shouts and runs into the passage. William appears again and they search together, opening doors and calling for the servants to help. Within half an hour the whole house has been checked and Bess is getting frantic.

"Where can she be? Surely she has not left the grounds!"

"Could she have taken a horse?"

"The stables are locked, the gatekeeper would never have let her go."

"She is playing a jape on us!"

"If it is, I do not find it funny. We must find her and quickly!"

Several of the servants are sent to search the outbuildings and grounds, returning with dejected faces.

"She cannot have gone far; she is not dressed," Bess tries to reason and looks at William for inspiration.

They are standing in deep thought in the Hall when Bess notices a movement out of the corner of her eye, Arbella has appeared from the direction of the kitchen. She is carrying what looks like a chicken leg, and has obviously been eating, as the remnants of food are down the front of her nightclothes.

"Where on earth have you been hiding? We have searched the whole house!" Bess is furious and desperate to shake some sense into her. "The servants have better things to do than spend their time looking for you, as do the rest of us. Whatever were you thinking of?"

Arbella is unperturbed. "I was hungry," she announces and continues gnawing at the meat. "I have been in the game larder. I saw someone looking for me but I hid. Was that not clever of me?"

Bess and William can only look at her in disbelief. "Tell the other servants she has been found," Bess says to William. "After breakfast we must have an urgent meeting, and I will write back to Lord Burghley."

Beckoning to the chief steward, she quietly tells him to lock all the external doors so that Arbella cannot go outside. The windows too, must have the handles removed for the time being. She is not taking any chances, given Arbella's current state of mind. It will be inconvenient for everyone else, but it cannot be helped.

"If you have had enough to eat now, perhaps you had better go back to bed," Bess tells her.

"Yes," she replies dreamily. "I will do as you say."

She ceremoniously hands the chicken bone to the nearest servant and wipes the grease down her nightdress, before walking past everyone to go upstairs, humming a tune as she does so. The servants melt way and Bess is left to follow her, unsure of what her granddaughter will do next.

૭૩૮૦

Hardwick Old Hall, Derbyshire

My good Lord Burghley,

Your letter arrived at dawn this morning and has troubled me greatly. The thought of wicked people attempting to capture my dear Arbella for their own ends is truly shocking, but we must admit to ourselves that such plots are no less than we expected. My diligence in protecting Arbella continues to be of the highest level. I never permit unknown or suspect persons entry to the house, and Arbella is not permitted to walk outside alone at any time. I do not allow her to go to anyone's house, although she would wish it. She is with me almost every hour of the day, or at least very nearby. Do not think that she lacks company though; my house has enough to keep her occupied. At night, she shares my bedchamber and when I wake she is the first person I see and the last before I close my eyes.

I plan a visit to Chatsworth with Arbella shortly, where the arrangements will be just as stringent at all times. Please reassure Her Gracious Majesty of my continued devotion to this task, and of my continued humble desire to serve her at all times. This letter has been written for me by my son William, as I have a great pain on one side of my head and I am unable to write this morning. Written this day xv September 1592

Elizabeth Shrewsbury

Hardwick Hall – March 1593

"I forbid it Charles! It is absolute madness!"

"You will not stop me, lady mother, I mean to show my friendship for Gilbert."

Bess looks at him in annoyance as they face each other across her desk. Timothy has been sent from the chamber and William stands behind his mother, where he has positioned himself.

"Why should you get involved with Gilbert's problems? He would not rush to defend you I am sure."

Charles had been reluctant to visit Bess, as he knew she would try and stop him from going through with a duel against his old friend John Stanhope, in two days time.

"I do not understand what this is all about," says William. "It seems to be a lot of fuss over a weir, which Gilbert has no rights over anyway."

"You are both acting like spoilt children," says Bess. "I know that Gilbert holds a grudge because he was not granted the posts of Earl Marshall of England and Lord Lieutenant of Nottinghamshire. He expected it on the death of his father, but we cannot be sure that John spoke in favour of his own brother for the posts, and not Gilbert."

"John promised to speak in his favour and clearly reneged on his word. I do not blame Gilbert for being angry."

"But they have been friends for so many years!" exclaims Bess.

"You should not have become involved in this dispute," William scolds.

Charles gives him a withering look. "Why does William have to be here, lady mother? This is none of his business. He is always at your side these days, it is very tedious for the rest of us."

"He is here because I wish it."

"I would speak to you alone." He folds him arms obstinately.

"I will get to hear it all anyway, you might as well let me stay," William mutters.

"You may be our mother's favourite, but my life is not your concern, so you can go back to your bookkeeping."

"I do not have favourites, Charles! For the sake of peace, leave us William." Bess raise her eyes to heaven. "Are you boys never to grow up?"

After he has gone, Bess asks Charles to pour them both some wine from the flagon on the table at the side. She studies his back with affection, broad shouldered and fit, he has recently remarried and it suits him, for he looks better than she has seen for a long time.

"Well, what about this attack on the weir?" she asks as he hands her the glass.

"Gilbert says the local people have been disadvantaged since the Stanhopes built it," he replies.

"How so?"

"It creates a sediment which means they cannot wash their linen."

"I heard his men were breaking it up with pickaxes, how does that help the situation? I suspect Gilbert is not at all bothered by the weir, but used it as an excuse to cause trouble."

"You do not understand how very upset he was by being passed over for those posts, he saw it as an insult to the family name and a lack of confidence in his ability."

"This duel of yours will not solve the problem, it will only make matters worse. Can you not see that?"

"I want to defend the good name of my friend. I know you disapprove of my friendship with him and you are not on speaking terms any more, but you must understand that our friendship means a lot to me. This feud will not go away..."

"...so you think by getting yourself killed in a duel that will be the end of it."

Charles touches the hilt of his sword lightly. "It is not I who will be injured. I am a first rate swordsman, as you know. I have insisted on certain terms which he has agreed to, so it is all arranged."

Bess tries one more time. "If this matter is not settled quickly it will affect Arbella's standing at Court. For her uncle to be seen brawling with a man such as Stanhope will be very damaging. If it comes to it, the queen will take Stanhope's side, as she knows him better than you. There is one thing that her majesty will not tolerate, and that is fighting courtiers. It is a big mistake Charles, to antagonise a man on the rise at Court, I learnt that from your grandfather."

"Yes, yes, I know it is flattery, favours and gifts that have more influence. I refuse to bow to such superficial means."

"It may be superficial, but it is how to survive. Had I not be able to play the game by their rules, how long do you think I would have lasted? I would be a nobody, married to some obscure squire in the country and living off a pittance."

He laughs at the very idea.

"No lady mother, you know as well as I do that would never have happened. For once, you will not have your way, I will not be dissuaded. " He gets up and drains his glass. "I must ride south at once, I am already behind time by calling in to see you."

"Where is this duel to take place?"

"On Lambeth Bridge at dawn."

"I beg you to take care, Charles! Please think again about this foolish enterprise."

He pauses as he pulls on his gloves. "Do not fret lady mother, I shall return afterwards and we will toast my victory."

"Will you write word of the result as soon as it is over?"

"I will do better, I shall come back to Derbyshire at once. I have my new wife Catherine to come back to now."

Charles kisses her cheek briefly and she watches him leave, fighting back the tears she does not want him to see. When William returns a few minutes later, he finds her sobbing quietly and he can say nothing to reassure her.

ೞ෮

Lambeth Bridge, London
(Two days later, 6.55am)

Charles has been up since 5am, unable to sleep. Bess has not been the only one to try and dissuade him from this course of action. His new wife Catherine, her pale face edged with anxiety, also begged him not to go through with it, but Charles has his mother's stubbornness and will not be swayed. Sword fighting and fencing are sports which he has always enjoyed, winning prizes at Eton and becoming so good, that he would give informal lessons to other pupils. Gilbert is touched by his friend's loyalty, not having the wish to engage in a duel himself, although his wife Mary has said she would happily take on the whole of the Stanhope family if she could. He knows she would too, for her strong and dominant personality is comparable to Bess'. She has the same determination, although she lacks her mother's charisma, political awareness and business mind. Having heard that Charles, her favourite brother, is to fight this duel, she berates Gilbert and accuses him of "letting Charles do his dirty work." Gilbert tells her that no one can persuade Charles not to go through with it, but she does not want to believe him.

Charles is excited rather than nervous. He knows he is the more capable swordsman, but there is always the possibility that something could go wrong on the day. Jarvis Markham, his second, sensibly steered him away from the taverns last night, and made sure he was in bed by ten o'clock. The morning has dawned bright and dry, the sun casting sharp shadows on the water as it gently laps along the banks of the Thames. The two of them wait patiently on the bridge, talking quietly and scanning the road for Stanhope. A small crowd of early stallholders has gathered, realising that something is going to happen and do not want to miss it; a duel is especially exciting for them because such events are illegal. Already they are betting on a winner. Charles has made certain conditions, which Stanhope has agreed to honour; the main one is that the men will fight in their shirtsleeves. Just a few minutes after 7am, Stanhope and his second appear, there is a murmur of anticipation from the crowd.

"Cavendish," says Stanhope curtly, by way of greeting. He is paunchy and does not look as ready as Charles.

"Stanhope," replies Charles, equally blunt, and begins to take off his cloak. The seconds mark out the area to be used and the weapons are examined. Then Charles notices that Stanhope has not taken off his doublet.

"We agreed shirtsleeves, or have you forgotten?" he growls.

"No, but I have a cold, I will have to keep it on," replies Stanhope defiantly.

Jarvis immediately approaches him and feels it. "This is a very thick doublet, you will have to remove it."

"I will not."

Charles feels it for himself and shakes his head in disbelief. "I am not fighting you with that on! Do not be ridiculous, take it off and let us continue. I want my breakfast."

He gives a few parries with his sword, eager to start the fight.

"I will not remove it." He stands looking at them and Charles gives a laugh of disbelief.

"Well perhaps you should have my doublet too, if you have a cold." He gestures for Jarvis to hand over his own. "We cannot have you suffering can we? I shall stay in my shirtsleeves, then at least one of us will be dressed honourably."

There is a ripple of laughter from the crowd, who can hear the conversation and begin jeering. Both Charles and Jarvis are now chuckling, but Stanhope is adamant that his doublet remains on.

"If you will not remove it then we must call it an unequal match," says Jarvis.

"I agree, the fight cannot go ahead," echoes Stanhope's second.

Charles is furious but there is nothing he can do.

"Oh, I see this was all a deliberate ploy on your part to avoid the fight! I might have know you would resort to such a pathetic deception. I think that you have realised you would never win against a superior swordsman like myself."

"We shall take our leave." Stanhope puts on his cloak again, and looks at Charles with as much dignity as he can manage after such a loss of face.

"Your friend the Earl of Shrewsbury has not heard the last of this! Tell him we shall see him in the Courts," he threatens.

With this, they turn on their heels and disappear, the sound of jeering and sniggering from the crowd following them until they are out of sight. With the release of tension, Charles and Jarvis are now shaking with laughter and have to sit down to regain their composure. Applause breaks out from the crowd and they give a mock salute to them in acknowledgement.

"Come on Charles, let us find some breakfast. I have worked up quite an appetite."

Linking arms, they make their way over the bridge and the crowd reluctantly disperse; there is to be no duel after all.

଼ଃଓ

It is only two months after this failed duel that Bess decides to move to Chatsworth until the New Hall is finished. Aware that Anne finds her presence awkward, she thinks it is best to distance herself, and visit regularly, instead to check on the progress of the building work. Arbella's health has improved and she seems more settled for the time being, writing long letters in her neat hand to her Aunt Mary, Gilbert's wife, as well as the Earl of Essex. Bess could prevent this communication, but is aware that Arbella will find a way of reaching them anyway. Also indirectly, it is a way for her to keep in touch with Mary and find out her news as her own contact with the Shrewsburys has been minimal since George's death. It is therefore quite a surprise one morning, when a servant announces that Mary has arrived without warning, and is waiting in the Hall. She goes at once to greet her and they exchange the briefest of kisses.

"Mary, how good it is to see you. I hope all is well with everyone; I do so miss your girls, Mary,

Elizabeth and Alathea, I think of them often," she says wistfully.

"We are all well, lady mother. I hope you do not mind me coming to see you, I was passing and thought I would call in."

Bess knows this is a lie, but says nothing. She has a good idea of the reason for the visit and they sit by the fire as servants bring refreshments, Bess waving them away when they have finished.

"Arbella seems in good spirits," observes Mary. "You know she writes to me? Of course you do, you know everything."

Bess lets this comment pass and waits for Mary to get to the point.

"The weather does not get any better," says Mary, sipping her wine and looking through the window.

"No, we have had a lot of rain." The two women both study the contents of the glasses and after half a minute, Bess takes the initiative.

"I am delighted to see you after all this time, but I am wondering what has prompted you to visit me."

Mary gets up and walks about restlessly, clearly uncomfortable about it.

"You have likely guessed the reason for my visit. I may as well come out with it. We are in debt, even worse than usual. Our expenses far outweigh our income."

"No changes there," Bess cannot resist commenting.

"Gilbert is alienating all his family, one by one. He has challenged his brother Edward to a duel over a silly lease, but Edward has more sense and refused to fight his own flesh and blood. Now he is claiming that Edward is trying to poison his gloves, of all things!

You must have heard about the ambush of the Stanhopes in Fleet Street?"

"Oh yes, I heard about it."

"That was so shameful."

"No more shameful than your message to Sir Thomas Stanhope."

"How do you know about that?"

"My dear Mary, he has sent details of your comments to Lord Burghley. Apparently when her majesty found out, she was not very complimentary about you."

At this, Mary looks annoyed, but quickly recovers her composure. "What did she say?"

"That you lead Gilbert in all things, or words to that effect."

"I wish he would take notice of me then he might not be making such a mess of his life. Gilbert is so afraid now that he will only eat at home when we are in London, as he thinks the Stanhopes are out to poison him. I am at my wits end with it all!" She begins to cry and Bess frowns.

"You have my sympathy Mary, but as I know myself, when a woman is married to a man whose personality and intelligence is no match for her own, there is trouble."

"We do try to economise, but we have a certain status to maintain when we are in London. Everything is so costly!"

"I suppose you want me to help you. How much does Gilbert need?"

Mary looks at her through tears of self-pity. "A thousand pounds would go far to reduce our liabilities."

Bess hides her shock at the sum, which is more than she imagined.

"Will you promise me that you will try to manage the accounts better in future? I have always kept a meticulous record of where my money is spent, whether it is given to the poor at the gates or spent on gifts for the queen. Do you write all your expenditure down as I suggested?"

"I must confess I do not have your discipline for bookkeeping."

"It is not discipline Mary! You need to know exactly where the money is being spent! You have never wanted for anything in your life, so you have no knowledge of fighting for your rights as I myself have had on many occasions. I was not born with a knowledge of how to handle my finances, it is a skill I have had to learn."

"Yes, that is all very well, but some of us do not have your knack of making money, we are not as talented."

"It is not a question of talent, but simply living within your means. I have offered to help Gilbert to manage his money and I am more than happy to do so, but he has made it clear he does not wish it."

"But we are the Earl and Countess of Shrewsbury now! How will it look to everyone if cannot live as we should?"

"You must give fewer parties, buy less meat, avoid card games, cut down on your servants, make do with old clothes; I could go on."

Mary holds up her hands in mock horror and sits down again.

"Please do not continue, lady mother. It all sounds too depressing." She sniffs and regards her mother anxiously.

"I will loan you and Gilbert the money, but you are aware that he still owes me £1,000 from last year when he wrote that it was a particularly difficult period for him."

"Yes, I did know about it. We are grateful," she adds and finishes her drink in one gulp.

"I will arrange for the money to be sent over this afternoon," Bess tells her.

"Thank you," Mary says, her head bowed.

"I assume now you have got what you wanted, you will be leaving."

Mary has wiped her eyes but she remains tearful.

"Is there something else you wish to tell me?" Bess asks.

"It is just …," she hesitates, then her words come tumbling out.

"Gilbert is very disappointed with his life. When the old earl died, we assumed that all his titles and honours would be passed to Gilbert. As you know, this has not happened and he feels very resentful, especially as the two most important posts were given to Stanhope. He believes this is very unfair. He will not listen to me when I tell him that such posts have to be earned, not just given out like sweetmeats. He says I nag him all the time, which I suppose I do occasionally, but he makes me so cross with his constant moaning and blaming everyone else when anything goes wrong. His father had a bad opinion of me and Gilbert has started to agree with his viewpoint. Soon we shall have no-one in the Shrewsbury family speaking to us, as he has had bad words with all of them."

There is a long silence after this speech and Bess gives a sigh.

"What do you expect me to do about it?"

"Nothing!" Mary stiffens with animosity. "You did quite enough by arranging my marriage to him in the first place. I wish I had been born Frances, she was allowed to marry for love and is so happy now with Henry and the children."

"But she is not the Countess of Shrewsbury, as you are. You were pleased enough to be joined to a family such as the Shrewsburys at the time, I seem to remember."

"The title only came to me because Gilbert's older brother died. I did not seek it."

"But you enjoy the prestige and power it gives you, what woman would not?"

"This discussion is unhelpful, I shall go now." She stands up impatiently. "I thank you for the money, lady mother. Gilbert will write and show his gratitude, I shall make sure of it."

After a cursory embrace, Mary hurries out to her waiting carriage. Bess watches her depart from the window and turns away in resignation; it depresses her to acknowledge that her daughter only sees her when she wants money.

꼐꽁

Hardwick Hall – November 1595

"You had no right to ask the Earl of Essex to visit without my permission! Have you also asked his wife?"

"No, of course I am not interested in his wife, that dull as ditch water, Frances! Why should I not ask him, he is my good friend? The best friend I have. Because he is a favourite of the queen, you cannot forbid it; he is coming for my twentieth birthday and you cannot change it."

Bess and Arbella, now back at Old Hardwick Hall, are eating breakfast when Arbella makes this announcement, much to the fury of her grandmother. William and Anne sit in silence, watching and listening as they try to eat.

"You will change it, you will write today and cancel the visit."

Arbella looks at Bess triumphantly. "It will look very strange if I do that, lady grandmother; the queen knows of it."

Bess reflects on her last encounter with the earl and realises she will have to do some quick thinking. She finds him a dangerous adversary due to his unwholesome influence on Arbella, and his streak of self-destructive ambition, which she recognised some while ago. It will not be possible to stop the visit now, she realises that much, but she can certainly have control over the circumstances under which Arbella will see him in her own home. It also occurs to her that the visit will serve as a reminder to the queen that Arbella is still unmarried, and has not been to Court for these three years, so it is not all unwelcome news.

She smiles and pushes her plate away, wiping her mouth on a linen napkin.

"Very well child, I shall entertain the earl as you wish for your birthday, and I shall do so with good grace, although it goes against my better judgement to have him here."

Arbella looks smug. "Good, I am glad you have seen the sense of it, lady grandmother."

"I will start to plan his welcome at once." She turns to William, "Will you write to all the family and say I shall expect them to join us?"

William nods in acquiescence, his mouth full of food. Arbella's face falls at this instruction.

"Oh no, it is not necessary for all the family to be here as well! I want it to be an informal visit, he will only be joined by two friends."

"Arbella, his visit is a great honour," she says smoothly. "It would be unthinkable not to invite the family and our friends in the neighbourhood, especially for your birthday."

"But I had planned it to be a very quiet visit … "

"It is out of your hands now, Arbella. There will be many people wishing to meet him and spend time in his company, we must not deny them the opportunity."

"As long as I will have some time with him, I suppose it will be all right."

"Do not get your hopes up, child, I doubt there will be any time for you to see him unless it is in sight of everyone."

"But it is my birthday!" she says petulantly.

"And you shall have a wonderful time, as you always do on such occasions."

Bess gets up and Arbella can only glower in frustration that she has been out manoeuvred by her grandmother, and it looks as if the visit will not be at all what she had hoped. William and Anne exchange a look of despair, the frequent clashes between Bess and Arbella make for an uncomfortable atmosphere in the house, but they can do nothing to help ease the tensions between the two women. By the time of Arbella's birthday and the Earl of Essex's arrival, Bess has ensured that everything possible has been done to provide the best comfort, food, lavish entertainment, hunting and sport for her guests. On the second and last evening, Arbella is becoming desperate to spend some time alone with her hero. She has been thwarted at every turn by circumstances, and Bess always seems to be one step ahead of her. The earl is never seated next to Arbella at any meal, William and Charles monopolise him at every opportunity, apparently eager to hear of his military views on defeating the Spanish or subduing the Irish. Bess keeps him occupied from dawn to dusk with every outdoor sport that she can offer. All the frustrated Arbella can do is gaze forlornly at her hero from the other side of the table.

Bess has avoided any conversation with the earl other than banal pleasantries, but she finds herself unavoidably alone at the table with him during a dance. He pours himself some wine and leans back in his chair as if quite at ease.

"It must have cost you dear to allow my visit, countess"

"Do you mean in monetary terms or my conscience?"

"Nothing so sordid as to refer to the cost. Of course I meant you do not wish me to be here with access to your precious jewel." He looks across at where Arbella is dancing reluctantly with an elderly friend of the family.

"Have I given you that impression?"

"No, you have been the perfect hostess. I shall tell the queen I was treated like a king when I return to London."

"I believe you could easily become accustomed to such treatment," replies Bess lightly.

"What are you implying? That I have the highest of aspirations?"

"I am implying nothing, but in truth you cannot deny it, can you?"

"I think you are trying to trap me, countess!" He laughs. "All I wish to do is to serve our queen. As you can see from the honours she gives me, my efforts are much appreciated."

Bess stays silent and he lights his pipe, blowing smoke over her and laughing to himself.

"Still no husband for your prize jewel," he says and shakes his head. "She must be wondering if she is ever to marry, at twenty years of age, she is not so young."

"A suitable husband will be found, in good time," replies Bess.

"Of course, I am sure they are queuing up all over Europe for the privilege. Whether or not the queen will ever give permission for her to marry is another matter."

"There is still plenty of time, do not trouble yourself to give it any thought."

"I do not, countess, I have much more important matters to occupy me." He leans across and lowers his voice, "You do me wrong to believe that I wish to seduce your granddaughter. I am an honourable man, despite what you may think of me. I feel sorry for Lady Arbella, she is a sweet girl who is a pawn in a game over which she has no control. She has an unhappy life and I am afraid for her as I cannot see that it will improve."

"Arbella does not need your pity!" responds Bess crisply. "What a shame your visit will end tomorrow. Excuse me."

She gets up and he places his hand over hers in a firm grip.

"If I have spoken out of turn, you must forgive me. I am a soldier first and foremost, my language is sometimes clumsy."

Despite these sentiments, apparently expressed so sincerely, Bess pulls her hand away and with a cold stare at him, she makes her way over to where William is standing and watching the dancing.

"Is everything all right, lady mother?" he asks, having seen the way Bess left the table.

"Quite all right," she replies. "The earl and I do not always agree on certain matters so our conversations are always lively."

They look at each other knowingly.

"I see," he says. "Our guests will be leaving tomorrow and you can relax again."

"How is Anne this evening?"

"Tired, little Gilbert is teething and she attends to him herself rather than leave it to the nurse. She is not getting much sleep."

"Being with child so soon has not helped matters," Bess tells him, a slight reproach in her voice.

"I know, it was not our intention, but you will soon have an army of grandchildren to dote on at this rate."

"And I love them all," she says, her mood changing whenever they are mentioned. "But I am weary tonight, I shall go to my bed."

Signalling for Ruby, who waits in the corner, she takes her arm and they leave together. William is suprised; he has never known his mother to retire this early before.

෴

New Hardwick Hall is still unfinished, but Bess is impatient to live there, so she decides to move in anyway, in time to celebrate her seventieth birthday. Anne and William's son Wylkyn (7) is now a boisterous, energetic boy, but there is great sadness when their son, Gilbert, dies the year before, as well as two daughters who do not survive infancy. Their only daughter alive now is little Frances, but Anne is expecting another child due in the spring of 1598, much to everyone's joy.

෴

31 October 1597

Today the two houses are in a state of disarray, as all the household items that Bess has been storing over the years are moved into the New Hall. There is furniture from Chatsworth brought over in covered carts, protected against the drizzle that began at first light. Crates, carpets, trunks and coffers containing clothes, linens, bedding, paintings, thick curtains, rugs, plate, Arbella's books, her lute, virginals and personal possessions are all gradually put into place before Bess' birthday on the 4th of November.

A family celebration is planned, this time organised by William and Charles, and they are in the kitchen to look at the food for the big day. In one of the pantries the cook has placed dishes of venison, geese, peacocks, pheasants, partridges, larks, quails, capons, a swan and a whole pig roast. A long oak table holds large silver plates of salmon, turbot, anchovies, oysters and eel in vinegar sauce, together with bowls of green salad leaves such as mint, fennel, watercress, cucumber and parsley. There are dishes of boiled potatoes for those daring enough to try such a new vegetable. They inspect the cheese and custard tarts, preserved fruits, jellies, marzipan moulded into flowers and animals, their delicate edges tinged with gold leaf.

"A fine feast," murmurs William, his mouth watering.

The cook stands watching, his hands on his hips, coughing noisily if either of them look likely to sample any of the food. They manage to leave with a pasty each, and eat it standing by the blazing fire in the Hall.

"Our lady mother seems in good health," observes Charles. "She is indestructible."

"Indomitable."

"Inexhaustible." They both laugh.

"Infallible?"

"No, I cannot allow that one!" Charles almost chokes on a piece of pastry.

"Seriously, she is upset that you always take Gilbert's side against her," William says.

"She misjudges him all the time. They do not always have to be enemies, think how well they used to be together. I sometimes used to think she preferred Gilbert to us."

At this William looks astounded. "I have never thought so."

"Well, Gilbert and Mary need my friendship as never before. I am not going to forsake them just to keep our mother happy."

"I think you are making a mistake. Gilbert has a lot of his father's personality. Do you not see how he has been making trouble for his family and friends?"

"He has never made trouble for me."

William makes a sound of defeat and changes the subject; an argument with his brother is the last thing he wants. "Has work commenced on your own new house at Kirkby-in-Ashby yet?"

"They are laying the foundations as we speak, in the meantime I am renting Welbeck Abbey from Gilbert, Catherine likes it there."

"Have you seen the outside carvings here at the top of the towers yet?"

"No, the stonemasons were still working on them the last time I looked; what has been done?"

"Come and see for yourself."

William and Charles make their way towards the front door and walk outside until they are about forty feet away, before turning round to face the front of the house. Charles gives an enormous gasp of awe, staring up at what he sees. For Bess has proclaimed her wealth and power to the world; her initials ES stand in large carved letters at the top of the six roof top corner pavilions. Resting above each set of initials, sits the coronets of a countess, surrounded by stone scroll embellishments. The building itself, made of sandstone from Bess' own quarries, is dominated by windows which become bigger as they reach the upper floor; already the locals have a rhyme about it, '*Hardwick Hall, more glass than wall.*' There can be no doubt who the house belongs to, nor the achievements and confidence of its builder and owner. The two brothers do not speak, but look at one another in wonder; this is a triumph of self-promotion on a grand and magnificent scale.

From her bedchamber window, Bess sees her two sons standing and admiring her initials, and smiles to herself. Her expensive new home is the result of years of careful planning, and she is delighted with the effect.

"Am I to have my own chamber at last, lady grandmother?" Her thoughts are disturbed as Bess sees Arbella coming towards her.

"Not exactly, child. There will still be a bed in my own chamber, but there is a smaller chamber for you, which you may use as a study, and sleep in when I think it is safe to do so. Your lady-in-waiting will have a chamber adjacent to you."

"I am twenty-one years old now!" She exclaims with feeling. "I should have my own chamber, it is so unfair!"

"I quite agree, but this is the price you must pay for being who you are. Would you rather be a maid living in the servants quarters with two coins to your name?"

"Yes! I think I would, for nothing could be worse than this captivity. Mr. Starkey tells me I am lucky to be so protected from the world; what does he know?"

"He is right, the world can be a bad place." Bess links arms with her. "Come with me, I will show you the rest of the house, as much as we can see. You will like living here, we shall be very comfortable together."

"Until I marry," adds Arbella quickly.

"Of course, but in the meantime you must continue with your studies, learning Spanish and Hebrew and reading the classics. Mr Starkey tells me that you are doing very well and working hard. Wylkyn has learnt much from your Latin lessons with him."

"He is a sweet child, I enjoy our time together and I am pleased to teach my cousin."

"Good. There is much to keep you occupied here, Arbella, if you will only seek it out. You must make the most of these days, so that when you eventually become a wife and mother, you will be the greatest accomplished lady in the land and the envy of everyone."

Looking unconvinced, Arbella allows Bess to lead her round the parts of the house that are habitable. No expense has been spared in the interior decoration either. The symmetry of the chambers and expanse of natural light that floods through all the glass windows, give the house a delicate, almost spiritual atmosphere. There is a soft sheen on the exquisitely carved oak wall panelling and overmantels, which Bess caresses sometimes, as if to reassure herself of their beauty. It is unlike any other house that either of them have seen. But Arbella cannot share her grandmother's enthusiasm, finding the light, airy space intrusive and threatening. There seems no escape from the relentless luminosity in each chamber. She nods silently as Bess chatters away to her, the pride in her voice all too evident.

Compared to Chatsworth, the New Hall is smaller and less fussy. But it is the magnificent Great High Chamber, on the uppermost floor, that Bess is most proud of. This is the place where she hopes to entertain Queen Elizabeth, although men are still working on finishing the plasterwork frieze, which tells the story of Diana the Huntress. Once this is complete, splendid tapestries will be hung along the walls, rush matting laid on the floors, and furniture brought over from the Old Hall, where it is being stored. Bess can hardly wait to entertain here.

The first Christmas festivities to be held in the New Hardwick Hall are fast approaching, and the servants are working hard to get everything ready. But Anne has been constantly sick during her present pregnancy, and spends most of each day in bed, her spirits low. Even William cannot cheer her with talk of their new home at Oldcotes, which should be ready for completion soon.

Over the next few days, family and friends start to arrive to celebrate Bess' birthday; they stand and look up in wonder at the carved initials before entering through the front door. She welcomes them all herself, explaining the reasons for a certain design, and pointing out areas of special interest as they tour the house. As queen of all she surveys, she sits in the new Long Gallery, surrounded by everyone, always the centre of it all. She listens, gives advice, laughs and watches her beloved children and grandchildren as they grow up. In quieter moments, she reflects on her seventy years, and thanks God she is still fit and healthy. Neighbours that she has lent money to, regard her as a lifesaver, as they do not know who else would help them out of financial difficulties. The fact that she insists on their land as security for loans does irk some of them, but not enough to shun her generous hospitality and friendship. There is still no news from the queen about Arbella's future, and Bess notices that her granddaughter seems to be shrinking under the strain of her restricted life, not eating much or joining in with card games any more. She has become very secretive, taking letters and running upstairs to read in private, then either burning or hiding them. Bess knows that not only is she in contact with the Earl of Essex, but also with her uncle Henry, whom she suspects is very sympathetic to her plight. But it is Anne who causes the most concern over the next few weeks. Her ankles have started to swell and she complains constantly of severe headaches. She looks very unwell, her face is puffy and there are dark shadows under her eyes.

Bess is sitting with her one February afternoon; the sky is grey, and rumbles of thunder are heard as the light begins to fade. Anne is laying on the bed, too exhausted to speak, but stares at the window, while Bess sponges her forehead with rosewater.

"Will you have some warm mead, my dear?" Bess asks her, holding the goblet to her lips.

Anne shakes her head, and suddenly clutches her stomach, groaning in pain.

"Is it your time? I will send for the midwife."

Bess immediately calls for servant and tells them to summon not only Mistress Flack, but also William. "She has started early, God willing all will be well," Bess tells a tense William when he arrives from the hunting field, his cloak and boots wet with mud.

He goes to Anne's side and is shocked by her appearance; beads of perspiration are trickling down her ashen face as she rolls from side to side in pain. Mistress Flack does not take long to arrive, and after rolling up her sleeves, carries out an examination. When she has satisfied herself, she goes over to where Bess and William are waiting anxiously outside the chamber.

"Lady Anne's condition gives me cause for concern, your grace. How long has she been like this?"

"We sent for you at once when she began to complain of pain, but she has not been herself all through this pregnancy."

"How bad is it?" William's voice is shaking with fear.

"I cannot say, sir. I will do my best but I must warn you to be prepared for the worst. I have seen mothers like this before ..." her voice trails off and she looks back at the bed.

William gives a gasp and Bess puts her arm round him. "Come away and let Mrs Flack carry on, there is nothing we can do here. It is in God's hands now."

For the next ten hours, the Old Hall is wracked with Anne's cries, which gradually become fainter and fainter as her strength gives out. Everyone else waits downstairs in desperation and helplessness; William pacing up and down like a caged animal, Bess trying to concentrate on her sewing, and Arbella biting her nails as she turns the pages of a book. Finally all is quiet and then they hear the sound of a crying baby.

"God be praised!" William cries and runs up the stairs, Bess and Arbella following behind. They crowd into the chamber as Mrs Flack is wrapping the baby in a blanket.

"A baby boy, he seems bonny enough," she adds encouragingly and hands him to William.

"And my wife?" His gaze moves to the bed but Anne has her eyes closed, oblivious to his presence.

"She must rest," Mrs Flack instructs them. "You have a wet nurse ready?"

"Yes, she is waiting to be called. A woman from the estate, we have used her before," Bess replies, and looks lovingly at her new grandchild.

"What will you call him?" she asks William.

"James I think, after your brother."

Bess smiles and holds the baby's little hand tenderly.

"We must get your mother better now, James."

"Amen to that," says William and hands him to Bess while he goes to comfort Anne. She is unresponsive to his solicitous murmurings, but he holds her hand and strokes it. The fear is still there gripping the pit of his stomach; he turns to Mistress Slack as she gathers up her instruments and soiled linen.

"Thank you," he tells her simply. "Please go to the kitchen for some refreshments."

She nods, and says she will be back in the morning, before curtseying and leaving the chamber. Bess kisses baby James before placing him in the hastily prepared crib, and leaves the three of them alone while she gives orders for some nourishing soup and fresh linen to be brought up.

Arbella is still at the door, wide-eyed and curious. "We will return later when Anne is stronger," Bess tells her.

"Will aunt Anne be all right?" whispers Arbella.

"We shall have to see, child. Do not worry now, the worst is probably over."

But Bess has a terrible foreboding about Anne. Such fancies have no place in Bess' usual outlook on life, but this time she cannot help but think there will be another death in the family before long.

୦୪୬୦

1598 – 1599

Bess' worst fears were realised when Anne dies less than four months after Bess and Arbella move into the New Hall, but James thrives and is doted on by everyone, especially Bess. Lord Burghley is also dead. Bess is still in contact with officials at Court, including Sir Robert Cecil and Sir Walter Raleigh; she sends them occasional gifts of food or silver plate. The bad feeling between the Stanhopes and Gilbert has not gone away, as Charles finds out, to his detriment, one morning in June 1599.

"Will you take the new mare this morning, sir?"

They are outside the stables where grooms and stable lads are busy going about their early morning chores: sweeping the yard, polishing harnesses, mucking out and preparing the cart horses for work in the fields. As befits a gentleman of means, Charles has a variety of horses for different purposes. There are palfreys for long distance riding, coursers for hunting and some large Flanders horses for heavy work such as transporting goods. Charles has an expert eye and runs his hands over the mare's flank. He usually buys them from a breeder such as Sir Nicholas Arnold or the horse fair at

Ripon, but this one has recently come from a neighbour. She is a beautiful four-year-old chestnut with white markings on her forehead. Charles is paying a visit to a kiln he is having built near where his new house is to stand, and he wants to check progress on the work.

"She is smaller than I remembered," he replies and the groom raises his eyebrows as he holds the reins.

"Try her out, the ride to the kiln is not long, sir. The lad says she responds well and has a soft mouth."

"Very well, although I have a feeling she might be more suitable for Lady Catherine. We shall call her Lucky. Have my hunter saddled and ready for when we return within the hour."

The groom murmurs acknowledgement, and Charles mounts with ease and rides to the gates where his brother-in-law Henry, and his page Lance, are waiting, also on horseback. They set off at a gentle pace, the roads are good for a change, there has been no rain, so the dust swirls beneath the horses hooves, making clouds at their feet. In ten minutes they are in the open countryside of Nottinghamshire and they can see their destination, less than a quarter of a mile away. Laughing and relaxed in the morning sunshine, it seems they have no cares in the world.

Then Charles looks towards the brow of a hill to the right, and sees a large group of riders galloping towards them, about half a mile distant. He reins his horse in and they all stop. "Who is that at such a pace?" he frowns, squinting against the sun on the eastern horizon.

"They cannot be heading for us," replies Henry, shielding his eyes. "They must veer soon one way or the other."

"I am not so sure," Charles says slowly.

They watch as a dozen determined riders gallop nearer and nearer with frightening purpose and speed; the horses hooves thundering towards them, the riders in a frenzy of determined unity. As they approach with each second, they show no sign of deviating from the course leading them to where Charles and the others are waiting in the middle of the road. "God's blood, they are coming straight for us!" Charles shouts. "Separate quickly!"

They spur their horses in different directions, Henry and Lance manage to make some ground, but despite brave Lucky's efforts, Charles is slower and the riders are soon almost upon him. Not one of the riders has chased the other two, so it is clear to Charles at once that he is the intended victim. With a shout of anguish, he is thrown to the ground as Lucky stumbles on gravel. Dazed and hurt, he looks up to see two masked men pointing their pistols at him, less than fifteen feet away. They are masked, but their eyes are cold and determined as they loom over him. There are rallying shouts, the sound of swords being unsheathed, horses neighing in confusion. He tries to draw his sword, but before he can reach it, two shots are fired and he feels a searing pain shoot up his leg. Crying out in pain, he falls back and his attackers laugh as if they have performed a conjuring trick. Charles loses consciousness for a few seconds, but on recovering, is reassured to see that Henry and Lance have turned round and are already fighting. Outnumbered, with only a dagger and sword between them, they charge into their opponents' horses, unseating several riders in the process, whilst wielding the weapons with enough accuracy to injury two more. Some of the attackers have had enough already and disappear with speed, one exits on foot, limping and holding his arm. Henry and Lance dismount and continue fighting on the ground. The clash of steel on steel glinting in the sunlight fills the air, and Henry also manages to land some well-aimed punches to his opponents. Lance, although of slight frame and short, is as tenacious as a terrier; thanks to having four older brothers, he knows how to take care of himself in a fight. Charles can only watch in frustration from the sidelines, clutching his right leg, which by now is bleeding badly.

By this time, alerted by the noise, twenty or so workmen at the kiln are running towards the scene and Charles notices them with a sigh of relief. The remaining attackers realise they have lost the advantage, and either re-mount, riding away at a gallop, or run off without their horses. Two of the men lie inert in the road, perhaps unconscious or dead. Henry and Lance run over to Charles and attend to his leg wound, tying it as best they can with their shirts to staunch the bleeding. The attack has lasted less than five minutes, but caused mayhem. The worst Henry and Lance have suffered is some bruising, but they are much more concerned about Charles.

"I am fine," he insists, although his expression tells a different story, and he grimaces as they tighten the makeshift bandages. "Someone needs to look at Lucky, she may be injured too."

Henry and Lance look at each other grimly, they know that Charles must have the bullet removed quickly. Henry takes charge, and as soon as the men from the kiln are close enough, he tells them to bring a litter at once to transport Sir Charles back home, and someone to ride urgently to the physician and tell him to attend without delay.

A handful of men run back to carry out his orders, and the others round up the horses and weapons left behind. Lance goes over to the attackers on the ground and turns them over with his foot. He does not recognise them, but they are both dead, one has bled heavily from his chest and the other has a gaping head wound where he fell, most likely hitting a nearby rock.

"God's Blood! I could do with a drink! I hope the physician can give me something for this pain, I have never felt the like before."

Charles closes his eyes and he starts to shake with shock. Lance murmurs words of manly comfort as Henry tries to distract him.

"I am trying to deduce the reason for the attack, it was completely unprovoked! They were not robbers, they asked for nothing; they were only interested in you, Charles. Do you have any idea what motive they might have had?" Henry asks as they put their weapons away and sit beside him, mopping their faces with handkerchiefs.

Charles opens his eyes briefly. "Stanhope was amongst them," he manages to mutter, his breath laboured and erratic.

"That bastard!" exclaims Henry.

"Must be revenge for when I laughed at his doublet on Lambeth Bridge."

"That was six years ago," Lance says incredulously.

"Do not try to talk, Charles," Henry tells him. "Save your strength. The litter will be here shortly, we are not far from home and you will soon be right again."

His words do not fool anyone. They have all heard of men who have had to have limbs amputated from such pistol wounds, or died from the infections that took hold afterwards. They attempt to move him to a more comfortable position and he lies back, trying not to think of the agony from his wound. As he waits underneath the warming heat of the summer day, his friends loyally by his side, Charles has time to think of what the consequences of this cowardly attack might be for him. It seems unimaginable that one minute he is riding in the sunshine with his friends, laughing and talking, and the next he is lying wounded on the ground, bleeding and in pain. He is a very active, fit man of forty and has every intention of staying that way for as long as possible. The best surgeon available will be at his disposal, but there is no guarantee that the outcome of his treatment will be successful. Having forgotten all about the duel, this attack has come as a great shock, and at the moment he knows he cannot think clearly. He was certainly unaware that Stanhope had been planning anything. Henry and Lance are looking at him anxiously.

"Are you all right?" Lance asks him. "Where is that damn litter?" He gets up to look.

"Stanhope has a prestigious post at Court does he not?" asks Henry.

"Treasurer of the Queen's Chamber, no less. You can imagine what the Stanhopes had to do to get it for him," replies Charles through gritted teeth.

"He will not keep it after this cowardly attack."

"We shall see; he has powerful friends at Court."

"Your mother, the Dowager Countess is not without influence," Henry reminds him.

Charles thinks there is not much that even Bess can do about the situation. They sit and wait, looking round uneasily in case of a second attack, but no one passes. At last the litter arrives and he is lifted carefully onto it. Henry and Lance sit beside him to begin the slow, careful ride home where Catherine and the physician will be waiting. Getting justice for the attack is not a priority over the next few days, but Charles will not be in a position to do anything about it for a while.

ೞ಄

New Hardwick Hall – 1601

"Has the rider delivered any letters yet today?" Arbella asks a servant one afternoon as she sits, bored and discontented, watching the sleet as it falls against the latticed windows.

"Yes highness, he arrived about an hour since. The Dowager Countess has all that was delivered."

Arbella gives a sniff of disapproval and goes to Bess' study, where without knocking, she storms in and demands to see her letters. Bess is in the middle of a meeting with William and Timothy and looks at her with a frown of annoyance.

"Have you forgotten your manners that you come into my chamber so rudely?"

"Why are all my letters given to you first? They should be left on the hall table for me."

"All correspondence is brought to me because this is my house. Even William's letters come through me, do they not William?"

"It has never been a problem for me, lady mother," he dutifully replies.

"You see? Do not fret Arbella, I do not open the letters, even though I could open yours if I chose to."

She begins to shift through the ten or so letters on a pile beside her and singles out one, which she hands to Arbella.

"From the Earl of Essex," she tells her.

An expression of delight crosses Arbella's face at this news. "I shall read it upstairs."

"Do not enter my chamber again without knocking, child," Bess tells her sternly, but Arbella is already running upstairs, the letter clutched to her breast. Timothy gets up and shuts the door.

"One wonders what the earl has written about his recent exploits," William says. "Or perhaps we should ask ourselves what Arbella finds to write to him about?"

"She will write about her unhappy life here with me, I expect."

"If the news is to be believed, he will not be writing letters for much longer," says Timothy.

"He does have a certain following. The people did see him as a hero after the victory at Cadiz. Then he spoilt it all by his foolhardy management of the Irish expeditionary force and negotiating with that rebel Tyrone in Ireland," William's voice is derisory.

"I always knew his ambition would be his downfall," Bess says and opens one of her drawers.

"Robert Cecil has kept me up to date with all the earl's plots and plans." She puts half a dozen letters on the desk.

"Read them if you will. I am going to speak to Arbella and will return shortly, then I want to talk to you both about an inventory I wish to be made for the new house. I shall have a new will drawn up, so you will need to contact my lawyers," she pauses. "Master Hardy will do it."

She follows her granddaughter upstairs and finds her on the bed, avidly reading the letter. Arbella looks up crossly; she had been hoping to have some rare privacy.

"I must speak to you about the Earl of Essex," Bess tells her firmly.

"If you are going to say that he has displeased the queen, then I already know about it."

"Do you? How much do you know?"

"What do you mean?"

"He is in serious trouble, he may lose his head."

At this, Arbella goes pale. "No, that will not happen! The queen adores him, she would never do such a thing."

Bess sits down with a sigh of reluctance. "Child, you must understand that he has started to take too much on himself in matters of state, often without the queen's knowledge or consent. He has been secretly negotiating with the Irish leader and made agreements with him that were not to our advantage. He has publicly insulted the queen, even half drawing his sword on her when she boxed his ears ..."

Arbella gives a cry of frustration and puts her hands over her ears.

"I will not listen any more! This is all lies!"

Bess pulls her hands away. "You can listen and you will! He is a traitor. Robert Cecil tells me ..."

"Oh that dwarf would say anything to gain favour! He hates Robert and is jealous of him! It is not difficult to know why is it?"

"Arbella, Robert Devereux is on the way down, very publicly and very dramatically. I want you to realise that his end will be coming soon and there is nothing you can do about it. I know you are fond of him ..."

"You have never liked him!"

"My feelings towards him are irrelevant. I maintain a relationship with him as he is the queen's favourite, but no, compared to his stepfather the Earl of Leicester, he is not someone I would call a friend."

"Why do you always spoil everything for me?"

"What do I spoil for you? You have a family who love you and everything money can buy, you are a very lucky girl."

"Am I?" she cries, throwing the letter on the bed in a fit of temper. "I do not think so. Look at this house you have built for yourself …"

"And for you."

"No, lady grandmother, this house is not for me. It is for you, everything about it has your mark on it. Do you know the only part of me that is here; is my coat of arms, placed in a corner out of the way? In years to come, that will be the only record that I, Arbella Stuart, Countess of Lennox, was ever here. History will remember you, with your almshouses at Derby and your huge initials at the pinnacle of the towers here, but me? No, I shall die in this corner of Derbyshire, old and lonely, the best part of my life gone, spent waiting for a husband that others say they will find for me. Now I must watch my younger cousin Elizabeth plan her wedding, have you any idea how it makes me feel? No, you do not care!"

After this long speech, she starts to bang her head against the wall; Bess gets up quickly to stop her. It is not the first time she has acted in this self-destructive manner, but Bess considers it to be nothing more than dramatics from a young woman seeking attention.

"Now, child, calm down. It is not as bad as you say. You must not get so upset."

Arbella slides down the wall and sits on the floor as if exhausted by life itself. Bess sighs, impatient to get back to work.

"Are you still here?" Arbella looks up at her.

"Am I not always here for you?"

"Yes," she nods miserably. "You are always here and I am always here. You are my destiny and I am yours. I shall be quiet now."

"I shall send for your lady-in-waiting."

"I do not wish for her! Why can I not be left on my own?"

"I thought she would be able to comfort you, someone nearer your own age."

"No you did not. You have your servants to spy on me all the time. I long to be alone, with my own thoughts. Is that such a crime?"

"Of course not." Then Bess has an idea and forces her voice to be cheerful.

"Would you like to come to one of my jewellery caskets and choose a pretty brooch or ring? I think that would cheer you up."

Arbella shakes her head, for once unimpressed by this offer.

"I do not want your brooches or your rings or anything you can give me. I want the Earl of Essex to stay alive and be unmarried, I want to leave this house forever and never return, I want a husband and a home and children of my own to love and cherish."

She recites all these requirements with a monotonous tone before ending by crying out in despair, "I want my own life! Why is that so impossible?"

"We cannot always have what we want," Bess tells her gently.

"You did!" she retorts fiercely.

Bess is not going to crouch down to Arbella's level, and after a few moments she quietly leaves the chamber to return to her meeting with William and Timothy. Meanwhile Arbella remains on the floor staring straight ahead. She makes a pact with herself; if the earl is executed, she will take matters into her own hands and do something positive to change her life before she is completely suffocated by her captivity. Getting up abruptly, she goes over to a secret drawer in her desk and removes a letter. Hiding it from her grandmother is essential as it is from her Uncle Henry, and as far as she knows, Bess has not seen it. She reads;

My dear niece Arbella,

I read your letter with great sympathy as I understand all to well the overwhelming force of my lady mother's personality, made all the more difficult by your being kept as a prisoner. It may reassure you to know that many people are dismayed at your lack of freedom over so many years, and feel it is very unjust. My lady mother has had much practise in her role as jailor, and one I fear she takes to with consummate ease.

I wish to help you in any way I am able, as I realise you have no other family member to turn to. When the time is right, we shall be able to take you away from Hardwick and your life will truly begin anew. I am in contact with people who strongly sympathise with your position, to the extent of endangering their own lives.

But we must be very careful, as I am sure you realise. Hide this letter or burn it, for if it was to fall into the wrong hands, you know what the consequences would be. Wait patiently, for I will not let you down, I remain your affectionate Uncle Henry.

Written this day v March 1600 at Tutbury Castle.

Arbella reads it again and yet again before taking it to the fire and watching it burn. Already an idea is beginning to form in her head, but she needs to think more deeply about it. Having Uncle Henry on her side is reassuring, and she does not feel quite so alone.

※

February 1601

Another person who is sympathetic to Arbella is her tutor, Mr Starkey. The two of them spend time each day in each other's company at her lessons. He is a chaplain by profession, but has an extensive knowledge of the classics, as well as languages such as Hebrew and Spanish. A quiet, reserved little man, he finds Arbella to be an excellent pupil who has above average intelligence. It is now two weeks since the execution of the Earl of Essex for treason and when the messenger arrived with the news, Arbella had hysterics and nothing could calm her for several hours. Eventually she fell into an exhausted sleep, watched over by Bess and her maid. Reluctantly, she returns to her studies within days, but everyone can see she is withdrawn and quiet; spending hours on her own in her small study off the bedchamber that she is still forced to share with Bess. Mr Starkey shares the concern of the household, and decides to broach the subject over lessons.

"I was shocked to hear the news of the Earl of Essex, I know he was a good friend to you. I think you have taken it badly, and I cannot help but feel that you have much on your mind."

Arbella looks up from her book and her expression is neutral. "I am quite well Mr. Starkey. I hope you do not think my studies are suffering."

"Not at all. You are still a diligent pupil, one of the best I have ever had the privilege to teach. No, I am simply concerned that, well, given the life you are forced to lead here, a virtual prisoner…"

He realises he has said too much, and looks about nervously, but Arbella lowers her voice. "You are kind to be concerned. My life is one of misery and loneliness, despite all the luxury of my surroundings. The dowager countess still treats me as if I were a young child, and not a grown woman. You have seen for yourself how I am made to suffer …" She begins to cry, and Mr Starkey looks at her apprehensively.

"… but I am in the process of planning my escape from here. You must keep it a secret of course, I know I can trust you, you are a dear friend."

"Oh, I wish you had not told me about this plan," he replies nervously. "For if I am asked, I shall have to tell the truth. I am honoured to be considered your friend, but I am only your tutor."

"You will not be asked, and I would not expect you to lie for me. My uncle Henry is going to take me away from this place. Will you help me too? Please say you will."

This was not what he was expecting, and caught unawares, he can only stare at her in dismay.

"I can see you are reluctant and I understand, of course. But ask yourself this question, if you shall not help me, will you not have it on your conscience that you passed by on the other side and refused to help another fellow Christian in distress? I would beg you on my knees if it would sway your decision."

"Oh, please do not even think of it!" he replies, horrified at the idea.

"This is the depth of my despair, Mr. Starkey. You have no idea how I envy the women servants here, they have a freedom denied to me, they can pass through these wretched gates and go where they will. Anyone within these walls can do so, except me, and yet I am the highest-ranking woman in the land after her majesty. Do you think that is fair? Do you think that is right?"

"No! I do not, highness. I wish to help but I do not see how someone as humble as myself ..." His voice trails off half-heartedly. She leans forward on the desk, her face earnest, her eyes brimming with tears.

"But you will not have to do much, perhaps take a letter or perform a minor errand. It will be enough that I have someone in the house that I can trust to act for me, and not my grandmother. Do not forget that one day I shall be in a position at Court to return your favour. How would you like to be the tutor to royal children?"

He does not reply, and Arbella presses home her point.

"Just think of it. You would have fine clothes, a handsome salary, even more than you receive here, all the benefits and privileges of a royal tutor, as well as access to the royal family. It is every humble tutor's dream, is it not?"

His mind is racing now with the possibilities of a position at Court, something that he had always thought was beyond his reach. She is right, what tutor would not wish of such a life? He smiles and gives a solemn bow.

"You may rely on my help for this matter, highness."

Arbella claps her hands and wipes her tears away. Her plan is falling into place, slowly but surely.

25 December 1602 – Hardwick New Hall

Christmas Day dawns with dark clouds rolling across the red streaked sky and a sharp, fierce wind from the north that finds its way through all the many windows of the new house. It blows around the chambers from the rooftops down, reaching every corner, permeating cupboards and drawers, so everything feels icy cold to touch. It brushes the backs of peoples' necks and turns their fingers numb. The inescapable whining moan never seems to lessen; making windows rattle and draughts race through open doors. As servants go back and forth to the brewing house, dairy and smithy that are close by, they are bent with the effort of remaining upright. The workmen do not appear today, but are in their homes celebrating as far as their means will allow, with their families.

Bess is now seventy-four years old, and each day tries to ignore her ageing body's aches and pains. With great reluctance, she has taken to using a walking stick, which gives warning to the servants as they hear it tapping along the stone floor towards them. She has also acquired Caesar, a little brown dog of dubious ancestry that terrorises the Irish wolfhounds as they lie in front of the fire. Cossetted under the many layers of scarlet wool blankets and bed hangings on and around her bed, she knows the best way to keep warm even in the bleakest of Derbyshire winters. Her bedchamber fire is always kept burning brightly, and she has started to work here lately, as it is by far the warmest place in the house. She has been pleased with Arbella's behaviour these last few months, noting that she has not been complaining or disagreeable at all, but quietly working at her studies. Now that she is over three score years and ten, Bess re-wrote her will last year with William and Arbella as the main beneficiaries. Mary and Charles are notably omitted, due to their taking Gilbert's side over legal wranglings against her, but she has already been generous with gifts of money and land to them both. She also was able to read through the completed inventory of the New Hardwick Hall and reflect on everything therein, a tidy sum's worth by any standard. Another task completed, was the commission of her burial tomb, made from stone mined from her own quarries, to await her final resting place in Derby.

She is spending the Christmas celebrations with William and his new wife, Elizabeth. Their children, Wylkyn and James, together with the Pierrepoints, Frances, Henry and their children, Bessie, Robert and Grace, all of whom arrived a week ago, are also staying. As Ruby dresses her hair, now faded to white, she watches Arbella who has her back to them as she lies on the bed. It occurs to Bess that she has not had a proper conversation with her granddaughter for a few days.

"You may go now," she tells Ruby who puts down the comb before curtseying and leaving. Arbella turns over with a grunt of displeasure.

"Why can I not have my own chamber in the new year? It is always so very hot in here!"

Bess finishes arranging her hair, and looks over at Arbella with some impatience.

"I feel the cold more than you do. My bones are much older; and you know why I must have you near me."

"No-one is going to kidnap me here! I am too well guarded and locked up all the time."

She gets up and walks over to one of the many large windows, gazing at the outlook she knows so well. From this view, the sodden fields stretch into the distance as far as the eye can see. There is no sign of life, except the sheep huddling under the trees for shelter. She gives a loud, frustrated sigh.

"How much longer will I have to stay here?"

"Do not keep asking me that question," replies Bess, her voice straining to be patient. "I do not know, how many more times do I have to tell you? If I knew, then I would say so."

"But what will happen when the queen dies?"

"It is not for you to speculate! Do not even think of the queen dying, it is tantamount to treason."

"It is just between the two of us. We are alone."

"It makes no difference." Bess goes over to her and holds her shoulders in both hands. "I know you are unhappy and wish to be far from here. If I could change it, I would, but there is nothing I can do."

Arbella pulls away from her. "I do not believe you! You like having me here with you. You enjoy keeping me in your control all the time. I hate you!"

"You do not mean that, child. You are upset. I thought that lately you were coming to terms with your situation."

"Well I am not, nor will I ever."

"Let us go to breakfast, and after we have been to chapel, we can all open our presents. Will it not be pleasant to spend this special day with all the family?"

She does not reply and Bess ushers her through the door to join the others. The new chapel is on two floors, the upper level for the family, and the lower level for the servants. It has fine embroidery of the Crucifixion and three pictures of the Virgin Mary on the wall. The communion rails have been carved from oak trees on the estate and, on fine days, the sunlight streams through the windows, reflecting the wood that has been so carefully polished with bees wax. As Mr Starkey welcomes them, he notes that Henry, Grace, Mary, Gilbert, Charles and Catherine are absent, but it is not his place to ask the reason.

Arbella stops at the entrance to remove a stone from her shoe.

"Are you all right, Arbella?" asks William solicitously, coming after her.

"Oh yes, uncle, please continue without me, I shall be there shortly; I have forgotten my prayer book."

He carries on and in less than half a minute, everyone is inside the chapel and she is alone. She runs back downstairs and looks around quickly for a particular servant. She finds him giving instructions to a maid, and interrupts them without preamble.

"Dodderidge, I must speak to you."

He looks at her in surprise as the maid curtseys and leaves them. The Hall is deserted and Arbella produces a letter from her gown, which she furtively holds out to him.

"Highness, what is this?"

"It is letter to Lord Hertford. I want you to take it to him at once."

Dodderidge has known Arbella since she was a baby and is one of Bess' oldest and trusted servants. He is known for his discretion, which is why she has chosen him. Puzzled and uneasy, he hesitates and scratches his baldhead.

"Is it from the dowager countess?"

"No, of course not! It is from me, and my lady grandmother must not know about it. I have chosen you to help me. You must hurry, go now, while everyone is at prayer."

"I cannot leave the house today, highness. It is Christmas morning, I have my duties. You realise Lord Hertford lives just outside London, it will take me days to reach him."

He still has not taken the letter and she thrusts it into his hand.

"I will say you have received bad news from your family and that I gave you permission to go."

"I am not sure …"

She looks up him beseechingly. "Please do this for me, I beg you to help me."

"What is in this letter?"

"My uncles Henry and William are involved in a plan for me to marry Edward Seymour, Lord Hertford's grandson. You must tell him to bring Edward here in disguise, under the pretext of wanting to buy land, then I shall be able to escape with them. You are my only hope, I shall kill myself if you do not do it."

At this last declaration, his expression changes and he nods slowly. "Very well highness, if it is that important to you, I shall do it."

"Thank you. Thank you, I am so grateful. My uncle Henry is waiting outside the gates with a horse for you. Go at once, there is no time to lose!" She turns and runs back to the chapel, her face flushed. Unnoticed, she slips into place at the end of the pew, as the first hymn is starting. Her heart is beating fast; she feels a strange excitement that at last, she is beginning to take control of her life. This secret is the result of a plan that has been going round and round in her head for a long time. If no one can find her a husband, then she will find one herself.

ଔଚ

3 January 1603 (Nine days later)

The Christmas celebrations at Hardwick are as lavish as usual, and Bess is enjoying spending time with her family and friends. The days have taken on a routine of their own; the gentleman like to hunt or fish, sometimes the ladies will join them if the weather is dry. Or there is hawking, when the older children are allowed to join the adults. In the evening, Bess has organised entertainment, and there are plays, musicians and dancing, as well as card games, indoor bowls, chess and poetry readings. There are discussions about the recent plays by William Shakespeare and Ben Johnson, the writers that everyone is talking about. This afternoon, Bess sits in her carved oak chair; complete with it's padded velvet cushions, near the fireplace in the Long Gallery, the largest chamber in the house, although not as grand as the High Great Chamber will be when it is finished. There are other chairs and stools together with window seats in every window, so there is plenty of space for everyone. A recent portrait of Bess herself, as well as the queen and Arbella, hangs on the walls with other family likenesses, and two long tables are covered with silk carpets, one is a beautiful blue Turkish one, admired by all who see it. The nursery maids have just taken the children to bed, and everyone feels replete after another feast of assorted food and best wine.

Bess surveys the scene with satisfaction. Her most ambitious project of a new Hardwick Hall is now almost complete, and her family are enjoying the benefits. Every time she is in the garden and looks up at the tops of the corner towers, she sees with pride and satisfaction, her own initials E S – proof if any were needed, of how far she has come in life. There can be no doubt now of her wealth, power and influence. Having learnt from building all her life and taking note of the designs of other great houses built by her friends, Lord Burghley and Sir Christopher Hatton, she had a very clear idea of what she wanted. William and his family now live nearby at Owlcotes, while Bess and Arbella live here with the ladies–in-waiting, gentlemen and servants. Security is always a priority, and there are guards stationed at the entrances, day and night. But for once, the threat of an imminent kidnap of Arbella is forgotten, and the family are enjoying a game of indoor bowls after supper, amidst much noise and hilarity. The servants have just lit the candles on the wall sconces, providing welcome light in the midwinter afternoon, and the roaring fire provides a cosy atmosphere in contrast to the inhospitable evening outside. Suddenly Bess notices a servant running in towards her and he bows, aware that his announcement will cause much consternation.

"Sir Henry Brounker, a Royal Commissioner, is here to see your grace, by the queen's command."

She looks surprised, which quickly turns to shock. William notices and goes to his mother's side.

"What is it, lady mother?"

The servant repeats his statement. This time the whole gallery hears and there is immediate silence. Everyone realises this is very serious. Arbella takes herself quietly to an obtrusive corner and waits, her eyes darting nervously from Bess to William. Bess has visibly paled at this news and William places his hand on her shoulder as if to reassure her. "Is he alone?" he asks the servant.

"Yes sir."

"You had better show him up."

The servant disappears and Bess looks up at her son. "What can this mean? Sweet Jesu, William, for the first time in my life, I feel quite faint."

He sits beside her; they know they only have a few minutes before he is in the room.

"It must be serious to send a Royal Commissioner during the Christmas celebrations. They are not sent without good reason."

Bess tries to compose herself and takes a few sips of wine. Downstairs, Sir Henry is looking up at the long, imposing stone steps of the ceremonial staircase that leads to where he has been told the family are all gathered. He is middle aged, overweight and tired after riding from London, where he was enjoying the festivities with his own family. Breathing heavily, he trudges after the servant, mopping his brow with the exertion of the climb.

"Why does your mistress not entertain her guests on the ground floor?" he grumbles, as they are only half way up. "New fangled ideas," he mutters to himself.

The servant does not tell him that this is a deliberate plan by Bess to emphasise her advantage when her guests eventually reach her. The symbolism of the unusually long climb upwards to be received by Bess is often not realised until guests are later able to reflect on it. They are not the only ones though, to resent the number of steps. The servants, having to walk up and down their own wooden staircase daily, have no great liking either for this topsy-turvy arrangement of new accommodation. They finally reach the door.

"Mind the step, sir," the servant tells him as he reaches for the knob.

"Wait!" Sir Henry commands and he takes a few seconds to recover his breath, aware that he is now red faced, as well as wet and travel stained. He brushes his cloak and puts his handkerchief away, but there is nothing else for it, he must continue with his task. He nods and the servant opens the door before announcing him. Blinking at the assault on his eyes from the bright colours of the richly coloured wall tapestries, the scene that greets Sir Henry is like a tableau. All the figures are standing poised as they wait, regarding him curiously as he approaches Bess, who by now is calmer, although she is still pale. He gives a courtly bow.

"Sir Henry, you are most welcome." To her dismay, Bess finds her voice is not strong as usual and she clears her throat self-consciously.

"Countess, I apologise for this intrusion. I have been commanded by her majesty the queen to ride here without delay on a matter of great importance."

"May I first offer you some refreshment?"

"Thank you, I have need of it, but first I must speak to you privately."

Bess gets up and indicates for them to go the other end of the gallery, some one hundred and fifty feet from where she is seated. Taking some deep breaths, she tries not to show her acute anxiety. "Sir Henry …this is most unexpected. I trust her majesty is in good health?"

"The queen has asked me to extend her gracious favour to you, and hopes to find you well."

"Forgive me, I am rather overcome with the surprise of your visit. I am at a loss to know why you are here in the middle of our Christmas festivities."

"Do not be alarmed, countess, I am to reassure you that you yourself have nothing to fear, and that I am to give you this letter from her majesty at once."

Bess takes the letter with the queen's own seal and opens it, her hands trembling.

"I see," she says after reading it. "You wish to speak to my granddaughter, the Lady Arbella. May I be permitted to know the reason?"

"Not at present, countess. All will become clear shortly I hope. Where may I see her in private?"

"There is an antechamber over there you may use. I shall have some refreshments brought up for you." Bess waves to the servant standing nearby, and orders him to take their visitor there. After Sir Henry is shown where to go, Bess scans the chamber for Arbella, who is trying to look inconspicuous.

"Arbella! Come here." Still no one has moved or spoken, but it is clear now who is the reason for this intrusion.

Arbella, her head low in diffidence, approaches her grandmother, but will not look her in the face, preferring instead to study her hands and occupy herself with a broken nail.

"What is this all about?" Bess hisses at her.

"I am sure I do not know, lady grandmother."

"You have been up to no good, have you not?"

"Why do you always think the worst?"

"Is your Uncle Henry involved in some way? Tell me the truth, I shall find out in the end."

Arbella does not answer, and Bess points to the door of the antechamber.

"You are to speak to Sir Henry Brounker alone. Do not disgrace me, Arbella!"

William joins his mother, his face full of curiosity.

"Have you managed to find out why he is here?" he whispers, as the others begin to talk amongst themselves once Arbella has left.

"The letter from the queen said that I was to allow Arbella to be questioned, that is all. No hint of the reason. I have no idea at all why he is here, but Henry may be behind it."

"Can you still not bring yourself to ask the others to our family gatherings?" he asks.

"I could not ask Mary to join us without Gilbert of course, but she does not seem interested in me, except when she wants money, and Gilbert is always bringing some legal suit against me."

"And Charles?"

"He is more loyal to Gilbert than to me, which I find very hurtful; I think Gilbert has turned him against me. It means I do not see his two boys, William and Charles."

" I know you miss seeing the grandchildren, your jewels as you call them."

Her eyes become misty and William hastily changes the subject. "You know Charles has definitely abandoned the building of his new house since the attack?"

"I did hear he rather lost the will to build there after what happened, understandable I suppose. He was lucky not to lose his leg. All I could do was send Dr. Hunton to attend him."

"And Stanhope has never been called to answer for his actions on that day, what a disgrace!"

Glancing over to the door where Arbella and Sir Henry are closeted, they can only hear a muffled conversation, Sir Henry's deep tones asking the questions and Arbella's much lighter voice replying. Bess and William, along with everyone else, continue to wait as patiently as they can. It looks as if it is going to be a long night.

※

Sir Henry pours himself a glass of wine and studies Arbella, who is sitting demurely and looking at him expectantly. He has never met her before, and is surprised that she bears no similarity in looks to her Cavendish family. She is very pale and rather delicate, and her large blue eyes are now looking at him without blinking. His own daughters are of a similar age and if they were in such a predicament, he knows they would be much afraid. He had been dismayed at the idea of having to ride a hundred and fifty miles in mid-winter, but a royal command cannot be refused. There was little time to prepare either; her majesty wanted him at Hardwick without delay. A politician and soldier, he served in Ireland and more recently in Scotland, so time with his family is particularly precious. Robert Cecil put forward his name to the queen and she has no reason to doubt his suitability for the job. Sir Henry explains who he is, and that the queen has sent him to question her.

Arbella nods calmly and waits, seemingly unperturbed. He stands by the fireplace, his back erect and confident, sure of his authority.

"Her majesty has commanded me to thank you for the Christmas gift you sent her."

"I am pleased that it was favourably received."

"But there is a matter that the queen has taken very unkindly. Have you an idea what it could be, Lady Arbella?"

"No, I have not."

"I suggest you think carefully. Is there nothing you wish to tell me? About a letter that you have sent recently?"

"I do not know of any letter. I have written nothing."

He produces the letter from his bag, which he shows her.

"Is this your handwriting, Lady Arbella?"

She looks at it closely and shakes her head.

"No, I have never seen it before."

"Are you quite sure?"

"Of course I am! Someone has taken liberties with my writing, no doubt for their own ends."

Then he gives her a second letter.

"Here is a letter written by you to the queen. The writing is identical. Do you still deny any knowledge of it?"

"Oh, that letter, I may have written it after all," she admits lightly and two red spots appear on her cheeks. "But I have never seen the other letter until now."

"You would do well to answer my questions truthfully, this is a very serious matter."

"You have not yet told me why you are here."

His voice becomes softer.

"It is not unusual for young people such as yourself to make mistakes. I am here to help you, trust me. How did you think you were going to marry Edward Seymour? Who was going to assist you? You need not fear that I will tell your grandmother, what you say will just be between the two of us."

"I do not know what you mean, I have never made any plans about marrying anyone."

"But the writing on these two letters is the same, look for yourself."

"Someone has forged my hand."

"Why would they do that? Why would Dodderidge, one of your grandmother's best servants, spend five days travelling in the middle of winter, to deliver a letter that is forged?"

"I am at a loss to tell you," she responds stubbornly. "I hardly know this man."

"I have his confession here; he says he has known you since you were a child."

Arbella does not reply and shifts position in the chair. He moves closer and the odour of his wet clothes mingled with horse sweat, makes her wrinkle her nose distastefully.

"Well, let me remind you of the facts, Lady Arbella. On Christmas Day you dispatched one of your grandmother's servants, Dodderidge, to ride at once and take a letter to Lord Hertford. He arrived five days later while the family were still celebrating the Twelve Nights of Christmas. In front of witnesses, Lord Hertford was told that your uncles Henry and Sir William proposed a marriage between his grandson, Edward Seymour and yourself. To facilitate this marriage, Lord Hertford was to come to Hardwick

Hall, disguised and under the pretext of selling some land ..."

He pauses to judge Arbella's reaction to this summary of her plan; she hardly seems to be listening, but is looking intently at the embroidery on her gown.

"He was to identify himself to you by producing a letter from his late wife's sister, the Lady Jane Grey, of all people."

He waits a few moments and allows the name of the unlucky claimant to the throne, to penetrate Arbella's apparent indifference. When she still does not respond, he is more direct.

"How do you know the style of Lady Jane Grey's handwriting?"

"I must have seen it somewhere."

"She was executed almost fifty years ago!"

"Oh well, my lady grandmother has letters from those days. Did you know she keeps a likeness of Lady Jane beside her bed? No, I suppose you would not. Yes, she knew the Grey family when she was younger. Did you know that? No, perhaps not." She gives a high-pitched laugh and he regards her with a perplexed expression.

"Can you explain yourself, what do you have to say?" She looks at him with a smile. "What do I have to say about what?"

"Lady Arbella, you must answer my questions. Did you intend to marry Lord Hertford's son, Edward? It seems an unlikely match, he is only seventeen and you are at least ten years older."

She glares haughtily at him. "I do not think I intended to marry him, no."

"You do not think so," he emphasises and shakes his head. "Your letter suggests that you did. You must know if your uncles were planning a marriage for you."

"They may have done, I really could not say." She starts to get up. "I must go now, you are confusing me."

"No, you may not leave until I say so!" He blocks her path, his voice commanding.

"How dare you tell me what to do, do you know who I am?"

"Yes, you are Lady Arbella Stuart, and I am commanded by the queen herself as I have already said. You are to remain here until I decide you may leave."

"I have to stay here?"

"I repeat, until I say otherwise!" She sits down again, biting her nails nervously. Sir Henry pulls up a chair to sit opposite her.

"Why did you write that letter?"

"You mean the letter that Dodderidge took?"

"Are there any other letters?"

"I am not sure."

"The letter that Dodderidge took for you, who else helped you with it?"

"I asked my tutor, but he is not here. He said he would, but he will not be here until Easter. I cannot wait to get married until then, but I would never offend her majesty and if I have, then I am heartily sorry, for I did not mean to."

"Who is your tutor and where is he now?"

"Mr Starkey, I think he is with his family. He is very kind to me, the only friend I have in this house."

"Is he? I will need to question him."

"Oh no! You cannot do that, he knows nothing, nothing at all. I was going to ask him to help me. But he cannot help me if he is not here can he?"

"Have you ever met Edward Seymour?"

"I do not think so."

"And yet you wish to marry him."

Arbella begins to laugh.

"Yes I did, what a strange thing to wish for; all women should marry. That is why my uncles helped me. Are you married, Sir Henry?"

"You are trying my patience Lady Arbella! Are you trying to be deliberately obstructive?"

"No ... it is just that ... my memory. I cannot think when you keep asking me so many questions."

"Very well," he replies. "Perhaps you can tell me in your own words how this idea of marrying Edward Seymour first came to you."

"The idea came to me a long time ago, or was it only last week? I do not know, does it matter?"

"Yes it does matter; you must try to remember."

"You see I am kept here as a prisoner. I am not allowed to see anyone or do anything. I have ideas, but I must repress them and they come to nothing. Husbands are not that easy to find, not good ones. Sometimes I think I will go quite mad, yes mad! What would everyone say to that?"

He regards her thoughtfully.

"I think you are tired. Would you find it easier to marshall your thoughts if you wrote everything down?"

"Yes, most definitely. I can write very well, you know. I have been told that my handwriting is very fine indeed, you can see for yourself from my letter to the queen. My lady grandmother has spent so much money on my education, which is as good as the queen's herself. I can definitely write on my own, without any help from anyone."

The words come tumbling out in a garbled rush and he gets up, bemused by her change of mood.

"You should go to your bed now and tomorrow I shall read what you have written about this affair. Make no mistake, Lady Arbella, I mean to find out everything, one way or another."

She looks at him coolly before leaving, passing Bess and William outside without a word.

"Please come in," Sir Henry asks them.

"Has Lady Arbella answered your questions, Sir Henry?" asks Bess, now hardly able to contain her anxiety. "If so, we should like to know what all this is about."

"She has not answered any of my questions, countess. In fact, she is very distracted. I fear she is not quite well."

He looks over to the remainder of the family who are still waiting in the Long Gallery, surreptitiously watching, and shuts the door.

"We must speak privately."

He pauses to gather his thoughts, before telling them the details of how his visit has been thought necessary by the queen. Bess is so enraged that she interrupts him mid sentence.

"This is absolute nonsense! What is the girl about? She knows only the queen may decide such matters."

"I cannot speak for my brother Henry, but I can assure you I would never entertain such an outrageous idea," William tells him emphatically.

"God's blood! You cannot believe that my son William was involved in this foolhardy scheme. My eldest son, Henry, yes, he may be foolish enough, but this is complete madness, Arbella has lost her wits! How was this letter sent?"

"One of your servants, Dodderidge, rode to Lord Hertford's house with it. He has been arrested, pending my investigation."

"Dodderidge? I thought he was visiting his family. Did he know the contents of the letter?"

"We cannot be sure, he is denying any knowledge, of course. He told us that she threatened to kill herself if he did not help her."

Bess and William both look horrified at this news.

"So you can understand that the queen became very concerned when she found out, and I was dispatched here right away."

"How could she do this? After all I have done for her. That ungrateful girl! I have a good mind to box her ears!"

Bess starts to move towards the door, but Sir Henry raises his hand in a gesture of restraint.

"Leave her be, countess. She is going to write a statement, which I shall look at in the morning."

"May I be permitted to read her letter now, Sir Henry?"

"I do not see why not." He hands it to Bess and she studies it with a growing sense of fury.

"I should have guessed she would do something of this nature. I have been so careful over the years but it has not been enough." She looks at him anxiously. "I hope her majesty does not believe that we had any part in this ridiculous idea?"

"Please do not distress yourself, countess. My first impression of your granddaughter leads me to believe that she has a hysterical nature. Is that the case?"

"She chafes at her isolation here with me, what young woman would not? Perhaps it has affected her reason. I struggle to cope with her at times, I must admit."

William puts his hand on her arm in a gesture of concern.

"Lady mother, I think you should rest now, all this has been a shock for you. I will call for Ruby and she will help you to lie down."

Bess nods dumbly, and allows herself to be persuaded. It has all been stressful and she is feeling slightly overwhelmed.

"I shall write to the queen and reassure her of my ignorance in this matter. Her majesty cannot believe I had any part in it. Please excuse me, Sir Henry."

"Of course," he says. "I shall await Lady Arbella's written statement tomorrow, which I hope will make more sense than our conversation a few moments ago."

William returns with Ruby who helps Bess to go to her chamber. When they have gone, William turns to Sir Henry, his face serious.

"The care of my niece is becoming too much for my lady mother. As you can see, she is of advancing years, and this latest upset is very trying for her."

"Yes, I can see it is a difficult situation."

"My niece is of a romantic disposition, with a vivid imagination. I think her attempt to arrange a marriage for herself is an indication of how desperate she has become."

"I agree, but she must not be allowed to imagine that such ideas are within the realms of possibility, her majesty will decide if and when a marriage will take place."

"Of course," William replies. "We are all aware of it, Lady Arbella is too of course. I cannot think what happened to make her believe she could possibly marry anyone in this way."

Sir Henry stifles a yawn, he is now very tired and it is getting late. William is apologetic. "Forgive me, you must be in need of a rest yourself after your long journey. You will stay with us of course, I will have a servant show you to one of the guest suites and send up a tray of food."

"Thank you, I fear there is little more I can achieve tonight."

William leaves him alone, and hurries away to tell the others and order the preparation of a bedchamber for their unexpected guest. With a few moments to himself, Sir Henry wanders back into the Long Gallery, his hands behind his back, ignoring the family gathered at the far end. He peers at the wall hangings, the carved frieze above the chimneypiece and the two alabaster statues of Justice and Mercy, for he has heard tales of this fine house with its costly furnishings and adornments. He is disappointed to find it gaudy and ostentatious, too much for his own taste. On his approach to the house earlier, he could not help but see the initials ES and he shook his head in disapproval at such blatant self-promotion. But he knows that Bess is highly thought of by the queen, so he will keep his opinions to himself.

As for the Lady Arbella, he is beginning to question her sanity after speaking to her just now; but he is prepared to give her the benefit of the doubt, and see how lucid she is after a night's sleep. He yawns loudly and hopes the guest bedchamber is comfortable, which given the quality of everything else he has seen so far, is highly likely, thank the Lord.

☙❧

BESS

Palace of Whitehall, London

To Elizabeth Talbot, the Dowager Countess of Shrewsbury.

Countess,

I have been commanded to write to you by Her Gracious Majesty Queen Elizabeth, regarding the matter of your granddaughter's latest behaviour and continued presence at Hardwick Hall with you. Sir Henry Brounker returned to Court on 13 January and reported that Lady Arbella had been led astray by base companions. He was able to reassure her majesty that the attempted effort to secure this foolish marriage with Edward Seymour, was nothing more than a half-baked plan that would never have been successful. He also feels that Lady Arbella is being kept too strictly, which may be detrimental to her health, and concluded that Lord Hertford was completely innocent of the whole affair. It is to be regretted that your sons, Henry and William, have been implicated, but no evidence has been found against them. I am to inform you that the queen wishes your granddaughter to remain under your care, and knowing how your wish is to continue serving her majesty, this reply will no doubt be welcome to you.

I have also written to your granddaughter today, urging her to live in good harmony with you and with a warning that any similar transgressions in the future will not be so gently dealt with by her majesty. I should also add that in my own view, the disparity in age between these two people is so great, that the idea of a marriage would be quite ridiculous, and the plan was doomed to fail from the start.

Written this day xv of January 1603 by Sir John Stanhope, Vice-Chamberlain to Her Majesty Queen Elizabeth.

16 February 1603

Now the dust has settled from Arbella's failed bid to escape and marry Edward Seymour, the atmosphere at Hardwick is very strained. The letter written by John Stanhope only added to the humiliation felt by the family. Bess cannot bring herself to relax the strictness of the enforced regime and is puzzled as to why it should be, given the events of the last month. She has told Timothy to intercept Arbella's letters intended for local neighbours who are sympathetic to her. Meanwhile Arbella writes again to the queen begging to be allowed to come to Court. She is not speaking to her grandmother now, which makes for an even tenser atmosphere between the two of them.

After having breakfast on a tray in her bedchamber, Bess settles down to look at her accounts. Caesar sits quietly at her feet and she will occasionally stroke him, which he accepts regally as if no more than his due. All around her the house is busy and she can hear the servants cleaning floors and attending to the fires. The relentless winds earlier in the year have subsided and given way to thick white snow, which gently coats the house and surrounding countryside, whilst long icicles hang like jagged teeth above the windows. She pulls her shawl more tightly around her shoulders and dips her quill into the black ink once more. Just then there is a rustle as some thick parchment is pushed under the door and she hears fading footsteps. Puzzled, she goes over and picks it up, recognising Arbella's neat, slanting handwriting on the first page, but which deteriorates so much that by the last page, it is virtually indecipherable.

After ten minutes of careful reading she says aloud to herself "Oh dear, what are you thinking?"

There is nothing else for it. Calling for Ruby who is sewing in the adjoining chamber, she tells her to bring Arbella without delay, then she waits. Ruby appears with Arbella almost at once before tactfully leaving the chamber. Bess is shocked by Arbella's appearance, for she has lost weight since Christmas, and looks gaunt and tired.

"Will you sit, child?" She asks her gently, but Arbella shakes her head. Bess holds up the letter and waves it like a flag in front of her. "Whatever do you mean by sending me this rambling and incoherent letter? You claim to have a secret lover, who will help you to escape! What madness is this?"

Arbella stares at her blankly and remains silent.

"Who is this man and how did you meet him? I am waiting!"

Reluctantly, Arbella finally replies, but her voice is cold and hard.

"I am not going to tell you; it is my secret."

"What is wrong with you? Why are you acting in this way?"

"You think to control my life, but I have many friends that you know nothing of, and they have promised to help me escape."

"And where would you go?"

"Far away from here!" She cries passionately. "My lover is very powerful, of royal blood and Scottish."

Bess gives a disbelieving laugh. "You will be telling me it is King James himself, next!"

"You would not be wrong."

"Arbella, what are you saying? That is not possible."

"I have said too much, I will say no more of him." She puts her hand over her mouth in a childish gesture, and Bess throws the letter on the desk.

"Put this silly notion from your mind. I do not think you realise what a lucky escape you had last month. Sir Henry believed you were lead astray by your so-called 'friends'. Meanwhile, I was left to reassure her majesty in the strongest terms that I had no knowledge of your plans."

Bess winces as she sits down, gripping her stick for support.

"I have given you the best of everything, the finest education and clothes. I have introduced you to everyone who is important at Court and you have lacked for nothing. It has taken me a lifetime to build the relationship I have with the queen, and now she trusts me implicitly. Your behaviour threatens everything I have achieved over the years. I cannot begin to tell you how disappointed I am with you."

"It is not my fault! You have driven me to it. If I had been allowed to live at Court and marry, everything would have been different. You could have tried harder with the queen to gain my freedom!"

"I did try, often, and to no avail. These schemes of yours, these mad ideas have got to stop, Arbella."

"Is it any wonder I have ideas, the life I am forced to lead? No one understands me here; I am not living the life of a royal princess as I was born to. I am just growing older and more miserable. Well, I will not stand for it any more, I have had enough. My secret lover will come one dark night and take me far away from this hateful place, and we will be married and live happily ever after. What do you say to that?"

"I say you have childish dreams that are not of the real world. I will write yet again to the queen and request that you go to Court, away from Hardwick, since you are determined to make trouble. I cannot be responsible for you any longer."

Arbella finally begins to sob and runs to the door, turning once to glare angrily at her grandmother.

"That would please me beyond words! I do not wish to remain here another minute!"

"Come back here at once! I have not said you may leave; how dare you turn your back on me!"

But Arbella rushes out and Bess gets up to follow, hampered by age, she is not as fast.

"You are a wicked, selfish child!" she screams at Arbella's back. "If your parents could see you now, they would be ashamed. After all I have given you, the best of everything, and this is how you re-pay me! Your uncle Henry is only helping you for his own ends, can you not see it? You do not deserve to call yourself a Stuart..."

But Arbella has fled downstairs, knocking over a servant bearing a tray and disappeared from view. Bess rubs her forehead wearily, closes the door and returns to her desk. She picks up her quill to write to the queen once more as promised, although she doubts anything will happen. She is seriously worried that if Arbella continues to be so wayward and unpredictable, they will both end up in the Tower, and Bess, the richest woman in the land, apart from the queen, will be powerless to stop it.

༺༻

In another part of the house, Arbella's tutor, Mr James Starkey, having returned earlier than expected, is sitting alone at his writing table. On it there are several books left out from the day before that he has not yet put away. His chamber is simply furnished, and quite unlike the lavish surroundings of his employer; but it does have a small fireplace that is plentifully supplied with coal. There is a narrow bed, a wooden chair and a small, folding table upon which sits a blue and white china jug and bowl, together with his most precious possession, a Bible. The carpenter has put up some shelves to hold the books that Bess has bought for him to teach Arbella; sometimes he reads them by the light of the candle when he cannot sleep. He has not moved for the last two hours, but stares through the window at the snow. The fire has gone out and with it any warmth, so his limbs feel cold and stiff, but he does not care.

Mr. Starkey is a creature of habit, every morning he rises at 6am to pray before breakfast, then returns to his chamber to prepare lessons for Arbella. His usual day passes quietly and he is not required to teach William's children any more, as they have moved to Owlcotes and the eldest, Wylkyn, has started school. On Sundays and Feast Days, he is kept busy in his role as chaplain, but when possible, he loves to walk and climb in the Derbyshire hills. The other servants look askance as he sets off in a stout pair of boots, with a knapsack containing a drink and a book, returning at dusk with his cheeks glowing and ready for a hearty meal. When Arbella first asked him to help her, he was flattered. But in the days that followed, he realises it would be very dangerous for him to be involved. Then he thinks he is already involved, by the simple fact that she has confided in him. Who is going to believe that after all the time they have spent together with their books, that he is not an accomplice to any of her ideas? He has heard about the failed marriage plan from some of the servants, they have spoken of little else recently. Without expression, he listens to them telling the tale and does not betray his fear that he could be found to have been a part of this marriage plan, and possibly taken to the Tower and found guilty of treason. The thought of it fills him with such terror that he cannot swallow and has to leave them quickly, only to be violently sick as soon as he reaches the relative safety of his chamber. Thoughts of escape are quickly dismissed, he knows that they would find him soon enough, and he does not have the funds to pay for a passage to France where he would be safe.

Some of the servants think Lady Arbella has a streak of madness; they talk of her unpredictable outbursts and sometimes strange conversations that the family tries to hide. Most of the seventy servants that Bess employs, know her to be a spoilt, haughty young woman and they are indifferent to her trials and tribulations. But Mr Starkey knows her better than any of them and has seen her struggle with her emotions and in despair over the unfairness of her captivity. Is it her fault if she is haughty? For has not her grandmother brought her up to believe she is a royal princess who must be addressed as 'highness'? Is it her fault if she is spoilt when her grandmother has given her the best that money can buy, all her life? But he says nothing and keeps his counsel when they discuss her. If he was ever to talk about her, he would tell them that he admires her intelligent and enquiring mind, surely so unusual for a woman; and believes that she is, in fact, cleverer than some of the men he has met in his lifetime. Added to which, she is quite beautiful in his eyes, with her soft and sensitive nature. The truth of it is that he feels very sorry for her. Often he watches with sadness as she cries during lessons, or tells him of a particular grievance; he aches to put his arm round her, to hold her close and make everything right.

Jolted out of these thoughts, he picks up his quill. It is a great effort for him to move and write now, but he forces himself, and after fifteen minutes he has painstakingly written three short sentences. Just as slowly, he puts down the quill and carefully props the letter up against his books so that those who will find him can see it. He stands up; stretching stiffly and quietly manoeuvres his chair under a ceiling beam before reaching under his bed where he has hidden a length of rope. All his movements seem to require a great effort and are taking all his concentration. He is very tired. Slowly he takes off his boots and puts them neatly beside the desk before climbing on the chair. He feels that he is dreaming; his senses are heightened so that the wooden seat feels harder than usual against his bare feet. There is a pounding in his ears and the only thing real to him is the roughness of the rope and the overwhelming smell of fear as he swallows the bile from his stomach.

It is a tremendous struggle to throw the rope over the beam and tie it round his neck; it takes him several attempts before he is satisfied. The sweat from his hands has made it slippery and by the time he manages to do it, he is panting heavily.

A floorboard creaks as someone walks past his door and he stops to listen intently. No one has ever been into his chamber, it is his own private space, and now at this moment, he is glad of it.

Seconds pass and he fleetingly remembers he has not set Arbella's work for the next day, but it does not matter any more. He hopes she will remember him kindly and not judge him harshly. "Forgive me Lord!" he cries, then with a grunt, he kicks the chair from under his feet.

The last thing he sees is the bright sunlight glinting on the snow covered Derbyshire countryside, hurting his eyes.

○○○

Hardwick Hall,

Derbyshire

My dear Uncle Henry,

We awoke this morning to find my faithful tutor, James Starkey, has taken his own life by hanging himself. This has been a terrible shock to me and the household. I find myself trembling so much that I can hardly write at all and my mind is overwhelmed with the thought that he was so unhappy, yet we did not see it or were able to help him. To take one's own life is a terrible sin and I know he must have been desperate to do it. Sometimes I can feel myself sinking into such depths of despair that I imagine taking one step further and … but no, I will not write down such thoughts. You must forgive me, I am very upset by this news. He has been a good friend to me and I am very saddened that he should choose to end his life. May God have mercy on his soul. My lady grandmother has told me that in all likelihood, he was afraid that since Dodderidge was arrested, a charge of treason would be brought against him. Although she has not said as much in words, I know she considers his death to be as a result of my plan to marry Edward Seymour. To conclude that I am in some way responsible for his death hurts me deeply.

I wish I could say to her that it is not I who is to blame, but rather the circumstances, which have forced me to take such drastic action to secure myself a husband. We all know who is responsible for those circumstances.

This has made me all the more determined to escape from my lady grandmothers house for I feel that if I have to live here a moment longer, I am very much afraid I will truly go mad. I have written again to her majesty begging to be allowed at Court, but the queen is very ill, possibly dying, so I doubt she has even seen my letter. I have told my lady grandmother that I will refuse food until I may be allowed to leave this place, such is the despair I am forced to endure. Your recent letter proposing to take me from here within weeks did give me some hope, and I beg of you with all my heart to implement the plan at once. I will be ready, day or night, but we must take great care. My lady grandmother is still ever watchful of me, and her spies are everywhere. I wish you good luck and God speed with this endeavour.

I remain your ever loving niece, Arbella, dated this day vii February 1603

Arbella takes the news about Mr Starkey so badly that she has to be confined to her bed for several weeks. She is laid low with stomach pains, vomiting, aches in her muscles and painful redness of her skin.

Disorientated and restless, she is unaware of the family who watch her anxiously. Dr. Hunton tries various remedies such as the application of leeches and some herbal medicines he has made himself, but all are unsuccessful. He advises rest and Bess realises there is nothing he can do to help her. But it is not just Arbella who is affected by Mr. Starkey's suicide. For a long time afterwards there is an air of shocked disbelief at Hardwick. Bess has never experienced such a tragedy with any servant before, and in her letter to his family, she expresses her deep regret, whilst praising his many good qualities. He is, of course, buried in unhallowed ground, and although Arbella wants to attend the funeral, she is too ill to do so.

A new chaplain will have to be found, but Bess is now reluctant to engage a replacement tutor for Arbella, fearing that another man will unwittingly be drawn into her granddaughter's wayward schemes. For moral support, Bess has summoned William and Elizabeth to visit, and they arrive as the weather is just beginning to feel warmer in March. The snow has melted and the first of the snowdrops are coming through the ground. After the usual greetings, they sit down to eat, but there is a conspicuous space where Arbella should be seated.

"Will Arbella not be joining us, lady mother?" asks Elizabeth as they help themselves from the assorted dishes on the table. "You mentioned that she spends a lot of her time writing at her desk."

"Most of which is complete nonsense," says William dismissively, as he peels himself an orange.

"This refusal to eat is making her ill. I am very worried about her, but Dr. Hunton says there is nothing that can be done," replies Bess.

"Have we tried that hard? We should force her to eat," he says emphatically. "Hold her down."

Bess and Elizabeth look shocked. "You cannot force anyone to eat," Elizabeth tells him firmly.

"I agree," says Bess. "What you suggest is very undignified."

"So is fading away due to lack of food. Typical female hysteria!"

"I am not subjecting her to such violence. She will start to eat when she realises this protest will not achieve anything."

"Shall I try to talk to her?" asks Elizabeth.

No one has a chance to reply as two servants enter at speed, out of breath from running, and bow in unison.

"Your grace, there are two men demanding entry at the gate," one of them announces.

"Do these men have names?" asks William.

"One is Sir John Stapleton, sir, and the other is your brother, Henry Cavendish."

"Stapleton, the Catholic?" queries William and looks at Bess in surprise.

"I knew he was in the area, I have had my men around the village on watch over the last few days. What do they want?" she says.

"Henry Cavendish wishes to speak to his niece, the Lady Arbella, your grace."

"Does he?" Bess is unperturbed and carries on eating.

William gets up, "I will go and speak to them."

"No, William, sit down." She turns to the servants. "My son may come inside and speak to Lady Arbella for two hours, tell him, no more. Stapleton is not to be admitted under any circumstances."

The servants bow again and make their way back to the front gates. Bess wipes her mouth on a linen napkin and looks at Elizabeth, who is watching the proceedings with fascination.

"Elizabeth, would you be so good as to ask a servant to find Arbella, and tell her that her uncle Henry is waiting at the gates to see her?"

"Of course." Elizabeth gets up and disappears, leaving Bess and William to wait.

"What is Henry up to now?" asks William with a frown.

"We shall shortly find out I think, come with me."

William helps his mother up and they walk over to the window that overlooks the front gates. They watch as the servants are seen conveying her message, and Henry dismounts before the gate is unlocked and passes through. Stapleton stands holding the reins of both horses.

"Are you just going to let them walk around the grounds?" William sounds surprised.

"My men have their orders, they will not be able to take her."

"I hope you are right."

Elizabeth joins them at the window and they see Arbella come towards her uncle. Even from this distance she does not look well, and leans on Henry for support when she reaches him.

"This situation with Arbella is intolerable for both of you, for all of us. And Henry is not helping matters as usual," observes William.

"I had expected no less of Henry. It has to continue as long as the queen lives. We are all at her mercy."

"And when she no longer lives, what then?"

"William! To talk thus ..." exclaims Elizabeth, shocked by his question.

"Do not be alarmed, Elizabeth," Bess is quick to reassure her. "Such talk will be all over Court, whispered in corners of course. And we are amongst friends here."

"Has the queen named a successor yet?"

"Has she ever done so? No, but King James has been secretly establishing himself here in recent years. He has a son and heir, so there will not be much doubt about it."

They are interrupted by another servant. "Your grace, the Lady Arbella and Sir Henry wish to speak to you."

"Bring them up," Bess replies with some reluctance.

She gestures to William and Elizabeth for them to sit down on the seat by the window, and brings herself up to her full height, breathing deeply to calm herself. After a minute Arbella appears on Henry's arm, and they position themselves about ten feet from where Bess stands. Henry gives an exaggerated bow and has a supercilious expression on his face. Arbella looks defiant, although it is clear she is unwell, her skin is pinched and as white as a sheet.

"So Henry, what brings you to see me after all this time?" Bess asks wearily.

"My lady grandmother ..." begins Arbella.

"I addressed the question to my son. Be silent until you are spoken to, Arbella!"

Henry's expression does not change. "I am pleased to see you looking so well, lady mother. And William, I see you are still trying to ingratiate yourself with the one person who holds all the purse strings."

William makes a half movement to get up, but Elizabeth puts a restraining hand to stop him. Henry turns his attention to William's wife.

"And Elizabeth, how are you finding your new life inside the Cavendish family? Very cosy is it not? Our mother is not on speaking terms with most of her children, despite claiming to love us all."

Elizabeth looks at him stony-faced and does not reply.

"My visit here today is merely to see my dear niece and take her for an outing. The weather is so fine today …"

"… so you thought she would benefit from a change of scenery. How very thoughtful of you Henry," Bess finishes for him.

He smiles, "just so. If you have no objection, we are ready to leave at once and will be back by nightfall."

"And where are you planning to go?"

"Not far, lady mother. Do not be alarmed, I shall take great care of your jewel."

"I cannot allow you to take Arbella, the reasons are well known to both of you. Why do you come here and disturb me with these outlandish schemes?" she demands.

"I can tell you why!" interrupts William, getting up. "Because he always likes to cause trouble."

"You keep out of this! It has nothing to do with you. If you had been a better uncle to Arbella, she might not be so keen to leave here," Henry retorts.

"You are deliberately going against the wishes of the queen if you think to remove Arbella."

"For all we know, the queen may already be dead; I would not trust Cecil an inch."

William gives a dismissive laugh. "When the time comes, our niece will go to Court, but it will have nothing to do with you. Anyhow what exactly did you plan to do with Arbella? Where would you go?"

"We have friends in the West Country," replies Henry evasively.

"He means Edward Seymour, Lord Beauchamp," says Bess and they all look at her, now it is Henry's turn to laugh.

"Of course you know all about the plan, lady mother, I should have guessed. Nothing happens that you do not know about."

"What is this?" asks William.

"There are rumours that he has raised an army with the help of the French, to support Arbella's claim to the throne."

Henry looks sheepish, for even as Bess tells them, it sounds too preposterous to think that anything will come of it.

"So this is your grand plan, is it? To place Arbella in danger; do you realise what will happen if there is a challenge to the succession? Arbella could be tried for treason and sent to her death!" William is red faced with anger. "Go back to your mistresses Henry, and keep out of matters you do not understand!"

"Will you two be silent!" Bess cries with exasperation.

"May I be allowed to speak now?" Arbella's voice is heard at last. "Are you telling me I may not go with my uncle?"

"Yes, as well you know child, you may walk with your uncle in the grounds, under guard, but that is all. You did not expect anything more, did you?"

"You see uncle Henry, I am a prisoner just like my aunt, the Scottish Queen; and we all know what happened to her!" Arbella pulls herself away from Henry and begins to walk up and down in agitation. "I have pains throughout my body, why is it I cannot sleep? Why do I sometimes feel so confused and do not know where I am? Do you know what I saw last night, the ghost of Mr. Starkey, he was running through the grounds. If he was here now, he would know what to do, when is he coming back, he has been away for so long …?"

"Arbella, you must go to your chamber and lie down, you are not well," Bess tells her in alarm.

"No!" she shouts in reply. "I shall not go to my chamber. I have no chamber, there is only your own. I shall spend some time with my uncle who has been kind enough to come and visit me."

Henry takes her arm again and guides her towards the door. "This is what you have driven her to, I hope you are satisfied," he says with a reproachful look at Bess.

"I have driven her to nothing. She is ill and should be in her bed; do not let her get overtired," Bess urges as they leave, although they give no sign they have heard her.

"Henry is looking old, his lifestyle must be catching up with him," muses William, who pours himself some more wine. "Shall I go after them?"

"There is no need, I have taken care of it," Bess tells him and sits down heavily.

Elizabeth has been watching the scene in amazement, and had not realised the extent of the animosity between the family members. But she is not stupid, and knows it is Bess who holds all the cards in this game, for the moment.

༄

"Open up and let us pass at once!" Henry commands as he stands at the gates with Arbella.

A curious crowd has gathered, craning their necks to see the latest Cavendish family disagreement.

"The old countess is not letting her leave," someone says.

There are cries of "shame!" which heartens Arbella's resolve, but her exit is blocked by a dozen burly men, all in the Cavendish livery, who regard them impassively.

"Did you hear my uncle? I command you to open these gates!" Arbella shouts to them. The men remain still, staring straight ahead. "Who is in charge here?"

"I am, highness." One of the men steps forward and Henry goes up to him, his voice low.

"I will give you money if you let us through, here, a gold coin."

"I cannot take it, sir. I have my orders."

He looks up to where Bess is watching the proceedings with William and Elizabeth.

"Come along man, can you not see the cruelty of keeping the Lady Arbella here against her will? Look, I will make it two gold coins, you cannot refuse now."

"Sorry, sir. I take my orders from the countess, no-one else," the man replies and turns back in line with the others.

Arbella stamps her foot in frustration and whispers to Henry, "it is no matter, I will pass anyway, they will not dare to lay a finger on me."

But Arbella is in for a shock if she thinks the men will shrink from physically restraining her. As she comes forward to push her way through the line, they hold firm and two of them grasp her shoulders, their arms locked. With the little strength she has anyway, she quickly realises that they are not going to budge. Meanwhile Henry is trying to pull her towards the gate and an unseemly scuffle takes place. The men position themselves to stand between Arbella and Henry, slowing pushing Henry one way and Arbella the other.

"Let … me … pass!" She pants.

"Henry, what is happening?" John Stapleton is still holding the horses in the lane, unable to see them.

"They will not let Lady Arbella out!" Henry shouts as Arbella is pushed further and further back from him.

"I will have to leave," he tells her. "It is too dangerous, I fear you will get hurt; I will think of another plan"

"No, no! Do not leave me here!" she wails. Just as Henry is finally pushed through the gates, he looks up at the window where Bess is watching, and scowls at her in sulky displeasure. There is a slam as the gatekeeper shuts the door firmly and locks it. Arbella collapses to the ground in a torrent of frustrated and angry tears.

Upstairs, Elizabeth turns to Bess. "May I go her?"

Bess nods. "Take her straight to bed. I will send up a camomile tisane to calm her."

Elizabeth runs outside, and they watch as she helps Arbella to her feet. Now the gates are secure, the men disperse to their other duties and leave the two women to make their way back inside the house, Arbella leaning heavily on Elizabeth for support. Henry is still cursing as he mounts his horse, and they ride off at a gallop;

Arbella hears them leaving and gives a cry of despair. It has been a humiliating failure for Henry, and he will be in no hurry to try again.

William helps Bess to sit down again, concerned that she looks so strained. "That was well done, lady mother," he tells her. "Your men are very loyal."

"Yes," she agrees with a hint of resignation. "Some of them have been with me for many years, and their fathers before them. This story will be all over the village by the end of the day."

"You cannot stop it from being talked about."

"But it makes me look so heartless."

"People know it is not you, but the queen who insists that Arbella is kept here."

"Do they? Sometimes I am not so sure. Arbella has convinced herself that I am responsible for all her misery. No matter how many times I tell her, she does not believe me."

"She does not wish to believe you. It is easier for her to blame you, than to blame the queen."

"But I know now that the queen will not allow her to marry while she is still on the throne. It has taken me years to realise it. There was never going to be any marriage, to a foreign prince or a noble Englishman. It was all a sham."

"While the queen lives, yes, but afterwards there will be hope surely?"

"Who knows? We shall have a Stuart king. Years ago I had high hopes that he might marry Arbella, but that was not to be either."

"They say the Danish Queen Anne is unhappy in the marriage and James is a poor husband. At least Arbella is spared that fate."

"Yes, poor Anne, I hear he prefers the company of men."

They look at one another meaningfully. James' preference for men, and the honours he showers on his favourites, are well known.

"I am getting so tired of these episodes with Arbella," she says wearily. "It is not what I had planned for my old age. All I want is to live quietly and peacefully here, seeing my family and working at my business interests. I do not have the same energy to cope with it all. Arbella hates me in a way that no grandchild should, I can see it in her face when she looks at me, despite all I have done for her over the years. I have loved that child as if she was my own; I would die for her." She looks at him with tears in her eyes. "The one thing that I wanted for so long will never happen. I have achieved much, it is true, but pleasing the queen and doing my duty has brought about the breakdown of my relationship with Arbella."

"She is not the easiest of people, so highly strung and emotional."

"I should not have spoilt her so much, it has not done her any good. I could not help it, William, when her parents died and Margaret Lennox too, she had no-one else but me."

"You must not feel guilty, you did your best for her."

"Whatever shall I do if James wants to keep her here too?"

"He will want her at Court," he hastily reassures her. "She is a Stuart and his cousin. Once he is king, he will send for her, I am sure of it."

"But when he sees her! So very underweight and ill. They will all think I have been neglecting her."

"No, they will not think that, lady mother. You are worrying too much."

Bess wipes her eyes and gets up. "This has not been a good start to your visit and I am sorry for it."

"We wish to help in any way we can. Why do you not go away for few days and have a rest? Perhaps stay with the Manners family at Haddon Hall, I am sure they would be delighted to see you; Elizabeth and I will stay here with Arbella."

"I shall think on it, thank you, William," She looks at him tenderly. "I sometimes wonder what I would do without you and Frances, my only two children now to still be part of my life."

"Now then, do not become maudlin, it does not become you."

"A sign of old age," she replies. "I miss my other grandchildren more than I can say. One day I may be reconciled with Mary and Charles, but Henry …"Suddenly she becomes decisive. "I have had enough of their antics; I shall add a codicil to my will revoking the bequests I have made to Henry and Arbella. They both go too far."

William sees the set of her jaw, and does not attempt to persuade her otherwise.

"Come, you must show me the work in the gardens. We saw the men digging as we arrived."

They make their way outside and William gives a sigh of relief that he has managed to distract his mother from her problems and worries. He hopes for all their sakes that the death of the queen will be soon.

ଔଃ

27 March 1603

The letter that Bess and Arbella have been so urgently waiting for finally arrives just before dark, carrying news that the queen has died three days previously and James VI of Scotland is now James I of England. When Bess opens it, she is alone, but quickly summons everyone, from William, Elizabeth and Arbella, to the lowest and youngest servant in the house. It takes some time for everyone to assemble, but this is an historic moment and she wants to give it due recognition.

She stares at the writing, almost disbelievingly that it has finally happened. She knew the queen when she was still Princess Elizabeth, and they did indeed 'grow old together.' As godmother to both Henry and Charles, she was a part of their lives, albeit at a distance. Bess is acutely aware that it is the end of an era and brings uncertainty for the future. She makes the announcement without fuss and it is received quietly with a few sobs from the women. Most of the ladies, gentlemen and servants have known no other monarch and they shake their head sadly. Arbella receives the news with apparent calm and runs back to her chamber to order the packing of her clothes in readiness. But she still has to wait for the new king to send for her.

಄ೞ

April 1603

William and Elizabeth leave at once for London where they will wait for King James to make his entry into the city and take his throne. Other members of the Court have already made their way to Scotland to be amongst the first to swear allegiance to him, and Bess has heard that Gilbert intends to invite the king to stay at his house in Worksop as he travels south. She has a pang of envy which she quickly supresses. The house at Worksop is the one that George built so proudly and which cost him so much money. He would have been pleased beyond words to know that James will be staying there. Bess realises that her own dreams of entertaining royalty at Hardwick will never come true, and she thinks to herself that Gilbert and Mary will no doubt be even more out of pocket after entertaining the king and all his retinue. Bess has no choice now but to move her granddaughter to an antechamber just off her main bedchamber, but the two women are still within sight of one another. When the letter from King James finally arrives, Bess asks a servant to bring Arbella at once.

There is a knock at her study door and Arbella comes in, looking gaunt with dark shadows under her eyes.

She crosses her arms and stares at the floor; her gown looks too big, as if it has been made for someone else.

"Sit down, child" says Bess gently. "How has it come to this between us? Will you not even look at me?"

"I prefer to stand." She looks up, focusing on the parchment which rests in front of Bess. "Is that the letter from King James telling me I can leave now?"

Bess exhales heavily.

"Since the death of our dear queen, I have been waiting to hear my instructions regarding your care. I have now heard and I wanted to tell you without delay. His majesty has decreed that you are to go to the Earl of Kent as soon as possible, from there on to London when the king himself arrives, and you can join the royal party."

Arbella does not respond and Bess wonders if she has heard.

"Well, child, this is what you wanted, you will soon be gone from this place."

"Why do you still call me 'child'? It is many years since I was a child, I am now a woman!"

"I call you "child" because to me, I will always see you as that little girl when you first came to live with me. I am sorry if you do not like it."

When Arbella finally looks at her grandmother, all the years of frustration and heartache are visible in her face. "Has the king given any hint of what my future holds?"

"Not yet, but he will. You are the highest-ranking female relative of the late queen. And you are a Stuart, as is the king himself."

"Will I have to attend the late queen's funeral?"

"Of course, it will be expected of you."

"I was often refused permission to come to Court and see the queen when she was alive, why should I go now that she is dead? I do not see why I should. No, I shall not attend the funeral!"

"But you must go to the funeral, Arbella, it would be unthinkable for you to refuse."

"There is no more 'must' from you, lady grandmother. I am free of you now, do you not understand? I can do as I wish."

"No, you will not be able to do as you wish. That is something you will have to learn. There will be restrictions at the Court of King James, and you will have to make your own way there. I do not think it will be easy for you, but I hope that you will remember all I have taught you and be a credit to your family."

"Is that all you think about? What people will say?" Arbella leans on the desk, the veins on her painfully thin arms are like the twisted roots of a tree. "My parents would never have allowed me to be a prisoner here away from all the excitement of the Court and London. I will never forgive you for it!"

"Your parents could not have prevented it, just as I have not been able to. You have not had such a bad life here Arbella, you have had every luxury in life and your education ..."

"My education! Yes, much good it has done me!" She spits the words out. "I hear the king despises educated women, and thinks they should not be taught anything. My costly education will do me no good at Court whatsoever, you have wasted your money!"

"I did my best for you. I have always loved you and always will."

"Do not talk to me of love! I should have been loved by my husband, if I had been allowed to have one. You have never been concerned for me; I have just been a pawn in your grand schemes. You have always been driven by your ruthless ambition, which has dominated your life and been the ruin of mine! I used to think your husband's speeches about you were the result of his confused and jealous mind, I certainly know better now."

"Without my ambitions my family would not be where it is today. You would not have had fine gowns and jewellery and servants …"

"… I care nothing for all that!"

"That is easy for you to say, child."

"Will you stop calling me that!" she screams.

They regard one another in silence, then when Arbella speaks first, her voice finds a new confidence.

"Well, all your hopes for me have come to nothing. The great Bess of Hardwick, with all her power and money, has not been able to marry me off to a prince, nor secure me a place at Court. I have never wished to be queen; I have only ever wanted a normal life. How does it make you feel to know those years have been wasted? Shall I tell you how I feel?"

Bess does not get a chance to reply as Arbella continues, hardly pausing for breath.

"The years spent with you have been like a torture for me, I am like a fly caught in your web, trapped and alone. But you did not care did you? As long as you can plan a glittering future for me and tell yourself I am destined for greatness, you are content. Well I have news for you, I am not destined for a crown and I never have been. If I had been born a man then it would have been different."

"This is not all about your feelings!" responds Bess. "Of course you are angry and resentful about your life, but I have done my best for you in difficult circumstances. I could not go against the queen, I had no choice but to obey, you must see that. Was it so wrong of me to hope you would eventually have the best marriage in the land? Why must my family always make me feel guilty for wanting the best for them?"

"Because it is not about the best for them is it? It is the best for you. We must all conform to your wishes and if we do not, then we are cast out. Uncle Henry lives a miserable life in Tutbury Castle because you do not help him, your own flesh and blood. Uncle Gilbert, Aunt Mary and Uncle Charles are all estranged from you. What a family we are!"

"That is enough!" snaps Bess. "You are quick to judge, but you do not know the whole facts. In any case, such matters are no concern of yours."

Arbella gives her a triumphant look.

"The king will decide what is best for me now. Let us pray he is not afraid to have me near to his person, and will give me some hope for a happier future."

"That is also my wish for you," Bess says quietly, her anger quickly disappearing.

"Am I free to go now?"

"Yes, I will arrange transport at once to take you to Bedford at first light tomorrow. You may take all your servants of course. Will you write to me?" She cannot control the tremble in her voice; she has never felt so vulnerable. The question hangs in the air unanswered; Bess can hold back her tears no longer and buries her face in her hands.

"You are breaking my heart!" she sobs.

Arbella stares at her with fierce hatred before leaving quietly, her head held high and ignores the stares of the servants scrubbing the stone floor outside the door.

֍

Hardwick Hall Gardens – August 1603

On warm summer afternoons, Bess likes to take the air and walk round the gardens, her stick a useful aid, as she is sometimes a little unsteady on her feet. Caesar is also slower as he follows her, sniffing and digging the flowerbeds whenever the mood takes him. There is a gentle breeze blowing which ruffles her hair beneath her white cap, and she pushes some stray tendrils back into place. The soft cooing from the dovecote and a gardener turning the earth with his spade are the only sounds. There is nowhere on earth she would rather be than here. Since Arbella's departure it was surprising how quickly the house found peace again. It was as if a great weight had been lifted, not just from Bess' shoulders, but also from the servants, who now only had an old woman to care for. As long as they all go about their work efficiently, their mistress is content and leaves them to get on with it. Her business affairs are just as complex and successful, although now she tires easily and feels the cold winters more than ever. As William is often in London attending to his duties as a Member of Parliament, Timothy has taken over his share of the work and Bess rewards him well for it, increasing his salary proportionally. Frances and Elizabeth visit her each week, usually separately, to make it two visits for her, instead of one. Elizabeth does not particularly relish each visit, but William has asked her specifically to check on his mother while he is away, so she feels obliged. Bess hears the coach arriving and walks along the path to greet her outside the door. As always, Elizabeth is a picture of beauty and elegance. She has dark, glossy hair and a porcelain complexion, made all the more attractive by her deep blue eyes and generous mouth, which is usually quick to smile. William's two sons have accepted her easily enough, although she finds being Bess' daughter-in-law a more daunting role. As the coach draws to a halt, she gives Bess a wave.

"You are late, Elizabeth! I was expecting you over an hour ago."

"I am sorry, lady mother, we were delayed by one of the horses shedding a shoe." She descends from the coach and kisses Bess on both cheeks. "How are you?"

"Hungry. I have been waiting for you and did not want to start the meal without you."

They make their way indoors and out of the bright sunshine. The table is already laid with different cold dishes and as soon as the two women appear, a servant starts to pour wine. Caesar is barking wildly for some reason.

"What is the matter with Caesar?" asks Elizabeth, watching him out of the corner of her eye.

"You seem to have upset him. He was all right until you came," Bess replies and helps herself to a portion of pickled fish and green herbs.

Elizabeth bites her lip; she can see the visit is going to be one of those days when nothing she does is right. Bess gives him a morsel of fish and he is quieter, eventually sitting at her feet.

"Have you heard from William lately?" she asks.

"Yes, he usually writes every day with his news."

"Do you not think you should be with him in London, as a dutiful wife?"

"I care little for London, it is noisy, smelly and crowded. I prefer to be at home."

"I understand how you feel, but I am sure William misses you."

"He is too busy to miss me, anyway he will be home again soon."

"I have good reports of Arbella, she is happy at last with Gilbert and Mary at Court."

"I am pleased for her, life has been difficult in the past."

"Not just for Arbella!" Bess retorts sharply. "I have also had much difficulty."

"Of course, I did not mean to suggest …"

"People always take her side, but it was not easy for me either."

"I know, but she has made a good impression at Court and Queen Anne likes her, which must please you."

"It would please me more if the king would increase Arbella's pension. Robert Cecil has asked me to help with it, but I am not going to give her more money to squander. I have told him I am not willing to do it; I think he was quite surprised. She will have to start being nicer to me, they all will."

"I hope you do not include William and myself," says Elizabeth lightly.

"No, and I hope you never give me cause to say it."

There is an uncomfortable pause and Elizabeth searches for something to neutral to say, but Bess is already ahead of her.

"You said you would bring Wylkyn and James to see me today."

"Actually, I said I would try, but Wylkyn is still at school and James has a bad cold, so I thought it best to leave him at home."

"It is many weeks since I have seen James. He will forget what I look like, I have bought him a Bible; I know he is only young but he will learn to read it as the years pass."

"How kind of you! We have already got one for him, so now he will have two."

"Why did you feel the need to get one when I told you weeks ago that I had ordered one?"

"No lady mother, you did not tell us."

"I beg your pardon, Elizabeth, I most certainly did. In this very room when we were eating, just as we are now."

"I have no recollection, I am sure I would have remembered."

"Well my memory is as good as ever; you must have forgotten."

"I think not," Elizabeth replies testily, suddenly tired of her mother-in-law's mood. Bess looks up from feeding Caesar again. "Whatever is wrong with you today, Elizabeth? I have never known you to be so rude."

"There is nothing wrong with me. I rather think it is you who is not quite well."

"What do you mean?"

"First you berate me for being late, then you react harshly when I mention Arbella's life being difficult. You try to make me feel guilty because the boys are not with me, and you have accused me of lying over a book!"

"You exaggerate! Just because I am getting old it does not mean I am unwell. I really do not know what is wrong with you all, I try to do my best, but it is impossible to please everyone. There is only Frances and William of my children who are still close to me. Henry will always be my bad son, Charles takes Gilbert's side all the time and Mary wants nothing to do with me. It is a different story when they all want money, of course. As for Arbella, do you know she has not sent me one letter since she has been at Court? She has hurt me most cruelly. I do not see why I should always be handing out money to my ungrateful family."

Bess is angrier than Elizabeth has ever seen her. It is obvious that she has been waiting for a while to tell someone about it.

"I am sorry that you feel like this, lady mother, but please do not take it out on me. These are matters I am powerless to control. Although I am needed at home, I come here each week because William wishes it. I do not take kindly to this treatment." She stands up abruptly. "I shall take my leave, you must excuse me, I have a bad headache, good day, lady mother."

"Yes, please go, I would hate to think you are forced to come and visit me!" Bess says as she glares at her departing back. Caesar begins to bark again, aware that the two women are disagreeing, and follows Elizabeth to the door, snapping at her ankles.

"When are you going to discipline this damn dog?" she yells furiously, and lifts her skirts in an attempt to fend him off with her foot.

The little dog backs off and runs back to Bess, still barking. The servant clears away Elizabeth's plate, his eyes downcast.

"Clear it all," she tells him. Calling Caesar, she goes outside again to sit on one of the seats under the shade of the oak tree and reflects on Elizabeth's sudden departure. She was right, Bess did find fault with her from the moment she arrived, she could not seem to stop herself.

"What is happening to me?" she murmurs to Caesar as she strokes his back. "I am spending too long alone and in my own company. Now I have upset Elizabeth, and she probably will not come to see me again."

The dog looks up at her trustingly.

"And I am having a conversation with my dog, this is what it means to be old."

She closes her eyes and rests awhile; it is too warm to do anything else.

☙❦☙

When William hears of the argument between Bess and Elizabeth, he is very concerned and tries to reconcile them. Elizabeth refuses to visit Bess, claiming she is too ill to travel and tells William she is not returning to Hardwick until her mother-in-law apologises. After several visits between the two women and using all his diplomatic skill, William finally persuades Bess to send over an apologetic letter, together with the gift of a silver and emerald brooch, which is enough to pacify her daughter-in-law, and everything returns to normal.

But in March 1605, Bess takes to her bed with a high fever and a hacking cough that keeps her awake at night. William is worried enough to stay at Hardwick and supervise her care personally. He tells her one morning that Arbella has asked the king for permission to visit her.

"And what did his majesty reply?" she asks in a thin voice, in between fits of coughing.

"He was delighted to think there could be harmony between you again."

"There has not been harmony between us for some years," responds Bess sadly.

"And also that you treat her kindly and generously, for his sake."

"Get paper and quill William, you can write a reply for me."

"It can wait, lady mother. You are not well enough."

"No, I shall dictate it now."

Knowing better than to argue, he goes over to her desk and picks up the quill. She cannot bring herself to write directly to Arbella, but tells him to address the letter to the king. He waits as she struggles for breath, but she is determined to speak.

"I find it very strange that my granddaughter, Arbella, should wish to visit me and that she has asked for news of life at Hardwick Hall. If your majesty may recall, she could not wait to leave my side and escape from her life here, which has caused me much grief. If Arbella should doubt her welcome to my house, I may reassure her that she is doubly welcome because of your majesty's gracious attention. In response to your request that I should be monetarily generous to my granddaughter, I have already shown largesse towards her on many occasions, including the purchase of properties on her behalf to ensure an income that should be more than adequate for her needs. Of course she also has her State pension, as kindly sanctioned by your majesty."

Bess stops and Ruby helps her to sip some wine before continuing, saying each word slowly and with care. William still has his head bent over the paper, his quill scratching rapidly.

"I have also given Arbella a gold cup worth £100 and £300 as a gift, which cannot be said to show a lack of feeling or generosity. It is to be remembered that I do have other grandchildren who, although not as elevated in status as Arbella, have their own needs and my wish to help them is undiminished. Of course if my granddaughter wishes to see me, I shall be delighted to receive her, with your gracious permission. I remain ..."

She has a prolonged coughing fit and William finishes the letter with a flourish.

"I will send it right away. Arbella will be here by the end of the week I imagine."

Very tired now, she can only nod and he leaves her to rest. He thinks it will be good to see Arbella here again, but it seems Bess has not forgotten the past so quickly. By the time Arbella arrives, over a week later, Bess is feeling a little better and well enough to sit out of bed, close to the fire. She has dozed off, and does not hear Arbella come up to her and lightly touch her shoulder.

"Lady grandmother? Are you awake?"

Bess opens her eyes and blinks. She hardly recognises her granddaughter, who is dressed in a beautiful purple silk gown with matching cloak, a colour she has not seen her wear before now. Arbella has an air of sophisticated confidence that has come from her position at Court. The thin, pale woman of the past has gone.

"So, you are here at last. You are very welcome," she tells her, only just remembering in time not to call her 'child.'

Arbella gives a pretty curtsey and kisses her grandmother's cheek before pulling up another chair and sitting down opposite her. She quickly removes her cloak, as already she is very hot with the temperature in the chamber.

"How are you? I have been worried to hear that you are so unwell."

"I am better than I was last week."

"Is Dr. Hunton treating you?"

"Yes, he comes daily. You will see him no doubt, he often asks after you."

"He was always very kind to me."

"He is a good man."

"I have many stories to tell you about my time at Court."

"I am sure you do, William tells me you are enjoying all it has to offer. I wish you could have felt able to write and tell me yourself."

"Well I am here now," she says, looking round. "And glad to see everyone again. I know you will find it hard to believe, but I have been a little homesick," she confesses.

Bess laughs and shakes her head in disbelief. "You have a good way of hiding it."

"That is all in the past now. I am so happy at Court! The queen has made me her trainbearer and we are firm friends. You know we are the same age and find much to talk about. I sit very close to the royal family at formal events, always at the top table."

"Of course, I expected no less. And how do you find Queen Anne?"

"She is very patient with the king, who loves hunting. I declare he spends every spare minute possible with all his friends and makes a great fuss of them."

"William was grateful that you helped him to obtain his new title, Lord Cavendish, how splendid it sounds! And we shall have to get used to another new title for Robert Cecil, now the Earl of Salisbury."

Arbella shrugs as if it is a minor favour.

"I am glad to use my influence with the king," she says proudly.

Bess regards her shrewdly, it seems her granddaughter has finally grown up.

"And did you use your influence so that Mary was made a Lady of the Bedchamber?"

"I cannot take the credit for it, I think Mary has made a favourable impression on the queen."

"Does she still wear a crucifix under her gown?"

"You know about that?" Arbella looks surprised.

Bess does not answer but her disapproving expression says it all.

"She sends you her love," volunteers Arbella tentatively and waits for her reaction.

"Does she?" asks Bess, a little bitterly. "It is some time since I heard from her."

"I wish we could all be friends again. Aunt Mary and Uncle Gilbert are always so good to me."

Bess will not be drawn into this particular issue and after listening to Arbella telling her about their latest party and how lavish it was, she says she must rest before dinner.

"Will you join me downstairs, lady grandmother?"

"I think not." She stumbles over the words. "Movement is difficult for me, I am so stiff." Her gaze lingers on the view from the window. "I have not left this chamber for three months. You cannot imagine how much I suffer with this lack of freedom. I, who was always so active and busy."

"I think I can well imagine," replies Arbella slowly.

"I hope you are not comparing us! Our situations are very different. You always had youth and hope on your side. I have nothing except these four walls."

"So you are the prisoner now! How the tables have turned!" Arbella's voice is quiet, but there is no disguising the delight this information brings her. Bess seems not to hear. Arbella walks to the door and stares at the key in the lock. How easy it would be for her to lock Bess into the bedchamber! With a quick glance at her grandmother's back, she grabs the key and hesitates before pulling it out.

"Are you going to lock me in, child?"

Bess has not turned round, but her voice rings out across the space between them and Arbella freezes.

"Of course not, lady grandmother. What a foolish notion!"

There is a long pause, and then the sound of soft laughter from Bess.

"Do it, if it makes you feel better. It will make no difference to me."

Arbella leaves without replying and closes the door. She stands and stares at the key, turning it over in her hand, feeling the large scrollwork of Bess' initials at one end.

"Is there nothing in this house that does not have her stamp upon it?" she murmurs fiercely.

She thinks of all the years her grandmother held keys, for the Scots Queen as well as herself, and the heartache that it caused. This key is just like all the other keys in the different houses she has lived in, just a piece of metal. It cannot harm her now. She will not be kept under lock and key ever again. With one swift movement, she throws it at the wall and does not look at where it has landed, before hurrying to freshen up before supper. She is relieved to find her grandmother is not as ill as she has been led to believe; but she does not stay at Hardwick for long.

༺༻

1605 – 1608

*B*ess *recovers from her illness only to receive notice that Gilbert is suing her, claiming that she has cut down trees and mined for coal on land that was his, not hers. She has fought all her life for her rights and she is not going to stop now. Her victory is bittersweet as it did not help to heal the rift between them, and reconciliation seems as distant as ever. In the November of 1605, Gilbert is sent to the Tower for questioning over his alleged involvement in the Gunpowder Plot, but released shortly afterwards. The previous year Henry suffered the same fate over what was called the Bye Plot and Main Plot to assassinate the King and his son Prince Henry. Bess can only watch and fret over these events from the safety of Hardwick, but she does not help Henry when he again asked for a large sum of money to pay his debts. Still forced to live at Tutbury because he cannot afford to furnish Chatsworth, he becomes depressed, making life even more difficult for his wife, Grace. In September 1606 the whole family gathers for the wedding of Gilbert and Mary's youngest daughter Alathea, when Bess makes peace with Mary, Charles and Gilbert at last. But Bess' health gives cause for concern again in the winter of 1607-08.*

Hardwick Hall

The snow and ice began at the end of November, covering all of England and remained for eight long weeks; no one can remember a winter as bitterly cold. Rivers are frozen solid and on the Thames, horses can be ridden from one side to the other. People go about their daily business as best they can, wrapped and swaddled under layers of clothing, their breath visible in the air. Some people simply die of cold, found stiff and lifeless in their beds. When Timothy brings the daily sheaf of paperwork for her to check, her signature is shaky and she looks at it with a growing sense of her own mortality. Servants are kept busy carrying trays of food up and down stairs for her, as well as bringing coal to feed the insatiable fire and emptying the velvet covered close stool. Christmas is spent quietly, William and Elizabeth are at Court for the celebrations, all the more lavish as the King of Denmark is visiting his sister Queen Anne.

Bess is not well at all through these months, constantly battling with a persistent cough and sore throat. She loses her normally healthy appetite and sometimes only manages to sip a little broth throughout the day. Ruby is unwell herself, so a local gentlewoman and friend,

Mistress Digby, offers to care for her. At the beginning of January she is worried enough to send a messenger to London for William to return at once, and he hurries back up north to be at her bedside.

Elizabeth takes over the management of the house, supervising the servants and ensuring the smooth running of everything. William and Timothy ensure that her business affairs continue to be handled efficiently, as she would wish. William sits next to her bed and listens to her talk whenever she is well enough to do so. Each day takes on an almost surreal quality in the dim light of the chamber, contrasting with the still, stark whiteness of outside, where nothing is moving in the fields and even the birds are silent. Mistress Digby sits by the window, patiently attending to her, her sewing hastily put down whenever she is needed. The days are short and merge into one, they lose track of time and the house waits with bated breath. One morning as the snow falls softly and steadily, Mistress Digby appears as William and Elizabeth are having breakfast.

"My lord, her grace is asking for you, she is very agitated."

William puts down his spoon at once and runs upstairs to his mother's bedchamber, Mistress Digby following behind at a slower pace. When they reach the bed, Bess raises her hand and looks at him fretfully.

"I must talk to you about my will, I have been lying awake all night worrying about it. You must make sure all my wishes are carried out. I am relying on you, William, you are the only one who understands and is capable of continuing my work."

She coughs and Mistress Digby is immediately at her side, straightening her pillows and wiping her mouth.

"How are the negotiations progressing between you and Henry with regard to the sale of Chatsworth?" Bess manages to ask when she has recovered her breath.

"I have offered him £5,000 for Chatsworth with £500 a year whilst you are alive."

Bess manages a roguish look at him. "William! You know as well as I do, that he will never receive the first annual payment! I have lived for over eighty summers, I will not see another one."

"Lady mother, you will outlive us all."

She gives a croaky laugh, which quickly becomes another coughing episode, and he watches with concern as she recovers momentarily from it.

"I will go and make up another poultice for you," Mistress Digby tells her and goes back downstairs, not trusting anyone else to do it.

"Have you checked the water from the well?" she asks him, without preamble.

"The well? Why should I do so?" William replies, the puzzlement showing on his face.

"I am afraid it has been poisoned."

"No, you can rest easy, it has not been poisoned."

"Are you sure?"

"Quite sure, do not worry."

She mutters something under her breath and he wonders if she is thinking back to when her third husband, Sir William St Loe, died. It was never proved that his brother Edward murdered him, an event that she has not mentioned to him for over forty years.

"Are my builders still working?"

"Only just, the mortar is not setting properly."

"Tell them to pour boiling ale on it."

Closing her eyes, she drifts off to sleep again and he returns downstairs to find Elizabeth and Mistress Digby talking quietly.

"We think you should send for the others," Elizabeth tells him. "The end cannot be far off now."

"Yes, I agree. I will send a messenger at once."

He makes his way to the study with a heavy heart. His mother has been a constant and loving presence in all of his fifty-six years, and it will be hard to adjust to life without her. Dr. Hunton arrives the next day although there is little he can do, but Bess seems calmer if he is there. He says that Bess has a congestion on the lungs and her heart is weakened by old age. The days pass and Bess clings on to her life, drifting in and out of consciousness, whispering odd phrases or coherent sentences. There is always someone with her. The servants creep round the house, afraid to see her so struck down on her deathbed. Then one February morning William approaches her bed and whispers that Frances, Mary, Charles and Gilbert are on their way.

"So I am dying then," she says and gives him the ghost of a smile. "My building …?"

"Work has been stopped, it has just been too cold. Do not worry yourself about such matters now."

At this news, she seems to sink into the bed and he knows the reason. Locals say that when she stops building, she will die. He can think of nothing to say that will reassure her.

"Arbella?" she croaks.

Not trusting himself to tell her that Arbella has made excuse after excuse not to make the journey, he shakes his head, wishing it was not so. The faintest frown appears on her brow, but she betrays no other emotion.

The others arrive just as dusk is falling, their journey made hazardous by the deep snow and ice.

They are chilled to the bone, and after warming themselves by the fire in the Great Hall and drinking hot mead, they troop up to Bess' bedchamber and crowd round the bed. Shadows from the flickering candles dance round the walls and the sound of the howling wind echoes relentlessly up the valley. For a few minutes, no-one speaks, lost in their own memories and thoughts. All are shocked to see Bess, always so vital and alive, reduced to an inert, pale figure under the bedclothes. Dr. Hunton makes a tactful retreat downstairs, his patient is beyond help.

"Lady mother, we are all with you."

Frances reaches for her hand, already cold, despite the warmth given by the fire.

"Why is it is so unbearably hot in here?" mutters Henry, pulling at his shirt.

"Be quiet!" Mary tells him. "Show some respect."

"Too late for that." Charles leans against one of the bedposts and wipes his eyes.

"Is this the pearl bed that will be yours?" Gilbert asks and receives a glare from Mary for his trouble. He raises his eyes to heaven and pulls out his pipe.

"Gilbert! We do not wish to breathe the smoke from that wretched pipe. Take it outside!" Mary snaps.

"Why not wait in the antechamber, it is cooler in there?" Frances suggests. "Mary can stay with her now; we can take it in turns."

Mary sits on the edge of the bed and assumes a caring expression as she looks at her mother.

In the antechamber, they find extra chairs have been provided for them, and on the table, more food and drink. Charles puts another log on the fire and they sit uneasily to wait.

"Is Arbella not coming?" says Frances. "She does know, I assume."

"Oh yes, she knows all right. She is not going to put herself out," Henry tells them with a superior air.

"I see." Frances hides her disappointment at this news but says no more as she thoughtfully watches the flames.

"You have been very quiet, William, that is not like you," Henry observes.

"There is not much to say. I have spent the last few weeks here, at her side each day."

"Acting as nurse maid I suppose, how very heroic."

"One of us has to do it; the businesses do not run themselves. There will be a lot of administration afterwards, and I have orders from our lady mother for legacies and other legal matters."

"Of course you do," sneers Gilbert. "You are the only one she trusts."

"Why is that, Gilbert?"

"I do not know, could it be because you have always been the favourite?"

"If I have been the favourite it is because I have never disappointed her like the rest of you. I have always been loyal."

"Only because it suited you to do so."

"All you ever wanted was her money!"

"And you do not?"

"For the love of Christ, stop this bickering!" Frances tells them. "You will disturb her with all this arguing."

They look through to where Mary is whispering to Bess, who is now awake and seems to be responding to questions. William is alarmed, he does not wish Mary to be alone with Bess, as bequests could be promised without his knowledge and may cause trouble in the future. He goes to Mistress Digby, and tells her quietly to interrupt them without delay. After a minute, Mary joins her them, and the atmosphere is heavy with unsaid words and simmering resentments. Gilbert strides over to the table and helps himself to a large glass of claret.

"This is folly, she could linger for weeks; we all know how tough she is. I have business affairs to attend to, I cannot be waiting about here indefinitely."

"No-one is making you stay, you are free to go," says Frances.

"We all have other matters to attend to," Henry adds.

"You should not be here in any case; or you, Gilbert." William glares at them. "You both caused our mother a lot of heartache over the years."

"If she had a heart," Gilbert is heard to mutter.

"That is enough!" William's voice is strident, as he looks contemptuously at them. "You should be ashamed of yourselves. Our mother is on her deathbed and you are still bickering. You make me sick!"

He storms out and Henry exchanges a look of sympathy with Gilbert. The hours pass slowly. Servants bring more candles so that Mary and Frances can sew, whilst the men pace restlessly or read. They avoid each other's eyes and from time to time, one of them sighs heavily or yawns. Finally Charles can stand it no more.

"Well, I am for my bed. There is nothing more to be done tonight." He drains his glass and the others murmur agreement. Eyeing Bess cautiously, they all file out to make their way to the bedchambers that have been prepared for them. Mistress Digby has made herself comfortable in a nearby chair and her eyes are closed as William approaches the bedside. He looks fondly at his mother's face, now serene and at peace. She is still breathing, but only just, and does not seem to know he is there.

"The world will not see the like of you again." Leaning forward, he plants the lightest of kisses on her forehead. "You were one in a million."

As he walks through the door, a glint of metal catches his eye on the floor underneath a chest. Bending down, his hand reaches out and he is surprised to find the key to her bedchamber, usually kept on the inside of the lock. He places it in his pocket and goes downstairs to write again to Arbella. He wonders if she will regret not being here to say a last goodbye to her grandmother.

The End.

Authors Note

Bess is a character that has intrigued me for a long time. She has not had a particularly good press through the centuries, having been called a shrew, selfish and unfeeling, in the past. Her immense wealth and successful entrepreneurial skills must have provoked jealousy within the limited expectations and opportunities for women during the Tudor period. But she outlived four husbands, were they all taken in by her charms or has time distorted her true character?

Evidence from surviving letters written by eminent members of the Court of Queen Elizabeth 1st, show that she was highly respected and admired. The queen herself once said that there was no other lady in the land she loved so much. This contrasts sharply with the opinion of the Earl of Shrewsbury, her fourth husband, during the latter years of their marriage. But perhaps it is understandable when it is now thought he was suffering from the early onset of dementia, as well as being in constant pain from gout and arthritis. He was also having to simultaneously deal with Mary, Queen of Scots, as well as Bess and Queen Elizabeth, all strong-minded women, so it must have been quite a challenge for him at times.

After Bess' death, **William** was in sole control of her estate, and there was the inevitable wrangling and legal battles between the siblings over her will. He became the 1st Earl of Devonshire in 1618, before dying seven years later, outliving Henry, Charles and Gilbert.

Charles lived to be sixty-three, despite the bullet wounds, and his second marriage was a happy one. His bloodline lives on through the Dukes of Newcastle, Portland and the Barons Ogle.

Henry eventually sold Chatsworth to William for £8000. He had no legitimate heir and died the same year as Gilbert.

Arbella grew increasingly frustrated by the search for a husband and took matters into her own hands once more by secretly marrying William Seymour, (the brother of Edward, whom she had previously approached) in 1610. King James changed his mind about giving permission for them to wed, and Arbella was again imprisoned. She escaped, hoping to meet her husband and flee to France, but the plan went wrong and she was finally kept in the Tower of London, where she died in 1615, having become anorexic and depressed, her fragile mental state completely broken. It is now thought she suffered from porphyria, a hereditary genetic disorder, inherited from her Stuart line.

Mary Talbot helped Arbella in her attempted escape and was initially sent to the Tower for a year. She was accused of being 'obstinately Catholic' and King James suspected her of plotting to overthrow him. Having nursed Gilbert through his final illness in 1616, she was again sent to the Tower for refusing to answer questions, finally being released in 1623, when she was seventy. She died nine years later, almost as old as Bess.

If there are any historical inaccuracies I hope the reader will note that it is a work of fiction, although I have tried to stay as close as possible to the facts. There are some characters, such as Bess' mother, Elizabeth Leche, that are only briefly mentioned in the book, and this is partly because I felt the list of characters was already long enough. Bess' ambition to create a dynasty has been realised, as her descendants number the Dukes of Devonshire, amongst others.

If you are interested in finding out more about Bess, a visit to her magnificent home of Hardwick Hall in Derbyshire is highly recommended, together with the splendid Chatsworth House (although it is not the same building now that Bess commissioned.)

For more information log on to www.national/trust.org.uk/hardwick and www.chatsworth.org

Georgina Lee, Oxfordshire.

Lightning Source UK Ltd.
Milton Keynes UK
UKOW02f0824160915

258713UK00001B/24/P